Medillia's Lament II

"The Dark Waters"

A novel by Jody Clark

Enjoy the magic
of Maine!

Jody C

DEDICATION

To all my family and friends.
Especially Erica and Owen for their endless support and encouragement

ACKNOWLEDGMENTS

A special thanks to Marie Sapienza for the beautiful cover photo.
You can check out more of her amazing work at:
www.MNSImagery.com

Chicago – 1981

Like any college campus, the most popular nights to party were Friday and Saturday. Northwestern University was no different. This particular Friday, the parties would be some of the biggest of the year. It was the beginning of Northwestern's spring break and would be their last stretch of time off until finals in early May. The plan for most students was to party hard on Friday and then head out of town on Saturday to their official spring break destination. For most, that would either be Florida or Myrtle Beach. Hope Simmons would not be one of them. In the three years she attended Northwestern, she had been to a total of four parties; to all but one she was dragged by her roommates. The faces of her roommates changed each year, but the one thing they had in common was they all loved to party.

Hope was a straight-A student. She didn't drink, smoke, or partake in any promiscuous college-type behaviors. And despite her hippie appearance, she'd never even smoked pot. Even though she was against those things, she never once passed judgement onto those who did. *Whatever gets you through the night* and *To each his own* were two of her favorite sayings. She was kind, accepting, and one of the most non-judgmental people around. Unfortunately, this didn't prevent most people from making fun of her. She'd certainly be rich if she had a

1

dollar for every time someone said, "What kind of hippie doesn't like to get high?" Or "I thought all you hippies like to shag?"

Hope never considered herself a prude. She wasn't against sex, even sex before marriage. She just wanted it to be with someone special and have some meaning behind it. To her, it was a beautiful act between two people in love. Sadly, most of her peers looked at it as a competition. Two of her present roommates, Darcy and Dee, took it to another level. They actually had a small chalk board filled with tally marks for each of their conquests. Okay, maybe Hope was a little judgmental, for she looked at this act of keeping score as utterly disgusting.

Hope's grandparents lived only twenty minutes from the campus, and if she had her choice, she would have been just fine with commuting. Her grandfather was all about teaching her how to be independent. To him, living at home throughout college was simply unacceptable. He was constantly preparing Hope for the real world. Ironically, even though her grandparents forced her to stay in the school dorms, they regularly complained about her roommates over the years. Her grandfather called each and every one of them a bad influence and urged her to stay away from them. Her grandmother was famous for labeling them as *unsavory types*.

Being a junior, Hope decided to leave the tiny dorm rooms and get a place where she could have her own bedroom. The only way she could afford to do that was to shack up with multiple roommates—three, to be exact. A couple of weeks before school started, Hope responded to an ad in the paper. She was the final roommate, which meant she got the smallest bedroom in the house. This didn't faze her in the least, for if given the choice, she probably would have chosen the smaller room anyway.

Hope prided herself on being a minimalist. A bed, a dresser, and a small desk was all she needed. Oh, and a record player. Her music was very important to her. As soon as she placed those black, oversized headphones on, her problems seem to melt away. On the floor next to the turntable sat a milk crate filled with some of her favorite vinyl records. When she listened to her records, she always did it through headphones. Partly, so no one would make fun of her choice in music, but mostly, she did it out of respect for the rest of the house. Unfortunately, her roommates, especially Darcy and Dee, never returned the same courtesy. Whether it was in their bedroom or the living room, they loved to crank their music up. It wasn't that Hope hated their type of music, she just didn't appreciate the loudness of it. Not to mention, they had no reservations with blasting it at all hours of the night.

This was one of the many reasons Hope spent most of her time away from the house. She was either working, volunteering, or studying at the library. Tonight's place of choice was the library. Usually, she'd stay there well into the evening, but tonight she was on her way back home by 6:30.

Before she even opened the door, she could hear REO Speedwagon's "Take it on the Run" blaring out. That in itself would have been fine, but it was accompanied by her roommates loudly singing along. At that point, they were only buzzed, or else it would have been even louder and more off-key. Like always, Darcy and Dee were the stars. They were both standing on the couch using hairbrushes as microphones. Hope's other roommate, Robin, sat in the chair across from them and was doing more laughing than singing. Robin enjoyed drinking and partying with Darcy and Dee, but she was nothing like them.

"Hey, Hope. Where have you been?"

"The library," Hope said, hurrying across the room.

She crossed her fingers, hoping she could make it to her bedroom before any more questions came her way. She didn't even make it to

3

the staircase. "Did you say library?" Darcy said, turning down the music. "On a Friday night?"

Without making eye contact, Hope shyly shrugged and nodded. Robin knew how sarcastic and mean the girls could get, so she tried to save Hope by changing the subject. "Is that a new outfit? I love it."

Hope slowly looked down at her clothes. It was no secret that her style was different from most girls her age. She embraced a look from a different time; the fashion of a hippy, as most liked to say. Tonight, for instance, she had on a pair of tan corduroy bellbottoms with a high waist, and she paired it with a flowing floral print blouse and her signature Birkenstock sandals. Her look was as comfortable as it was eclectic, and she knew none of that was lost on her roommates. Darcy and Dee's eyes always said more than their mouths ever could, if that was even possible.

Sometimes, Hope felt that girls like Darcy and Dee were jealous of her—at least that's what told herself. She was distinctive looking and she knew it, even if her low self-confidence precluded her from admitting it. Hope had an unassumed beauty about her. She had effortless good looks and long, wavy hair that cultivated natural highlights whenever she spent enough time in the sun. She rarely wore makeup, and if she did, it was limited to lip gloss and some eyeshadow. She had a smattering of freckles that danced across her cheeks and the bridge of her nose. This made her somewhat unique and she never wanted to hide that feature with blush or foundation.

"Thanks," Hope quietly said. She gave Robin enough eye contact to show her appreciation. Her appreciation went beyond just the compliment. She knew Robin was trying to distract the girls from their catty comments. It didn't work.

"Thrift store shopping at its best," Dee murmured, loud enough for Hope to hear. "Not everyone can dress as cool as us," she confidently said, more to Darcy than to anyone else.

As she said it, Dee gestured to her own ensemble, which consisted of a barely-there short, black skirt and a bright green crop top. The neckline of the crop top was loose enough that it fully hung off one shoulder, nearly exposing a whole cup of her black lace bra. Modesty was certainly not one of Dee's strong suits. Nor was kindness, but not everyone could be as gentle as Hope.

Darcy didn't miss the opportunity to chime in. When she saw a chance to diminish someone else while simultaneously inflating herself, she always took it. "Yeah, you can tell just by looking at her that she's boring. Not like us. We're fun!" Darcy bumped hips with Dee while teetering on the couch cushion. This caused her drink to slosh out of her cup and spill down the front of her white cutoff t-shirt. In doing so, it became abundantly evident that Darcy had opted not to wear a bra on this particular evening. Hope would have been mortified, but not Darcy. She just looked down at her now exposed chest and shrugged, followed closely by a party girl "*Woo hoo*" and a healthy chug from what was left in her cup. Sobriety was definitely not in her cards tonight.

Again, Robin tried to prevent their comments from getting out of hand. She reached into the box of cassettes and said, "What should we listen to next?" And once again, her attempt failed.

"Were you really studying on a Friday night?" Darcy asked. "We don't even have classes next week. Who studies at the library on the first night of vacation?"

The two girls giggled at each other as they climbed down off the couch. Hope bit down on her lip and did her best to smile away her embarrassment. She should have just lied. She should have told them she was, well, anywhere else but the library.

Robin jumped in, sparing Hope from having to say a word. "And that's why Hope has the perfect grade point average, and you don't! Do you two even know where the library is?"

5

"Pfft, we'll take getting drunk and high over the perfect grade point average any day," Darcy said, giving Dee a high five.

Hope was tempted to mention that her grade point average wasn't exactly perfect (3.95), but before she could muster a word, Darcy got bored with the conversation and took another toke off the joint.

Already knowing the answer, Darcy held out the joint and sarcastically asked, "Do you wanna hit, there, Miss Brainiac?"

"Or how about we mix you a drink?" Dee said, motioning to the assortment of alcohol on the living room table.

With a straight face, Darcy replied, "Oh, come on, Dee. You know she doesn't drink alcohol. Maybe you should make it a *virgin*, like her."

She looked directly at Hope and made sure to accent the word virgin. As both girls cracked up laughing, Robin stood up and put an end to their sarcasm.

"Okay, girls, enough. You don't need to get drunk or high to have fun." Before Darcy and Dee could offer a snide remark, Robin continued. "You should come to the party with us tonight, Hope. I'm probably not gonna drink much, if at all. You and I can just stand around and make fun of all of the drunk idiots… like these two."

Darcy and Dee glared over at Robin and rolled their eyes. Hope had no intention of going, but she graciously smiled at Robin's gesture. She was always doing and saying thoughtful things like that. When it came to Hope, Robin tried her best to be inclusive. A few times a week, they would go out to lunch, and seeing as they had a class together, they also spent time at the library studying.

Robin had a lot of friends that she hung out and did stuff with, but for Hope, Robin was pretty much it. She was as close to a best friend as Hope had ever had. Even though Robin had many other friends, Hope was usually the first person she went to for advice. Whether it was homelife, school work, or boy troubles, Hope always seemed to say the right things. This was a bit ironic, considering Hope had no real experiences with boyfriends. Her only experiences were boys that were friends.

"You're gonna make a great therapist one day," Robin would often say.

For a split second, Hope considered saying yes to Robin's party invite, but she knew she had somewhere else she needed to be. Her big mistake was revealing where that would be.

"Thanks, but I'm spending the night over at my grandparent's tonight," Hope said, then quickly regretted it.

Nearly choking on her drink, Darcy snickered and loudly whispered, "Well that sounds way more fun than a college party."

Internally, Hope chastised herself. Why did she tell them where she was going? She really needed to learn how to lie better. Actually, she needed to learn how to lie, period. She was way too honest for her own good. Lowering her head, she turned and started up the stairs towards her bedroom.

"Hey, Hope," Robin called out. "What are you doing during vacation this week?"

Hope shrugged. "Nothing much."

This was as close to a lie as she could tell. The truth was, she planned on hitting the library, doing some volunteer work, and if the weather warmed up, she intended to take a stroll or two through Grant Park. Those were her *actual* plans, but there was no way she'd reveal any of that to the girls. Darcy and Dee would have a field day with that kind of information.

"You should totally come with us to my parents' lake house. They're out of town for the week." Robin was focused on Hope's answer and didn't notice Darcy and Dee's disapproving glares. Their looks didn't go unnoticed to Hope. "Come on, Hope. It'll be fun. There'll be plenty of single guys there, too," Robin said, with a convincing wink and a smile.

7

Hope thought about saying yes, not because of the guys, but just to see Darcy and Dee's heads explode. Robin continued smiling and awaiting an answer. Hope didn't actually say no, but her shrug and hesitation said it for her.

"Well, if you change your mind, let me know. We're leaving tomorrow afternoon."

"Thanks," was all Hope managed to say before finally heading upstairs to her room.

She truly appreciated Robin's kindness, and even though hanging out in a giant house on Lake Michigan sounded fun and relaxing, Hope knew she needed to be at her grandparents' house, at least for tomorrow. None of her roommates knew, but tomorrow was her birthday. That in itself was never a big deal to Hope, but what always happened *on* her birthday every year was a big deal—a phone call.

Hope waited for the girls to leave for their party before heading out to her grandparents' house. She arrived just after eight, and her grandmother seemed surprised to see her.

"Hope, what are you doing here?"

"I always spend my birthday with you guys, you know that."

Her grandmother sat up straight. "Tomorrow's your birthday?" she said with a puzzled look.

Her grandmother never forgot Hope's birthday. For a brief second, Hope was worried that early Alzheimer's was setting in. Her worry quickly dissipated when she saw her grandmother smile. Neither one of her grandparents had much of a sense of humor, so on the rare occasion that they cracked a joke, it always caught her off guard.

"You really didn't think I forgot your birthday, did you? I'm old, but not that old. But don't think you're fooling me... I know the real reason you spend your birthday with us."

Hope froze. Her heart raced. After all these years, her secret had been found out. She searched for an explanation but had no idea what to say. All she could come up with was, "You do?"

"Yup. And don't worry, I already picked up all the ingredients earlier today."

"Ingredients?"

"For your birthday breakfast?"

Just like that, the tension released from Hope's shoulders and she let out a sigh of relief. "Ohh, right… my birthday breakfast."

"What did you think I was talking about?"

"Sorry, I guess I just spaced out for a second. Long week at school."

Every birthday, for as long as she could remember, her grandmother made her homemade waffles with strawberries. She would top it off with whipped cream and rainbow sprinkles, and not to mention, a side of bacon and freshly-squeezed orange juice as well.

Hope looked around the living room and asked, "Where's Grampa?"

"Where do you think?"

Hope laughed and replied, "Down in the basement tinkering with his radios."

"You can go down and let him know you're here."

"It's okay. I don't want to interrupt. I think I might just do a little reading and call it a night."

"Sounds good, dear. I'll see you in the morning."

Most teenagers had every inch of their bedroom walls plastered with posters. And in addition to an unmade bed, every inch of their floor would be covered with dirty clothes. Hope was not like most teenagers. Whether it was her home or her dorm, her bed was always perfectly made, and there was rarely an article of clothing out of place. There were only two posters in her room. One of them was on the wall behind her bed and contained brightly colored flowers and a giant peace sign reading PEACE & LOVE. The other was pinned to the back of her door. It was a Grateful Dead poster with both the lightning skull and dancing bears logos on it.

On each side of her bed were two small wooden nightstands. The one on the left had an alarm clock and lava lamp sitting on top. Perfectly centered on the other one was a gray Panasonic tape recorder. All the buttons were black with the exception of the bright red record button. Placed neatly under her bed was a brown cassette case. She actually preferred vinyl over cassettes, which is why she chose to bring her record player off to school with her.

Not only did Hope do some reading before bed, she did some writing as well. Over the years, she had more diaries than she could count. She kept them all in a brown cardboard box, which was buried in the back of her closet underneath stacks and stacks of books. The books were more of a deterrent than anything. Just in case her grandmother was ever snooping, she wanted to make it as difficult as possible to get to the diaries. That being said, it wasn't like there was anything too juicy or scandalous—not at all, actually. It was just her thoughts and feelings on everyday life in general. That night's entry would be short, yet would turn out to be quite prophetic.

This is my last night of being 19, and although I don't feel like 20 will be much different, I do feel like something special is about to happen tomorrow. I can't put my finger on exactly what. It's just a feeling… a strong feeling.

The next morning, Hope awoke to the smell of bacon and coffee. Even though she never drank it, she loved the smell of freshly percolated coffee. A nice hot cup of tea was her drink of choice. Hope looked over at her clock: 7:50 a.m. Breakfast would be served in ten minutes. How did she know this? Because breakfast was always served at 8 a.m. Her grandparents, especially her grandfather, were very regimented on their daily routines. Breakfast at eight, lunch at noon, and dinner at five on the dot. Not to mention, almost every night at seven sharp, her grandfather would have a single glass of scotch as a nightcap.

Hope headed downstairs, and after making sure her grandfather had his black coffee, she fixed herself a cup of tea. No sooner did Hope sit down, her grandmother placed a plate in front of her. A huge smile filled her face as she stared down at the mountain of whipped cream and strawberries. It was so big she could barely see the waffle underneath. Her grandfather's breakfast was far more basic—a waffle, a sliver of butter, two shots of syrup, and three pieces of bacon.

Her grandmother wasn't much on vocally expressing her feelings, but Hope knew she did it through her cooking. Not to mention, when it came to Hope's annual birthday breakfast, her grandmother dug out her fine china plates. The only other time they were used were on the very, very rare occasions of a family get-together.

"So, do you feel any different?" her grandfather asked, just like he did every year.

She pondered, smiled, and then replied, "Nope, no different."

"Trust me, when you get to be our age, you'll definitely feel different. Bones creaking and muscles aching where you didn't even know you had muscles."

"Oh, don't let him scare you," her grandmother said.

"Not trying to scare her. Just making sure she enjoys being young… because it ain't gonna last forever… especially once you hit the real world."

"For heaven's sake, Raymond, let the girl enjoy being twenty. So, any big plans for your school vacation?"

Before Hope could say a word, her grandfather answered for her.

"I'm sure she'll be working quite a bit, not to mention, doing some extra studying. The school year is nearly over, and finals will be here before you know it."

Hope finished chewing then said, "I do have some studying to do, but my boss gave me the week off. He told me to enjoy my vacation."

Her grandfather paused mid bite and quickly said, "I hope you told him thanks but no thanks. Can't get ahead in the world that way. Besides, what would you be doing with your time if you weren't working all week? You know what they say, idle hands are the devil's workshop."

Without thinking too heavily on it, Hope blurted out, "Actually, Robin invited me up to her parents' lake house for the week. A bunch of us girls are going."

What was I thinking? She knew she should have kept that information to herself. She took a sip of tea, gulped it down hard, then prepared herself for her grandfather's disapproving comments. He spent the better part of ten minutes pointing out fault after fault of each of her roommates. He then gave reason after reason why spending the week with her friends was a stupid and irresponsible idea. At one point, Hope looked over at her grandmother, as if to beg her to throw a life preserver her way. She should have known better, for her grandmother rarely went against her grandfather.

"What your grandfather is trying to say is we just don't want you hanging out with unsavory types."

As soon as the unsavory-types line was played, Hope knew it was useless to even try to disagree. She conceded. "Yea, you're probably right. I'll just call my boss and tell him that I don't mind picking up some shifts this week."

"Don't call! Just show up," her grandfather said, wiping his mouth with a napkin. "Employers love go-getters. That's how you get ahead in this world, Hope."

Her grandmother nodded but said nothing. Ironically, Hope agreed with a lot of what he said. She knew the lake house would probably be a waste of time. It would just be a bunch of wild parties with tons of alcohol and drugs. Even though none of those were her scene, there were times she wondered what it would be like to let her hair down and just have some real fun; even if was with unsavory types.

Hope took a deep, calming breath and pushed the lake house out of her mind. It wasn't like she was going to accept the invitation anyway, so she knew there was no sense to dwell on it. Instead, she turned her attention back to her birthday breakfast. By now, the mountain of whipped cream was more like a molehill. After she had polished off her plate, Hope helped her grandmother with the dishes. When they finished, Hope grabbed a book and sat back down at the kitchen table.

"Wouldn't you be more comfortable reading in the living room?" her grandmother asked.

"I'm fine. I like feeling the warmth of the sun," she said, pointing to the large kitchen window.

"Suit yourself. I'm going to start some laundry. Do you need anything washed?"

"No, thanks. I'm all set."

Hope wasn't exactly lying when she said she liked to feel the sun's warmth while she read, but the real reason she chose the kitchen was for phone on the wall. It was the one and only phone in the house, and she needed to make sure that she would be the first to answer it when it rang. And not only was she positive it would ring, but she had a strange feeling that today would be different. She just knew it.

Sometimes it rang early on her birthday. Sometimes it rang late in the evening. Either way, Hope was determined to remain in the vicinity of the phone until it did. Her grandparents were intelligent people, which is why she couldn't believe they hadn't figured out her birthday ritual over the years. She knew for a fact they hadn't a clue, for if they did, they would have surely forbidden her from answering.

As she sat and read, she crossed her fingers that today's call would

13

come sooner than later. Fortunately, her wait would be short, and less than two hours later, the phone rang. She sprang to her feet, nearly knocking over her chair in the process.

"I got it! I got it!" she yelled, halfway across the kitchen.

Her grandparents didn't have the best hearing, and they seldom heard it ring right away, but still, Hope made sure to get to it before the second ring. With her heart already in her throat, she took a deep breath and picked up the receiver and answered.

***

Hope had barely entered the living room when she heard her grandmother's voice from down the hall. She was carrying a laundry basket full of clean clothes. "Taking a break from reading? Who was that on the phone?" she asked, before Hope had a chance to answer the first question. Hope froze. Her heart raced. She was the worst liar in the world and she knew it. Most years, if one of them asked who was on the phone, Hope would just say it was so and so wishing her a happy birthday. But this year was different, and it called for a different sort of a lie.

"It was… umm, it was actually my boss. He was wondering if I could work this week after all. He said he didn't need me until tomorrow, but I told him didn't mind coming in today. Employers love go-getters," she said, quoting her grandfather.

Her grandmother smiled. "He'll be very happy you took his advice. Make sure you go down in the basement and tell him before you leave."

"Okay, I will."

Hope never actually made it downstairs to see him. She was in way too much of a hurry. Instead, she rushed up to her bedroom and grabbed a jacket, her bag, and the cassette case. She then headed directly back to campus. On the drive over, she once again crossed her fingers. This time, she hoped that her roommates were still passed out from their big party. The last thing she wanted was to have to explain where she was going and why she was packing a bag.

She still couldn't explain it to herself, never mind to her hungover and nosy roommates. If anyone would understand, it would be Robin, but even still, there was no way she had enough time to fill her in on every crazy detail. Thankfully, her finger-crossing once again worked. Even better than still sleeping, her roommates weren't even home. They must have crashed at the party or at some random guy's house.

Not knowing how long she would be gone or where exactly she was even going, she hastily threw some clothes into a small suitcase. Before exiting, she stopped and looked over at her guitar case in the corner of her room. Without thinking twice, she grabbed it and took it with her. She had no intention on playing anytime soon, but there was no way she trusted her roommates around it for long periods of time—namely, Darcy and Dee.

She popped the hatchback on her Chevy Chevette, and before she placed her belongings inside, she removed a black bag that was off to the right. Inside the bag contained an emergency roadside kit her grandfather had put together for her back when she bought the car. Up until that point, she had never used or had even opened the bag before. But seeing as this would be the longest road trip she'd ever taken, she decided to at least peer inside.

There was an atlas, a giant Maglite, a pair of winter gloves and hat, a tightly rolled up blanket, and an assortment of tools; tools she had no idea what they were or how to even use them. Pretty much the only thing missing were road flares. Before zipping it back up, she removed the atlas and placed it next to her in the front seat.

If she sat there long enough, she would surely start to overthink what she was about to embark on. Hope was the type who weighed every pro and con before making any big decision in her life. Even the small decisions were carefully examined and over-examined before following through. Besides her grandparents, she was the least spontaneous person she knew. What she was about to do went against every ounce of common sense she had. With that in mind, she took one final deep breath then started the car and put it into drive.

2

Interstate 95 – twelve hours earlier

It was nearly three in the morning when the green, and mostly, rusted 1969 Dodge Dart came to a stop at the darkened Connecticut rest area. Seeing as the interior light had long since burned out, the man was forced to blindly search the floorboards on the passenger side. His hand frantically dug through piles of fast-food wrappers and empty cigarette packs until he finally found what he was looking for— a small bottle of vodka. At most, there was only a swig or two left, but he savored every last drop. He tossed the bottle back onto to floor and made a mental note to restock his supply sooner rather than later. He then fully reclined his seat and grabbed an old woolen blanket from the back and half-tossed it over himself. Out of his shirt pocket, he pulled out a crumpled pack of Marlboro reds, but before he could even locate his Bic lighter, his eyes fell shut and he was out for the night.

When he finally awoke the next morning, the sun was directly shining into his windshield. Exhausted and annoyed, the man shielded his eyes and turned his head towards the passenger side. And there, with his pudgy face pressed against the window, was a small boy. The boy's eyes moved from the piles of garbage in the front to the piles of clothes strewn about in the back.

"What the fuck you looking at?" the man yelled out. "Didn't your parents ever teach you to mind your own goddamn business?"

He then located and whipped his Bic lighter at the boy. It loudly clinked against the window, nearly breaking it. This caused the boy to bolt back to his family. The man was tempted to get out of his car and give the boy's parents a piece of his mind, but he didn't. His head was cloudy and his body ached, and he knew he needed to hit the road. He was on the final leg of his trip, and his destination was still a few hours away.

While looking out the window at the boy and his remiss parents, the man caught a faint glimpse of his own reflection. Not that he was one to ever really care about appearances, but even he acknowledged how rough he looked. Sitting in the same rumpled clothing that he had slept in for days, he considered the boy lucky that the window was up because he was saved from the strong scent of body odor that was emanating throughout the car. He couldn't remember the last time he showered or shaved, for that matter. His beard was long, unkempt, and scraggily.

On the rare occasion that he looked in a mirror, he could hardly believe how much gray was now in his beard. He'd grumble at the contrast it had to the hair on his head, which was still mostly dark and only appeared darker with each passing day that it went unwashed. It was long enough now that it hung over his ears and down onto his forehead. But cleaning himself up required ambition, and for that, he was sorely lacking.

Shaking free from his thoughts, he tossed the blanket into the back. He straightened up his seat, turned the key, and roared back onto I-95. He was barely out of Connecticut, and he had already polished off his last few cigarettes and added them to his list of supplies to buy once he arrived at his destination. He spent a good portion of the Mass Pike profusely coughing. At one point, it got so bad, his car veered into the next lane and nearly clipped a brand-new BMW. The woman laid on her horn and shot the man a *what the fuck* look. It was completely the man's fault, but that didn't stop him from flipping the woman off and shouting profanities.

"Fucking rich bitch!"

Although his coughing subsided, his nerves remained tense. Anxiously, his fingers twisted the tuning knob on the radio but he never settled on one station for more than five seconds. After a few minutes of this, his patience finally ran out, and he angrily turned the power off.

When his eyes returned to the road, he was in the midst of crossing over a large green bridge. That's when he saw it—the sign.

WELCOME TO MAINE – THE WAY LIFE SHOULD BE

He knew he was getting closer. He reached onto the passenger seat and grabbed an old worn-out atlas. He could only focus on the map for a few seconds at a time before the sounds of beeping horns snapped his attention back to the road. Once again, his car veered into the other lane, and once again, as if it was their fault, he flipped off the driver. After he lowered his middle finger, he snatched up the map and placed it directly on the steering wheel, in hopes of making it easier to study.

***

It was late morning when the Dodge Dart rumbled over the short causeway and entered Applewood, or as the sign read:

MAINE'S MAGICAL ISLAND

The man rounded the bend and found himself passing through a small marina. Most of the fishing and lobster vessels were already out for the day, but there were still a handful of boats and dinghies floating about. He noticed a large wooden pier with stacks and stacks of lobster traps on it, but what really caught his eye was a little seaside shanty called The Rusty Anchor Tavern. He definitely added it to his mental list of places to go to.

Moments after passing through the marina, the man slammed on his brakes. Luckily, there was no one behind him. He threw it in reverse and slowly crept backwards until the wooden sign he had just passed was once again visible. It was white with blue lettering and read:

THE GREAT BLUE HERON INN

High up on the hill was a very old and quaint looking inn. He placed his hand above his eyes to shield the bright sun. As his car idled, he just sat there staring up at the large old inn. His mesmerized look was eventually broken up by a loud horn beeping from behind him.

"Yea, yea! Relax, ya impatient prick!"

He continued mumbling profanities as he threw his car back into drive, and after shooting his middle finger out the window, he turned into the front entrance of the inn. There was only one other car in the driveway, but he parked as far away from it as possible.

He took his fresh pack of Marlboros and shoved them into his t-shirt pocket. The cigarettes, along with an RC Cola, were purchased at a gas station vending machine back in Massachusetts. The only other thing he grabbed from his car was a tattered old leather satchel. He slung it around his neck and made his way up the walkway.

The inn was three stories high with faded white clapboards and blue shutters. The front yard was small but was filled with well-manicured and vibrant gardens. In the center of the yard were three wooden lobster traps stacked on one another. Several multi-colored buoys adorned the sides of the traps. The small wrap-around porch was lined with white chairs, which alternated between wicker and Adirondack chairs.

The man ran his fingers through his scraggily beard. Its dark reddish color matched his hair, as did the hints of grey. The screen door loudly creaked as he swung it open. He entered into what appeared to be a common room. There were couches, chairs, and end tables with antique lamps placed on them. The walls were covered with plenty of old Maine photos. The man moved closer to get a better look at them.

"That was this place back in 1879."

The man spun around to see a pleasant looking woman smiling over at him. She looked to be in her fifties. She was dressed neatly in a dark pair of front-pleated slacks, a pale yellow cable knit sweater and a pair of penny loafers. Her auburn hair was pulled back into a chignon bun and the man noticed her matching pearl necklace and earring set.

He almost blurted out a snide comment about her being a modern-day June Cleaver, but he pulled back at the last second. He knew which side his bread was buttered on, and he couldn't risk her turning him away from renting a room.

"As you can see, it hasn't really changed much," she said, smiling.

The man cut right to the chase. "I need a room… for a week."

"Do you have a reservation with us?"

"No. Why? Is that a problem?"

"Not at all," she said. "We're still a month or so away from our busy season, so things are quite slow here at the moment. As a matter of fact, as of now, I only have one reservation this week. They should be checking in sometime tomorr—"

"Did I mention I needed it for a week?" David interrupted.

She smiled and nodded. "Why don't you come over here, and I'll get you signed in." She motioned to a small front desk off to the far right.

"I'll be paying cash," he announced, following her over to the desk.

"Sure. Whatever you like."

Before she could hand him a clipboard, he blurted out, "It's our anniversary later this week."

"Congratulations! We get a lot of couples here on—"

"I can get your best room, right?" he interrupted.

"I think you two will be very happy with your room," she said, handing him a clipboard and a pen. "If you could just quickly fill this out for me, that'd be great."

She could tell by his expression that he looked a little overwhelmed by the simple form. As he continued staring down at it, the woman took a moment to take in his entire appearance. His t-shirt was dirty and stained but was nothing like the condition of his blue jeans. They were ripped, filthy, and had random paint splatters about them. He smelled of cigarettes, alcohol, and BO; bad, bad BO. It was apparent that he probably hadn't showered in weeks. The man was only forty-two, but between the grey hairs and the heavy lines on his face, one could have easily assumed he was in his fifties or sixties even.

When he finally put pen to paper, his hand was shaking uncontrollably. Frustrated and impatient, he slid the clipboard back to her. She gave it a quick once-over, noticing that he left the address blank. The only thing he actually filled out was his name, and even that was illegible.

"Thank you, Mister…" she squinted down at the form trying her best to read his name.

"Simmons. But call me David, okay?"

"Very nice to meet you, David. I'm Janice." She politely smiled, holding out her hand.

He looked at her outstretched hand but didn't reciprocate.

Instead, he pulled out a wad of money and changed the subject. "I can pay cash, right?"

"Of course," she said, retracting her hand. After she handled the transaction, she grabbed a key off a hook. "If you'll follow me, I'll give you a tour of the place."

The first room they entered was the living room. It was a decent size area with a stone fireplace as its centerpiece. There was a couch, three armchairs, and a large Zenith console TV.

Janice pointed down the hall. "Our two first-floor guest rooms are down that way."

"Is that where you're sticking me?"

Janice smiled and shook her head.

"Those two are pretty basic. The special room I picked for you is up on the second floor."

Besides the two guest rooms, the first floor consisted of a small library, a sunroom, a kitchen, and a large dining room with an oversized pine table in its center.

"Will your wife be joining us for dinner tonight?"

"Dinner? Here? How much is that gonna cost me?"

"Not a thing," she said with a laugh. Breakfast and dinner are part of your stay."

"Oh. Okay. And no, Maggie won't be joining me for dinner. I wanted to get into town early to get things ready. I want everything to be perfect. Absolutely perfect."

"Aww, that's very sweet of—"

"Can I see my room now?" he said, once again interrupting her.

"Sure, of course. Follow me." Janice led him towards the staircase. "This inn has a total of eight guest rooms. Two on the first, four on the second, and two on the third. The two on the third are in the process of being remodeled. Of course, it's been in the process for three years now. It was my husband's big project."

"Sounds like someone's a procrastinator," he mumbled.

Without making eye contact, Janice replied, "He passed away two and half years ago."

"That sucks," David said, matter of fact.

Surprisingly, Janice seemed to not take offense to his insensitive comment. Instead, she sadly smiled and said, "Yes, it does suck." At the top of the landing, she pointed to her right. "There are two rooms this way and two rooms that way," she said, now pointing to her left. "Each side has a room with a private bathroom, and the other rooms share this one."

Janice motioned to a bathroom directly in front of her. She noticed his expression, and before he could blurt out his displeasure, she quickly quelled his worry. "Don't worry, Mr. Simmons," she said with a wink, "I gave you one of the rooms with a private bath."

"Damn right! I'm not paying all this money to share a goddamn toilet with a stranger."

Unbeknownst to Janice, David's comment was soaked in irony. Not only had he stayed at many places that shared a bathroom, but he'd also crashed at places with no bathrooms at all: Sidewalks, benches, cars. David followed her down the hall until they came to room 4.

"This is one of my favorite rooms of the inn," she said, allowing him to enter and inspect for himself. The room was spacious, well-lit, and had the biggest canopy bed David had ever seen. There was a nautical theme to the room with four framed pictures of scenic spots on the island. He then entered the bathroom. It was also good-sized with a shiny slate grey tiled floor.

"No shower?" he grunted.

"Unfortunately, no. Just the tub."

In the corner was a white porcelain bear claw tub. Janice braced herself and assumed David would demand another room, but he surprised her by offering up a shrug.

"Maggie loves taking bubble baths. She likes to fall asleep while reading in there."

"Sounds like my kind of woman," Janice said. She watched as David stepped out of the bathroom and gave another long look around the room. Finally, a slight smile formed on his face.

"It's perfect!"

This was the first time she had seen David smile. He walked over to the window, and his demeanor seemed to lighten even more.

"Good. I'm glad," Janice said. "Well, I'll let you get settled in. If you need anything at all, let me know."

David didn't respond. He was too busy staring out the window at the courtyard and the many flower beds down below. When he finally did turn around, Janice had already left. He closed the door, placed his satchel on a chair, then jumped face first onto the bed.

Within seconds, he began having another one of his coughing fits. David sat up straight, holding the side of his abdomen in pain. He climbed off the bed and began rummaging through his satchel. He pulled out a bottle of pain pills and a small bottle of vodka. When he noticed it was bone dry, he angrily slammed it onto his bed. He tossed back a few pills, grabbed his satchel, and made his way back downstairs.

Janice was in the middle of dusting. When she saw David, she paused what she was doing and asked, "Is everything okay with your room?"

"Yea, everything's fine," he said, walking towards her. "What restaurant do you recommend for our anniversary dinner?"

"Hmm, let's see," she pondered.

"It doesn't have to be fancy… just needs to be cozy and picturesque. Definitely picturesque."

"The Cliffside Restaurant," she said definitively. "It has only been

25

open for a few years or so, but they get nothing but rave reviews."

"The Cliffside, huh?" he said, running his fingers through his beard.

She smiled and nodded. "It's on the other side of the island."

"And it's picturesque?" he asked suspiciously.

"Very! My husband and I only went there once, but I highly recommend it."

Janice paused and took an inconspicuous glance at David's dirty and raggedy clothes and began to regret her recommendation. The restaurant didn't have a dress code per se, but if those were the only type of clothes he owned, he would most certainly feel out of place. Janice felt the need to point this out. "They are on the pricey side, though. There are a couple of other places that might be—"

"Nope! This place sounds perfect. Besides, money is no object. I've been saving up for this for a long, long time. Also, is there a flower shop in town? If not, I need directions to the best of the best!"

Janice chuckled at his enthusiasm.

"I'm overdoing it, aren't I?" he asked.

"Not at all. I think it's sweet. Your wife must be very special."

"She's one of the best things that has ever happened to me. Better than I ever deserved, that's for sure."

Unsure how to respond, Janice simply stood there, politely smiling at David.

"Is there a pay phone around here?" he asked.

"You're more than welcome to use our phone," she said, pointing to the black rotary phone sitting on the counter of the front desk."

"You sure?"

"I'm positive."

He mumbled what she assumed to be *thank you* then walked over to the phone. Janice made her way into the next room in order to give him some privacy. When she returned a few minutes later, he was off the phone and walking towards the front door.

"Did you make your call?" she asked.

He nodded and said, "Is there a store on the island where I can get some… some supplies?"

"Take a right out of the driveway. There's a general store a few miles up the road."

David confirmed what she assumed he meant by *supplies*. "Do they sell cigarettes… and booze?"

"I believe so," she said. It's a small store, but they have a little bit of everything there."

Satisfied with her answer, David just stood there nodding and running his fingers through his beard.

"Well, I should probably get back to work. The laundry isn't going to wash itself today."

Again, David said nothing. He adjusted his satchel then started to open the door. Janice took another long look at his clothes and decided to take a chance with an offer. "Actually, David, if you have anything you need washed, I'd be happy to throw them in."

David stopped at the front door and turned around and shot her a suspicious glare. Not wanting to offend him in any way, Janice was quick to clarify her suggestion.

"I saw your California license plate and just assumed you had a very long drive to get here. My husband used to be a truck driver, and whenever he got back from the road, I was always surprised at just how many dirty clothes he had."

David stood still and continued to glare. At any moment, Janice expected him to snap at her.

"How much is that gonna cost me?" he finally spoke.

"Oh, nothing at all. Just another perk for staying here. I offer it to all our guests," she lied.

His eyes remained on hers. She held a hopeful breath, for she wasn't sure if he had bought her white lie or not.

"I might have a few things in the car that could use some washing," he said.

Slowly, she released a relieved breath. "Bring them in and I'll get right on it."

He opened the screen door halfway then spun back around. "What kind of detergent do you use?"

Janice almost found herself laughing at his question, until she saw he was completely being serious.

"Umm, I use—"

"Because I don't like Ivory Snow or Bold."

"I use Cheer," she said, crossing her fingers this would be acceptable.

David paused a second. "All temperature Cheer, huh?" He pondered, and then bobbed his head in approval and walked outside. As the door shut behind him, Janice couldn't help but smirk at his response. There were many things about him that caused her to be a little suspicious and weary, but she was raised to never judge a book by its cover, so she was determined to give this stranger the benefit of the doubt.

A few minutes later, the front door swung wide open. Janice's eyes also swung wide open when she saw David standing there, buried behind a huge armful of clothes. "It might be a little more than a few clothes," he announced, making his way into the room.

"Oh, that's ok," she said. "You can just set them down right over…" David released the pile of clothes onto one of the chairs. "Sure, that chair is fine," she said with a smirk.

Without a word or even a thank you, he turned and once again exited the house. Janice was left staring and laughing at the giant pile of filthy clothes. As she made her way towards the chair, the pungent odor hit her and she was forced to cover her nose.

"Oh, Janice, what did you get yourself into?" she said aloud. She held her breath, scooped up the clothes, and made a mental note to give the chair a good spray-down with Lysol.

David followed her directions and found his way to the old general store up the road. They didn't have a huge section of hard booze, but luckily, all he needed was vodka. He purchased two small pints, two packs of Marlboros, and a bag of pork rinds.

He drove back towards the inn, but rather than turning into the driveway, he passed right by and headed for the tavern he'd driven by earlier. He pulled into the small marina and parked directly in front of the Rusty Anchor Tavern. David didn't realize it until he approached the door, but there was a reason his car was the only one in the dirt parking lot. Taped to the door was a makeshift cardboard sign.

OPENING AT 4PM TODAY, SORRY!

David grumbled some profanities then climbed into his car, slamming the door behind him. Seeing as he just purchased two bottles of vodka, it wasn't that he was lacking alcohol, but sometimes he enjoyed the social setting of a bar. This was also filled with irony considering he wasn't the most social person in the world.

Even though he had a perfectly comfortable bed back at the inn, he chose to recline his seat and nap in his car. It was more force of habit than anything. It felt as though he'd been on the road forever, and now that he had reached his destination, his mind and body were beyond exhausted. It didn't take long for him to fall into a deep sleep. The burning cigarette in his hand fell to the floor and luckily extinguished itself before causing any real danger. There were dozens of burn marks and holes on his vinyl seats and floor boards from this very occurrence.

When he finally awoke, the tavern was open, and there were at least ten other cars around him. He entered the local watering hole and sat at the very end of the bar. He treated himself to a Jack and Coke, and although this wasn't his usual drink, he seemed to enjoy the change of pace. Other than doing a little bantering with a few locals and the bartender, David kept to himself.

It was late in the evening when he finally returned to the inn. The place was extremely silent. Of course, all that changed as David drunkenly stumbled up the stairs, nearly knocking over two pictures along the way. At the foot of his door was a laundry basket filled with his clothes. They were crisply folded and smelled noticeable better than before.

It took him a while to retrieve the key from his pocket and even longer to get it into the keyhole. With his foot, he pushed the laundry basket into his room, shutting the door behind him. Before climbing into bed, he dug into his satchel and washed down some pain pills with a swig of vodka. He attempted to strip down to his underwear, but when his jeans got caught around his ankles, he quite literally fell into bed. The blanket over his body felt warm and cozy, and the pillow beneath his head was the softest thing he'd ever felt. Those would be the last thoughts to cross his mind that night.

3

If it wasn't for his uncontrollable coughing, David would have snoozed the day away. It had been weeks since he had slept in an actual bed. Groggy and still exhausted, he shielded his eyes from the sun glaring in through the window. When his coughing subsided, he clutched at his side and glanced over to the clock—11:45 a.m. He allowed his head to fall back onto the pillow, but a loud buzzing noise from outside prevented his eyes from closing. Even with the pillow thrown over his face, the annoying buzzing sound continued to reverberate around his head.

"Oh, for fuck's sake!" he yelled, throwing the pillow across the room.

He climbed out of bed and headed over to the half-opened window. Down below, a landscape company was mowing and weed-whacking the back yard. Annoyed, David slammed the window shut then made his way downstairs. Before he hit the final step, he was greeted by Janice.

"Looks like someone slept in today."

"Would have slept in longer if it wasn't for that damn company."

It took a second for Janice to realize what he was referring to, but when she figured it out, she offered an apology for the noise. "I'm sorry about that, David. That's my new landscaping company. They've been working extra hard getting this place ready for the season. You wouldn't know it now, but this place gets quite busy in another month or so. Believe it or not, I used to do all the gardening and upkeep myself, but it just got too much after my husband passed away."

David was barely paying attention. He seemed more concerned with taking one whiff after another of his shirt. "Are you sure you used all-temperature Cheer?" he asked. "This smells like a different brand."

Janice laughed and said, "I promise. I can show you the box if you—"

"Ya got any coffee?" he interrupted.

"The coffee station is still set up in the dining room. Help yourself. I can whip you up a late breakfast or an early lunch if—"

"I just need coffee, that's all." he said, walking towards the dining room.

She could tell he was in no mood for small talk, so she politely nodded and continued into the kitchen. When she returned, David was headed back upstairs with his coffee. It didn't take long for him to once again fall sound asleep in his giant canopy bed. It was nearly four o'clock before his eyes would open again. By then, Janice had long since finished her chores and was relaxing in a chair with a hot tea and a good book. She knew once the busy season hit, there'd be little or no down-time, so she took full advantage of the quiet afternoon.

Just then, Janice heard the front door slowly creak open. She assumed it was the Hendersons checking in. So far, they were the only new reservations for the day. "Oh well," she said, closing her book and climbing out of the chair. "So much for getting some reading done."

When she entered the foyer, she saw a young woman with her back to her. She was standing at the front desk and was about to ring the bell.

"Can I help you?" Janice called from across the room.

The girl's hand stopped short of the bell and turned around. Janice knew the Hendersons were a young couple, but this girl looked barely out of high school. It was Hope.

"Can I help you, sweetie?" Janice repeated.

Hope just stood there, fidgeting with her hands and searching for an answer to this woman's simple question. She nervously bit down on her lip, knowing full-well the answer was far from simple.

"Maggie! You're here already!"

Both Hope and Janice had confused looks on their faces as they turned to see David standing halfway up the staircase. With a smile and a mesmerized look, he made his way down the rest of the stairs. Janice joined him in staring over at Hope, whose face was now red in embarrassment. In truth, Hope was a spitting image of her mother; right down to the group of freckles on each of her cheekbones.

She once again bit down on her lip and quietly said, "I'm not Maggie… I'm Hope… your daughter."

Confused, David looked from Hope to Janice and then back to Hope. A bit embarrassed himself, he half-laughed and played it off. "I know who you are. Why wouldn't I know who you are? So, you've come to help with the big day, huh?"

"What?" Hope asked.

"You know what I'm talking about, silly. It's mine and your mother's anniversary in a few days. We've got a lot of planning to do, you and I." David then looked over at Janice and asked, "You have an extra room for her this week, right? I'll pay for her."

Janice herself was completely confused and unsure what exactly was going on. Hesitantly, she answered, "Uh, sure. Of course we can accommodate your daughter."

Hope didn't even get a chance to say a word say a word. "Well, why don't you have Janice settle you in, and we'll meet up later to go over the details for the week." Much more content than when he first awoke, David rushed back upstairs.

Hope thought of scenario after scenario on her long ride from Chicago to Maine. Some of the good ones involved her father greeting her with open arms. The bad ones involved David not even being at the inn. She did her best to prepare herself, knowing full well this trip was a long shot and that the whole thing could just be a giant dead end. The one scenario she didn't prepare for was her father mistaking her for her mother.

Janice had no idea what was happening, but she put on a warm smile and began to escort Hope up to her room. "Where did you drive in from?" she asked.

"Chicago," Hope answered softly.

"Chicago? I heard that's a beautiful city. Quite the long drive, though."

Janice brought her to a guestroom at the top of the stairs. Hope remained quiet, and Janice could tell that her mind was somewhere else. She led her to the room directly across the hall from David.

"It's a little small, but I think you'll find it to be quite cozy," Janice said, opening the door.

Hope quickly gazed around the room but was more concerned with what Janice must be thinking about this whole strange situation.

"I'm sorry for putting you in the middle of this, ma'am." Hope lowered her head, staring down at the floor.

"First of all, it's Janice, not ma'am. And second, I'm not exactly sure what I'm in the middle of, but I will say, he seems very happy that you're here to help plan the big anniversary. He's been excited about it ever since he arrived here yesterday. Your mother sounds very special."

Hope's hands started to once again fidget by her side. She rarely trusted people enough to tell them her true thoughts. Actually, it was less of a trust factor and more of a case of not wanting to bore people with her own problems or feelings. Hope sat on the edge of the bed then slowly raised her head up to the inn keeper. Janice's eyes seemed kind and full of understanding. So much so, that Hope let her guard down and opened up about what was going on.

"My mother… my mother died during childbirth. I never met her."

Janice clutched her heart. "You poor girl. I had no idea."

"Actually, until a few minutes ago, I'd never met my father either."

Janice's expression turned from sympathetic to confused. "What? I don't understand?" She took a seat next to Hope.

"I don't have a lot of details about what happened. I just know there were complications and that she passed away shortly after I was born."

The only person in recent memory that Hope had revealed this to was her roommate, Robin. She hadn't intended on it, but Robin took an honest interest in knowing more about Hope. So when she started asking about her family life, Hope just sort of told her.

With her eyes becoming red with emotion, Janice placed her hand on Hope's and said, "Oh sweetie, I'm so sorry."

Surprisingly, Hope's eyes remained dry. She was still reeling from the shock of seeing her father for the first time in person. Her uncle had shown her some pictures of him from when he was much younger, but seeing him now face to face, he didn't look like any of those photos, nor did he resemble the person she had imagined him to be.

"I guess soon after she died, my father just lost it… completely lost it. I… I haven't seen him since. My grandparents—"

Before Hope could offer any more details, the faint sound of a ringing bell echoed upstairs into the bedroom.

"That must be the Hendersons checking in," Janice said, standing up.

"I'm sorry," Hope said, "I didn't mean to interrupt your—"

Janice looked directly into Hope's eyes. "No interruption at all. I'll tell you what, as soon as you get your stuff settled in, why don't you come downstairs and I'll get you something to eat. Okay?"

Hope nodded in appreciation then softly said, "Thank you, ma'am."

"It's Janice. And you're welcome." She gave Hope a wink then headed downstairs.

As soon as Janice checked the young couple in, she scurried off to the kitchen and fixed Hope some food. Janice still had a bunch of questions for Hope but allowed her to eat in peace. She knew the young girl needed some space and a chance to process everything that just went down. Janice knew something was off about David from the moment he walked into the inn, but she had no idea just how bad it was.

***

About an hour or so later, David once again came down from his room. He snatched a handful of fresh-baked cookies from the counter and headed outside to the front porch. After he made quick work of the cookies, he wasted no time shoving a cigarette into his mouth. It wasn't until his second exhale of smoke that he noticed Hope sitting at the end of the porch. David took one more puff then made his way over and plopped down next to his daughter.

She had years to think of what she wanted to say to her father, yet now that she was face to face, the words seemed to escape her. He took the cigarette out of his mouth long enough to take a swig from his bottle. She watched but said nothing.

"So, you in school or something?" he asked, putting the cigarette back into his mouth.

"I'm a junior at Northwestern."

"Northwestern, huh? My brother went there."

"Yea, I know," she softly replied. She paused a second and said, "He told me."

"Oh, he did, did he? What are you two, best friends or something?"

"No. We just talk once in a while... and he always sends me a card on my birthday."

She hoped her last comment would cause him to mention the years of anonymous phone calls on her birthday. It didn't. Instead, he continued on with his sarcastic line of questioning. "How is my fuckin' brother doing these days?"

The truth was, she only talked to her uncle a handful of times a year. Back when he lived closer to Chicago, they saw and talked to each a lot more, but he moved to Europe back when she was six. *At least Uncle Jeremy made an effort to be in my life*, she thought. This was a lot more than she could say about her own father. That being said, she wasn't angry with him. Despite twenty years of abandonment, she was never really angry with him. Sure, there were times she felt it boiling just below the surface, but ultimately, she knew her father was unwell. It didn't take long before she realized just how unwell he actually was.

"When was the last time you talked to him?" Hope asked.

"My fuckin' brother? Pfft, it's been a long, long time."

She watched him nervously fidget with his hands as he stared out at the front lawn. It was clear who she got that habit from.

"Is my brother still selling drugs?"

"What? He works for a pharmaceutical company," she clarified.

"Eh, same difference. Is he still a Nazi?"

Hope couldn't tell if he was joking or serious, but she answered anyway. "Uncle Jeremy isn't a Nazi."

"Then why does he live in Germany? Huh? Huh?"

"Because that's where his wife is from."

David took another pull from his vodka and said, "She's probably a Nazi, too."

Just then, her attention turned to the side of the house as one of the landscapers came around the corner. The boy looked to be close to her age. Hope's look lingered long enough to see him slip off his Red Sox hat, revealing the tips of his perfectly blonde hair, which were dipped in sweat.

As if sensing her staring at him, he paused at the porch, lowered his sunglasses, and then threw his blue eyes in Hope's direction. They exchanged a quick smile with one another, and before he had a chance to see her blush, he turned and headed towards his truck. Her smitten trance was quickly interrupted by her father's comments. "That's the goddamn punk who woke me up earlier!"

Having no idea what he was talking about, Hope glanced over at her father. By the time she returned her look to the boy, he had already backed out of the driveway and was speeding away.

"So, what are they learning you over at that school of yours?" he asked.

"I'm majoring in behavioral health and psychology. I'd like to be a therapist one day." She looked over at him as if to gauge his reaction, but he had none. He just sat there, puffing and swigging away.

"Did you know your mother wanted to be a doctor?"

Slowly, Hope shook her head no. Her grandparents didn't talk about her mother much, but when they did, they would simply say she had all the potential in the world and that she was smart enough to do anything she wanted.

"Not a nurse… but a *doctor*," he clarified. She was that smart. Did you know she was the Victorian of her high school?"

Knowing he meant valedictorian, she laughed to herself then quietly said, "Like mother like daughter."

"What?"

"I also graduated at the top of my class," she said, hoping to get some sort of proud reaction from her father.

"Your grandparents must be through the roof. They always put a high stock in that sort of crap. They are still alive, aren't they?" he asked, not really caring either way.

Before she could answer, David began coughing.

"You okay?"

"Yea, I'm fine. Just coming down with something, that's all," he said, standing up. "I think I'm gonna go lay back down for a bit."

Without a goodbye or another word, David walked away from Hope and into the house. As soon as the door closed behind him, she lowered her head into her hands. She still wasn't sure what she even wanted to accomplish from her trip, but she knew it wasn't to watch him smoke and drink himself to death.

Frustrated, Hope stood up from her chair and headed towards her car. As she walked by the Dodge Dart, she couldn't help but to notice just how much of a disaster it was inside. The ashtray was overflowing with cigarette butts, and there were empty alcohol bottles and food wrappers strewn about. She assumed this must be her father's car, and she also assumed by the pillow and old blanket in the backseat that he'd been living out of it for a while now.

There was a part of her that wished she had never seen an earlier picture of her father. Maybe then, it wouldn't have been such a sad shock seeing him in the condition he was now. *No*, she thought to herself. *Either way it would have been depressing to see him like this.* Her heart broke for him. This would become a familiar feeling over the next week.

Out of her car, she grabbed a book then headed back into the house and settled herself into a cozy chair in the library.

"I see you've made yourself at home."

Hope looked up to see Janice standing in the doorway.

"This is a great room," Hope said with a smile. "I'd love to have one of these."

"One of my favorite rooms in the house. Feel free to read anything in here."

"Are these books all yours?"

"A lot are from my personal collection, but most of the books have always been here. This inn is actually one of the oldest buildings in Applewood."

In the corner of the room stood a wooden carving of a Great Blue Heron. Hope pointed to it and asked, "Did you pick out that name? The Great Blue Heron Inn?"

Janice joined her in staring at the carving. "Nope. It's always been called that. The Great Blue Heron is a very important symbol to the Natives of the island."

"Like a spirit animal?" Hope asked. "I saw a really groovy documentary about Native American culture, and on one of the parts, they talked about spirit animals and their meanings. I don't remember if they mentioned the Great Blue Heron or not. It was a while ago."

"Self-reliance and self-determination," Janice said, staring directly into Hope's eyes.

"Huh?"

"Those are two of the attributes of the Great Blue Heron. They prefer to be alone but can certainly flourish amongst others. The heron also acts as a guide and teaches you to find your true self, but to also discover your true gift as well." Janice paused, and then gazed deeper into Hope's eyes before continuing. "The native fishermen here believed it brought them good luck. Overall, the Great Blue Heron is one of the spirits that looks after this island and its people."

"Groovy," Hope said, smiling over at the wooden statue.

"I'm sure there's a book or two in here on spirit animals. Like I said, feel free to read whatever you like. As for me, I have chores to get done. The busy season will be here before I know it. If you need anything, let me know, okay?"

"Thanks, Mrs.—"

"Janice. It's Janice, dear."

"Thanks… Janice."

4

Out in the courtyard, David sat on one of the benches overlooking the water fountain. Dusk was just settling in, and the cool island air was starting to take hold. He only had on a blue shirt, but he had his vodka to keep him warm. His shirt was still stained and paper thin, but at least it was washed and smelling a whole lot better. Every so often, David found himself sniffing his shirt. It was hard to tell if he took pleasure in the fresh scent or if he was still questioning if Janice indeed used the proper detergent.

For what seemed like forever, Hope stood at the back door. She was carefully studying this man that in no way resembled the father she had envisioned all those years. He was only forty-two, but he was the oldest forty-two she'd ever seen. The lines on his face were from a long, rough life lived in a short period of time. There was a hardness about him.

The lines on his face and his overall appearance only added to the many questions she had for him. Knowing she didn't drive all this way just to watch him from afar, Hope took a deep breath then slowly opened the door and made her way towards her father. He heard her approaching, but never once looked over at her. His eyes remained on the fountain, and his lips remained swigging from his flask.

Hope sat on the other end of the bench but said nothing. It would be a few minutes before anything was spoken.

"You all settled in?" he asked.

She nodded, but her eyes were still focused on his bottle.

"Good. Tomorrow we can go check out this restaurant Janice recommended to me. If we like it, we can make a reservation for the big anniversary dinner."

Hope squirmed in her seat. Every time he mentioned her mother, it made her insides twist and turn. *Does he really think she's still alive? Has he thought this way the last twenty years?* These questions and more continued to weave in and out of her head.

"Oh, and we need to find a flower shop, too," he added. "I definitely need your help picking out flowers for your mother. I was never good at that sort of thing. I always went the typical red roses route, but this needs to be way more creative… way more stunning!"

Hope continued watching him take one swig after another. When he did pause, it was only to place a cigarette in his mouth. With his free hand, he searched each of his pockets for a lighter.

"Goddammit it!" he blurted out as his hand came up empty. "Where the hell is it? I just had that goddamn lighter a second ago." He looked at Hope and asked, "Got a light?"

"Umm, no. I don't smo—"

"Ahh, there it is!" he said, reaching into his front shirt pocket. "I knew I wasn't going crazy… crazier, that is," he said with a slight grin on his face.

Hope didn't return his grin. As a matter of fact, she didn't appreciate his humor at all regarding his mental health. And she certainly didn't appreciate him continuously drinking from his flask. She recalled all the times she had overheard her grandfather calling her father a no-good alcoholic. Actually, his exact words were "a no-good, drunken lunatic."

One time, when she was seven, she overheard him ranting and

raving to her grandmother about her father. He was yelling about how he had warned Maggie that David was nothing but trouble. "Once a drunk asshole, always a drunk asshole," her grandfather said. "That loony bin should have never let him out!"

Hope remembered sprinting into the living room and yelling at her grandparents for talking about her daddy that way. That would be the last time David's name would be mentioned in their house. But now, as she watched him smoking and drinking and barely acknowledging her existence, she wondered why she ever bothered to defend him.

"I need to get a card, too," he said, interrupting her train of thought. "I've never been much of a card person either—but this anniversary is a pretty big deal. Yea, I definitely need the perfect card."

The whole time David was talking, he was fumbling with his lighter in attempt to light his cigarette. At one point, the lighter slipped from his shaking hand and fell to the ground.

"Fuckin' lighter," he scoffed, bending down to pick it up. When he finally got his cigarette lit, he noticed Hope staring blankly at him. "What? Why the hell do you keep looking at me like that?"

"This is the first time in my life seeing my father. How am I supposed to look at you?"

She was a little surprised that she blurted that out, but it felt good to finally say at least one thing that had been on her mind. David seemed unaffected by her comment. He took a long drag off his cigarette then released a giant bellow of smoke.

"Did I mention that I need you to help me pick out flowers for our anniversary?"

Hope lowered her head, letting out a sigh.

"What's your problem? Don't you wanna help me plan the big day?"

Without thinking too hard, Hope uttered, "What I want is to just have a conversation with you."

"What the hell do you call this?" he mumbled with his cigarette dangling from his lips. He followed that up by polishing off the rest of his vodka.

She searched for something to say, but all she could come up with was, "That stuff is gonna kill you, ya know?"

She assumed her comment would cause him to lash out at her, but all it seemed to do was amuse him. He twisted the cap onto the bottle and shoved it back into his satchel. He took one last satisfying drag from his cigarette, tossed it into the fountain, and then stood up and started to head back inside.

"Really? You're just gonna walk way… again?"

She emphasized the word *again* and braced herself for what she was sure to be a caustic response. But again, he had no response except to continue walking towards the house.

"Where are you going? You seriously can't have like a five-minute conversation with me? You owe me that much."

He placed his hand on the back door, and without turning around, he announced, "I'll tell ya where I'm going. I'm taking a little stroll to that tavern down the road. If you wanna join me, so be it. If not… so be it."

Hope had no response, and even if she did, it wouldn't have mattered. David had already entered the inn, firmly closing the door behind him. She sat there a moment then leaned forward placing her head in her hands. With the exception of the running water in the fountain, the night air was completely silent.

***

When David arrived at the tavern, there were only a handful of locals scattered about. He sat in the same stool as the previous night and decided to go with another Jack and Coke as well. Just like before, each customer gave David a look, telling him they knew he was an out-of-towner. Their look was brief, for their attention quickly returned to the Red Sox game on the sole television behind the bar.

As David took a sip from his drink, he also focused on the game, but it was more out of boredom than anything. He had no real interest in the Red Sox or sports, for that matter. This wasn't always the case. He used to love watching and playing sports as a kid, but all that changed in his early teens.

Over the years, other things had taken over his main focus—things like: Holding down a job, finding a place to sleep at night, and more importantly, finding ways to numb his pain by keeping alcohol pumping through his veins. Unfortunately, all the alcohol in the world didn't prevent the voices in his head from getting stronger and stronger.

It didn't take long before he completely lost interest in the Sox game. He began stirring his drink with his finger and mumbling to himself. At one point, his mumbling got so loud that most of the bar was staring over at him. Unaware of their looks, he removed his finger from his drink and took a long, satisfying sip.

About halfway through his Jack and Coke, he heard the front door swing open from behind him. He didn't bother to turn around to see who entered. Instead, he focused in on an old Native American man sitting alone in the back corner. The old man's eyes widened, and he straightened up in his chair as best he could. David watched as a slight smile came over the man's face. Before he had a chance to turn around to see who he was staring at, she appeared next to him—his daughter.

Hesitantly, she slid out the stool and sat next to her father. David pretended not to notice, and instead, he glared back at the old man in the corner. He still wore a wide smile, and his eyes glistened as he continued staring over at Hope. David thought about giving the old man a piece of his mind, but he decided against it. Besides, he had more important things to do, like ordering another Jack and Coke for himself. The bartender was also staring over at Hope but for different reasons. His look was more out of curiosity. With all the empty seats around the place, why would this young girl choose to sit next to Mister Jack and Coke?

As the bartender moved towards them, David slid his empty glass forward and said, "I'll take another."

The bartender gave David a quick glance but turned his full attention to Hope. "What can I get you, dear?"

"Can I just get a ginger ale, please?"

David huffed and rolled his eyes at her non-alcoholic choice. When the bartender returned, he handed both of them their drinks. David took another long sip and did his best not to acknowledge his daughter. Hope nursed her ginger ale as her mind raced a mile a minute. She still had no idea why she had actually made the long trip to Maine, and she certainly had no idea why she was sitting at a bar next to a man who obviously wanted nothing to do with her. As her many doubts started to boil to the surface, she was tempted to just stand up and leave, but then it happened—he spoke.

"What the hell are you wearing?"

Hope had on her favorite bellbottom jeans. They were broken in in all the right places and fit her perfectly. There was good reason for them to be her favorite and she had no plans of retiring them any time soon, no matter how much shade was thrown at them. Paired with the jeans, she had on a blue and green batik camisole with a white jean jacket over it. The jacket had long tassels that hung like fringe under the sleeves. The tassels were long enough to be noticed but fine enough to not get in her way. She loved to fidget with the tassels and feel the weight of them on her arms. There was a calmness she felt in this particular jacket, and she couldn't help but feel grateful to be wearing it that evening while she tried to get to know her estranged father.

"What's wrong with what I'm wearing?"

"Nothing, if you're a goddamn hippy." Without giving her a chance to say a word, David changed the subject. "Do you realize the first time I met Maggie was right here at this bar?"

"Really?" she quietly asked. "I never even knew she had been to Maine before.

"Yup. Her best friend's parents had a summer place here, and coincidentally, my aunt and uncle had a place here as well. My brother and I used to come here in the summer... before he became a Nazi."

Hope rolled her eyes, but for the first time all night, a smirk appeared on her face. "I just assumed you guys met in Chicago."

David took another long sip but said nothing. Hope twirled the straw around her glass then asked, "What was she like?"

"Who? Your mother?"

"Yea. They don't talk about her much. Actually, Nana and Grampa rarely talk about her. Not about the stuff that matters anyway. I mean, I get it. I look like her, and my laugh is like hers, but... but I want to know what she was like as a person. Her favorite movies... the type of music she listened to. You know, that kind of stuff. The only thing they ever tell me is that she was super-smart and that she had so much potential, until..."

"Until she met me, huh?" David interjected.

"Actually, I was going to say, until she got pregnant with me."

"Is that what they told you?"

Hope paused then smirked and said, "No, they said it was because of you."

What appeared to be a smile crept onto David's face. "Yea, that's what I thought. Your grandparents never much liked me back then."

She took a sip from her straw and jokingly said, "They don't much

48

like you now either."

David looked over at his daughter and they both found themselves cracking a smile. For the moment, the tension was lessened, but that didn't stop David from continuing to poke fun of her jacket.

"For Christ's sake, Hope, take that damn jacket off! It's bad enough that everyone's looking at you like a goddamn tourist, never mind a goddamn hippy tourist! If you're gonna travel out of town, ya need to learn to blend in like me."

Hope obliged her father and slipped off her jacket, but she did it with a smile on her face. She knew full-well that there were more eyes on him than her. She placed the jacket beneath her, and as their conversation paused, Hope took a quick glance around the tavern. In the middle of the room, she noticed the cute boy from the landscaping company. He was sitting with a few of his buddies having drinks. Her look lingered long enough for him to notice her gazing over at him. He threw her a smile and a nod. Embarrassed that she got busted staring, she quickly looked away.

She was still blushing when her father blurted out, "*It's a Wonderful Life.*"

"Huh?"

"The movie… *It's a Wonderful Life…* ya ever heard of it?"

"Um, yea, but I've never really seen the whole thing. Just parts of it. Why?"

"It was your mother's favorite movie."

"Really?"

"She loved those magical types of movies. Ya know, like *The Wizard of Oz* and shit."

Hope smiled over at her father. *The Wizard of Oz* was one of her favorites as well.

"But to be honest, your mother wasn't really much of a TV or movie girl. But you can bet your bottom dollar that she always had a book by her side. Always."

Hope's smile grew, and she excitedly blurted out, "I'm totally like that, too!" Her excitement didn't seem to resonate with her father, for he was too busy jamming his finger back into his drink and stirring it.

"So, this is really where you met Mom?" she asked, looking around the bar.

David returned his attention to her and said, "Yup. It was there. Right *there*." He pointed to a spot across the bar. "That was where we had our first encounter."

"First encounter?" Hope said curiously.

"The first time we met, I was completely blasted. Shocking, I know." He continued staring intently over at the spot. "I remember it like it was yesterday. I walked over… well, I stumbled over and dropped some silly pickup line on her."

"And that worked?" Hope asked.

"God no. She told me, and I quote, 'Get your filthy hands off of me, ya creep!' She then proceeded to dump her drink on me."

Hope laughed. "Well that sounds like the start of a great romance."

"It was," he said with a straight face. "Because after I wiped the Pabst off myself, I knew without a doubt that I was gonna do whatever it took to win her over that summer."

"Wait," she interrupted. "If Mom had me when she was nineteen, that would mean she was drinking underage when you met her in her?"

David looked at her like she was nuts. "Yea, so. What are you, a cop?"

"No, I'm not a cop," Hope said, grinning. "It's just a little surprising that she would be at a bar drinking underage. By the way Nana and Grampa talk about her, she seemed too straight-laced for that."

David chuckled to himself.

"What? What's so funny?"

"Straight-laced? Maggie? Around them maybe. But trust me, your mother definitely has a wild side."

The fact that her father just used the word *has* instead of *had* in describing her mother, led her to think maybe he really did think she was still alive. Either way, she was still more than a little surprised that her mom might not have been as clean-cut as she thought. She liked that.

"And she really drank beer?"

"Yes, she drank beer. You don't think women like beer?"

"I know they do, but it's just…" she paused and let out a tiny laugh. "Pabst Blue Ribbon? Really?"

"You've got quite the stick up your ass, don't you?" he said, loud enough for multiple people to hear. He shook his head, mumbled something to himself then took another sip of his drink.

Still embarrassed from his comment, Hope finished her ginger ale and gave the ice at the bottom of the glass a swirl with her straw. After a few moments of swirling, she finally blurted out, "I don't have a stick up my rear. I'm just surprised learning these things about Mom. Like I said, nobody really talks about her… or you."

Uncomfortable where the conversation might be headed, David quickly changed the subject. "So, have your grandparents taken you on any vacations?"

His random question surprised her a bit, but she shrugged and answered, "Um, no, not really."

"No Disney World and shit?"

"No," she said, shaking her head. "Grampa hates big crowds, and Nana can't stand the hot weather.

David shook his head in disgust. "Yup, sounds just like Ray-Ray and Patty Cakes."

51

Hope nearly spit out her drink. No one *ever* called her grandparents that. They went by Raymond and Patricia—not Ray, not Patty, and certainly not Ray-Ray and Patty Cakes.

David started to take another sip, but quickly pointed out, "Now your grandparents definitely have sticks up *their* asses!"

Hope let out another laugh and said, "They totally do. To be honest, this is pretty much my first time outside of Illinois."

"Are you shitting me?"

"When I was a freshman, my roommate pity-invited me to go to Florida with her and her friends, but I had way too much schoolwork and studying to get done, so I—"

"Pity-invited?" he interrupted.

Embarrassed, Hope looked down at her glass. "I really don't have many friends... I kind of just keep to myself. So I'm assuming she just felt sorry for me... hence, she threw me a pity-invite."

David looked at her like she was crazy then said, "Who the hell cares why she invited you. You shoulda went! I can't believe you turned down a trip to Florida for some silly school work."

"It's not silly school work. I have to keep my grades up if I want to get to where I want to go." David shot her a look of disbelief. "Besides," she shrugged, "getting drunk all week and being hit on by immature college boys doesn't really sound appealing to me. Not to mention, they didn't even have a hotel booked. They were just going to find random people to stay with."

David laughed to himself and shook his head.

"What?" she asked. "I'm not like a prude or anything! I just like to have things planned out, that's all."

"Haven't you ever heard of spontaneity and living on the edge?"

"I can be spontaneous. I... I just like to plan it out first. I told you, I'm like Mom in that way."

"And I already told YOU, your mother could be very

spontaneous. Not to mention, she was the queen of living on the wild side."

Hope stole another look over at the cute boy then looked back at her father and said, "I was actually invited to go to a big house up at Lake Michigan this week, but—"

"Let me guess, it was another pity-invite?"

Sadly, she shrugged. "Something like that."

David shook his head, finished off his drink, and slowly climbed off the stool. "I'm gonna take a piss, and then I'm heading back to the inn."

"Oh, okay," she said, reaching in her macramé bag for her wallet.

"I got it," he said. "I'll meet you out front." He tossed some crumpled bills onto the bar and stumbled his way across the tavern, intermittently coughing as he walked.

Before exiting the front door, Hope made sure he made it into the bathroom okay. As soon as the bathroom door closed behind him, he clutched his side in pain. The coughing became more persistent. With his shoulder, he forcefully nudged open the stall door and began throwing up. It was mostly dry heaves, but what did come up was filled with blood. After he finished splashing his face with water, he reached into his satchel and pulled out his pain pills and popped a few into his mouth.

A cold chill was blowing in off the ocean, and as Hope stood waiting for her father, she put her jacket back on. She closed her eyes and took a deep breath of the salt air. When she opened them, she was surprised to see the cute boy from inside heading her way. With his Red Sox hat on backwards, he approached, smiled, and then said, "I saw you earlier today. I was doing some landscaping at the place you're staying."

If Darcy or Dee were here, they would have told her to pretend she didn't really remember seeing him. "Always play hard to get and act like you barely notice them," is what they told Hope on numerous occasions.

"I remember you," Hope said way too quickly. "You walked by me on the porch." She was never good at playing the mind games that other girls did.

"From Illinois, huh?" he asked.

"How'd you know that?"

"It's a gift," he boasted. "I can always tell what state people are from."

For a brief second, she almost bought into his *gift*, but then it hit her. "You saw my license plate earlier, didn't you?"

"I almost had you," he said, smiling and moving closer. "You a Chicago girl?"

"Yea," she curiously said. "How did you know that?"

"See, I told you I have a gift."

Hope thought for a moment and smiled. "That's the only city you know in Illinois, isn't it?"

He let out a laugh then raised his hands. "Busted."

The goosebumps on her arms were less about the cold wind and more about the cute boy, who was now standing within a foot of her.

"I'm Adam," he said, reaching out his hand.

"I'm Hope," she said, returning his gesture.

"Oh, in full disclosure," he said in an almost whisper, "I'm not really a fan of any of your sports teams."

Hope responded with, "In full disclosure, I don't really follow sports, so it's all good."

They both shared a laugh, and she allowed herself to quickly glance into his piercing blue eyes. His attractiveness was enough to not only make her cheeks blush, but to make her goosebumps have goosebumps. Moments later, the tavern door opened and David exited. He looked out into the parking lot just in time to see Adam writing something on Hope's hand. When Adam finished, he threw her a wink and a smile then made his way back into the tavern. As he passed by David, he gave him an acknowledging nod. David didn't return the boy's gesture. He simply shot a death-stare his way. By the time David got to Hope, she had a smitten glow about her.

"What the hell was that about?" he said, cutting to the chase.

"What? He's one of the landscapers at the…"

Before she could finish her sentence, David grabbed her wrist and looked at her hand. "What do we have here?"

"It's just his phone number, that's all."

David released her wrist and shook his head. "He wrote his number on your hand? What is he, like, twelve?"

"Relax. I'm probably not even going to call him. He's way out of my league—"

"Where the hell is your car?" he blurted out, looking around the parking lot.

"I… I walked over here just like you did."

David scratched at his beard and began to mumble to himself.

"I can run back to the inn and come back to pick you—"

"What, ya don't think I can handle the walk?"

The next thing she knew, he was already stumbling his way towards the road. Not much was said on the short walk back to the inn. It wasn't until they walked up the steps of the porch that he once again glanced down at her hand and shook his head in disgust.

She noticed his look and said, "You don't even know him."

"Doesn't matter. I know his type."

"Oh, really? And what's his type?"

David opened the front door and turned to his daughter. "Bad news. That's his type."

She followed him inside. "How do you know that?"

"Because we can smell our own kind," he said straight-faced. "Not to mention, wearing a baseball hat backwards is a dead giveaway. Classic dickhead move." David let out a big drunken yawn and said, "Night."

Hope peered up at the clock on the wall. "You're going to bed already? It's only nine-thirty."

She was secretly hoping they could continue their chat from earlier at the tavern. She still had so many questions to ask her father.

"Lots to do tomorrow. The big day is close at hand," was all he said.

Sympathetically, Hope watched her father slowly climb the stairs. Hearing him continually mention the big day, left her with an uncomfortable sense of sadness in her heart. Without turning back around, David yelled down from the top step. "Word to the wise— wash your goddamn hand!"

Her sadness was briefly replaced with a tiny smirk as he disappeared out of sight. Moments after he shut his door, Hope also went upstairs to her room, but she was only there long enough to grab her keys. She then headed back outside to her car where she opened her trunk and pulled out her guitar case. The case was worn and covered in stickers. In addition to peace symbols, flowers, and the Grateful Dead bears, there were also stickers with slogans on them – *Make Love Not War – Give Peace a Chance.*

The gravel path crunched beneath her feet as she followed it around to the courtyard in the back. It was beautifully lit by multiple strings of white lights. Hope placed the case at her feet and settled herself on one of the benches. Besides the running water of the fountain, the only sound that could be heard was the chirping of crickets.

Carefully, she pulled out her guitar and gave it a few strums. After a few minutes of hesitation, she decided to just go for it. The acoustic sounds from her guitar quickly drowned out the water trickling in the fountain. But it wasn't until she started singing that even the crickets stopped to listen.

The crickets weren't the only ones taking notice of her angelic voice. Up on the second floor, as David lay in his bed, his eyes slowly opened. Curiously, he pulled himself up and made his way over to the window. He cracked it open then knelt down on the floor. A proud, yet sad smile crept across his face as he listened his daughter. Eventually, David would pass out on the floor beneath the window, but not before listening to Hope's entire set of songs.

5

The next morning, David was surprisingly awake early enough to have breakfast with the others. It wasn't that he wanted to get up that early, but his dry, hacking cough made it impossible to stay sleeping. When he reached the dining room table, Janice was placing a large plate of blueberry pancakes in the center.

"Good morning, David," she said, and then motioned for him to sit wherever. "Help yourself. There's plenty more where those came from. Let me go grab you a coffee."

David didn't say a word. He simply plopped down across from his daughter and began helping himself to the pancakes and bacon.

"Morning," Hope quietly said in his direction.

"Too soft," he said with a disgusted look. "I like my bacon crispy. Extra crispy, actually."

Just then, the other couple staying at the inn came downstairs. The Hendersons looked to be in their mid-twenties and both wore big smiles as they clutched each other's hands. If that weren't bad enough, Hope watched as the man peppered his wife's neck and cheek with kisses. David was too busy stuffing his face to notice their public display of affection.

"Morning, y'all," they both said in a sickly-sweet southern accent.

Hope put on her best fake smile and said, "Morning."

David said nothing.

"I'm Cindi Henderson. Cindi with an *i* not a *y*," she said, smiling.

"An *i* with a heart over it," the man specified, and then looked lovingly over at his wife.

"And this is my husband, Andy," she said in Hope's direction.

"Andy with a *y* and no heart above it," he said.

This caused them both to start to giggle uncontrollably. David paused his eating long enough to shoot them a disgusted look.

"Nice to meet you both," Hope softly replied.

"And you must be Hope?" Cindi said. "We ran into David earlier, and he filled us in on everything."

Wondering exactly what he filled them in on, Hope sat straight up and hesitantly asked, "He did?"

"Yup," Andy replied. "You're here to help plan the big anniversary."

Hope's smile turned less fake and more uncomfortable. She looked over at her father, but he was now showing disdain towards the non-crispy bacon.

"This is anniversary number three for us," Andy boasted.

Cindi quickly responded with, "Four years and two months since he proposed.

Just as quickly, Andy said, "Five years, seven months and three days since our first kiss."

Again, they held hands as they smiled and gazed into one another's eyes. The disgust on David's face grew even more than before. Hope took notice and thought for sure he was about to say something embarrassing. Luckily, the moment was interrupted by Janice placing more platters of food onto the table.

"This looks amazing, Janice," Andy said.

Janice smiled. "Dig in."

At any second, Hope expected her father to blurt out some

comment about the bacon, but he didn't. He actually seemed to be thoroughly enjoying his cup of coffee.

"This is really good coffee," he said to Janice. "Maxwell House?"

"You guessed it," she replied.

He nodded his approval then paused a second and said, "The bacon could have been crispier, but whatever."

Hope lowered her head in embarrassment. Andy and Cindi had no reaction. They were too busy feeding each other strawberries.

"I'm sorry. I'll have to remember you like it crispy next time."

"*Extra* crispy," he pointed out.

"*Extra* crispy," she repeated, then winked and exited the room.

Not much was spoken over the next few minutes. Between David picking crumbs out of his beard, and the happy couple feeding each other food and playing footsie under the table, Hope just sat there. As uncomfortable as it was, it was much better than the dialogue that ensued.

Hope wasn't much of a conversationalist, yet was forced to answer question after question from the happy couple. Questions like: Where are you from? Where do you go to school? What are you majoring in? Blah, blah, blah. She wasn't even sure why they asked her, because every time she began to answer, they interrupted and told their own life stories. Just when she thought it couldn't get worse, they turned their questions to David.

"So what do you do for work, David?"

Hope sat up in her chair. She too was curious to hear his answer. David finished off the rest of his coffee then looked over at the couple and said, "I work for the government."

Hope slumped back down in her chair. She knew this was a bullshit answer.

"Oh, nice," Andy said. "Doing what?"

"I'm not at liberty to say," he said, picking another crumb from his beard. "It's top-secret type of shit. I mean, I *could* tell you… but then I'd have to kill ya."

Unsure how to react, their bubbly smiles disappeared. David's look was deadpan, borderline crazy. Finally, he let out a laugh and clapped his hands together. It took a second, but the happy couple joined in. Everyone began laughing. Everyone except Hope. It was apparent that no one, including her, was getting a real answer from David about anything. She hoped they would revisit their question, but they didn't. Instead, they did what they did best—talk about themselves.

"My sweetie over here is a truck driver for Schlitz beer," Cyndi proudly boasted.

"And this cute little thing works for Montgomery Wards. She's the manager of the Appliances department."

"Appliances *and* TV department," Cindi corrected. "I just got promoted."

"Pumpkin! Why didn't you tell me?" Andy said, clutching her hand on top of the table.

"I was just waiting for the right moment." She beamed, grabbing his hand tighter. As they gazed lovingly at one another, Hope had a look of someone who had just thrown up in their mouth. David's attention was focused on something completely different.

"Schlitz, huh? You get free beer and shit?"

Andy turned to David and gave him a proud nod. David gave him an approving smile then leaned back into his chair and said, "Good gig."

By the time breakfast was over, the only thing Hope had learned about her estranged father was that he liked his bacon crispy—extra crispy. Hope also made a promise to herself that if she ever dated or married someone that she would never EVER use pet names to address them.

***

After breakfast, Hope took a long bath, which gave her plenty of time to come up with a game plan. There'd be no more dancing around subjects. She would ask him everything that had been on her mind for years. Hope had no idea how long she'd be staying at the inn, so she knew she needed to get her answers quick.

When David wasn't in his room, Hope wandered around the house and finally found him out back sitting by the fountain. It was only eleven in the morning, and David was already washing down his fifth cigarette with vodka. She knew she had her work cut out for her, but she was determined to get some answers. She took a seat next to her father and decided to start slow.

"How about the Hendersons? They seem quite in love, huh?"

Without so much as a smile, David flicked his cigarette into the fountain and said, "I give them two years before they're at each other's throats and divorced."

It was a negative and jaded response, but one that Hope completely concurred with. She figured it was as good a time as any to ask her father some questions.

"So, what *do* you do for work? Like, *really* do?" She asked her question with a smile on her face as if it would make him open up to her easier. It didn't work—at all.

"Did you wash that stupid phone number off your hand yet?" he said, lighting another cigarette.

Unphased by his deflection, she pressed on. "Seriously, what do you do for work? Your license plate says California. Is that where you live? Have you been there this whole time?"

She simply had way too many questions pent up to take it slow. Unfortunately, she quickly realized that David had no intention of answering any of them. Instead, he untwisted the cap off his vodka and took another swig.

"I'm thinking we should hit the flower shop first and get something good picked out for the big anniversary. It needs to be colorful. Your mother loves—"

It was at that point, Hope did something highly uncharacteristic. She temporarily lost her patience. "Enough! Enough with the stupid anniversary talk! She's dead. Mom is dead!"

She immediately regretted her outburst. David shot her a glare but said nothing. He then took a much longer swig off his vodka. As a matter of fact, he didn't stop until every last drop was polished off.

Hope softened her tone, almost pleading with him. "I just... I just want—"

"What? What the hell do you want from me?" he said, raising his voice.

"Answers," she said, almost whispering. She fought back the tears welling up in her eyes and gave him a pleading look.

"You want answers, huh? Like how I've never held a job for more than a month? Or how I've lived in more shelters and halfway houses than I can remember? Or how about the fact that I have to beg, borrow and steal for money? Shall I keep going?"

As Hope searched for something to say, a few tears broke free and ran down her cheek. David fumbled with his pack of cigarettes, but his hands were shaking too much to get one lit.

"How's that for answers?" he shot in her direction. Just as quickly, he continued his sarcasm. "Don't tell me you're speechless? Aren't you gonna psychoanalyze me now? Isn't that what your shrink school teaches you to do? Huh?"

Hope lowered her eyes to the ground.

"What next? You gonna tell me I drink and smoke too much? Save it! I don't need you to try to fix me. I'm unfixable! Understood?"

Sympathy, embarrassment, and anger, were just some of the emotions swirling around Hope's head.

"I… I can't do this," she said, finally breaking down. "Why did you even invite me here if you weren't going to talk to me? You obviously wanted me here or else you wouldn't have—"

"I have no idea what you're talking about," he said, turning away from her.

"I knew I shouldn't have come. It was stupid to think that after all these years we could maybe…" Too overcome with emotion, Hope turned and ran up the cobblestone path and into the house. By the time her foot hit the staircase, tears were pouring from her eyes.

She grabbed what few things she had in the room and then rushed out of the inn. She couldn't get to her car fast enough. Her hand shook as she unlocked and opened her door. After she tossed her things into the backseat, she steadied her hand and attempted to place the key in the ignition.

With the car now started, she just sat there trembling. Placing her hands over her face, she lowered her head onto the steering wheel and continued bawling her eyes out. Just then, the passenger door swung open and David plopped himself into the seat. Startled, Hope raised her head and looked over at her father.

He placed a cigarette into his mouth, shut his door, then casually said, "Let's go check out that restaurant Janice recommended and see if we can get a reservation for the big day. I think she said it's on the other side of the island."

The whole time he spoke, his focus remained straight ahead and not on his daughter. Hope wiped her tears and sat there confused and speechless. He was acting as if nothing had just gone down between them. David wasted no time in lighting his cigarette, and although he cranked his window down a bit, it did little to prevent smoke from filling up inside. Hope hated, absolutely hated cigarette smoke, but she couldn't bring herself to say anything about it. As a matter of fact, she couldn't bring herself to say anything at all. It wasn't until David asked her a question that she finally uttered a word.

"So, how long have you been playing?"

"What?"

He motioned to the guitar in the backseat. "I heard you playing last night.

"Oh," she said, embarrassed that someone had actually heard her.

"You didn't suck," he said, matter-of-factly.

Hope smirked at his feeble attempt at a compliment.

"You were actually pretty good." This time with more sincerity.

"Thanks."

"Did you write those songs yourself?"

"Yea."

"You in a band or something?"

His question caused her to chuckle. "God no."

"What do you mean, God no?"

"I don't really do so well in front of people."

By the look on her father's face, she could tell he was expecting her to elaborate. She wiped the remaining tears from her cheeks then took a deep breath and continued.

"I pretty much went my entire high school career being invisible. I'm still not sure how I mustered up the courage, but when I was a senior, I signed up for our annual talent show. And for some insane reason, I decided to play one of my originals. I had this stupid vision that after I finished my song, everyone would be clapping and giving me a standing ovation. It's like, I thought if I let them see a piece of me, then they might see me differently. Stupid, I know."

David took a long drag from his cigarette then tossed it out the window. "What happened?" he asked.

Hope's face turned red and she felt herself slumping in her seat.

"Um… about halfway through my song, I heard a bunch of people snickering out in the audience."

David shrugged his shoulders. "So. Those kids are just mother fucking idiots! You should *never* care what people think."

Hope also shrugged then continued. "Anyway, I was so embarrassed that I stopped playing and rushed off stage. That's the first and last time I've ever played my own stuff in front of people."

David paused, gave her a deadpan look and said, "Well that's just plain stupid."

"Whatever. It's not that big of a deal. It's just a silly little hobby anyway."

David shook his head in disgust. "That statement has your grandparents written all over it."

Hope smirked. "They might have called the guitar a giant waste of time."

"Ha!" he yelled, smacking his hand on the dashboard. "I knew it! Leave it to them to suck the creativity out of a person. They were always doing that to your mother. Did you know she used to write poetry?"

Hope shook her head no.

"Of course you didn't! Why would they ever mention that? To them, her poetry was also a giant waste of time."

As Hope sat there in her car, the fight she just had with her father was the last thing on her mind. At that moment, all she really cared about was hearing more about her mom.

"Were they good… the poems?"

"How the hell do I know?" he said, throwing up his hands. "They were too deep for me to understand. Besides, it had nothing to do with whether I liked them or not. It was just Maggie being creative and writing from her heart. How can anyone ever judge that? Never mind call it a waste of time!"

Hope smiled. She'd only been around her father for a day, but that was one of the sweetest things he had said so far. For whatever reason, she started the car and began to drive to the other side of the island towards the restaurant her father had spoken of.

"You do realize, if it wasn't for playing the guitar, your mother and I would have never gotten together?"

"What do you mean?" Hope asked, curiously looking over at her father. "Are you saying *you* play guitar?"

"Once upon a time I did."

"How exactly did the guitar help you and Mom get together?"

He smiled as if he was waiting for her to ask that. "Remember I told you I spent the entire summer trying to win her over?"

"You mean after that night she dumped her beer on you?"

David nodded. "As a matter of fact, it was the very next day that I put my plan into motion."

Hope adjusted herself in the seat, preparing to listen to her father's tale.

"I kind of knew the guy that was dating your mom's best friend, so I paid him five bucks to do a little recon for me."

"Recon?"

"Yup. I had him discreetly find out what some of Maggie's favorite songs were, and I quickly learned them on my guitar. Then I—"

"Wait," Hope interrupted. "What kind of music was she into?"

"That's not important right now. What's important, is the fact that I was such a skilled musician that I learned a bunch of songs just like that!" he said, snapping his fingers.

David then gazed out the window and appeared to be caught in a brief moment of nostalgia. He remembered their tiny apartment in the southside of Chicago. He also remembered Patsy Cline blaring out on Maggie's turntable every night when he returned home from work. As soon as he walked in the door, she would start singing "Crazy" or "I Fall to Pieces."

No matter how shitty his work day was, Maggie's singing always put a smile on his face. He constantly told her she had the most beautiful voice he'd ever heard. "Angelic," he called it. He swore there would never be a voice as beautiful as hers. That theory would be proven wrong when he heard his daughter singing in the courtyard the night before.

"What happened?" Hope asked, pushing him out of his deep thoughts.

"What?"

"You said you found out some of the songs Mom liked, so you could learn them on the guitar."

"And learn them I did! I taught myself like five of them in less than a day," he boasted.

"Wow."

"Damn right wow. Don't let this broken-down exterior fool ya. This alcoholic and poisoned brain is much smarter than people think. Well… at least it used to be. I was a goddamn musical genius, I tell ya!"

Hope grinned. "I can't believe you used to play the guitar," she said, more as a statement and less as an accusation. He took it as the latter.

"Are you calling me a liar?" he snapped.

"No. Not at all. I just—"

"Can I finish my damn story now?" He let out an exasperated sigh then continued. "So, after I learned a bunch of songs… in less than a day I might add… I had that same guy do a little more recon for me. I had him find out when and where Maggie would be at certain times."

Hope laughed. "You stalked her?"

"I wasn't stalking her! I was being romantic!"

She continued to laugh and said, "Is that what you told the cop when he gave you a restraining order?"

"Ha fucking ha! There weren't any restraining orders, smartass. That's the problem with youth today. You don't have the creativity or the patience for the art of romance."

"That's not true," she replied.

He shot her a dubious look then reached over and grabbed her wrist. On her hand was Adam's name and number. It was a little smudged and faded but was still legible.

"I stand corrected," he said. "Writing your name and number on a girl's hand is *very* romantic… and *very* fucking creative."

She started to retort but realized he was kind of right. She shrugged in agreement, conceding his point. As he released her wrist, he seemed happy with himself.

"I really don't know where I'm going, by the way," she said, motioning towards the road.

"Just stay on this road and you'll be fine."

As she continued driving, David's eyes became fixated on the many keys dangling from her keychain. "What are you, a janitor or something? Why do you have so many damn keys?"

Hope smiled then looked down at them and began to explain each of their purposes. David lost patience after the third key. "Hey, did I tell you I taught myself like ten of Maggie's favorite songs in a day? Less than a day, actually."

She nodded yes but still said nothing. There were so many questions she had for her father, but she decided to hold off and to focus more on how her mother and father met. It seemed like the one subject he enjoyed talking about with her.

"Tell me about some of the places," she said.

"What?"

"Tell me about the places that you showed up and stalked Mom… Umm, I mean, *romanced* her."

David's face had no reaction to her little joke. Instead, he pondered a second then let out a smile of his own.

"I'll do better than that," he said excitedly. "How about I take you on a tour of all our special places that summer?"

"I'd like that. I'd like that a lot," Hope said with a smile.

"Alrighty then. Stop the car and turn around! First stop, the general store."

"What about the restaurant you wanted to check out?"

"Eh, we can do it another time."

She gave him an acknowledging nod then turned around in a random driveway and headed back towards the other side of the island. As David sat there, he found himself giving the collar of his shirt a whiff. He seemed surprised yet very pleased with its fresh scent.

"How about some tunes?" he said, reaching for the knobs on the radio. For the most part, all he came across was static. There were only two stations he could get to come in clear. One of them was playing disco, and the other was country music. David angrily voiced his displeasure with both.

"Jesus Christ! Doesn't anyone play good music anymore?"

"I'm not sure if you'll like any of them, but my cassettes are down there." She pointed to the brown case in between David's feet.

He reached down, grabbed it, then placed it on his lap and popped it open. His expression went from puzzled to disgusted. As Hope concentrated on the road, she could hear him mumbling his displeasure of the list of bands. Bands like: Cat Stevens, Joni Mitchell, Simon and Garfunkel, and plenty of the Grateful Dead.

"For the love of Christ! You really *are* a goddamn hippie, aren't you? I want some real music!" he exclaimed.

"I think there's some Beatles in there," she said, assuming everyone loved the Beatles.

"I don't wanna listen to the goddamn Beatles," he grumbled. He started to shut the case but paused and slid out a Jim Croce greatest hits tape. "Is this the Leroy Brown guy?" he asked.

Hope nodded and joked, "Baddest man in the whole damn town."

David had no reaction to her comment, but he did place the tape into the player and seemed content as "Bad, Bad Leroy Brown" blared out over the speakers. For the first time since he climbed in, David began to scan the interior of her car. With the exception of the guitar on the backseat and the tape case on the floor, her car was spotless. The carpets were meticulously vacuumed and the dashboard appeared to be completely dust free.

"The old goat buy you this car?" David asked.

"Grampa? No. I paid for every penny of it with my summer jobs over the years."

"Not my type of car, but I guess it suits you."

When they arrived at the general store, Hope pulled into one of the spaces and put the car in park. She glanced up at the old store then looked over to her father and curiously asked, "This is one of the places you romanced Mom?"

"What? No," he said almost laughing.

"Then why are we here?"

"Duh! This is where we load up on supplies for our little road trip today." David reached into his front pocket and pulled out a crumpled twenty and handed it to Hope. He then dug his hand into his satchel.

"Grab me another one of these," he said, holding up an empty pint bottle of vodka. "Make sure it's *this* size and not the big bottle. I'm sure in the long run it's cheaper to buy the bigger one, but I prefer the pocket-size one." He winked and added, "Oh, and grab another pack of Marlboros, too."

Hope just sat there, staring at the crumpled twenty and the empty bottle of vodka. There was no way she wanted to be a part of her father's bad habits, especially when one of those habits directly contributed to her not seeing him all her life.

"Go ahead, take it," he urged. "Don't worry, there'll be enough money for you to get something for yourself."

Hope was torn. The last thing she wanted was to buy her father cigarettes and booze, but she knew if she didn't it would cause a huge blowup. She wanted to hear more about her mother, and she really did want to see all the places where her parents had first met. Hesitantly, she took his money and slowly exited her car.

"Oh, and grab me a bag of pork rinds," he said, before she closed her door.

Hope nodded and made her way into the store. She was immediately greeted with smiles and friendly hellos. It was as if she was a regular there. For as long as she could remember, she had been going to the White Hen Pantry just around the corner from her grandparents' house, but she had never once been greeted this warmly. She returned their smiles, and for a second, she almost forgot what her dreaded mission was in the store.

"Something I can help you find, dear?" asked the woman behind the counter. She had a somewhat dark complexion, and Hope surmised the woman was of Native American descent. Hope knew the woman would eventually see what she was purchasing, but she couldn't bring herself to announce it out loud.

"I'm all set. Thank you," Hope replied.

The more she wandered around the narrow aisles, the more she loved everything about the old general store: The amazing smell of fresh-baked goods, the large section of nostalgic penny candy, and even the wide wooden floorboards creaking beneath her feet. She wove her way in and out of the aisles, knowing full well she'd eventually reach the alcohol section.

It was tucked away in the back, and as she stood staring at the array of glass bottles, she couldn't help but wonder just how many lives had been destroyed by them—how many dreams had been destroyed by their contents. She thought about telling her father that they were all sold out, but she knew he would probably call her bluff and march into the store himself.

Reluctantly, Hope grabbed the pint of vodka and headed towards the register. On her way, she picked up a bag of pork rinds, a bottle of water, and a small bag of trail mix for herself. She assumed the woman behind the register would change her warm and kind look once she saw her purchasing the alcohol, especially considering it was technically still morning.

To Hope's surprise, the woman continued smiling at her in a sweet, non-judgmental way. Even when Hope quietly requested a pack of Marlboros, the woman's pleasant look never wavered. She even complemented Hope on her blouse. As the woman handed the change back to her, Hope felt the need to inform her that neither the cigarettes nor the vodka were for her. Without saying a word, the woman's smile told Hope that she completely understood.

When she exited the store, she found David leaning against her car smoking a cigarette. His eyes widened when he saw the grocery bag in her hand. They widened even more when he pulled out the pint of vodka. He wasted no time in twisting off the cap and taking a long sip. Hope stared at him but didn't say a word.

"Want some?" he asked, reaching the bottle out towards her.

"No. I'm good."

"Suit yourself." He took another swig then shoved it into his pocket. "See, pocket-size is the way to go." He gave her a wink and proceeded to climb back into the car.

"Where to?" she asked, buckling her seatbelt.

David ran his fingers through his beard, thinking for a moment. "It's been a long, long time since I've been here. Why don't you just drive around and let's see what comes back to me."

"Okay," she said.

They drove up the road and as Hope approached the four-way stop, a small wooden sign caught her eye. It had an arrow pointing to the right, and next to it was an outline of a lighthouse. The sign read HARBOR COVE PARK.

"Oh, we totally have to go there," she excitedly said. "I've never been to a lighthouse before. Well, not a real one anyway. I've driven by some of the ones on Lake Michigan, but—"

"No!" he said, grabbing the steering wheel before she could turn right. "I'm not ready to go there... not yet. That was one of our most special places."

Sympathetically, she looked at her father. The last thing she wanted was to upset him again. "It's okay. We can just go this way instead," she said, pointing to her left.

When he was satisfied that she wasn't going to pull a fast one, he released the wheel. She turned left then quickly tried to lighten the mood. "It must have been so groovy to come here in the summer. Especially to escape the brutal heat of the city."

David stared out the window and took a long pause before replying. "There's no place on earth quite like this island."

The way he spoke those words, Hope could tell he was becoming deeply lost in the past. She wasn't sure if that was a good thing or not, but for now, he seemed content. Hope decided to stay quiet and allow her father to remain in deep thought.

The road they were on was long and straight, and on one side, pine trees were lined as far as the eye could see. In contrast, the other side of the road was nothing but marsh land. Hope took the time to appreciate the beauty of both sides equally. After a few miles, they came across another wooden sign which read ISLAND AIR TOURS.

"Cool," Hope said. "I love watching planes take off. Do you mind if we check it out?"

"You're the driver, do what you want."

Hope found his statement slightly amusing, especially considering just five minutes earlier he was grabbing the wheel and preventing her from going where she wanted. She laughed to herself then turned left down a dirt road.

"Sometimes Grampa used to take me to a little airport outside the city, and we would just sit there and watch the planes take off and land. Pretty ironic, considering I don't think he's ever been on a plane. Either of them, actually."

"What the hell does that have to do with anything? You can still enjoy watching without doing."

Hope didn't really know how to respond. She was a little shocked that he was defending her grandfather.

"I suppose you're right," she said, watching him light another cigarette.

David pointed ahead. "Well, looks like you're outta luck."

Not only was the small parking lot and airfield completely vacant, but the building itself was all boarded up. She slowed the car to a stop and sighed. "Aww, it's closed." Most of the boards on the windows were spray painted with graffiti. "Oh, well. I guess we should get going," she said.

"You're not gonna at least walk around the runway?"

"Of course not. Look at all the signs." She pointed to the many NO TRESPASSING and PRIVATE PROPERTY signs.

David flicked his ashes out the window and grumbled, "What's your point?"

"My point? This is obviously private property. And trespassing here would be against the law."

David was laughing well before she even said the word law.

"Yea, we wouldn't want the fuzz to come get us. I'd hate to be arrested by Barney Fife."

Blankly, Hope asked, "Who's Barney Fife?"

"Are you kidding me? Don Knotts? The Andy Griffith Show?"

Hope shrugged. "I don't really watch much TV... not at all, actually. Although, I do watch that Lucy program with Nana once in a while."

"Looks like I've got my work cut out for me this week," he said, shaking his head. "Drive on, my little goodie-two-shoes."

For a brief moment, Hope was tempted to wander around the abandoned airfield just to prove her father wrong. The moment was short-lived, however, as she stared at one of the many DO NOT ENTER signs on the chain-link fence surrounding the runway. After a slow, disappointed sigh, she threw her car into drive and carried on.

Halfway down the dirt road, Hope asked, "So, you just want me to drive around? Like, with no real destination?"

By now, David had already lit another cigarette and was bellowing smoke in her direction. "Do you have something better to do?" he asked.

"Well... no. I just—"

"And what the hell is wrong with driving around with no destination? That's the best kind of driving."

Hope wondered if that's what he'd been doing the past twenty years—just driving around with no real destination. If so, how far did he stray from Chicago? Did he ever come back? Did he ever try to see her? Did he even want to?

"Hello? Earth to Hope."

"What?" she said, snapping out of her thoughts.

"I said, since when does a stop sign mean stop forever? Are we gonna drive somewhere or not?"

Hope had no idea how long she had been stopped.

"Oh... yea... I'm sorry."

"So?? Have you figured it out yet?" he asked.

"Huh? Figured what out?"

"Jesus Christ, Hope! What's wrong with you? Have you figured out which way we're going? Left... or right. It's not that damn complicated."

If she ever wondered why her grandparents always called her a space cadet, this would be the perfect example.

"I'm sorry. I'm just not sure where to..." Just then, she remembered she had grabbed a little one-page map of Applewood when she went into the store earlier. She pulled it out of her pocket and began to study it.

"How about the Willows? It's a park over by where we're staying."

"Go wherever you want. I just don't want to sit at this stop sign all damn day."

Hope turned right and headed back to the marina area. The park was tucked off the beaten path and took its namesake from the three beautiful willow trees in its center. Another highlight of the park was the narrow river, which ran along its edge. Besides the one young couple having a picnic on the grass, Hope and David were the only ones there.

"Wow!" she exclaimed. "This place is adorable. Such a groovy little park. I should have bought some more film for my camera while I was at the store."

"Shoulda, coulda, woulda," David mumbled, pulling the bottle from his pocket.

Hope's eyes tried their best not to focus on his drinking, but they lingered long enough for him to sense her disappointment. He thought about blasting a comment her way, but instead, he twisted the cap back on, and this time, he placed it into his satchel.

"I bet this is a great place to watch the sunset," she said, pointing to the other side of the river. It was a wide-open space with barely a tree in sight.

David's face softened and he nodded. "This was one of our favorite places to watch the sunset together."

"You and Mom used to come here?" she asked.

Again, David nodded and said, "After I won her over, of course."

Hope laughed. "I have to admit, I'm very curious as to how you did it."

He lit another cigarette then gazed around the park. Finally, he pointed over to one of the willow trees. "Your mother used to love to come here and sit under that tree and read."

"Really?" Hope said with a big grin.

"Either that, or she'd sit and read under that one over there."

She followed his finger to a large oak tree looming over the edge of the riverbank. Her grin grew even more. One of her most favorite things in the world was to wander around one of the many Chicago parks and cozy up under a tree with a good book. She loved knowing that her mother used to do the same thing.

"As a matter of fact, that goddamn oak tree nearly cost me a chance with Maggie."

Hope was still picturing her mother reading under the trees, so it took a second for her father's comment to resonate. "Wait… what about this tree?" she asked.

David huffed at having to repeat himself. "I said, that goddamn oak tree nearly cost me a chance with your mother."

"How so?"

He took a drag off his cigarette then began to fill Hope in. "My recon man told me that your mother liked to come here and read in the morning, so I decided to show up early and climb one of the trees."

She laughed. "Like a peeping Tom?"

"No… more like a serenading David," he said with the slyest of smiles.

"So, you climbed that oak tree with your guitar?"

"Yup. Way up there camouflaged in the leaves."

"But how did you know she'd be under this tree and not one of the willows?"

David shrugged. "Lucky guess. Besides, willow trees are horrible to climb… especially with a guitar."

Hope gazed up at the majestic oak and said, "So you waited for her to show up and then began to serenade her?"

"Well… kinda."

"What do you mean, kinda?"

"Ten seconds into the song, the goddamn branch broke."

Hope covered her mouth in shock, but more so to hide her huge grin. "Were you okay?"

"Most of the branches broke my fall, and luckily I landed in the water and not the ground. By the time I retrieved my guitar down the river and swam back to shore, your mother was long gone. But… while I was in the river, I did see her smile on her way out. That's when I knew—it was only a matter of time."

"You mean, a matter of time before she had a restraining order against you?" Hope said, giggling.

Unaffected by her joke, David stared around the quiet park and said, "I knew I was close to winning her over. Very, very close."

After leaving the Willows, they continued driving around and exploring the island. Over the next few hours, David told one outrageous story after another regarding his feeble attempts to win over her mother. Hope still had so many questions about his whereabouts over the past twenty years, but for the moment, she decided to keep them to herself. Truth be told, she was completely caught up with her father's stories of how he romanced her mother.

By the time they made it back to the inn, David looked exhausted and could barely keep his eyes open. No sooner did they enter the front door, David let out a yawn. "I'm hitting the sack."

"Kind of early," she said, looking at her watch.

"We all can't be young college kids. Some of us are old, broken, and tired." About halfway up, David paused then turned back around and said, "Maybe tomorrow I can show you the rest of the places that I made a fool of myself with your mother."

Hope smiled. "I'd like that." Before David reached the top, she called out, "Thanks."

"What the hell are you thanking me for?"

"For today. For telling me how you and Mom met. I'd never heard that story before. And for what it's worth, I don't think you made a fool of yourself at all. It was really sweet." She paused and said, "I wish I had someone put that much effort in getting to know me."

David hesitated a moment, and Hope thought he might actually offer her some kind and encouraging words. He didn't. He felt for his daughter, he truly did, but between his pounding head and the sharp pain in his side, David was in no mood to console her.

"Well, night," he said, and then disappeared down the hall.

Hope remained at the bottom of the staircase with a thousand thoughts running through her head. Most of them were sad thoughts, but she made a conscious effort to focus on the happy ones. She really did enjoy her day with her father. Despite his constant drinking and smoking, she loved hearing about her mother.

Just then, the front door opened, and Hope's train of thought was interrupted by the entrance of the Hendersons. They were both giggling and holding each other's hands as they entered. If that wasn't bad enough, they paused, giving each other multiple pecks on their cheeks. If Hope drank, she'd surely be doing a shot right about now. She cringed, and although she looked away, she could still hear their sloppy, wet, and extremely loud kisses. She knew if her father was witnessing this, he'd have no problem voicing his thoughts to the happy couple. Hope had a few zingers of her own, but there was no way she'd ever say them out loud. Instead, she did the only thing that seemed appropriate; she cleared her throat—twice. The first time was a little too quiet to overcome their obnoxiously loud lip-smacking.

"Oh… hey," Andy said, spotting Hope. "We didn't see you standing there."

"Sorry about that," Cindi said, wiping her saliva-coated lips. This place is just so beautiful. It's like we're on our honeymoon again." They both giggled then tightly clutched each other's hands. Hope did all she could to keep from throwing up in her mouth.

"Yea, this island is pretty amazing," Hope said, and attempted to walk away.

"Hey, we're gonna play a little Yahtzee in the other room. You're welcome to join us."

Before Hope could respond to him, Cindi interrupted. "But I thought we were going to play Parcheesi?"

For a second, Hope thought there might be a lover's quarrel about to brew. There was no such luck, however, as Andy was quick to respond to his wife. "You're right! I totally forgot that you said you wanted to play Parcheesi tonight. Sorry about that, sugar bear."

With sugar bear still hanging in the air, Cindi smiled and replied, "It's okay, honeybunches. We can play Yahtzee, if you want?"

A huge grin came over Andy's face as he looked into her eyes and said, "How about we play *both*!"

"You read my mind!" she said, giggling. She then planted another vocal kiss on his lips.

When they were finally done kissing and hugging and giggling and staring deeply into each other's eyes, they glanced back over to Hope. They thought for sure she'd jump at the chance to join them in their game night, but to their surprise, Hope was no longer standing there. In the midst of their public display of affection, she had discreetly slipped out of the room and escaped out the back door.

After grabbing the guitar from her car, Hope headed out to the courtyard. She randomly strummed some chords, but her mind was more focused on the events of the day. She really did love hearing her father talk about her mother and how they used to be when they were younger. Her grandparents rarely talked about her mother like that. They *definitely* never talked about her mother the way her father did. She also loved that her mother had a wild streak to her.

Hope paused her strumming for a moment and thought about her parents' relationship—relationships in general, actually. She was twenty years old and never truly had a real boyfriend, not a serious one anyway. Most of the guys she knew fell into the *just friends* category. Some by her choice, but mostly by theirs.

Her thoughts then turned to the Hendersons. They were much too sappy and over the top for her taste, but there was an aspect to their closeness that Hope found sweet. That being said, never in a million years would she ever, *ever* use pet names with her significant other.

The next thing she knew, she was strumming and making up words to a new song, which she called, "Sugar Bear and Honeybunches." Although it made her giggle, she eventually stopped out of guilt. She wasn't the type of person who made fun of others, especially their happiness. Instead, she began playing her favorite Jim Croce song, "Time in a Bottle." It was on the tape they had listened to earlier, and her thoughts naturally moved back to her father and the day they had just spent together.

6

A sense of excitement coursed through Hope's veins when she awoke the next morning. She was eager to see more places where her parents had once connected. She also hoped she could learn more about her father, but she knew she needed to be patient and take what she could get. After she threw on some clothes, she quietly crept downstairs. At the bottom step, she paused and strained her ear towards the dining room off to her right.

"Don't worry, they already ate and have headed out for the morning."

Hope let out a startled squeal and turned to her left. There, walking towards her and carrying a handful of clean towels was Janice.

"Sorry. I didn't mean to startle you."

"I was just... um..."

"Seeing if the Hendersons were still in there eating breakfast?"

Hope didn't say a word, but her expression confirmed Janice's statement. Janice looked around the room then whispered to Hope. "I've been trying to avoid them myself. Don't get me wrong, they're a very sweet couple, but... but their public displays of affection are a bit much for me."

Hope laughed and also whispered, "Not to mention, all the pet names they call each other."

"Oh Lord," Janice said, shaking her head. "If I hear pumpkin or pookie or sweetie pie again, I'm going to lose my mind."

"And don't forget honeybunches and sugar bear," added Hope.

Janice gave a repulsed shiver, causing both of them to crack up laughing.

"Why don't you make yourself comfortable in the dining room. After I put these towels away, I'll come fix you something to eat."

"You don't have to go through all that trouble."

"Hope, it's no trouble at all. Especially if you don't mind me eating with you. I'm starved."

"Of course. That would be nice." Hope then looked up the stairs and said, "I'm assuming he hasn't come down yet?"

Janice shook her head. "No, honey. I haven't seen him yet today. I'll meet you in there in a few, okay?"

"No hurry," Hope replied, making her way into the dining room.

About fifteen minutes later, Janice appeared with two plates filled with scrambled eggs, bacon, and some fresh fruit.

"I wasn't sure if you liked your eggs scrambled or over easy."

"Scrambled is perfect. I don't really like my eggs runny. Thanks so much," Hope said, grabbing the plate from her. "It looks great."

Most of breakfast was spent with polite small talk. Hope was quite amused to find out that Janice was also asked to participate in the Henderson's little Yahtzee extravaganza the night before. Both women began laughing but were quickly interrupted by the sound of loud, plodding footsteps coming down the wooden staircase.

"Looks like your dad is awake."

Hearing that simple phrase - *your dad*, still felt strange to Hope. It wasn't necessarily a bad feeling, just strange. As David neared the bottom, the front door swung open and the Hendersons entered the inn. In true fashion, they were giggling with their hands all over one another. The perfect storm was about to hit.

"Good morning, sleepyhead," Cindi announced in David's direction. "We just went for a nice walk on one of the tiny beaches here."

David stared blankly at them. "And I need to know this why?"

His gruff comment wasn't enough to deter Cindi's peppy mood. She smiled and said, "Looks like someone got up on the wrong side of the bed."

Janice and Hope overheard the exchange, and Hope crossed her fingers that David wouldn't cause a big scene. Even more so, both women crossed their fingers in hopes that the Hendersons wouldn't come join them at the table. Both wishes came true. Although David's bloodshot eyes held their glare for a moment, he said nothing. Eventually, he turned and headed into the dining room. Before rushing back out to do some sightseeing, the Hendersons sprinted upstairs to retrieve their camera.

"Morning," Janice said, standing up. "Would you like me to make you some breakfast?"

David let out an incoherent grumble. "Coffee. I just want coffee."

"Of course." Janice grabbed an empty cup and the pot of coffee off the counter from behind her.

His appearance, especially his hair, always had a disheveled look to it, but this morning it was taken to a new level.

"Are you feeling okay?" Janice asked, pouring his coffee.

"Yea, yea! I just slept like shit, that's all."

"I'm sorry. Was it the bed? Because I can move you to—"

"It wasn't the damn bed! I just didn't sleep well, okay?"

Knowing he was in another one of his moods, Janice said nothing and simply handed him his coffee. It was piping hot, yet David took a long, hearty sip. To the shock of both girls, he showed no ill effects of the temperature. After his third sip, he clanked the half-empty cup down on the table. "I'm going back to bed. Hopefully, those damn landscapers aren't going to be here!"

Janice didn't reply, but before David left the room, Hope cleared her throat and asked, "But I thought we were going to…" She never finished her sentence, for David had already exited and was plodding back up the stairs. Hope immediately lowered her head, and Janice could tell just how frustrated and confused the poor girl was. She gave Hope a sympathetic look then quietly began clearing their plates.

"I'm sorry he snapped at you," Hope softly said.

"Oh, honey, you don't have to apologize for him. Trust me, I don't take any of it to heart. How about you? You okay?"

Hope shrugged and nodded. Janice decided to take this opportunity to ask a question that had been on her mind since the day she showed up at the inn. "Can I ask you something? It's completely none of my business, and you don't have to answer if you don't want."

"No, it's fine. Ask me whatever you'd like."

"You said until now you'd never met or talked to your father before?"

Hope nodded.

"Then… how did you know he would be here? Was it because you knew this place was special to them and that it was their anniversary this week?"

Hope shook her head and said, "Actually, I had no idea they'd ever been to Maine before. And to be honest, I don't really think this is their actual anniversary week either. My uncle once told me that my parents eloped while my mom was pregnant with me."

The puzzled look on Janice's face grew as she asked, "So how did you know he was here?"

Hope took a deep breath. "For as far back as I can remember, every year on my birthday the phone would ring. And every year it was the same result. I'd answer it, there'd be a silent pause, and then they'd hang up. I'm not sure when I actually put it all together, but when I did, I knew it was him. My grandparents were always getting wrong numbers dialed, so they never thought much of it, but I knew the birthday call was him… I just knew it."

"Come to think of it," Janice said, with a bit of clarity in her eyes, "he did ask to use my phone after he checked in on Saturday."

"Yup, my birthday. Except this time was different. This time he called collect. When the operator asked me if I would accept the charges, all she said was that it was a call from the Great Blue Heron Inn in Applewood, Maine. I accepted the charges, and after about ten seconds of silence, the phone hung up and there was nothing left but dial tone."

"So, you just hit the road and headed all the way out here? Blind faith?"

Hope shrugged. "I just knew it was him. I knew it was his way of telling me where to find him. I know, I know, it all sounds so crazy."

"No, honey. Not crazy at all. I'm a firm believer that everything happens for a reason. You're meant to be here right now. You both are."

"I'm not too sure about that," Hope said, lowering her head.

"I'm certainly no expert," Janice began, "but I'm assuming he suffers from some sort of manic depression?"

Hope nodded. "My grandparents very rarely talk about my mom, and they talk about my father even less. My uncle has told me a few things over the years, but even he is pretty vague about my father's condition."

"Your uncle—as in your father's brother?" Janice asked.

"Yea. I used to see him when I was younger, but then he moved to Germany. That's where he lives now. We talk on the phone a few times a year, but our conversations are pretty basic. He doesn't mention my father, so I guess I've kinda given up asking about him. But yea, from what I've gathered over the years, he's got a lot of mental issues going on, not to mention, a huge problem with alcohol."

"Alcoholism is a terrible, terrible disease. I can't imagine combining that with manic depression."

Hope nodded then slowly raised her head and said, "And I still think he has these delusions that my mother is still alive. He must, or else why would he keep planning for this make-believe anniversary?"

Janice placed her hand on Hope's shoulder. "A broken heart can cause people to think and imagine things that others will never quite understand."

"I suppose you're right," Hope said.

"So, what's on your agenda today?" Janice asked.

"We were supposed to hang out, but I guess that's not happening any time soon."

"Not that you asked for my advice, but personally, I think you should get in your car and go drive around the island and do some sightseeing." Janice paused then smirked and said, "I'm sure the Hendersons would love some company." This caused Hope to let out a little laugh. "I'm just kidding. I'm not sure I'd wish that on anyone. I am serious about you doing some sightseeing. There are so many beautiful spots here."

"Yea, we went to some groovy places yesterday."

"Did you go up to Harbor Cove Park?"

"No, but we went to another park, though."

"The Willows?" Janice asked.

"Yea, that's it. It was so peaceful and quiet. Is that water part of the ocean or is it a river?"

"It's called the Alsigontekw River, but it's more like a giant stream than anything. It winds its way from the center of the island out to the ocean. Actually, if you go to the easternmost point of the park, you'll see the estuary where the river meets the sea."

"What was that name you said again?"

"Alsigontekw… it means river of many shells. If you look closely along the banking, you'll see that it's covered with them. The Willows is actually one of my most favorite places on the island. That being said, you do need to visit Harbor Cove Park. The views of the lighthouse and the Atlantic are stunning. Definitely bring a camera."

A part of Hope loved Janice's suggestion, but another part of her wondered if she should stick around the house just in case her dad came back downstairs. She didn't want to miss out on hearing more about how her parents met. It was as if Janice read her mind. "Besides, I'm sure David will be sleeping most of the day," Janice said. "He looked pretty exhausted."

Hope agreed and decided it was best if she took Janice's suggestion of roaming the island on her own for the day. Some people wouldn't be able to handle the *on your own* part, but Hope had mastered this. Whether it was the movies, or dinner, or a quiet night at the library, she'd spent a lifetime doing things on her own. That being said, there were many times she wished she had a companion; someone to walk through this world with. Sadly, she didn't even have a best friend.

"Why don't you go grab that camera of yours and get going," Janice said as she finished clearing the table. "I've got a nice pair of binoculars you can borrow as well."

Hope slid her chair in and started to leave the room. She stopped at the doorway then turned to Janice and said, "Can you—"

"Don't worry," Janice interrupted. "I'll keep an eye on him."

"Thanks," Hope said, smiling appreciatively.

Up in her room, she grabbed her camera, her guitar, and her jean jacket. On her way out, she paused by her father's door. She could hear him coughing, and although tempted to knock, she decided it was best not to bother him.

As soon as she buckled up her seatbelt, she popped out the Jim Croce tape and replaced it with *American Beauty* by the Grateful Dead. With "Sugar Magnolia" blaring out, Hope drove down the long driveway and began her sightseeing excursion. Her first stop was the marina just down the road. The small lot was already full, so Hope ended up parking over at the Rusty Anchor. Most of the vehicles at the marina were pickup trucks filled with lobster traps and other gear. Hope surmised they belonged to the local fishermen.

With her trusty Kodak Ektralite in hand, Hope headed straight for the long wooden pier. The morning sun glistened off the water, causing her to reach into her bag for her over-sized sunglasses. Stacks of lobster traps and piles of buoys lined the old pier. Every breath she took, the salt air entered her lungs and filled her senses. By far, this whole trip was the craziest and most spontaneous thing she'd ever done. Yet, as she stood there gazing out at the ocean and breathing in the salt air, she felt a sense of peace. It was a feeling that would stay with her long after she would leave Applewood.

Hope remained on the pier for the better part of an hour, just taking in all the sights and sounds; from the gentle lapping waves to the loud squawking of the many seagulls hovering above. While standing at the end of the pier, she watched a large boat make its way into the marina and dock. It was filled with passengers, and Hope assumed it to be some sort of tour boat. Her assumption was confirmed when she saw a line of people milling around a tiny wooden building in the corner of the parking lot. There was an A-frame sign out front reading LIGHTHOUSE & WHALE WATCHING TOUR.

Just then, the woman in the booth yelled out, "We'll be boarding in about fifteen minutes. And if you haven't got your tickets yet, we still have a few available."

Hope wanted to buy a ticket in the worst way possible. She'd always wanted to go on a whale watch. Her excitement was short-lived when she realized she hadn't brought as much money as intended. She left Chicago in such haste that she forgot to grab some extra cash from underneath her mattress. She had plenty of money for a boat ticket but had no idea how long she'd be in town. David claimed to have paid for her lodging, but she wasn't ready to put her trust in him yet. Honestly, she had a hard time believing someone who looked, smelled, and acted the way he did could have enough money for both of them to be there for a week.

Hope knew she also needed gas money to get back home, and heaven forbid, if something unexpected happened, she needed to have an emergency fund. At a young age, her grandfather had taught her to always be prepared and to smartly budget her money. Even when she was seven and had her first lemonade stand, he was preaching the art of money management. And out of the two dollars of profit, he made her give him half for savings. So as much as she wanted to go on the boat, she knew she needed to be prudent with her money—food, drinks, and necessities only.

Her next stop would be a return trip to the Willows. Although she enjoyed seeing it with her father, she wanted to truly soak it in on her own, unrushed. When she arrived, she was surprised to see that she had the small park completely to herself. Well, there was one other guest. Standing on one of the rocks in the river was a Great Blue Heron. Quietly, she slipped the camera out of her pocket and began to capture the sleek and regal bird. It was much taller than the wooden carving at the inn, but as it stood there perfectly still, it seemed to give Hope a sense of calmness.

After taking a handful of pictures, she stepped closer to the edge and peered down. Janice was right, there were tons of seashells clinging to the banking of the river. She started to climb down to pick a few up, but it was much too steep. Fearing she might fall in, she moved away from the river and back towards the center of the park. When she came across one of the willows, she remembered her father telling her how her mother would sit under them and read. With her bag slung over her shoulder, she decided to do just that. Her grandmother often talked about her mother's love of books, but to sit in the very same spot and read gave Hope a magical sense of connection to her mother.

She cozied up against the trunk and let the rest of the morning slip away. Before she knew it, two hours had gone by. Not all the time was spent reading. At one point, she placed the book back into her bag and pulled out her journal instead. She wanted to write down as much as she could remember from the previous day regarding some of the stories about her mother.

Hope probably would have stayed there all day enjoying the park's serenity, but her stomach was growling, and she desperately needed something to drink. She placed her journal and her book back into her bag and slowly stood up. A cool breeze blew through the willow as she stretched her arms to the sky.

She reached for her camera and noticed there were only three exposures left. Less than a minute later, she made quick work of them, for the Great Blue Heron once again returned to its perch on the giant rock in the river. There were dozens of parks in Chicago where Hope sat and read, but this one might have been the most beautiful and peaceful places she'd ever seen. As the breeze continued to blow through the willows, it was as if she felt a sense of connectivity with her mother. It was enough to send chills up her arms.

Harbor Cove Park was next on her list, but first she needed to stop at the general store. In addition to grabbing some food and a drink, she wanted to buy another couple rolls of film. She had a feeling her camera-happy finger would be busy up at the lighthouse. Yes,

Hope deemed rolls of film a necessity. She did, however, splurge fifty cents on a handful of postcards.

The same woman was behind the counter, and just like the previous day, she greeted Hope with a warm, welcoming smile. Hope had only been in town for a couple of days, but she felt more noticed than she ever did back in Chicago. More times than not, she felt invisible back home. Here in Applewood, it seemed as if people were seeing her—like, *really* seeing her. To her pleasant surprise, it was the person who noticed her exiting the store that shocked her the most.

As Hope opened her car door, a voice called to her from behind. "You weren't gonna call me, were you?" Hope spun around and saw Adam standing by his truck. Caught off guard, she appeared speechless. Before she could muster up something to say, Adam let her off the hook. "I'm just giving you shit. I didn't really expect you to call me anyway."

"That's not true," she finally said. "I was going to call... probably... maybe?"

He laughed. "Yea, yea, yea."

By now, Hope's cheeks were already a bright shade of red.

"Whatcha up to today?" he asked.

"Not much. Just doing a little sightseeing, I guess. How about you? No lawn mowing today?"

"Landscaping. I do landscaping, not just lawn mowing."

"My apologies," she said with a smile. "So, no *landscaping* today?"

"Nope. Day off." Just then, a car drove by the store and beeped at Adam. He waved then shot a hoot and a holler their way. "Those are my roomies," he said, turning back to Hope.

For a brief moment, there was an awkward silence as they both just stood there staring at each other. Well, he was staring at her, but Hope was having a hard time looking directly at him. She wasn't used

93

to having conversations with guys, especially ones as good looking as Adam.

"I should probably let you enjoy your day off," she finally said. She gave him a polite smile and as much eye contact as she could, and then she turned back to her car.

"Hey, Hope," he called to her.

Just hearing him say her name sent shivers up her arms.

"Yes?" she asked, turning back around.

"Here's an idea. How about you let me be your personal tour guide today?"

If her face wasn't red enough already, it certainly was now.

"Thanks, but I'm sure you have better things to do on your day off."

Adam thought for a second then smirked and said, "Nope. Not at all, actually. So, what do ya say, Chicago girl?"

"Sure," she said, beaming. "That would be groovy."

"Cool. Why don't you leave your car here and hop into my truck."

"Okay. Let me just grab my camera and lock up." Her statement caused Adam to start laughing. "What's so funny?"

"You locking your car. You're definitely a big-city chick. We don't even lock our houses here on the island."

"Sorry. Just a habit, I guess."

"You don't need to apologize," he said, motioning her to climb into his truck. "It's kind of cute."

Technically, Hope knew he was calling her *action* cute, not her looks per se, but her blushing face considered it all the same. From his pocket, he pulled out a pack of Winstons.

"You want a smoke?" he said, offering her one.

She fought back a disgusted look and politely responded, "No thank you."

"Suit yourself," he said, popping one into his mouth and then lighting it. Within seconds, the truck reeked of cigarette smoke. It was a smell that Hope usually detested, but in this situation, her nose made an exception.

"Ya ready?" he said. She nodded. "Alrighty then. Let's rock and roll." Adam revved the gas then squealed out onto the main road. He pressed play on his tape player and cranked up the volume. The next thing Hope knew, the truck was vibrating from the guitar sounds of Kiss.

"You a Kiss fan?" he loudly asked over the music.

She thought about lying, but her initial expression gave her away. Without even realizing it, a cringey look appeared on her face.

"Are you kidding me? Who doesn't like Kiss?" Adam turned down the volume slightly then motioned to a small black suitcase of cassettes. "You can look in there and see if there's anything you like," he said.

Hope opened the case, and as she browsed through the titles, she made a more conscious effort to not allow her previous facial expression make another appearance. Not one of his bands appealed to her in the least. This was exactly how her father must have felt when he looked through her tapes. Just then, Adam's truck came to a halt at the four-way stop. Hope pointed to the HARBOR COVE PARK sign outside her window.

"Can we go out to the lighthouse?" she excitedly asked. "I haven't been there yet."

"Really? That's usually the first place tourists hit."

"It was actually on my list for today."

"The lighthouse it is!" he said. Once again he revved the gas and peeled out to the right.

As he sped down the road, Hope used that moment to nonchalantly close the tape case and place it next to her. A few minutes

95

later, his truck rumbled to a stop in a gravel parking area. It was a small lot and was already nearly full.

"Ready?"

"Ready," she said with a smile.

She grabbed her bag, camera, and one of the new rolls of film she had just purchased. She then climbed out of the truck. Before she shut the door, she started to press the lock down but felt Adam's eyes on her. He was smiling and shaking his head at her. She shut the door without locking it then looked back over at Adam.

"Atta girl," he said, giving her an approving wink. He then tossed his cigarette to the ground and stomped it out with his work boots.

Adam led her to a small hill, and as they climbed the built-in steps, Hope was still blushing from his wink. She watched as he pulled out a tin of Skoal and placed a pinch in his mouth. Everything about him was exactly the opposite of what Hope looked for in guys; from his brash, cocky attitude, to his loud raucous music, and definitely his disgusting smoking and chewing habits. As a matter of fact, she couldn't count the number of times she had made fun of other girls who fell for guys like him. But between his perfectly feathered-back hair and his sky-blue eyes, she was indeed willing to overlook the rest. Hope's enamored feelings were put on hold when they reached the top step.

The park was bigger and more open than the Willows but contained fewer trees. Even with the sun tucked behind a grey cloud, the grass seemed extra green. Gravel paths wound their way around the park, and there were colorful flower beds scattered about. In general, the entire park was much more landscaped than the Willows.

"Did your company do all this?" she asked.

"Nope. Our fucking competition has this account."

Smartly, Hope held back on the many adjectives she was about to use in describing the perfectly manicured park. Just then, the sun emerged from behind the large dark cloud. Its brightness was blinding and caused Hope to reach in her bag for her sunglasses.

"Nice shades," Adam said, shielding his eyes from the sun. "Speaking of which, I left mine in the truck. I'll be right back, okay?"

"I'll be here," she said.

As Adam headed back to his truck, Hope continued up the path. Off to her left, she noticed a handful of families. Most were sitting on blankets enjoying their picnics. On one of the blankets sat a mother, a father, and their young daughter. She looked to be around four or five, and Hope's mind was immediately transported back to when she was that age. It seemed like forever ago, but she remembered going on picnics with her grandparents. Grant Park was their go-to spot of choice. Most of the memories were hazy at best, but for whatever reason, she vividly remembered sitting on a large multi-colored blanket eating peanut butter and jelly sandwiches—with the crust cut off. She always had to have the crust cut off.

Just as she was getting lost in thought, the sound of children's laughter snapped her out of her flashback. On the grass to her right were a group of little kids playing what appeared to be freeze tag. She gave them a smile then continued up the path. When she reached the end, her eyes and mouth gaped open. She found herself standing at the edge of a cliff with the entirety of the Atlantic Ocean sprawled out before her. She quickly fumbled with her camera, loading a new roll of film into it. Before she started taking pictures, Hope closed her eyes and took a deep breath, allowing the salt air to fill her lungs.

Slowly, she opened her eyes. A smile appeared on her face as she gazed out at the sparkling blue sea. Between the intoxicating scent of the salt air and the glistening of the waves, Hope was truly in awe of its beauty. From the fishing boats to her left to the small flock of seagulls squawking directly in front of her, Hope excitedly began snapping one picture after another.

She then focused in on her right to the crown jewel of Applewood—the lighthouse. After another half dozen pictures, Hope took a long, curious pause. She squinted her eyes, staring just out beyond the lighthouse. She removed her sunglasses, and then took the binoculars from around her neck and lifted them up to her eyes. She focused on a tiny section of the ocean. It seemed a bit different from the rest. The waves there seemed rougher, and its color seemed darker.

"Whatcha looking at?" asked a young voice from behind her.

Startled, Hope let out squeal. She then spun around to see a little girl standing there looking up at her.

"Sorry. I didn't mean to scare you," the girl said.

"It's okay. I scare easy," Hope said and laughed.

The girl had dark hair and looked to be around eight years old.

"I love your braids," Hope said, pointing at the girl's hair. "I wish I could do mine as good as yours."

The girl smiled, but her attention remained on Hope's binoculars.

"See anything good with those? Sharks? Whales?"

"No, nothing that cool. Wait… do you really have them around here?"

Before she burst out giggling, the girl held her serious look for as long as she could. "No, silly. The water is too cold here for sharks. We do have whales, but they live wayyy out there."

"I didn't really think there were sharks around here," Hope said with a smirk.

The young girl continued to giggle. She then asked, "Can I try them out?"

"The binoculars? Sure."

Hope handed them to her and watched as she scanned the ocean, finally focusing in on the lighthouse.

"Wow! I've never seen the lighthouse like this before. It's like, so close I can almost touch it."

Hope grinned and turned her thoughts back to the rough waters out past the lighthouse. "Hey, do you know why that little section of the ocean looks so much darker than the rest?"

Slowly, the girl lowered the binoculars from her eyes and looked up at Hope and said, "What did you say?"

I was just wondering why that area out past the lighthouse looks so different than the rest of the ocean. The waves look bigger and rougher, and the water looks way—"

"You can see it, can't you?" the girl interrupted.

"See what?" Hope asked.

"The Dark Waters," the girl said wide-eyed.

"Is that really what it's called?"

The girl nodded.

Hope started to laugh and said, "Well, I guess that's what I see then."

Still in shock, the young girl said, "You really can see it, can't you?"

Hope was becoming more amused. "Am I not supposed to?" she said with a chuckle.

"I've never met anyone that could see it."

"You're pulling my leg again, aren't you?" Between the way the girl looked, and the way she shook her head no, Hope was starting to think she was being completely serious. "Are you telling me you can't see it either?" Again, the girl shook her head no. "Here, try to see it with the binoculars," Hope urged.

She peered through the binoculars and looked out where Hope was pointing to. "Just past the lighthouse... over to the right... can you see it?"

The girl lowered the binoculars and softly said, "No."

"There's no way... I can't be the *only* one who sees it." Hope turned and looked all around her. It was as if she was searching for someone, anyone who could validate her vision. Unfortunately, there was no one near them. Everyone was off in the distance doing their own thing. Hope turned and gazed back out to the ocean. Even without the binoculars, the small dark area was plain as day.

Quietly, the girl uttered, "I've never seen it for real, but I've had dreams of the Dark Waters."

Hope looked down at the girl and curiously asked, "I don't get it. What exactly are... the Dark Waters?"

The little girl's eyes fell toward the ground. "It's an old legend... It's where the Evil Spirit lives."

Her tone was completely serious, but Hope continued to think she was just putting her on. "Ahh, an old legend, huh? So, where does this Evil Spirit come from?"

The girl hesitated a second. "I'm... I'm not supposed to talk about it."

"What? You're not supposed to talk about the legend?"

"Or the dreams," the girl said, still looking down at the grass. "Or else my mom will make me go back to that feelings doctor."

It was at that point Hope realized the girl was being sincere and telling the truth. She also assumed by *feelings doctor*, the girl was referring to some sort of a therapist, which only added to her curiosity. Before Hope could say a word, the little girl raised her head and looked across the park at her mother and siblings. Her mother had just finished packing up from their picnic and was waving for the girl to return.

"I gotta go," she said, and then turned and rushed off.

Hope watched the girl scamper across the grass back her family.

"Geesh, I leave you alone for five minutes and you're scaring off little kids."

Hope turned to see Adam walking up the path. He wore dark sunglasses and was in the midst of grabbing his baseball hat from his back pocket and placing it on his head—backwards.

"Ha, ha," she said. "I'm not scaring anyone off. I am, however, gonna need to buy some more film today. I've already gone through a half a roll."

"Yup, a true tourist through and through."

"Oh, come on. You have to admit, this is like the most beautiful place in the world."

"I don't know about that," he laughed. "But it's okay, I guess."

Hope rolled her eyes then found herself looking back over at the little girl and her family. By now, they were nearly out of sight. She couldn't help but to think about the girl's comments regarding the Dark Waters. Even stranger, was the fact that she claimed no one else could see it. Hope knew that children were prone to exaggerate, but the little girl seemed totally serious. She pondered a second then decided to use Adam as a test subject.

"Hey, seeing as you're my tour guide today, what's that dark spot out beyond the lighthouse?"

Adam casually slipped his sunglasses down to the bridge of his nose then gazed out to where she was pointing. "Ummm, I'm not really seeing what you're talking about."

"Here, try these," she said, handing him the binoculars from around her neck. "It's out past the lighthouse and off to the right."

Adam spent the next thirty seconds scanning the ocean. Finally, he handed the binoculars back to her and said, "Sorry, but I don't really see any dark spots. It was probably just that giant cloud from earlier casting a shadow onto the ocean."

As he raised his sunglasses back up, Hope looked up at the sky. The large cloud had long since passed, and the sky was bright blue without another cloud in sight. Hope took another quick peek in the binoculars, and there, as plain as day, were the Dark Waters. She thought about pleading her case with Adam but decided to leave it alone.

They spent the next hour winding their way around the many paths of the beautiful park. Not another word was spoken about the Dark Waters. As a matter of fact, Adam seemed to do most of the talking. This was more than fine with Hope, who wasn't much of a conversationalist anyway. It wasn't that she didn't have things to say, but she was just used to hanging out with herself. Not to mention, she was still a bit shocked that this cute boy chose to spend his day off with her.

"We can head out whenever you want," she said, lowering the camera from her eyes. "That's the last picture, I promise."

"You do realize you said that three pictures ago, right?"

"Sorry. I just can't believe how gorgeous this place is."

"Relax, Hope. I'm just giving ya shit. But you really shouldn't waste all your photos here. Our tour has just begun." Adam ran his fingers through his hair, readjusted his baseball hat, and then motioned for Hope to follow him back down to the parking lot.

"Ya hungry?" he asked, climbing into the truck.

"I'm starving. That's why I stopped at the store earlier." She smiled and lifted up her small brown grocery bag.

"Get anything good?" he asked.

Hope nodded and pulled out a shiny apple.

"That's what you bought?" he said in disbelief.

"And a bottle of water."

"I thought you said you were hungry?" he said, and laughed. "Let's go get you a real meal."

She placed the apple back into the bag and softly answered, "Okay."

She turned away as to avoid him seeing her face turn red. She couldn't remember the last time a guy offered to take her out for a meal. When she finally did look his way, he was shaking his head and grinning at her. She had her camera strapped to her left wrist and the giant binoculars were still dangling from her neck.

"What?"

"You're like the classic tourist, that's all. It's not a bad thing, but… definitely a tourist."

Awkwardly, she slipped off the camera and binoculars and placed them in her bag on the floor. "Happy?"

He continued laughing and said, "You're still a tourist. So, besides a healthy apple and water, what else did ya get at the store?"

She looked over at the brown bag and blushed. "Film and postcards," she said, shaking her head. "I really am a tourist, huh?"

"Relax, city girl, I'm just giving ya shit again. I bet I can guess which ones," he said, looking back at the bag.

"Huh?"

"I bet I can guess which postcards you bought."

She smirked. "Okay, go ahead." She pulled out the cards and held them where only she could see them.

"One—the boats in the marina. Two—some sort of card with lobsters on it. Three—sunset at the Willows. And the rest are probably sunrise pictures at the lighthouse. How'd I do?"

She looked down at the postcards and smiled. "Wow, you're good. You got them all… except I do have a really groovy one of the lighthouse at night. It has stardust falling all around it and says Applewood, Maine: Home to Medillia's Lament.

Adam smacked the steering wheel and said, "Aw shit! That's like the most classic tourist card we have! How the hell did I forget that one?"

Hope giggled as she stared down at the postcard. "What is Medillia's Lament, anyway?"

"Just some silly Indian story. This island has more Indian legends and fairy tales than you can shake a stick at."

"What's the story behind Medillia's Lament?"

He shrugged. "I don't know. Something about a star that crashes and turns Applewood into a magical island or some shit."

"Awww."

"Don't tell me you believe in that stuff, do you?"

"No, but it's a nice thought. It's kind of cool to think that this place is full of magic, don't you think?"

"Trust me, there's nothing magical about this island. As a matter of fact, as soon as I get enough money saved, I'm outta here!"

"Oh yea? Where to?"

"It doesn't matter. Any place is better than this hole in the wall."

Hope disagreed. Applewood was one of the most beautiful places she'd ever seen. She knew Adam was probably suffering from the *grass is always greener syndrome*. She knew this because she too suffered from it. Chicago was far from a hole in the wall, but ever since she was little, she wanted to get out and explore the world.

As Adam pulled out of the parking lot, Hope stared down at her postcards. In particular, she focused on the Medillia's Lament card. She loved thinking that Applewood was magical. It had been a long, long time since she put any stock into that sort of thing. When she was much younger, she used to love watching *The Wonderful World of Disney*. Back then, she believed with all her heart in magic and happily ever afters. Those beliefs slowly waned over the years.

Adam took her to the local diner for lunch. He had an extra greasy double cheeseburger with fries and a chocolate shake. Hope had a garden salad and a glass of water. Needless to say, Adam threw more than one joke her way. She was unaffected by any of his playful jabs. After all, she was still pinching herself that someone as good looking as him was sitting across from her.

Even though lunch went well, when they were finished, Hope just assumed he'd call it a day and bring her back to her car. She assumed wrong. Before he even started his truck, he turned towards Hope and said, "If you want, we could make our way to the center of the island and drive up to Mount M?"

She did her best not to seem too eager and excited. "Sure, wherever you want. Wait, there's a mountain on this island?"

"Well, I wouldn't really call it a mountain, but it's the highest point on the island. There's not much to do up there, but I'm sure we can find a couple of good spots to take pictures. And if you're up for it, we can always explore the Devil's Lair."

"The Devil's Lair? What's that?"

"It's a giant rock formation with a cave winding its way through its center. Most of the cave is narrow, but there's one spot in there that opens up into a giant room. It's got a bunch of those pointy rock thingies hanging from the ceiling."

"Stalactites?"

"Huh?"

"Stalactites. That's the official name of those pointy rock thingies," she giggled.

"Cute *and* a brainiac" he said, flashing his pearly whites. "Nice."

Hope had been called a brainiac many times in her life, but the cute comment was a new one to her. As her face turned twenty shades of red, she did her best to deflect his compliment. "That place sounds groovy."

"Yea, it's a great place to party and get wasted."

"I'd love to go there sometime," she said.

Adam's lips formed a sly smile. It took Hope a second, but she realized he must have assumed that she was referring to wanting to get wasted there. Before she had a chance to clarify, Adam said, "The Devil's Lair it is."

He revved the gas then threw it into drive. As he peeled out, Hope nervously bit down on her lip and crossed her fingers that she hadn't given off the wrong impression. But the wink and the twinkle in his blue eyes said differently. Not that it was a bad thing to think about being alone in a cave with Adam. As a matter of fact, for a brief second, Hope allowed herself to fantasize about kissing his lips, and maybe even running her fingers through his thick, wavy hair.

Hope felt the heat flowing off her blushing face and quickly turned away to avoid any sort of eye contact with Adam. She certainly wasn't used to being in such close proximity to a guy she found attractive. It was usually from far across the room, and almost always, the guy had no clue she even existed. Not to mention, most of the time the guy had an attractive girl by his side; one that Hope could never dream of competing with.

As they neared the center of the island, her thoughts turned to his comments regarding the cave being the perfect place to party. Did he plan on taking her there to get drunk? Did he have alcohol with him? Before her eyes could scan the truck, Adam's comment put her worries at ease. "Shit! I should have swung back to the store and grabbed some booze."

She quietly let out a sigh of relief and said, "It's okay. I'm sure we can have fun without it."

Once again, she meant it in an innocent way, but once again, Adam's smirk took it differently. She thought about commenting on how much she enjoyed hiking and exploring, but she decided to remain quiet. It wasn't long after Adam turned left down a dirt road that he let out another expletive. "Fuck!" he said, slowing the truck down to a complete stop. Just up ahead was a construction sign boldly reading ROAD CLOSED. "Shit!" he exclaimed, turning down his radio. "It's still like a mile away, and I sure as hell ain't hiking it from here." Hope was glad that she had held off on telling him how much she enjoyed hiking. He obviously wasn't a big fan of it.

"It's okay," she said. "Maybe another time."

Adam proceeded to aggressively do a three-point turn, and as he sped off in the opposite direction, he said, "Don't worry, there are plenty of other hidden gems around the island." He thought a second then winked and said, "And I know the perfect place."

At any moment, Hope expected him to crank the volume back up, but he didn't. As a matter of fact, he surprised her by turning it completely off and asking her about herself.

"So, I assume that grumpy dude you were with the other night is your father?"

Hope nodded and quietly answered, "Yes."

"Yea, the angry glare he shot at me had father written all over it. He did not like me one bit," Adam said and laughed.

"Don't take it personally. I don't really think he likes anyone."

"Is this like a father-daughter trip or is your mother here, too?"

Hope thought about being vague with her response, but ultimately decided to be honest. "No, it's just us here. My mother passed away right after I was born."

"I'm sorry. That's some pretty heavy stuff. You and your dad must be close then, huh?"

Again, it would have been much easier to give Adam a vague answer, but for whatever reason, she told him the truth—the truth about everything. Even though she had just told Janice these same things a couple days earlier, this was different. This was a boy. A cute boy. She couldn't remember the last time she told a cute boy this much about her life, especially so quickly. Like an avalanche, once she started, she couldn't hold back. By the time they arrived at their next stop, she had filled him in on pretty much everything. It wasn't until he turned the key off that she caught herself.

"I'm sorry, I didn't mean to bore you with my life story."

"No, not at all. Bore away," he said and winked.

It was more of a twinkle than a wink, and it was enough to cause Hope to completely forget what she was talking about. Just in case her face was blushing again, she turned to her right and looked out the window. Adam had parked on the side of a dead-end road.

"Where are we?" she asked.

They both climbed out of the truck, and Adam pointed to the houses across the way. "There's a private cove out behind those trees."

"And by private, you mean only the people in these houses are allowed there?"

"Something like that," he said, and then motioned her to follow him. "There's a path behind this house over here. And it looks like we're in luck… no cars in the driveway."

Directly on the edge of the yard was a NO TRESPASSING sign. Adam noticed her trepidation and did his best to ease her mind. "Relax, Hope. The sign is just for show. No one's ever enforced it. Trust me, it'll be fine."

He then reached his hand out for hers. As she took it, her worries instantly faded away. They entered the back yard and walked past a small white gazebo, enroute to the path through the woods. Almost immediately, Hope could hear the sounds of the ocean out in the distance. It became louder as they moved closer. It wasn't long before the path opened up, revealing the sand and sea.

"Oh, wow," she said, releasing his hand and reaching for her camera. "This is gorgeous." She quickly took a few pictures and said, "And I can't believe there's no one here."

"Like I said, it's a hidden gem. A lot of the locals don't even know about it."

As they headed straight for the shoreline, rocks and shells crunched beneath their feet. Besides the occasional seagull squawking, the only sounds were the waves breaking against the sand. Hope immediately slipped off her sandals and walked ankle-deep into the water.

"Wow! That's cold," she exclaimed.

He laughed. "Well, yeah. It's Maine, not Hawaii."

She exited the water but continued walking barefoot along the sand. "Thanks for bringing me here," she said. "I love it. And thanks for showing me around today."

"You don't have to keep thanking me, Hope. It's really not a big deal."

"Still, I just want you to know I appreciate it."

As he was prone to do, Adam ran his fingers through his hair and adjusted his hat. He then flashed a smile and once again grabbed her hand. "Come on, there's some place I wanna show you."

They continued further up the cove and moved away from the shore and closer to the tree line. He led her to a group of three large boulders, which were in an almost cave-like formation. It was slightly uphill and appeared to be on high enough ground so that the tide never reached it. In the small sandy area between the boulders, there were remnants of a camp fire along with more than one crushed Budweiser can.

"It's not the Devil's Lair, but it's another cool place to come hang out late at night."

"The water doesn't come up this far?" she asked.

"Not unless it's a big storm."

Before Hope could notice, Adam nonchalantly kicked sand over an old condom wrapper.

"Wanna sit for a bit?" he asked, motioning to the ground.

"Yea, sure."

She tossed down her Birkenstocks and sat around the makeshift fire ring. Adam joined her and sat much closer than she expected. Not that she was complaining, it just caught her off guard. She wasn't cold, yet chills ran up and down her arms. Adam took notice and said, "Aww, are you cold?"

He didn't wait for a reply. He slid even closer and placed his arm around her. What happened next caused her heart to race and her goosebumps to become more prominent. He kissed her. Softly at first but then more passionately. Hope was in heaven, yet her goodie-two-shoes instincts took hold and she pulled away.

"Did I do something wrong?" he asked.

"No, not at all. I… I don't usually do this with people I just met."

"I'm sorry," he said.

"Oh, no. It's totally not you, Adam. I guess I'm just old-fashioned in that way."

"Believe it or not, I am, too. I don't usually do this with strangers… especially ones from Chicago." His smile was enough to put her at ease, but not nearly as much as his next comment. "I guess I just don't consider you a stranger. After hanging out with you all day and listening to your story, I just can't believe how similar we are."

"Similar? How so?" she asked.

"Well… I didn't say anything earlier, but our backstories are kind of the same."

"They are?"

Adam took a deep breath. "I lost both my parents when I was six."

"Oh my God, Adam. I'm so sorry."

From that point on, Hope sat back and listened intently as Adam filled her in on his tragic past. When he was finished, Hope slid closer and grasped his hand. Her heart was saddened, yet her eyes glistened at their serendipitous connection.

"Thanks for trusting me enough to share that with me," she said, sympathetically looking into his eyes.

"Thanks for listening. You're easy to talk to. I know it sounds stupid, but it feels like we've known each other forever."

She tightened her grip on his hand and said, "I don't think it's stupid at all. I… I actually feel the same way about you."

Adam continued to gaze into her eyes. That was all it took. With his free hand, he brushed the hair from her face and leaned in for another kiss. This time, Hope didn't pull away. She ignored her inhibitions and went with the moment. Even when she felt his hand on her breast and his tongue enter her mouth, she went with it.

There was no telling how far they would have gone if they weren't interrupted. The interruption came in the form of two young children, who had sprinted ahead of their mother down on the beach.

"Were you two kissing?" the young boy said, giggling.

The little girl quickly added her two cents. "Eww! Germs!"

By now, Hope's face was bright red. Sheepishly, she smiled as she straightened out her top. Adam's look was far from sheepish. In hopes that they would buzz off, he shot them an angry glare. The kids were oblivious and were more interested in exploring the tiny cave.

"Whoa! Did you guys have a campfire in here? Cool!"

Moments later, their mother appeared in the entrance, and after profusely apologizing, she dragged her two kids out of the cave and back to the beach. Adam and Hope were alone again, but it was obvious the moment had passed.

"I should probably head back to the inn," she said. "I bet my father is wondering where I am."

Hope knew the chances of David being awake, never mind worrying about her, were slim to none. It just seemed like the right thing to say.

"Yea, sure. Whatever you want." Adam stood up and smiled, but on the inside, he was still pissed at the little kids for ruining their make-out session. Not much was spoken as he escorted her through the cove and back up the path to the truck. When they finally arrived back at the general store, Adam offered up a suggestion. "What are you doing later tonight?"

She shrugged. "I don't have anything planned, why?"

My roommates and I are having a little party. You should come. And we can go out for dinner first, if ya want?"

Dinner *and* a party? Hope had just been officially asked out on a date. Her insides were about to burst, but she made sure her outside remained as calm as possible. She didn't want to seem like getting asked out was a rarity, which was exactly the case.

"That sounds groovy," she said, stepping out of his truck.

"Cool. I'll come get you around six. And maybe we can pick up where we left off."

Before he could even wink at her, Hope's face had already turned the all too familiar shade of red. She didn't respond to his comment, but she did manage to once again thank him for an amazing day of sightseeing.

"You don't have to keep thanking me," he said. "I'll see you at six."

"See you at six," she echoed, and then climbed into her car. She waited until his truck had completely pulled out of the parking lot before letting out an excited shrill.

7

It was late afternoon when David finally opened his eyes. His pounding headache had subsided and even the sharp pain in his side had lessened a little bit. Both of his arms, however, were bright red from excessive itching. The scratch marks from his long unkempt nails made it appear as if his arms had been attacked by a pack of wolves.

His tired bones creaked as he climbed out of bed and made his way towards the window. He gave the shade a tug then quickly released it, causing it to shoot up the window and loudly recoil. Shielding his eyes from the bright afternoon sun, he scanned the courtyard. He was hoping to see his daughter sitting by the fountain playing guitar, but to his disappointment, the bench was empty.

Just as he turned away from the open window, he heard laughing coming from one of the flower gardens. He strained his eyes out to the right, and there, walking between the gardens were the Hendersons. They were giggling and appeared to be feeding each other fruit.

"Are you fucking kidding me? Goddamn lovebirds make me sick!"

He grabbed the shade and hastily yanked it shut once again. He continued mumbling under his breath and walked over to his satchel at the foot of the bed. He mumbled even more profanities when he realized he was once again out of alcohol. After latching the satchel back up, he slung it over his shoulder and left the room. Out on the front porch, Janice was watering one of her many flower pots. She paused when she saw David exiting the front door.

"Good afternoon, David. I hope you were able to get some rest?"

David said nothing, but he did nod his head.

"You certainly picked a good week to come," she said. "You couldn't have asked for better weather."

Again, he nodded then made his way over to one of the porch chairs. Janice watched as he placed his satchel beside him and carefully lowered his body into the wicker. It wasn't until he lit his cigarette and let out his first exhale of smoke that he spoke. "She around?"

"Hope?" Janice asked knowingly. "No. I gave her a few sightseeing suggestions this morning, and she's been out all day. I can't believe she's never seen the ocean before. I guess you take those things for granted living here all your life. She seemed very excited to be out here on the coast. Definitely one of the perks of my job."

"What's that?"

"Getting to see the excitement of people visiting this beautiful place for the first time. It never gets old."

Janice continued watering her plants, and David continued puffing away on his cigarette. After taking a long, deep drag, and without making eye contact, David muttered, "Sorry about snapping at you earlier."

"No need for apologies, David. I'm sure this week has been hard on you." She paused a moment and continued. "I didn't realize you had been here before. Hope tells me you met your wife in Applewood? You must be shocked by how much has changed around here."

"So much has changed—period," he said, finally making eye contact. Janice knew he was referring to more than just Applewood. "She's just so big… so grown up now. And I missed it. I completely missed it."

114

David's broken voice revealed his grief. As Janice walked towards him, she placed the watering can down on the porch and swiped an ashtray off one of the tables. She settled next to David putting the ashtray at his elbow and watched him extinguish the butt in it.

"You shouldn't be so hard on yourself, David. Besides, from the looks of it, she turned out to be an amazing young woman."

David grabbed another cigarette and began to light it. "Want one?" he asked, holding the pack in front of her.

"Oh, I haven't smoked in years."

David started to put the pack down next to him, but stopped when he heard her say, "You know what, maybe I will take one."

He smiled and handed her a cigarette and lit it for her.

"My husband hated me smoking," she said. "If he was here right now, I'd never hear the end of it."

"Your secret's safe with me."

The fact that Janice had joined him in a smoke seemed to allow him to let his guard down a bit. It turned out to be the longest conversation Janice had with him since his arrival days earlier.

"I'd offer you some vodka, but I'm fresh out."

"Ha. That's something I definitely don't do anymore. Actually, even back in my heyday, I was never much of a drinker," she said, half expecting a sarcastic response. To her surprise, his response was far from sarcastic.

"Good for you. I wish I never touched the stuff. I wish I'd done a lot of things differently."

His words oozed with regret, and after taking a drag off her cigarette, Janice sympathetically said, "Luckily for us, tomorrow is always a brand-new day. A brand-new day where we can start all over again."

"I used to think that, but… but I'm afraid my brand-new days are long gone. I'm just a broken man who has finally reached the end of the line."

That would be as dark as the conversation would get. The rest of their time on the porch was spent smoking and talking about more lighthearted subjects. Even though Janice was just over ten years older, David was surprised how much they had in common. They reminisced about their first cars then both recited each and every car they had since.

"How long have you owned that one," she said, pointing out to his Dodge Dart."

"Oh, I don't own that. I just stole it to make the trip out here. It woulda been an awful long walk from California."

Even though they both laughed out loud, Janice got the strange sense that David wasn't really joking. She decided it best, however, not to pry too much. He was in a rare good mood, so the last thing she wanted was to alter that in any way. They stuck to small talk and things they had in common.

By the time Hope arrived back to the inn, David and Janice had polished off nearly half a pack of cigarettes. As soon as she saw Hope pull in, Janice extinguished her butt into the ashtray. It was like a role reversal; one where the adult hides their smoking from the child. Hope was in such a good mood that she barely noticed the guilty look on Janice's face.

"Hey, you two," Hope called out. "Nice to see you out on the porch enjoying this beautiful day."

"I was just telling your father that you guys picked the perfect week to come to the island."

"Agreed," Hope said, climbing the steps. "It was absolutely gorgeous today. How are you feeling?" she said, in her father's direction. He didn't reply. Instead, he lit another cigarette and blew a giant puff her way. Her eyes widened when she saw the full ash tray on the table next to him. "Holy cow! Did you smoke all those today?"

116

He gave his daughter a snarl and said, "Someone has to make up for all you non-smokers." He then turned to Janice and gave her a quick wink. She smiled and used that moment to make her exit.

"Oh my," she said, pretending to look at her watch. If we want to eat by six, I guess I need to get dinner started." Before heading inside, she turned back and said, "Thanks for the chat, David."

He gave her a slight nod but was more focused on trying to blow the perfect smoke ring. Hope was in such a happy mood that she didn't even seem bothered by the amount of smoke being blown her way. She was about to ask how his day was, but David twisted the rest of his cigarette into the ash tray and stood up and said, "I think I'm gonna go lay down for a bit. Come get me when dinner is ready, okay?"

She followed him inside and said, "Umm, I actually have plans for dinner tonight."

David started up the staircase but paused halfway up. "What do you mean you have plans? With who?" Slowly, he turned back around. Her embarrassed expression gave it away. "You've got to be shitting me! You called that loser lawn mower boy, didn't you?"

"No. No, I didn't."

Incredulously, David looked down at his daughter.

"I didn't call him. We just sort of… ran into each other today. You know, serendipity like."

"Seren what? I'm telling you, Hope, this idiot is bad news!"

"Oh, God. Now you're sounding like my grandfather. Adam and I had a groovy time sightseeing today, and—"

"You spent the day with him?"

Hope stood her ground. "Yes, I did. Adam is actually very sweet and funny. And believe it or not, we have a lot in common."

David bellowed a loud, sarcastic laugh and said, "How much can you have in common? The hoodlum mows lawns for a living."

"At least he has a job." She immediately regretted her comment.

She thought about apologizing, but David seemed amused by her jab and let out another laugh. Hope decided to skip the apology and leave well-enough alone. "I don't want to fight, okay? I'll see you later tonight after the party."

"Party? What party?"

"He's taking me to dinner and then to a party at his place."

"The hell he is!"

Hope placed her hands on her hips. "Are you kidding me? You're really gonna play the concerned parent? You're about twenty years too late for that!" Before storming up to her room, Hope uncharacteristically blurted out, "And just because you're an asshole, doesn't mean all guys are!" With that, she rushed upstairs to change for her date.

Hastily, she went through her suitcase, wishing she had brought more clothes—especially clothes for a hot date. She ended up picking out the one dress that she packed with her for the trip. It was a white muslin material with cap sleeves and a gathered waist, which had a bit of floral embroidery that matched the flowers scattered along the hemline. This dress was shorter than the other dresses she typically wore, but the fullness of the layered skirt made her feel more covered than most shorter dresses ever did.

Because this was a date, Hope slipped into the bathroom to perch on the side of the tub for a quick shave of her legs. After a swipe of lotion and splash of patchouli, she was ready to slide her feet into her Birkenstocks and dash out the door. At the last second, she grabbed her white fringe jacket, more for comfort than warmth. Hope's nerves were dancing at the thought of an actual date, but definitely in a good way.

When she finished getting dressed, she decided it was best to wait for Adam out on the porch. By the time she plopped herself into one of the chairs, her blood was still boiling from the earlier confrontation she had with her father. She couldn't believe he had the nerve to say those things. She also couldn't believe she used the word asshole. For the most part, Hope was a soft-spoken and an extremely calm, cool, and collected woman. It took a lot to get her blood boiling and for curse words to fall from her lips. Usually, her blowups were few and far between, but ironically, her next one was only minutes away.

Hope closed her eyes and took several deep breaths. Just when she had finally calmed down, she heard the creak of the front door. She opened her eyes and saw Janice's smiling face staring over at her.

"I'm sorry. I didn't mean to wake you up."

"It's okay. I wasn't really sleeping. Just trying to calm my nerves down a little bit."

"Ahh. Your father?" Janice knowingly asked.

Hope frowned and nodded.

"I'm sorry, dear. I wish I knew what to say."

"I appreciate that, but I'm the one who decided to come here. I should have known what I was getting myself into."

Janice gave her a soft, sympathetic smile then said, "Hopefully my famous pot roast will cheer you up."

"Actually… I'm going out for dinner tonight."

"Oh, okay. Where are you and David going?"

A smile formed on Hope's lips. "I'm going out with a boy," she said, blushing.

"I see," Janice said, returning Hope's smile. "Look at you. You're in town for only a few days and already have yourself a date."

"I'm not sure I'd call it a date."

"Anyone I know?" Janice asked.

"His name is Adam. He's actually one of the guys who does your landscaping."

"Ahhh, you must be talking about Adam Briggs. How did you guys meet?"

Hope filled her in on everything from writing his number on her hand to him being her tour guide throughout the day.

"Sounds like you two made quite the connection. I have to admit, I don't really know him that well. I just hired his company last month. I do know his parents, though. Every so often, I host a girls' night here and we all play cards and drink wine. His mother usually shows up for that."

The smile disappeared from Hope's face and was replaced by a confused look. "His aunt and uncle, you mean?"

"His aunt and uncle?" Janice asked, equally confused. "I have no idea who they are, but I was referring to Adam's parents, Gretchen and Jeffery Briggs."

Hope thought for a long moment then began shaking her head in disgust.

"Are you okay, Hope?"

"I have horrible judgement in guys, and I'm probably the most naïve girl in the world, but other than that, I'm fine." She lowered her head into her hands and let out a giant sigh. "I honestly thought we had a special connection, but I should have known that he only made up that story so he could…"

Janice didn't need Hope to finish the sentence. She had been around the block enough to know exactly what Adam's intentions were. The old wooden porch boards creaked as Janice walked over and placed her hand on Hope's shoulder. "Falling for guys' lines happens to the best of us. Don't be so hard on yourself, kiddo." She released Hope's shoulder and said, "The dinner offer still stands, okay?"

Hope lifted up her face enough to give Janice an appreciative half smile. Not long after Janice headed inside, Hope began to chastise herself. "You're such a fool, Hope! You really, really are. Like someone as good looking as him would actually be into you anyway."

The more she thought about Adam making up that story about

his parents, the more her self-pity turned into anger. Just then, as if right on cue, Adam's truck rumbled up the driveway. Hope noticed there was another guy sitting up front next to Adam. Both of them had their hats on backwards. They sat in the idling truck for a second before Adam finally got out and started walking towards Hope.

She stood up from the chair, and her hands began to tremble in anger. Slowly, she walked down the steps and met him halfway up the driveway. By now, Adam's friend had also exited the truck as if to allow Hope to sit in the middle closer to Adam.

"Wow, you look great," Adam called out. "We just have to drop my roommate off at our house, then we can go out to eat. Okay?"

With each step she took, her anger grew. It wasn't until they were face to face that she finally lost it. Like, *really* lost it.

"You lying son of a bitch!" she yelled, and repeatedly began smacking him. Adam raised his arms, deflecting most of her swipes. Both boys were in complete shock. Although, his roommate's look was a bit more bemused than shocked.

"How dare you play on my emotions with your fake sob story! And for what? Just to get into my pants?"

At this point, both boys had smiles on their faces.

"Get the hell out of here!" she yelled, giving him one last smack. "You friggin' dickweed!"

Adam slowly backed up towards his truck and pretended to surrender by raising his hands in the air. Hope turned and started to head back to the porch.

Adam's roommate laughed. "Holy shit, man! That's one crazy hippy-chick!"

"Yea. It runs in her family," Adam said, loud enough for her to hear.

His comment stopped her dead in her tracks. Her anger boiled over, and she once again lost it. Without thinking clearly, she marched over to the stack of decorative lobster traps in the front yard. She snatched two buoys off the traps and angrily rushed towards the boys. Seeing this, they both jumped into the truck. Adam quickly threw it in reverse and hit the gas. Before she could reach them, the truck peeled out and sped backwards. Frustrated and defeated, Hope unsuccessfully threw the buoys at the truck.

Long after they drove off and faded out of sight, Hope just stood there, upset and fighting back tears. From the large window in the dining room, David, Janice, and the Hendersons, all witnessed what just went down. Hope did her best to collect herself before heading into the house. She took several deep breaths, brushed away her remaining tears, and then bravely entered the dining room. Janice greeted her with a warm, sympathetic smile.

"If it's okay, I guess I will be joining you for dinner," Hope quietly said.

"I already set a place for you," Janice said, pointing to the seat next to David.

Hope forced a tiny smile, mouthed the words *thank you*, and then took her seat. Neither one of the happy-go-lucky Hendersons made eye contact with Hope. They thought about trying to lighten the mood with a silly anecdote, but after witnessing Hope angrily wielding those buoys, they decided it was best to sit quietly and eat their dinner.

David also didn't make eye contact or say a word, but that was only because he was more concerned with filling his plate and stuffing his face. Hope knew it was only a matter of time before he uttered the words, *I told you so.* But he never did. He never uttered any words, for that matter. No one did. The entire meal was uncomfortably silent. David was the first one finished.

"Thank you, Janice. That was the best pot roast I've had in a very long time."

"Why, thank you, David. I'm glad you enjoyed it."

David gave his mouth and beard a final wipe with his napkin. "I think I'm gonna take a walk down to the Rusty Anchor for a little dessert… if ya know what I mean."

The Hendersons were still so uncomfortable sitting there that they almost volunteered to join him. After David left, Andy and Cindi quickly finished eating and politely excused themselves to go upstairs. Hope barely seemed to notice that everyone had dispersed. She spent the entirety of the dinner lost in her own little world.

Janice stood and cleared everyone's plates and brought them into the kitchen. When she returned, she noticed Hope's plate was still full. She'd done more playing with her food than eating it.

"I'm sorry I didn't eat much. It was really good, though. I guess I just wasn't that hungry."

"Oh sweetie, you don't have to apologize."

Hope stood and began helping to clear the table.

"And you certainly don't have to help me clean up."

"It's okay, I want to."

As she picked up her plate, her gaze moved from Janice to the dining room window. She focused on the stack of lobster traps out in the yard.

"Sorry about the buoys. I promise I'll pay for them."

"Oh nonsense," Janice said with a smirk. "They're a dime a dozen around these parts." Janice paused and looked out at the two buoys laying on the ground further down the driveway. "Impressive throw, though. The Red Sox could use an arm like that."

A slight smile crept onto Hope's face.

"Boy's suck, don't they?" Janice said, laughing.

"They really do," Hope said. "They really, really do."

They continued laughing as they carried the rest of the dishes into the kitchen.

"I was gonna fire that company anyway. I liked my old company better," Janice said and smiled.

"You don't have to do that, Janice."

"Eh, they're way overpriced. Besides, us girls need to stick together, right?" Janice gave her a wink then took the dishes from her hands. "I've got these. Why don't you go relax."

"Are you sure?"

"Positive."

"Thanks… for everything."

After sharing a quick smile, Hope finally exited the kitchen and made her way into the library. She did her best to get lost in her book, but the thought of Adam's smug and lying face kept her from fully concentrating. She sat there for a good two hours but barely made it through a chapter. Realizing it was pointless, she closed her book and decided to head up to bed. Just as she climbed out of the comfy chair, she heard the front door open and close. The sound of footsteps moved closer, and within seconds, David appeared in the doorway. He placed his satchel on the floor but didn't say a word. He simply stood there looking over at his daughter.

After a night of drinking at the tavern, Hope was sure this would be the moment that he blasted her with the *I told you so* comment regarding Adam. She looked over at him and waited. When he still said nothing, Hope shook her head and blurted out, "Go ahead. You might as well get it over with and say it. I know you've been dying to all night."

He looked at his daughter for a moment then turned his attention to the old grandfather clock in the far corner of the room. It was just before 10 p.m.

"I'm heading to bed," he finally said. "Night."

He picked up his satchel and turned and headed upstairs. Surprised by his words, or lack thereof, Hope slumped back into the chair. She almost seemed disappointed, even a little hurt that her father

124

didn't care enough to give her the *I told you so* speech. Her grandparents would have wasted no time in telling her how she had screwed up. They could be pains in the ass, but at least she knew they cared.

Just then, David popped his head back into the library. "Depending on how I'm feeling tomorrow, maybe we can do some more exploring of the island. I still haven't shown you where your mother finally said yes to dating me."

Hope's mood immediately lightened, and a glimmer returned to her eye. "I would love to… thanks."

The final word of her sentence fell on deaf ears, for David had already turned and was headed upstairs. For the moment, the excitement of hearing more about her parents far outweighed the disappointment of the earlier incident with Adam.

8

Hope didn't see her father again until nearly noon time the next day. When David finally made an appearance downstairs, Hope greeted him pleasantly. Although she played it cool, she had been anxiously waiting and pacing around the inn for hours. As soon as she heard his heavy feet coming down the steps, she bolted into the kitchen. No sooner did he enter the dining room, Hope handed him a hot cup of coffee.

"Black, right?"

With no real acknowledgement, he grabbed the cup and took a huge sip. Hope cringed. She still couldn't understand how something so hot could have little to no effect on him. He barely took a second sip before Hope asked him the question that had been on her mind all morning. "Are we still going to drive around the island today?"

As she awaited his reply, she placed her hands behind her back and crossed her fingers. His eyes were still half closed, and she imagined his head was still pounding from whatever he'd been drinking the night before. At any second, she expected him to bail on her and to grumble something about heading back up to bed. In one not-so fluid motion, he pounded down the rest of the coffee. "I'm gonna head upstairs," he said, handing the cup back to Hope.

Her heart sank, but before she could let out a disappointed sigh, David followed it up with, "I just need to take a shit first, and then we can go sightseeing. I'll meet you in the car in a few."

And just like that, her spirits were lifted. It took him more than a few minutes to make it to the car, but Hope was just happy that they would be spending the day together. So, once again, with no real destination in mind, Hope drove around the island listening to her father tell story after story of the summer he met her mother. He wasn't as talkative as the last time, but his mood swings were less prominent than before.

At times, he seemed quiet, anxious even. She assumed it was because tomorrow was the big anniversary, and she could only imagine how hard this must be on him. She also wondered how he would be tomorrow. Would he be extra quiet? Extra grouchy? Extra drunk? Sadly, she feared it would be the last two.

As Hope's Chevette puttered down the road, she turned to her father and asked, "Where was your aunt and uncle's house? And whereabouts on the island did Mom stay?"

"Jesus Christ! I can barely remember last week, never mind a million years ago." She started to reply, but David blurted out, "Right here! Pull over right here!" They had just rumbled over a tiny wooden bridge and David motioned for her to park on the side of the road. "Come on," he said, getting out of the car. "I want to show you something."

She promptly removed her keys from the ignition and followed him onto the bridge. David smiled and leaned up against the old wooden railing.

"Is this it? Is this where Mom finally said yes to you?"

"No, no, no! This isn't where I won her over. I just wanted to show you just how wild and spontaneous Maggie really was. Your mother loved bridge jumping."

Assuming he was putting her on, Hope grinned and said, "Nooo."

"Yesss! I told you, there's probably a lot about your mother that your grandparents never mentioned."

Hesitantly, Hope approached the railing and looked down at the water below. When she actually thought he might be telling the truth, she turned to him and asked, "You and Mom really went bridge jumping?"

"Not me," he said, backing away from the railing. "I'm scared of heights. Climbing that damn tree was as much height as I could handle. But your mother had no fear. Yup, she sure loved her some bridge jumping. She said it was the best adrenaline rush in the world. She used to dare me to jump with her."

"And you never did?"

David paused a long moment then said, "Just once. I was pretty wild and reckless myself, but I had no desire to do it again." He smirked. "I remember her trying to peer-pressure me by calling me a big chicken. After she finished doing some sort of clucking routine, she smiled then proceeded to jump on in."

"Really? She jumped… just like that?" Hope looked from her father to the water and then back to him again.

"Yup, just like that. I told you, your mother had quite the wild and spontaneous streak about her."

Hope wasn't sure what she enjoyed more; the thought of her mother being spontaneous and jumping, or the glowing look on her father's face as he recalled the past. He popped another cigarette between his lips and began walking back towards the car. Hope remained a second longer, staring down at the river below. She shivered at the thought of jumping. She agreed with her father on this one. Heights were not her friend. When she returned to the car, David had already pounded down a sip or two of vodka.

"Continue on?" she asked.

He nodded then took one more swig before shoving it back into his satchel. Apparently, Hope's look lingered a bit too long, which caused David to quickly blurt out, "Are we going or what?"

Her red Chevette crept back onto the road and headed towards its next destination. Little did she know, it would be discovered by complete accident. Hope was trying to find the semi-private beach that Adam had taken her to. Despite the deceitful memories it contained for her, she thought her father might enjoy walking through the quiet and peaceful cove. Perhaps the salt air might do him some good.

Hope couldn't quite remember where the cove was, and after unsuccessfully trying several different roads, she was becoming frustrated. "Darn it! This isn't it either."

"Where the hell are you trying to go?" he asked.

"There's kind of a private cove around here with a nice little beach. I thought we could take a walk on it."

"You've been there?" She nodded and watched a sly smile appear on his face. "So, my little Miss Goodie Two-Shoes was trespassing?"

She rolled her eyes and replied, "No, I wasn't trespassing. It's not *really* a private beach… just kind of a hidden entrance, that's all."

"Uh huh," he said, continuing to chuckle to himself.

"Not that it matters anyway," she said. "I can't seem to find the road. Now I'm not even sure if I'm in the right area or not." Starting to get irritated, she turned the car around and headed back towards the main road.

"Stop!" David yelled and pointed out the window. "Right there."

She hit the brakes then followed his finger to a house set just off the road. "No," she said. "That's not where the entrance is."

"Entrance? I'm pointing at the house, ya fool. That's the house where your mother stayed."

Hope's disappointed demeanor immediately changed to an excited enthusiasm. "Really? That's where Mom and her friend stayed?" David didn't respond, for he was already out the door and walking towards the property.

After properly putting her blinker on and pulling over to the side of the road, Hope joined her father in the front of the mailbox. The house was a quaint Cape with grey cedar shakes and black shutters. The second floor had two dormers, and David motioned up to the one on the left. "That's the bedroom where your mother and her friend stayed… or so I thought."

Curiously, Hope smiled at her father. "Oh boy. Sounds like another crazy story is about to be told."

David continued staring up at the window then finally began his tale. "It was just after midnight when I rolled up and parked my car… just about the same spot where you parked. I grabbed my guitar, a couple of candles, and I walked over here."

Hope followed her father onto the lawn as he began to reenact that fateful night.

"Aww, you brought candles? How romantic."

"The street and sky were pitch black, so the candles were more used for light… but yeah, I was also being romantic and shit." David moved forward and positioned himself directly below the left dormer. "I thought it was my lucky night because your mother's window was the only one open in the whole house. So I lit the candles, placed them behind me and began my serenade."

As David started to pantomime playing guitar, Hope interrupted and asked, "What song were you playing?"

He stopped his pretend strumming and shot back, "It doesn't fuckin' matter what I was playing. The song choice isn't important… it's not the meat of my story. Do you wanna hear this, or what?"

She did her best to hold off a smile. "I'm sorry. By all means, get to the meat of the story."

Luckily, David was refocused on the window and didn't see Hope's smile break free.

"Just as I started my first verse, I heard a sound from over there."

He pointed to a rhododendron bush at the corner of the house. "A couple of seconds later, standing five feet in front of me, was a goddamn skunk! We became locked in a staring contest, but I continued strumming and singing. I wasn't about to let him interrupt my moonlight serenade."

"You mean, your candlelight serenade? Because you said the sky was pitch…" She stopped her joking comment as soon as David shot her a glare. "Sorry." She smirked. "Go on."

He let out another huff before continuing. "Just after I finished the first verse, the fuckin' skunk began to raise his tail at me."

"What did you do?"

"Instinctually, I started to back away, but… but I accidentally knocked over one of the candles… which accidentally caught the grass on fire."

"Oh my gosh!" Hope covered her mouth laughing. "That's horrible."

"Still not the meat of the story," he sternly said in her direction.

She raised her hands up in apology then motioned for him to go on. After one last irritated huff, he once again began to reenact the scene.

"So, not only do I knock over the candle, but as I'm backing up, I slip on some dog shit and fall on my ass. That's about the same time the light went on upstairs. And there, staring down at me through the window was a cranky old lady. She had these crazy pink curlers in her hair."

"An old lady?

"Yup."

"You had the wrong window, didn't you?"

"I had the wrong damn house!"

"Wait… what? So this wasn't where Mom stayed?"

Nope," he said, doing an about face. "She stayed in *that* house over there." He shook his head and pointed to the place across the street.

"Ahhh," she said, smiling. "Faulty recon info, huh?"

He stared her dead in the eyes before finally succumbing to a smile himself. "Don't even get me started on that damn recon guy," he said.

The two of them walked side by side off the property, climbed into the car, and slowly headed out. Hope's mind kept picturing the scene her father had just painted so perfectly for her. The mere thought of his serenade gone wrong kept her amused long after they drove away. So much so, she forgot all about searching for the hidden entrance to the cove. By the time she even thought of the beach, her father was in the midst of another one of his coughing fits. She knew better than to ask if he was okay, and she certainly knew better than to suggest he go see a doctor. He reluctantly took the bottle of water that she slid his way, but when his coughing continued, she decided it best to head back to the inn. His hacking cough finally slowed just as she was about to turn into the driveway.

"Where are you going?" he asked.

"Back to the inn."

"Whatever. I guess you don't wanna see where I finally won Maggie over."

"Of course I do. I just thought you might want to rest for a while."

"I can rest when I'm dead. Besides, I slept all goddamn morning. I'm wide awake and raring to go."

"Where to?" she asked, driving past the entrance to the inn.

David instructed her to head towards the Applewood Country Club. They passed by it earlier in the week on one of their drives. It was much smaller than most country clubs, but with the Atlantic Ocean as its backdrop, it more than made up for its size. There were two tennis courts, a large outdoor pool, and the golf course was only nine holes rather than the typical eighteen.

There were about a dozen cars scattered throughout the parking lot and Hope was able to find a spot right up front. After a few minutes of just sitting there and staring up at the building, Hope asked, "So this is it? This is where Mom finally said yes to you?"

David nodded, slung his satchel over his shoulder, and exited the car. Hope locked the doors and hurried after her father. As they headed up the brick pathway towards the front door, Hope asked, "Did you two meet playing golf?"

"Golf? God no. Only rich, entitled pretty boys play that sport... and I use the word *sport* loosely."

"Did you meet her playing tennis?"

He stopped walking long enough to shoot his daughter a glare. Although his mouth said nothing, his eyes clearly stated that he was even more offended that she assumed he would ever be caught dead playing tennis. They entered the country club, and Hope watched David briskly walk past the sign, which read PLEASE CHECK IN AT THE FRONT COUNTER.

The woman behind the counter was too busy reading a magazine to notice them rushing by. It wasn't until David was about to enter the small banquet room that she finally spotted them.

"Excuse me, sir... can I help you?" she asked, moving towards them. Hope froze and turned around to look at the woman.

"Don't worry about her. Come on, follow me," he said, opening the door to the room.

Hope was torn. Should she follow her father's orders, or should she stop and listen to what the authority figure had to say? The decision was made for her as David grabbed her arm and pulled her into the room with him.

"What are you doing?" she whispered. "I don't think we're supposed to—"

"Will you just relax and quit being such a worry wort."

133

By now, the woman had caught up to them.

"Is there something I can help you two with?"

Without hesitation, David asked, "Do you do weddings here?"

"Why yes, we do. Are you a member?"

"Do you need to be a member to have a wedding here?"

"Unfortunately, yes. All of our functions here are for members only."

"Well, I guess I'll become a member then," he said.

Hope gave her father a look of surprise, but it was nothing compared to the look she was about to give him.

"My daughter here is getting married this summer."

"Congratulations," the woman said with a big smile.

After Hope's face turned a bright red, she forced a smile back at the woman.

"A very expensive wedding, if ya know what I mean," he said with a wink.

"Excellent, Mr…?"

"Mr. Simmons," he said. "But you can call me David."

"Well, David, shall I get the paperwork started for your membership?"

"I'd like to take a little tour of the grounds first. You know, to see if this place is good enough for my little girl."

Hope continued to blush.

"Of course, of course. Would you like me to show you around?"

"No, that won't be necessary. I'd prefer if it was just the two of us, if you don't mind? That way we can talk openly about our thoughts on your little country club."

"Yes, of course. If you need anything, I'll be back at my—"

David had already turned and was heading across the room. "Sounds good," he called out. "Catch ya on the flipside."

He made his way over to one of the servers. She was placing trays of finger sandwiches on a table in the center.

"What do we have here?" he asked the server.

"The golfers are having a little get together after their tournament today."

As soon as the server turned away, David grabbed a handful of finger sandwiches. He immediately shoved one into his mouth and then carefully placed the others into his satchel.

Hope nervously looked around to see if anyone else had witnessed this blatant act of stealing. "What are you doing?" she loudly whispered.

"What?" he asked blankly. "Oh, did you want one?"

"No, I don't want one. I can't believe you just—"

David didn't give her a chance to finish her thought. He was already walking through the sliding glass doors onto the back deck. Reluctantly, Hope followed her father. As they both stood on the large wooden deck, David scanned the grounds left to right, finally focusing on a well-landscaped area. There were at least fifty white folding chairs neatly placed in rows. They were all facing a giant trellis, which was covered in beautiful flowers. Hope followed him onto the grass and listened intently as he began his final story of how he met her mother.

"Apparently, Maggie's friend had a wedding to attend here, and she invited your mother to tag along. It was this super-extravagant affair. Lobsters, steak, an open bar, a live band... you know, the works."

Hope joined her father in the front row, and they both had a seat in one of the white folding chairs.

"As soon as I found out about the wedding, I rented myself a fancy monkey suit. That's slang for tuxedo."

"Yes, Dad, I know," she said, leaning back in her chair laughing.

"Of course you do, Miss Big College Girl. Anyway, there must have been at least a hundred people at the wedding. I made sure I sat at one of the tables in the way back and pretended to be a friend of the groom."

"You just showed up at a wedding that you weren't even invited to?"

"Yea, so what. What were they gonna do, call the wedding police? Besides, I've done it dozens of times since. Some of my best meals came from weddings. Can I get back to my story or what?"

Hope grinned and nodded for him to go on.

"The summer was half over, so I knew it was now or never. Towards the end of the reception, I made my move. The band had just left the stage for their final break of the night. Hesitantly, I walked down to the stage and picked up one of their guitars."

By now, David had climbed out of his chair and was standing under the trellis and was once again reenacting the whole scene as he told it.

"I grabbed the microphone and turned it on. The feedback was so loud and ear-piercing that it echoed throughout the whole place. At that point, there was no turning back. I certainly had everyone's attention. It was do or die. When the feedback stopped, I gave a quick little speech then went into the song."

"Do you remember what you said… in your speech?"

"What I said?" he repeated. "In my speech?"

David looked at his daughter and raised his eyes up to the sky. He stared long and hard at the handful of white puffy clouds floating by. He then turned his attention back to Hope.

"I remember exactly what I said. I spoke into the microphone and said, 'I'm sorry for the interruption, but while the band takes a quick break, I'm gonna play you all a song. This one goes out to a very special girl. A girl who I haven't stopped thinking about since the first time I laid eyes on her. A girl who I've been tirelessly and unsuccessfully trying to pursue all summer. And she might not realize it right now, but I know that we're meant to be together. Not only is she going to be the love of my life, she'll be the love of all my lifetimes.'"

Hope placed her hand over her heart and gushed. "Awww, you said that?"

"What? Ya think I'm lying?"

"No, not at all. What you just said might be one of the most romantic things I've ever heard."

"Damn right," he said, proudly nodding. "Anyway, I ended my speech by saying, 'Maggie, this one's for you!'"

"I love it!" Hope said, standing up from the chair. "What did she say after you played the song?"

"Aren't you gonna ask what song I played?"

Hope smiled and joked, "I didn't think it was the meat of the story."

"Well, in this case, smartass, it is. It was your mother's all-time favorite song, 'Can't Help Falling in Love' by Elvis. Personally, I've never been a huge Elvis fan. His music never did anything for me, but your mother loved him. *Heartthrob* was the word I believe she used. Obviously, she never got to see him towards the end of his life. Her little heartthrob certainly never missed a meal." At that point, David reached into his satchel and pulled out the remaining sandwiches and asked, "You sure you don't want one?"

After Hope smiled and shook her head no, David proceeded to one-by-one scarf them down.

"I bet fat Elvis could have pounded down a hundred of these," he mumbled with his mouth full. When he finished chewing and swallowing the sandwiches, he blankly looked over at Hope and asked, "Where was I?"

"Playing the Elvis song for Mom."

"Ah, yes," he said, tugging on his scraggly, crumb-filled beard. "As I played, I could see that everyone was trying to figure out who this

Maggie chick was. Except for the people at her table, no one knew who she was. Of course, that was all about to change."

"What happened?"

"Well, when I finished the song, the crowd naturally erupted in applause. Like I said before, I used to be a bad-ass performer."

Hope rolled her eyes and smiled, but she continued to listen to her father's story.

"So, while the crowd was giving me a well-deserved ovation, the band made their way back onto the stage. I handed the lead singer the microphone, and he quickly announced that he was dedicating their next song to me and Maggie. Your mother immediately started covering her face in embarrassment. The crowd started chanting for us to dance, and the next thing I knew, we were getting ready to dance in front of the entire wedding."

Hope's face beamed. She absolutely loved hearing her father recall these stories about her mother.

"I'm not gonna lie, I was scared shitless," he said.

"Scared? You just sang in front of a hundred strangers."

"Singing and slow dancing are two different things. I thought my heart was gonna jump out of my goddamn monkey suit."

Hope continued to grin and asked, "Did you guys say anything to each other… while you danced?"

"Not a word. I was completely lost in the moment… and lost in her eyes. Hell, I was just doing my best not to step on her toes." He paused and uttered, "Crying."

"You were crying?" Hope asked.

"No, ya fool! The song that the band was playing… 'Crying' by Roy Orbison."

"Ohhh," she said, sweetly smiling. "So you two didn't say *anything* to each other?"

"Not until the song was over. I was so nervous that I just started to walk away without a word. That's when your mother shot me a puzzled look and said, 'That's it? Aren't you forgetting something? Isn't this the part where you ask me out?' I think I told her something about not wanting to ruin the moment. I assumed the dance was as good as it was gonna get. She gave me this huge smile and said, 'That's too bad, especially considering I don't have plans tomorrow night.' Before walking off, she turned back to me and said, 'Oh, and when you come pick me up, you might want to watch out. Rumor has it, there's an angry skunk roaming around. Not to mention, a crazy arsonist setting fires to people's lawns.' She then flashed me her beautiful smile, winked, and spun around and walked away. And the rest is history."

Without a shadow of a doubt, this was the best story Hope had heard all week—all her life, actually. Her sweet moment was briefly interrupted by the woman from the club rushing over to hand David some paperwork to fill out. The moment totally ended when David ripped them up and mumbled something about how only idiots put celery in chicken salad. He then grabbed Hope's arm and stormed out.

From there, Hope continued to aimlessly drive around the island. Even though the country club ended with another one of David's angry outbursts, the story he had just revealed remained in her heart and reflected across her face.

David was quick to nod off, so Hope remained quiet and wound her way towards the center of Applewood. It took her a second, but as the trees thickened and the road darkened, she began to recognize where she was. Adam had taken her up that road in attempt to drive up to the Devil's Lair. Hope drove around the corner, and just like the previous day, she eventually encountered the same road closure sign and barricade.

"Darn it. Closed again," she said, loud enough to awaken her father.

His eyes remained closed, but he shifted his weight and replied, "What's closed again?"

"Just this giant rock formation called The Devil's Lair. It's supposed to have some groovy caves to walk—"

David's eyes popped open. He sat straight up. "We're not going up there! Do I look like the type of person who enjoys wandering through a goddamn cave? Huh?"

By now, Hope was used to her father's outbursts, but this one seemed a little strange.

"How the hell did you hear about this place anyway? Huh?"

There was no way she was going to bring up Adam's name, so she played it off by saying, "I... I just read about it, that's all. I heard it was a fun place to—"

"There's nothing fun about caves! They're cold, dark, and pointless. Jesus, Hope! Sometimes I wonder what the hell goes through your head. It's amazing you've made it this far in life without my help."

David's comment had set her up perfectly. There were at least a dozen comebacks she could have blasted at him, but she chose to remain quiet.

His eyes remained focused on the roadblock. Sternly, he said, "I'm exhausted. Take me back to the inn."

Hope said nothing. Instead, she slowly backed her car into the small turnaround. Before she even had a chance to put it into drive, David was putting the finishing touches on his pint of vodka. He tossed the bottle out the window then dug into his pocket for his pack of smokes. Although tempted, Hope kept quiet regarding her father's blatant act of littering. As a matter of fact, she drove the rest of the way to the inn without so much as a peep.

9

When they arrived back at the inn, David wasted no time in heading straight up the stairs. When Janice asked if he'd be joining them for dinner, he mumbled something about not feeling well then disappeared into his room, slamming the door behind him.

"Looks like it's just you and me, kiddo," Janice said, in Hope's direction. "I'm making my famous chicken noodle soup and homemade buttermilk biscuits."

Hope politely smiled, but her attention was still focused on her father's exit.

"Should be ready in about an hour. That'll give you a chance to relax and unwind from your day."

Hope started to nod in agreement but paused and thought for a second. "Actually, I might take a quick ride up to the lighthouse. It was almost too bright to take pictures the other day. Should be perfect now that the sun is on its way down."

Janice smiled and said, "I knew you would love that place. It's some of the best views on the island... maybe in all of Maine."

"Definitely a huge contrast from Chicago," Hope said.

"I bet," Janice said, making her way out of the room. "Take your time, sweetie. The soup will be ready whenever you get back. And feel free to borrow those binoculars again."

As soon as Janice left the room, Hope exited the house and drove back up to Harbor Cove Park. It wasn't as busy as the last time, but there were still a handful of families enjoying an early evening picnic out on the grass. There were also more than a few couples walking hand in hand throughout the paths. Naturally, she thought of her time spent with Adam. Her stomach turned. It wasn't like they were ever a couple, but still, the reminder of that deceitful day caused her to once again chastise herself for being so stupid.

Not wanting to let those regretful thoughts get the best of her, Hope decided to do what she came there for. She slipped the camera out of her pocket and made her way towards the cliff's edge. As she neared the end of the path, she noticed a familiar figure sitting on one of the benches. It was the little girl from the other day.

"Looks like you love this place as much as I do." Hope said, approaching her from behind. The girl jumped and spun around. "Sorry, didn't mean to scare you. I guess now we're ev—" Hope cut her last word short when she realized the young girl was crying. "Oh, honey, are you okay?" Hope asked, moving closer.

The girl nodded and quickly attempted to swipe her tears away. Without thinking twice about it, Hope sat down on the bench and attempted to console her. After a few minutes of silence, Hope finally turned to her and said, "I didn't catch your name the other day. I'm Hope."

Barely making eye contact, the girl softly said, "Charlotte."

"Aw, that's a beautiful name. Nice to meet you, Charlotte."

"Nice to meet you, too," Charlotte said, wiping the last of her tears away.

"I know you don't know me at all, but I'm a pretty good listener if you want to talk about it."

Charlotte shrugged, and Hope knew if she was going to talk that it needed to be on her own terms and not forced.

142

"Or we can just sit and look out at the ocean."

And for the next five minutes, that's just what they did—sat quietly and gazed out at the Atlantic. It wasn't until Hope began looking through the binoculars that Charlotte finally spoke. "Can you still see it… the Dark Waters?"

Hope could absolutely see the small darkened area of the ocean, but she was unsure how to answer. She still couldn't believe that she was the only one who could see it. For a moment, Hope thought about answering no, but she couldn't bring herself to lie. If she wanted Charlotte to trust her enough to talk, then she needed to be completely honest with her.

"Yea. I can still see it," she said.

"And it's over there?" Charlotte asked, pointing out past the lighthouse to the right.

Hope nodded.

Charlotte paused and looked over at the binoculars and asked, "When you look at it through those, do you ever see… do you ever see anyone out there?"

A bit confused, Hope shook her head no. "Why do you ask?"

"Forget it," Charlotte said, lowering her eyes.

Hope stared over at the young girl and wondered why she was so focused on this whole Dark Waters thing. *This couldn't possibly be the cause of her tears, could it?* She decided to press a little more. "Seriously, sweetie, why are you so curious about what I can and can't see out there?"

Still looking down, Charlotte shrugged and said, "You'll just laugh at me."

"Oh, Charlotte, I would never."

Even though she believed that Hope was being genuine, Charlotte continued to hesitate. Not wanting to push too hard, Hope placed her hand on Charlotte's shoulder and said, "It's okay. You don't have to tell me. But just know, I would never *ever* dream of laughing at you."

She slid over a few inches to give Charlotte some space. Again, Hope leaned back and stared out at the ocean. She made a conscious effort to focus on the fishing boats over to the left of the lighthouse. She still had no clue what was going on with the Dark Waters, but she knew it was causing this young girl some sort of stress. It would be another two minutes before she realized just how much stress and heartache this strange anomaly was causing the poor girl.

"I can't see the Dark Waters when I'm here, but… but I see it in my dreams," Charlotte finally said.

Hope moved her gaze from the boats over to Charlotte. Although she had many questions, she remained quiet. Instead, she warmly looked into Charlotte's eyes, allowing her to continue.

"I've had the same dream for as long as I can remember. It's like I'm hovering above… watching him try to swim… but the waves are too big… and dark. They're so dark and scary. I can see and hear him, but… but he never sees me."

Hope was completely confused and her questions were multiplying by the minute, but she held off and let Charlotte continue to speak.

"I try to yell to him, but nothing ever comes out. Do you ever have a dream like that where you try to say something but you can't?"

With a confused look still on her face, Hope slowly nodded.

"You think I'm crazy, don't you? It's okay, everyone else does, too."

"Oh, honey. No, I don't think you're crazy at all. I just don't… get it. Who exactly is this person in your dream?"

Charlotte paused and answered, "My dad."

"Dreams can definitely be scary… and confusing. I've had so many dreams that make absolutely no sense at all. Have you told him about the dream? Your father?"

Again, Charlotte lowered her eyes to the grass beneath her feet and sadly said, "He died when I was only two. I actually don't even remember him."

Hope let out a sigh and slid back closer to the young girl. Sympathetically, she placed her arm around her. It was all making sense to her now. Hope had taken enough psychology classes over the years to realize that this was very typical considering the circumstances. People, especially kids, who have lost someone close to them, tend to see them in their dreams. And it's certainly not unusual to dream of trying to save that person—especially unsuccessfully.

That being said, she knew Charlotte was much too young to understand the psychology behind her trauma. Hope knew she simply needed to reinforce the fact that Charlotte's dream was quite normal, and more importantly, that she certainly wasn't crazy.

"Believe it or not, I know exactly how you feel. My mother died right after she gave birth to me, so I never knew her at all. I'm twenty years old now, yet I still have dreams about her."

Unfortunately, Hope's comments did little to ease Charlotte's mind.

"No, you don't understand. They're *real*. The dreams are *real*!"

The way Charlotte raised her voice, Hope knew better than to downplay her feelings. She decided on a different approach and calmly asked for more details about the dream.

"The ocean is so dark that it's practically black. And the waves are so huge… and they keep crashing down on him… pushing him under…" The more detailed Charlotte got, the more the tears began to once again well up in her dark brown eyes. "He looks like he's drowning. I want to tell him that I'm there… and ask him how I can help, but… but I can't speak. I try so hard, but…" By now, the tears were freely running down her cheeks.

Instinctively, in a maternal fashion, Hope pulled Charlotte's head into her chest. "Oh, sweetie, I'm so sorry. I'm so, so sorry."

145

When Charlotte finally composed herself and sat back up, she looked out to the ocean and said, "It always ends the same. Over and over, he yells something out… and then I wake up."

"Do you remember what he yells out?"

Without breaking her gaze at the water, Charlotte replied, "Help her—to help us."

"Help her to help us?" repeated Hope. "Do you know what that means?"

Charlotte shook her head no. Hope was at a loss as to what to say to the sad little girl. She recalled an old professor of hers who used to pride himself in analyzing dreams. If only he were here now. He'd certainly be able to figure out the meaning of Charlotte's dream.

"Can I ask you a question? And you don't have to answer me if you don't want."

"Okay," Charlotte softly replied.

"How did your father die?"

Charlotte just sat there, staring up at her. She stared so long that Hope was sure she had crossed the line with her question. Just when Hope was about to apologize for being too nosy, Charlotte looked out at the ocean and answered, "Plane crash… right there."

Charlotte's finger was pointing directly in the area of the Dark Waters. Chills ran up and down Hope's arms. Before she could console the saddened little girl, a voice called out from behind them. It was Charlotte's mother letting her know it was time to leave. Hastily, Charlotte wiped her remaining tears and jumped off the bench.

"I gotta go," she said, starting to walk away.

"Hey, Charlotte," Hope called after her. "I'm truly sorry about your father."

"Thanks," she said, in barely a whisper. "And thanks for being so nice to me."

"Of course, sweetie. And don't worry, everything you told me is just between us. I promise."

***

Just as Hope arrived back at the inn, Janice was ladling the soup into two bowls. "Why don't you meet me in the sunroom?" Janice said. "I think we'll eat in there tonight."

"Do you need any help?" asked Hope.

"Nope, not at all. Go make yourself comfy, and I'll be right in."

Moments later, Janice returned with two bowls and a small basket of biscuits.

"Voila, my famous chicken noodle soup."

"It smells amazing," Hope said, placing the bowl in front of her.

Janice smirked. "As you've probably noticed, I refer to everything I make as *my famous*."

A smile finally appeared on Hope's face. "Everything I've had so far has definitely lived up to that reputation."

"Why, thank you, honey. I appreciate it."

"Mr. and Mrs. Henderson out for the night?" Hope asked.

"I think they took a little excursion further up the coast for the day."

"Sounds fun," Hope quietly said, helping herself to a biscuit.

Janice could have continued the small talk all night but decided to go directly to the heart of the matter. "I take it things didn't go well with your father today?"

Hope finished chewing and replied, "Actually, it was a pretty good day. Just ended on a bad note, that's all. Things were mostly going great, but then all of a sudden he got irritated and blew up at me." She looked deeply into her bowl of soup and continued. "He's not well... mentally or physically... and I have no idea what to do to help him."

"Oh, honey. It's not your job to help him. I fear that one day you'll get crushed under all that weight you put on your shoulders."

Hope shrugged and looked away. After another spoonful of soup, she said, "Seriously, we were having a really good day… and then he just freaks out over some silly caves. Caves we couldn't even get to because the road was closed."

"Ahh, the Devil's Lair, up at Mount M, huh?"

Hope nodded. "You've heard of it?"

Janice laughed and leaned back. "There's not a place on the island I haven't heard of. A lot of old legends up at Mount M."

"What's the M stand for?"

"It's short for Madahôdo, which is the Abenaki word for bad spirit."

"Ahh, so I guess calling the caves the Devil's Lair makes sense. Sounds pretty ominous."

"I think you'll find this island is full of old legends. I'm sure I have a book or two in the other room that tells all about them."

Hope made a mental note to search out those books later in the night, but for now, she decided to take the opportunity and push the topic a little further. She desperately wanted to ask about the Dark Waters, but ultimately, she hesitated. She was afraid Janice would start asking her own questions. The last thing she wanted was for someone else to find out that she could see something that no one else could. Instead, she approached it in a roundabout sort of way.

"What do you know about the plane crash that happened years ago?"

With a spoonful of soup halfway to her mouth, Janice stopped cold. "How did you hear about that?" she asked, lowering the spoon back into the bowl.

Hope shrugged. "Just overheard some people talking about it, that's all."

Janice slid her bowl forward and leaned back in her chair. "That crash shook this island to the core. It'll actually be six years ago this July. Yet another horrible incident to hit Applewood."

"There've been other plane crashes?" Hope asked.

"No. Usually it's boating accidents or drownings."

"Really? That's horrible."

"Yes, it is. Applewood is a beautiful and magical island, but it's certainly not without its share of tragedies over the years."

"Were there a lot of people on the plane?"

"Three. The pilot and a young couple."

"Did you know any of them… personally?"

"I didn't know the young couple. They weren't from around here… but I did know the pilot. Kyle was a native islander here. He was a good man."

"I heard it happened just past the lighthouse." Janice nodded, and Hope pushed further. "Did they ever find the cause of it?"

Janice gazed out the window at the setting sun. After a long pause, she turned back to Hope and said, "Nope, they didn't. Whatever it was, I'm sure it wasn't Kyle's fault. He'd been flying his whole life… and he owned that tour company for years and years."

Again, chills ran up Hope's arms when she realized Janice must be talking about Island Air Tours. That's why the place was abandoned. It must have been closed ever since the accident. Hope's thoughts then turned to the little girl. Her heart absolutely broke for Charlotte. Actually, her heart broke for everyone involved: Kyle, his family, and even for the young couple. Hope decided to leave the conversation at that. There was no need to bring up the Dark Waters, and there was certainly no need to tell Janice what Charlotte had confided to her.

"So, tomorrow's the big day, huh?" Janice asked, changing the subject. "I'm sure that's probably part of the reason your father is on edge. A special day like that must be extremely hard on him."

"Yea, I know. And I have no idea what to expect tomorrow. Well, except that I'm sure he'll be drunk the whole day."

Janice gave her a sympathetic look and said, "Maybe he'll surprise you."

"I doubt it. But thanks."

Janice didn't really know what else to say, so she reverted back to small talk. "Want some tea and dessert?"

"No thank you. I'm all set," she said, watching Janice stand and clear the bowls. "Do you want me to—"

"I appreciate it, but I think I can handle a few dishes. If you need anything else, just let me know."

"Thanks."

After Janice disappeared into the kitchen, Hope relaxed in the sunroom a little while longer. She intended on going into the library to do some reading, but instead, she went out and grabbed her guitar. She walked around back to the courtyard for a little evening strumming.

The story her father told her at the country club had been stuck in her head all afternoon. She loved how sweet and romantic it was. Hope didn't tell her father earlier, but she wasn't a huge Elvis fan either. For her, his music was simply take it or leave it. More times than not, she left it. That being said, the next thing she knew, her fingers were mysteriously attempting to learn the song.

She remained in the courtyard well into the night perfecting her version of "Can't Help Falling in Love." Every so often, she looked up at her father's window wondering if he was listening. Secretly, she hoped he was. Unfortunately, even though his window was cracked open, David heard nothing. Hours earlier, he washed down a few pain pills with his vodka, and he'd been passed out cold ever since.

By the time 10 p.m. rolled around, Hope's fingers were tired and worn. She returned the guitar to the trunk and decided to head up to her room and hit the sack. Her head was spinning with thoughts, and although exhausted, she knew sleep wouldn't come easy. Part of her was extremely nervous about what tomorrow would bring. She could only imagine how drunk her father was going to be. A sick and anxious feeling entered the pit of her stomach.

Around midnight, her thoughts turned from her father back to the previous day's events with Adam—more specifically—Adam's deception. At that point, the feeling in her stomach switched from anxious to angry. How could she have fallen for his stupid lines? More importantly, how could she ever believe that a guy like him would fall for a girl like her? Both mentally and physically exhausted from the events of the day, Hope pushed these thoughts from her mind. It was nearly 1 a.m. when she finally dozed off. Her sleep would be short-lived.

"Pssst… hey… time to get up."

Assuming she was only dreaming, Hope rustled a bit, but her eyes remained closed. It wasn't until she felt the heavy hand of her father on her shoulder that she opened her eyes.

"Come on, get up," David said, giving her shoulder another good shake.

Startled at the sight of him staring down at her, Hope quickly sat up. Groggy and confused, she wiped the sleep from her eyes and looked over at the window. It was still pitch black out.

"What are you talking about? What time is it?" She focused over at the clock next to her bed. It read 2:52 a.m. "It's only three in the morning?" she said, still gathering her bearings.

"I know. That's why we gotta get going. Meet me downstairs in five minutes."

Before she could utter a word, David had flipped on her light and left the room. Hope knew the anniversary day was going to be unpredictable, at best, but she certainly didn't expect it to start at three in the morning. She let out a giant yawn and a sigh then slowly climbed out of bed to get dressed.

As tempting as it felt to stay in her comfortable nightgown, she knew she better change. There was no telling what the day held in store for her, so she'd need to be prepared. Hope slipped into her favorite bellbottom jeans that were still laying on the bedside chair from the night before. She grabbed a brightly-colored tie dyed Grateful Dead t-shirt from her suitcase. For a brief moment, she considered foregoing a bra because she hardly ever wanted to wear one to begin with, much less at the ungodly hour of 3 a.m. But alas, reason took over and she opted for the bra. Hope slid her feet into her well-worn Birkenstock sandals and headed out.

As she quietly tippy-toed down the staircase, David impatiently called up to her. "Come on, let's go!"

"Relax. I'm coming," she loudly whispered.

By the time she hit the bottom step, David had already opened and exited the front door. Curiously, Hope followed him outside onto the porch. She then watched David attempt to open her locked car door.

"What the hell are you doing locking your car? We're in Maine for Christ's sake!"

Hope was still half asleep and way too exhausted to offer a retort. She fumbled around her bag, pulled her keys out, and proceeded to unlock her door. She climbed in and popped the lock on David's side. He was still mumbling about her locking her door in Maine as he sat in the passenger seat.

With her sleepy eyes bearing down on him, David smiled and said, "Ready?"

"Ready for what? Where exactly are we going at three in the morning?"

"Where are we going?" he repeated, as if taken aback. "I'll tell ya where we're going. We're going to be wild and spontaneous! It's about goddamn time I teach you how to live on the edge."

"If this involves breaking into the store to steal alcohol or cigarettes, then you can most definitely count me out!" She crossed her arms and threw a stern look his way.

David laughed. "Relax, kiddo. I have plenty of alcohol right here!" From his jacket pocket, he pulled out a full pint of vodka. "Plenty of smokes, too," he said, unwrapping a new pack of Marlboros.

She shook her head and watched as he took a quick swig and proceeded to light one up. Hope was not amused, and she continued sitting there with her arms crossed. "I'm not starting the car until you tell me exactly where we are going!"

He shrugged. "I don't know where we're going. I was assuming you knew where your little loser lawn mower boy lived."

Her eyes widen and her curiosity was piqued.

"So, do you know where he lives or not?"

Hope hesitated but nodded. Adam had pointed out his house to her on their drive that day. "Why do you need to know where Adam lives?" she asked.

David took a long drag from his cigarette and attempted to blow smoke rings. "Oh, didn't I mention my spontaneous and wild lessons might involve a little revenge on that piece of shit? Or as you called him, Mister Easy On The Eyes."

Hope had no idea what he had up his sleeve, but she found herself turning the key and starting the car. As she pulled out of the driveway and onto the main road, she was still leery of what his master plan was. The closer she got to his house, the more her sensibilities kicked in. She was still angry as hell at Adam, but she was also worried about what her father was planning on doing.

"You're not going to beat him up, are you? Because you can get arrested for that, ya know? And that would make me an accomplice... and I can get arrested, too... and I've never been arrested before...

and—"

"What the hell are you babbling about?" he said.

"I'm just saying I don't want to spend the rest of the night in jail."

"Nobody's getting beaten up. And nobody's spending the night in jail. Relax and just drive," he said.

His reply seemed to calm her for the moment.

"Oh, okay," she said. "But what the heck do you have planned then?"

David said nothing. He simply smiled and gave his satchel a pat.

"What's in your bag?" she hesitantly asked. "Are there eggs in there? Are we going to egg his house? Because that is vandalism, and you can get arrested for that, too."

David shook his head, looking at her as if she was crazy.

"What? Why are you looking at me like that? I'm sorry if I'm not a seasoned criminal."

Again, he shook his head and chuckled at her nonsense. Hope took a left turn onto Adam's road.

"Whoa! A left turn without using a blinker? You can probably get arrested for that, too," he said with a loud laugh.

Hope glared at him but said nothing. She continued driving until she reached Adam's house. She parked along the sidewalk out front.

"What are you doing?" he asked.

"What? This is his house."

"Well don't park in front! Pull up the street a bit. And lose the headlights for Christ's sake!"

She shut off the lights and crept up the street until David told her to stop. She then put the car in park and turned the key off.

"Now what are you doing?" he asked in disbelief. "Leave it running! You always leave the get-away car running. Pffft… rookie."

"Sorry," she said, turning the car back on.

Hope watched as David scanned up and down the darkened road.

There were no street lights and most of the houses were pitch dark.

"Now what?" she whispered in his direction.

David looked over at her brightly colored tie-dyed shirt and then began to take off his jacket. "First of all, put this on. Or else you'll stand out like a sore thumb."

The jacket smelled of cigarettes and BO, but Hope was too concerned with David's plan to really even notice. When she finally had the jacket on, he motioned for her to follow him. They made their way back up the street. There were a few cars in Adam's driveway and a faint, flickering light coming from one of the windows. Hope followed close behind as he crept between the shrubs along the house. He paused when he reached the living room window.

"Now what?" she whispered.

"A little recon," he whispered back.

He placed his finger to his lips and motioned for her to remain crouched down. Slowly, he stood up and peeked into the window. The flickering light was coming from the large console television set. The programming had ended for the night, and it was nothing but static. When David was satisfied with what he saw, he crouched back down and smiled over at his daughter and said, "It's go time."

Relieved, she nodded and started to head back towards the car.

"Pssst!" he loudly whispered. "I didn't mean it was go-back-to-your-car time! I meant *go time*... as in..." he pointed at the front door.

Slightly embarrassed by her confusion, she returned to his side near the front steps. Again, he put his finger to his lips and he placed his hand on the door knob.

"Wait," Hope interrupted. "What are you doing? That's breaking and entering."

David ignored her comment and continued to twist the knob. He grinned when he realized it was unlocked. As he quietly opened the door, he turned to Hope and said, "See, it's not breaking and entering.

155

It's just entering."

"It's definitely trespassing," she mumbled under her breath.

He shot her a look then waved at her to follow him in. There were dozens of Pabst cans strewn about, not to mention, a couple of boys passed out on the orange shag carpet. On the couch, there were two heads poking out of a blanket—a male and a female.

"Is that him?" David asked Hope.

She took a couple steps forward and peered in closer. Relieved, she shook her head no.

"Bedroom," he said, then headed down the hallway.

Hesitantly, Hope followed, making sure to avoid the minefield of beer cans. The first doorway they came to was the bathroom. David entered.

"Hey, that's just the bathroom," Hope whispered. "He's not in there."

"I know. I have to take a piss," he said matter-of-factly. He pushed the door half closed behind him and proceeded to urinate. When he finished, he exited and boasted a proud smile. "You didn't even hear me go, did you?" he asked. "The key to a silent piss is throwing layers of toilet paper in the water first. And obviously don't flush after."

A blank stare was all Hope could muster. She wondered what other sage tidbits her father could offer, and then cringed at the thought. David continued up the hallway to the next door. Carefully, he pushed it open. The bedroom was way too dark to see anything. David pulled out his lighter and flicked it on. Nervous that they'd get caught, Hope immediately looked over at her father, but his attention was focused on something else. She tracked his eyes over to the bed, and there, laying uncovered were three individuals.

Hope held her breath as David moved the lighter closer. Sandwiched between two girls was Adam's roommate. Hope cringed in disgust as David mouthed the words, *Is that him?*

Still disgusted with the half-naked threesome, Hope shook her head no then turned and left the room. David held his look a bit longer. After he joined his daughter back in the hallway, he grinned and said, "Looks like someone had a good time tonight."

"Eww, gross," she softly said.

"What? I thought you hippies were into the whole peace, love, and orgy thing?"

She looked at her father but said nothing. Hope knew the way she dressed, the music she listened to, and even some of her care-free beliefs were most definitely hippy-esque. But when it came to love and sex, she believed 100% in monogamy. Just the fact that she kissed a boy she barely knew went against her better judgement.

"That must be Romeo's room," he said, pointing to the final door at the end of the hall.

Hope's heart raced as she watched her father slowly turn the knob and open the door. There were a couple of candles burning, so David didn't have to use his lighter. She followed behind him, and her eyes immediately focused on the bed. More specifically, she focused on *who* was in the bed. The candles provided enough light for her to clearly see Adam laying there with some young blonde girl.

The blanket was half-thrown over their legs. Adam was wearing nothing but a pair of Fruit of the Loom tighty whities. But the girl, however, appeared to be naked. For completely different reasons, David and Hope found themselves staring at her exposed chest. She was on her back, so her ample Double D breasts were on full display. Self-conscious of her own looks, especially her much smaller breasts, Hope sadly looked away. Once again, David held his look a little longer before turning back towards his daughter.

By now, Hope's eyes were on Adam. She still couldn't believe she allowed herself to fall victim to his pathetic charade. It was obvious to David just how hurt she was. He was tempted to put his arm around her and console her, like he had wanted to do all his life, but he didn't. Instead, he gave her a nudge and said, "Ready for the plan?"

"You still haven't even told me what the plan is?"

Deviously, David smiled and took the satchel off his shoulder and placed it on the floor. Hope's mouth and eyes popped open as she watched him carefully reach in and pull out a lobster—a live lobster. It had two thick rubber bands binding each of its claws.

"What in the heck are you going to do with that?" she asked.

"It's not what *I'm* gonna do… it's what *you're* gonna do." He smiled and attempted to hand her the lobster.

"No way!" she loudly whispered, backing up.

"Just think, that blonde bimbo could have been you. I'm sure he dropped her some lines, fed her some beers, probably smoked a joint or two… and the next thing ya know, wham bam thank you ma'am!"

Hope looked over at the girl and then to Adam. Even as he slept, he looked cocky and full of himself. She honestly thought he was different. She honestly thought he cared about her. She told him personal things—things she rarely told anyone. And just like that, her veins were pumping with anger. David knew she was ready, and he once again held out the lobster.

Reluctantly, and more than a little grossed out, Hope reached out and took the lobster from him. He motioned her to follow him over to the foot of the bed. He grasped the blanket and slowly began pulling it until it was off of their legs. The final tug caused Adam to move around. Through the flickering light of the candle, they watched Adam move from his side and then to his back. He ended his movement by slightly spreading his legs a bit.

The smile on David's face beamed as if he had just won the lottery. He reached into his pocket and flipped open a jackknife and cut the bands off. He turned to his daughter and gave her a nod. With her arm outstretched, she nervously leaned forward. By now, the lobster was sprawling and angrily snapping its claws all about. Hope closed her eyes, let out a tiny squeal, then cringed as she placed the lobster on the sheet between Adam's legs. While Hope was cringing, David was doing all he could to not crack up laughing.

As the lobster made its way closer to Adam's groin, David knew it was time to make their escape. He gave Hope's jacket a tug, and she followed close behind as he hastily headed back down the hallway. In the living room, David paused long enough to swipe an unopened can of Pabst. Before the front door had completely shut behind them, David had already popped the tab and was taking a celebratory swig.

Hope's adrenaline was in high gear, and she excitedly turned to her father and said, "Do you actually think it will bite him in the—"

Just then, they heard Adam let out a loud, blood-curdling scream.

"Does that answer your question?" David smiled, and then took off running up the street. "Go, go, go," he yelled as they both jumped into the car.

Hope threw it into drive and sped off.

"*Woo hoo!*" he screamed. "I honestly didn't think that shit would work!"

He pounded the rest of his beer and proceeded to crush the can and toss it out the window. Hope thought about giving him a quick lecture about littering, but she was still riding her high from the lobster shenanigans. When they got back to the main road, Hope still hadn't wiped the smile off her face. David took notice.

"Living on the edge feels pretty good, doesn't it?"

Not wanting to admit he was right, she shrugged and did her best to wipe the smile away. A few minutes later, it found its way back to her face. "That was the loudest scream I've ever heard," she blurted out. As she continued driving, they both cracked up laughing. David gazed over at her with a saddened pride.

It was just after 4:10 a.m. when they returned to the Great Blue

Heron Inn. Quietly, they crept back up the stairs. David paused when they reached her doorway. He knew there was a part of her that was still hurt by the whole Adam debacle, but no matter how much he wanted, he couldn't find the right words to say to her.

"Well, we should get some sleep. Don't wanna be tired for the big day tomorrow."

Hope nodded and began to open her door. She knew tonight's events were her father's way of trying to ease her heartache. She wanted to thank him, but she too couldn't find the right words to say.

"Hey," he called to her.

"Yea?"

He hesitated a second then mumbled, "Um, night."

"Goodnight," she replied, and slowly closed her door.

David remained in the hallway, sadly staring at her door. After a few minutes, he headed to his own room.

10

Despite not getting to sleep until the wee hours of the morning, Hope found herself wide awake at 8 a.m. Her hair was a wild mess, and she was still dressed from the night before, but she made her way downstairs for something to drink.

Good morning," Janice called out just as Hope hit the bottom step.

"Morning," Hope replied, letting out a giant yawn.

Janice took one look at her and said, "For someone who went to bed early, you look like you've been up all night."

Hope smirked and let out another big yawn. "I could definitely use a nice hot cup of tea."

"Good, because your father wants you to meet him at the diner."

"He's already awake?"

Janice nodded. "He was actually up hours ago. He wanted me to tell you to meet him there whenever you woke up."

"How... how did he seem?"

Janice thought for a second and answered, "Umm, different."

"Different how?"

Janice started to reply but paused as if to choose her words carefully. "Maybe you should head over and find out for yourself."

Hope continued to stand there, unsure what to think or expect.

"Different doesn't always mean bad," Janice said with a wink, and then walked out of the room.

Janice's comment appeared to have lighten Hope's anxiousness, and she turned and hurried upstairs to get ready. Usually, Hope wasn't very picky about her wardrobe, but considering her father had built this day up all week, she knew she needed the perfect outfit. She only brought a limited amount of clothes on her spur-of-the-moment trip, yet as she stood in front of the mirror, she had the hardest time picking out what to wear.

She knew they were going to a nice restaurant for dinner, but she was hesitant on wearing her best outfit now, especially considering she had no idea what her father had planned for the rest of the day. Hope changed from outfit to outfit and did it all over again. Finally, after what seemed like forever, Hope settled on an ecru-colored peasant blouse and her trusty second-favorite pair of bellbottoms, but just in case she changed her mind, she decided to bring her entire suitcase as well.

It's better to be too prepared than underprepared. That's what her grandmother always told her. Speaking of grandparents, Hope knew she should probably give them a call. With her bag of clothes clutched in her right hand, she hurried downstairs in search of Janice. She found her on the east side of the inn getting ready to do some laundry.

When Janice saw Hope approaching, she gave her a puzzled look and said, "Oh, you're still here? I assumed you left a while ago."

Hope let out a sigh. "I have no idea what we're even doing today, so I couldn't decide what to wear."

Janice glanced down at the suitcase in Hope's hand and said, "So you decided to bring them all?"

Again, Hope sighed and gave Janice a shrug.

"Well, I guess it's better to be too prepared than—"

"Underprepared," Hope finished her sentence. "My grandmother tells me that all the time."

"Sounds like a smart woman," Janice said, shutting the lid to the washing machine.

Hope nodded. "Speaking of which, would it be okay if I used your phone to call them?"

"Of course."

"I'll give you money for the long-distance charges," Hope said, digging her hand into her pocket.

"We already went over this, Hope. Don't even worry about it. Okay?"

"But…"

"Okay?" Janice said sternly, yet with a smile.

Hope knew it was pointless to argue. "Okay," she agreed. "I really do appreciate it."

"I know you do. You better get going. You don't want to keep your father waiting."

Hope started to leave but turned back around. "You know what we're doing today, don't you?"

Janice innocently shrugged, grabbed the basket of folded towels, and then exited the laundry room. "Have fun," she announced as she walked past Hope.

Hope followed behind and made her way to the phone at the front desk. She picked up the receiver and dialed the number. On the third ring, her grandmother answered.

"Hello?"

"Hey, Nana."

"Hope! Where in the heck are you?"

Hope's heart began to race as she searched for what to say. "Ummm…"

"I tried calling you last night. Your roommate told me she hadn't seen you all week. And she said it looked like your bed hadn't been slept in all week either."

Hope's heart continued to pound faster as beads of sweat began to run down her forehead. She was horrible at lying, and she hated doing it, but it was certainly better than the alternative. Her grandparents would flip their lids if they knew where and who she was with.

"Umm, yea… I've actually been putting in late nights at the library with my study partner, and then I've just been crashing at her house."

"Your study partner? Who's that?"

"Umm, my study partner is…" Just then, Janice walked by Hope, giving her a smile. "My study partner is Janice."

"Janice? I've never heard you mention a Janice."

Her grandmother was famous for asking a million questions, and Hope silently cursed herself for not having a full detailed story already made up in advance.

Without thinking too much on it, Hope blurted out, "She's just a girl in one of my classes. She's kind of struggling and asked for my help."

There was a long pause on the other end, and Hope thought for sure her grandmother would call her bluff.

"Well," her grandmother's voice finally broke, "just make sure it doesn't take away from your own study time."

"No, not at all," Hope pointed out. "Anyway, I just wanted to call and say hi. I'll probably stop by on Sunday."

"Okay, dear. I'll cook something special for lunch that day."

"Sounds good. I'll see you then. Oh, and say hi to Grampa for me. Love you."

Within seconds of hanging up, Hope let out a huge sigh of relief. For the time being, her grandparents had no idea where she was or more importantly, who she was with. Everything would be fine as long as she made it back to Chicago by noon time on Sunday. She wiped the remaining sweat from her brow and headed for the front door.

***

As Hope entered the center of town, she spotted her father's car. It was parked along Main Street directly across from the diner. She pulled into the vacant spot behind him, took a deep breath, then shut the ignition off. After she let out a long exhale, she placed the keys in her purse and exited the car.

The diner was only thirty feet away, but it might as well have been a mile. So many thoughts rushed through her mind. First and foremost, what did Janice mean when she said her father seemed different? *Is he full-on delusional? Does he think my mom is going to show up today? More importantly, is he once again going to confuse me for her?*

The closer she got to the front door, the more the sick feeling in her stomach grew. She barely remembered opening the door and entering. It wasn't until the waitress called over to her that she snapped out of her haze.

"Just one?" the waitress asked, grabbing a menu.

"Actually, I'm meeting someone. I think he's here already," Hope said, and then began to scan the diner. The place was only half full, and when her search came up empty, she let out an embarrassed laugh. "I guess he already…" Before Hope could finish her sentence, she saw someone waving at her out of the corner of her eye. It wasn't until she did a double take that she realized the man was her father.

"Is that who you're meeting?" the waitress asked.

Hope's mouth opened but no words came out. All she could do was nod yes. The waitress led her over to the table, and Hope's mouth remained gaped opened, and her eyes didn't once stray from her father. Not only was his scraggly beard completely shaven, but his long, wild

165

hair was neatly cut short. His jeans and shirt were familiar but appeared to have been freshly washed *and* ironed.

"Can I get you something to drink, sweetie?"

It took a second for Hope's eyes to break away from her father.

"Could I just have a hot tea, please?"

"Milk with that?"

"Yes, please. And some honey, if it's no trouble?"

"You got it, sweetie." The waitress then turned her attention to David. "More coffee?"

He answered her by sliding his empty cup in her direction.

"Decaf, right?" she asked. His face contorted, but before he could lash out and set her straight, she smirked and said, "Just kidding, sweetie." She then turned and walked away.

His expression lightened, and he even let out a slight chuckle. "Ya hear that? She called me sweetie," he boasted. "Probably the new look."

Hope's lips curled into a smile. "Yea, let's talk about this new look," she said. "What the heck happened to you?"

"What do mean? I went to the barber next door and got a cut and shave first thing this morning."

"I see that," she said, still grinning.

"Although, I should have done it my goddamn self! The son of a bitch charged me eight bucks! Not to mention, he talked funny. Everyone around here talks funny."

"It's called a Maine accent. I kind of like it," she replied. "And I like the cut and shave, too. I think it was worth every penny. Besides, it makes you look younger."

David pondered her comment and nodded his head in agreement. "That's probably why the waitress calls me sweetie."

Hope smiled. "Not to burst your bubble, but I think she calls everyone sweetie. Job requirement."

Right on que, the waitress returned with Hope's tea. "Here's your tea with honey, sweetie," she said, placing it in front of her.

David looked from the waitress back over to Hope. She smirked and gave him a shrug.

As the waitress poured coffee into David's empty cup, she asked Hope, "Do you know what you'd like to eat?"

Hope quickly glanced at the menu. "I think just the tea is fine."

"Nope," David interjected. "You need to eat something. Big day ahead of us. She'll have the Island Special," he announced to the waitress. "Make sure her eggs are cooked well… no runny shit. She hates that."

"And for you?" she asked David.

"Just the coffee for me."

"You got it, sweetie. Thanks."

She picked up the menu from the table and headed towards the kitchen. David slid the coffee cup in front of him and began pouring copious amounts of sugar in it. When he looked up from his cup, he noticed Hope just sitting there staring at him.

"What? Don't even think of giving me a lecture about the amount of sugar I use."

"How… how did you know I don't like my eggs runny?"

David shrugged but was too busy adding more sugar to further respond. Hope was actually too busy staring at David's new look to further delve into her eggs question. About halfway through breakfast, Hope noticed that the ashtray on the table was empty and perfectly clean. It was then she realized her father hadn't lit up once since she sat down. The way his fingers were continuing to fidget, she just assumed he must have been completely out of cigarettes.

As she ate her breakfast, her look went from the ashtray to her father's appearance. She still couldn't believe he shaved and got his hair cut. Even though it made him look younger, the weathered lines on his face were of a man well beyond his years and who had lived a long hard life.

"I still can't believe I didn't even recognize you when I came in earlier. What made you do it?"

Self-consciously, he ran his fingers across his clean-shaven cheek and then through his short hair.

"Don't get me wrong, I like it," she pointed out.

David took the final sip of his coffee, and without making eye contact said, "Your mother hated facial hair. No shave, no kisses. That was her rule." David glanced at the bill and threw down some money. He placed the empty coffee cup on top then looked across at Hope and said, "Ya ready to go?"

Hope nodded and slid her empty plate forward. She climbed out of the booth and followed her father towards the front door. He stopped short and turned to her and said, "Why don't you meet me out front? I need to piss out some of that coffee I just drank."

"Okay. Do you want me to hold your satchel for you?"

He looked at her as if she'd lost her mind. "No. Why would I want you to do that?" Not waiting for a response, he continued on towards the bathroom in the back.

Once inside, he made his way over to the urinal and placed his hand on the wall and began to urinate. Just as he was finishing up, he began to have another one of his coughing spells. He zipped up his pants and clutched at his side. Along with some painkillers, he pulled out a half-full bottle of vodka from his satchel. He looked long and hard at the bottle and even went as far as untwisting the cap, but he never lifted it to his lips. He forced himself to twist the cap back on and returned it to his satchel. He tossed the pills into his mouth then stuck his head under the faucet to wash them down. Luckily, by the time he made it outside, his coughing had subsided. The last thing he wanted was for his condition to detract from their big day. Hope was sitting on the bench out in front patiently waiting for him.

"Where to?" she asked.

"The general store for supplies. You drive."

And by supplies, she assumed he meant alcohol and cigarettes. He might have gotten a cut and a shave, but she knew his vices would remain. David stood by the passenger side waiting for her to unlock the door.

"It's unlocked," she said, opening her door without the keys.

He gave her a surprised look, smiled, then climbed in the car and said, "Atta girl."

Slightly proud of herself, she returned his smile and drove up the road to the general store. As soon as she put the car in park, David presented her with a crumpled twenty-dollar bill. "Just get some snacks and drinks for the day," he said.

As if waiting for more detailed instructions, she took the money and paused. When he said nothing, she decided to clarify his request. "Anything in particular?"

"Surprise me," he said. "Just no diet soda shit. I like the real deal."

"Snacks and drinks. Anything else?" she asked, knowing full well he'd request a fresh pack of Marlboros.

"Nope. That's it. But make it snappy, though. We have places to see, things to do."

With that, she shut the door and headed into the store. She hurried through the aisles grabbing bottles of water, trail mix, and some fresh fruit for herself. For her father, she bought a bag of pork rinds and a couple of bottles of RC Cola. When the woman at the counter asked if there was anything else she could get her, Hope was tempted to ask for a pack of Marlboros. Not because she wanted to support his habit, but because she had a feeling he'd flip out if she came back empty handed. She pictured him having one of his mood swings and yelling at her for not buying him cigarettes or booze.

169

When she got back to the car, however, he didn't so much as peek into the bag to see what she bought. "Let's get a move on," was all he said.

"Where to?"

"Down to the marina."

Hope pulled out of the parking lot and onto the main street. She just assumed the Rusty Anchor was her father's destination. He must have planned on starting their day off with a stiff drink. It wasn't even ten o'clock in the morning yet. There was no way the tavern would be open. She mentally prepared herself for him ranting and raving about the place being closed. Neither of them said a word on the short drive, and it wasn't until she pulled into the dirt parking lot of the tavern that David finally spoke.

"What the hell are you doing parking here? I said the marina, didn't I? The less walking the better for these old legs."

"Oh…okay," she said, turning her wheel hard to the left. As she did a U-turn, she quietly let out a relieved breath. She pulled into the heart of the marina and David hastily pointed to an empty spot for her to park in.

"Much better," he said, getting out of the car. "Grab some of the stuff you bought and throw them in your bag thingy. Oh, and bring your camera, too."

"Where are we—"

"Let's go, let's go!" he clapped impatiently.

Hope quickly grabbed the food and drinks and shoved them into her bag. Before exiting the car, she picked up her camera from the center console.

"Do ya want to put on something warmer?" he asked.

The sun was shining brightly, and it was nearly seventy degrees. She had on a long sleeve blouse and seemed quite content.

"No, I think I'm fine," she replied. "Why, where are we—"

Again, David interrupted. "Suit yourself. Let's get a move on."

She followed him to the small shanty-like shack at the foot of the pier. There were a handful of people gathered out in front. David paused and began digging into his satchel. Curiously, Hope's eyes moved through the people, but it wasn't until she spotted the familiar A-frame sign that she knew what they were doing.

"We're going on a whale watch?" she excitedly asked.

"If I can find the damn tickets," he grumbled, still rummaging through his bag. He then shoved his hand into his jacket pocket and pulled out two tickets. "Always the last goddamn place you look."

Hope's face was beaming as she moved closer to examine the tickets. "We're really going out on a whale watch!" she exclaimed. "Maybe I should go back to the car and get another roll of…"

Just then, the tour guide announced that they were starting to board the boat now. For the moment, Hope forgot about her film and everything else, for that matter. As they boarded the boat, she wanted to clutch her father's arm as if to relay her appreciation and excitement. But she didn't. She paused, and her mind quickly took her back to all the times that she watched other kids excitedly clutch at their parents' arms. She remembered how it always made her feel lonely and out of place.

"Over here," David said, pulling her out of her little flashback. He was already on the boat and was leaning against the railing looking out to sea. Hope joined him by his side and immediately took out her camera preparing for a morning full of picture taking.

"I've never been on one of these before," she said.

"You've never been on a boat?"

"I meant I've never been on a whale watching tour. I've been on a boat up at the lake, but—"

"This is definitely not like the lake," he interrupted. "Hopefully you don't get seasick."

Ironically, not long after the boat left the dock, it was David who ended up getting seasick. After hurling multiple times over the edge, one of the tour guides escorted David below the deck to lay down. Hope tried to follow to help take care of him, but he loudly insisted that she leave him be and go enjoy the tour. Reluctantly, she followed his orders and headed back up.

Just as she made her way back to her spot, the tour guide pointed out the lighthouse just up ahead. "It's one of the oldest and most famous lighthouses in Maine," he said.

Everyone moved to the right side of the boat to get a better view. Most of them had their cameras pressed against their eyes and were snapping one picture after another. Hope also started to make her way over to that side, but stopped as something caught her eye. Up ahead and off to her left, she once again saw it—the Dark Waters.

It covered a much bigger area than she had originally seen from the shore. For the most part, the ocean was calm that day, but within the Dark Waters, the waves were much higher and choppier than the rest of the sea. At one point, it looked as though the water was swirling as if in a giant whirlpool. Hope found herself mesmerized with a sick feeling in her stomach. The next thing she knew, she raised her camera and began taking pictures of it. She was the only person on that side of the boat.

"What do ya see out there?" the tour guide called to her. "Did you spot a whale?"

The word *whale* was all it took for everyone to rush back over to her side of the boat.

"Where? Where is it?" they shouted, as they peered out to where the Dark Waters were.

"I don't see it."

"I don't see a whale either," another said.

"Um... no... it wasn't a whale," Hope said. "I was just taking some pictures of the... of the ocean.

A disappointed groan emitted from the passengers, and one by one they filtered back towards the other side of the boat. *Charlotte was right*, she thought. *People really can't see this dark area of the ocean.*

Hope joined the rest of the passengers and even took a few lighthouse pictures of her own. When the lighthouse was well behind them, Hope headed down to check on her father. He lay curled up with his eyes closed. The bucket on the floor next to him was empty, so Hope took it as a good sign that his stomach might be feeling better.

"Any whale sightings yet?" he asked, as she started to leave.

She stopped and turned back towards him. His eyes remained shut, but his body began to rustle about.

"No, not yet," she answered. "How are you feeling?"

He let out a grumble. "Good thing I didn't eat anything this morning. Although, I think I puked up a lung earlier."

"Is there anything I can—"

"Nope. I'll be fine. Ya better get back up there. You don't wanna miss the perfect shot."

Hope felt bad for her father, but she nodded and obliged his order. Even though the sun was brightly shining, the ocean breeze made it feel at least twenty degrees colder than it was inland. Her thin blouse was no match for the sudden change in weather. Goosebumps ran up her arms, and she chastised herself for not bringing a jacket with her.

The boat headed south towards a handful of tiny islands. The tour guide continued to ramble on about the history of area, but not once mentioned anything about the legend of the Dark Waters. Hope was just about to ask him about it, but was interrupted by an excited shrill from one of the passengers.

"Look! Look!"

Hope, like the rest of the passengers, hurried to the other side of the boat. Everyone seemed to be pointing to a group of rocks on the edge of a tiny island. Her eyes sprung wide open when she saw a handful of seals sunning themselves on the rocks.

Without hesitation, she raised her camera and began taking pictures of them. She only had twelve exposures left on the film roll, so she was careful not to waste any. All in all, she ended up with five perfect shots. The boat's engine idled as the passengers clamored, pointed, and took photos of the seals. The tour guide even passed around a couple pairs of binoculars so they could all get a much better view.

The faces of every single person on the boat were beaming. From the bits of conversation she overheard, it was obvious that she wasn't the only one seeing seals for the first time. As Hope continued to stare at the seals, the bright sun became enveloped in a large cloud. This made the temperature drop even more and caused Hope to cross her arms, rubbing them for warmth.

"I told ya, ya should have brought something warmer."

Hope turned and saw her father standing there holding out his jacket for her. He only had a t-shirt on underneath, so she was quick to politely decline his offer.

"Take it," he said a bit louder.

She hesitated but took it and threw it on. It was still warm from his body heat and was a welcomed gift against the cold ocean air.

"Thanks, but aren't you going to be—"

"I spent a whole winter sleeping out on the streets of Cleveland. I think I can handle this weather."

Her expression saddened. She hated when he revealed things like this. Picturing her father sleeping and freezing out on the streets for a whole winter caused her heart to ache for him.

Softly, she said, "I'm sorry. That's sounds horrible."

"Eh, it was only for one winter. Then I smartened up. If you're

174

gonna be homeless, you should do it in a place that's warm all year round. That's when I hitch-hiked down south. Ya don't have to worry about your fingers and toes getting frostbite… but you do have to worry about getting bitten by an alligator."

David laughed, but Hope didn't join him. She not only hated hearing about his hardships over the years, but she hated him joking and making light of it.

"With all the commotion, I couldn't sleep a wink down below. What's going on up here?" he asked.

He looked over at the group of passengers, who were still pointing and commenting. He then squinted his eyes and followed their gazes out to the rocks. It took him a second, but when he finally saw it, he blurted out, "Holy shit! Are those seals?"

Just like that, the smile returned to Hope's face, and she handed her father the binoculars. She watched as he focused in on them. Besides the lobster shenanigans the night before, this was one of the first times she'd seen him with a genuine smile on his face.

"Did you get pictures of them?" he asked.

"Yup! I definitely should have grabbed another roll of film, though."

Just then, the boat's engine started back up, and the group of seals slowly disappeared in its wake. Out of the six tiny islands around them, only one looked to be inhabited. That was where the boat's next stop would be. After it was tied and docked, Hope and David were the last two people to exit.

"Feeling better?" the tour guide asked David.

David's only response was a thumbs up.

"Explore as much of the island as possible, but don't forget, the boat leaves in exactly two hours."

"Thank you," Hope said, as they exited onto the old dock.

By now, the large cloud had passed on through, allowing the

sunlight to instantly warm the tiny island. It was nowhere near the size of Applewood and sat about ten miles off from the mainland. The centerpiece of the island was a classic old inn. It was much larger than the Great Blue Heron but lacked its cozy, intimate charm. That being said, its gigantic sprawled-out front porch and its white clapboard siding made it an instant coastal classic.

They stepped off the dock and followed the footpath up to the beautiful old building. There were at least a dozen white Adirondack chairs lining the wide porch. Most of them were occupied by people enjoying a cold drink and the perfect ocean view. Hope paused and pulled out her camera for a single shot of the inn.

There were multiple paths to choose from, but Hope picked the Loop Trail, which encircled the rocky edge of the island. At first, there was nothing said between Hope and David. They were both too busy taking in the beauty of the ocean and the island. After a few minutes, Hope stopped and turned to her father. "You doing okay? Do you need to stop and take a break?"

He shook his head no, continuing to admire everything around him.

"Did you and Mom ever come here?"

Again, he shook his head no and said, "But she would have loved it here. She definitely would have loved it here."

Hope took notice of him using past tense in talking about her mother. As a matter of fact, for the past day or two, he'd referred to Maggie in the past tense. For most of the week, he referred to her as if she was still alive, and each and every time, it made Hope uncomfortable and sad for him.

It only took about a half an hour to make their way around the entire coastal trail of the island. They meandered towards the center, but besides the inn, there were only a handful of buildings. Behind the inn was a large flower garden with ornate statues and bird baths strewn about. They walked the paths in between and admired the garden's beauty. Well, Hope did most of the admiring. David spent his time grumbling and complaining about the number of bees flying about.

Hope stuck her nose into one of the flowers, sucking in its sweet scent. She then looked around and said, "This is a lot bigger, but I think Janice's gardens are much prettier."

David didn't respond. He was too busy swatting something away from around his head. She could tell he was starting to get a little more irritable, and she knew he was probably getting tired from all the walking.

"Do you want to go sit on the front porch for a bit?" she asked.

"As long as these goddamn bees don't follow me," he huffed, continuing to swat at them.

Hope looked closely but couldn't even tell if there were really any bees flying around his head or not. She knew it was time for a break.

"Come on, let's go out front," she said, motioning for her father to follow her.

Most of the chairs were taken, but Hope found two rockers available at the very end of the long porch.

"Is this okay?" she asked.

His shrug was indifferent. He placed his satchel on the floorboard then carefully lowered himself into the chair. As he sat down, the chair immediately began rocking backwards then forwards.

"Jesus Christ! Now I'm gonna get seasick from a goddamn chair."

"We can go find someplace else to sit if you—"

"Whatever… it's fine," he mumbled, attempting to sit perfectly still as to stop any sort of rocking motion.

Hope, on the other hand, took full advantage of her chair. She kicked off her sandals, crisscrossed her legs beneath her, closed her eyes, then gently rocked back and forth. When her eyes reopened, she took a deep breath, inhaling as much salt air as possible.

"This place is absolutely beautiful," she said, gazing out to the sparkling ocean.

David didn't respond at first, but eventually mumbled, "I'm glad you like it."

She turned towards her father and was just about to thank him, but he interrupted her instead. "What the hell is going on over there?"

A group of people had formed on the edge of the island and were pointing at something out in the water. The woman sitting next to David responded with, "It's probably a seal. There's one that likes swimming over in that area. I think he enjoys showing off for the crowd."

And just like that, Hope sprung to her feet and slipped her sandals back on. She grabbed her camera and turned to her father. "You coming?"

"I just got comfortable, for Christ's sake! You go on without me."

"Oh, okay. I won't be long," she said.

"Take your time," he said, in a softer tone. "It's not like I'm going anywhere."

Hope hurried down the steps and across the yard towards the group of people. As soon as she got to the rocks on the edge of the island, she saw it. There was a lone seal swimming about twenty feet off shore. Hope knew she only had a handful of exposures left in her camera, but there was no way she was going to pass up this amazing seal encounter.

Patiently, she waited for the perfect shot. Finally, after about five minutes of waiting and watching, the seal seemed to be posing for her. It was almost as if he was begging her to take his picture. Hope obliged by snapping two well-focused shots.

When she returned to the front porch, David was leaning against the railing and staring out across the lawn. Apparently, he had given up on trying to get comfortable in the rocking chair. Hope expected to see a cigarette dangling from his mouth or a bottle of vodka pressed to his lips. She found it extremely odd that it was just after noon, and she hadn't seen him do either all day. It was a pleasant change, but it still gave her a strange feeling inside.

"Was it a seal?" he called to over to her.

She smiled. "Yup. It was so groovy. He was so close to the shore. I got a couple of great pictures."

"Ya still got them snacks and drinks in your bag?" he asked.

"Uh huh."

"I'm not eating in these damn wooden chairs. My ass needs someplace more comfortable."

Hope gazed around and spotted a nice grassy area over by the water on the right side of the inn.

"How about over there?" she said.

He didn't answer, but he climbed down the stairs and paused as if waiting for her to lead the way.

"This spot okay?" she asked, pointing to freshly mowed area about fifteen feet away from the edge of the island.

"Whatever. Anything is better than those damn chairs."

Hope sat down and began digging through her bag. David joined her, but it took him much longer for his aching body to make its way to the ground. She placed the food on the grass between them and handed him one of his sodas.

"This is the type you like, right?" she asked.

He half-nodded but was more focused on rummaging through his satchel for a bottle opener. When he finally found it, he attempted to pop the cap, but his hands seemed weak and were shaking uncontrollably. Hope took notice and quickly offered her assistance.

"Here, let me get that for you."

Before his pride had a chance to deny her, she grabbed the bottle and opener and proceeded to pop off the cap.

"I could have done that myself, ya know?" he snapped.

She smiled and said, "I'm assuming that's your way of saying thank you?"

He huffed then took a long swig of the soda. As if preemptively, Hope opened his bag of snacks. David took notice but was much too hungry to verbally take offense. Hastily, he began stuffing his face with the pork rinds.

"Looks like someone's feeling better," she said, peeling her banana.

Pieces of food fell from his mouth as he responded to his daughter. "Let's just hope it all doesn't come back up on the boat ride home."

With her banana fully peeled, she offered some to her father. "Want a piece?"

"What the hell do I look like, a damn monkey?"

She grinned and took a bite. She was starting to get used to his brash sarcasm and demeanor. David watched her eat the banana and then nibble on some trail mix.

"Do you always eat so goddamn healthy?"

She shrugged. "I just think the body is a temple and you should take care of it."

Even as she was speaking the sentence, she knew how ridiculous it probably sounded to him. She prepared for a sharp quip or maybe a loud laugh, but David did neither. Instead, he tossed the pork rinds aside and did his best to stand back up.

"I'm gonna see if that place has a bathroom over there. I need to take a piss."

"Do you want me to come with—"

"I can take a piss on my own, thank you very much. Finish your shitty health food. I'll be back in a bit."

As always, he slung the satchel over his shoulder and headed off towards the inn. Hope finished the banana, neatly sealed the trail mix, then placed them into her bag. While she was in there, she pulled out her journal and a pen. The ocean breeze had subsided, and the sun felt much warmer than when they originally stepped foot onto the tiny island. She took off her father's jacket and placed it on the ground next to her. She took a deep breath of salt air and began to write in her journal.

David was told that the public bathroom was in the center of the island, and the one in the inn was for registered guests only. Of course, this didn't deter David from doing as he pleased. After threatening to urinate right there on the lobby floor, the woman threw her hands up and walked off in disgust. As soon as he entered the bathroom, he clutched at his stomach. It wasn't the same seasick feeling from the boat, but more of a sharp, excruciating pain. This was followed by a dry hacking cough. Hope was still writing in her journal when David returned to their spot on the grass.

"Everything okay?" she asked.

"Even better," he said, holding up a couple of candy bars. "I scored us some dessert from the vending machine inside. He displayed them in front of her and asked, "Which one do you want?" Before she could offer a reply, he blurted out, "And don't tell me you don't eat candy bars. Everyone loves chocolate."

She smirked and found herself reaching for the pack of Reese's Peanut Butter Cups. Happily, he replied, "Looks like it's Mr. Goodbar for me then."

Before Hope had even taken a bite, David had ripped open his bar and made quick work of it. "Looks like someone loves chocolate," she laughed.

"I don't eat chocolate as much as I used to, but I've been known to have a sweet tooth now and again."

As Hope took a bite of her peanut butter cup, David took notice of her journal. "Is that some sorta diary?"

She looked over at it and nodded.

"Your mother used write in those things constantly."

"Really? I didn't know that."

"Yup. And I hated it."

"You hated that she had a diary? Why?"

"Because I always assumed she was writing some bad shit about me."

Hope laughed. "I'm sure you were just being paranoid."

"One time, she wrote I was a giant pain in the ass and that I had the temper of a rabid dog." David took a sip of his soda. "I mean, it was the truth, but... but did she really have to write that shit in a damn book?"

Hope laughed and thought for a second. "Wait. How do you know what she wrote? Did you read her diary?"

"Damn right I did," he proudly boasted.

"You're not supposed to read other people's diaries. That stuff is supposed to be private thoughts only."

"Oh yeah? You're telling me I can't read your little diary?"

"Absolutely not!" she said, placing her hand on top of it.

"Why? Did you write some mean shit about me, too?" he said, more amused than anything. When she didn't answer right away, he pretended to be in shock and said, "Let me see what you wrote."

He jokingly moved his hand towards her diary, but she quickly grabbed it and held it out of arms reach. When she did that, a couple of Polaroid photos fell onto the grass.

"*Oooo*, what do we got here?" he said, snatching them up before Hope had a chance to beat him to it. "Hmm, lemme guess, pictures of your ex-boyfriend? They better not be another blonde hair, blue-eyed idiot... with their hat on backwards." He chuckled then took a closer look at the two photos. Almost immediately, his amused look dissipated. The first picture was of Maggie on her high school graduation day.

"I think Nana took that one," Hope quietly said.

The second Polaroid hit David even harder. It was a picture of Maggie laying in a hospital bed. She had just given birth to Hope and was proudly clutching her against her chest. Hope's squished-up face peeked out from a pink blanket. At first, Hope didn't say a word. She sat perfectly still and watched as her father sadly stared at the photo for the longest time.

"This is the only picture I have of us together." She then lowered her head and quietly said, "I don't have any pictures of you."

"Probably for the best. Pictures are overrated anyway," he said, tossing the photos back over to Hope.

"I don't think so," she snapped back. "I don't think they're overrated at all. These pictures are all I have to remember her by."

David looked away from his daughter, took the last swig of soda, and then stood up. "We should probably get a move on. I think the boat's gonna head back soon."

Hope swiped away the few rogue tears on her face and safely placed the photos back into her diary. She stuffed the book along with the candy wrappers into her bag and stood up. They made their way back to the boat in complete silence. Even when the boat shipped off, they both remained quiet. It wasn't until a younger couple approached David that the first words were spoken.

"Excuse me, sir," they said in David's direction. "Would you mind taking a picture of us?"

David turned and looked at them as if they had three heads. Assuming he was about to blurt out something rude, Hope stepped in and offered to take the picture herself. The couple lovingly placed their arms around each other and gave Hope a big smile.

"Thanks so much," they said, retrieving the camera back from

Hope. "Would you like me to take one of you two?" the woman asked.

Again, Hope knew her father was about to say something sarcastic, so she jumped in with, "Thanks, but—"

That's as far as she got before David interrupted and said, "Just make sure you get my good side."

The couple smiled over at him as Hope just stood there in shock.

"You gonna give them your camera or what?" David said in his daughter's direction.

"Um, yea, sure." Hope took the camera from around her wrist and handed it to the woman. At any second, she expected her father to say something like, *Ha! Just kidding. I'm not getting my goddamn picture taken.* But he didn't. As if prepping for the picture, David licked his fingers, ran them through his hair, and then leaned back against the boat's railing.

Hope was still taken aback, but she hesitantly moved closer to her father. They didn't place their arms around each other like the couple did, but they were close enough that their shoulders were touching. This was the closest they had physically been the entire week—the last twenty years, to be exact.

The woman placed the camera to her eye, took a step backwards and said, "Say cheese."

Despite neither of them actually saying cheese, they both managed a genuine smile.

"That was a good one," the woman said.

"Thank you," Hope politely said, retrieving the camera from the woman.

After the couple walked off, Hope searched for something to talk about with her father. There had been twenty years of silence between them, so she wanted to make the most of their time together. That being said, Hope had no idea what to talk about. The next thing she knew, she blurted out that she had spoken with her grandmother earlier in the morning. "They think I've been studying all week. I hate lying," she said, slumping her back against the railing.

"What they don't know won't hurt 'em. And obviously you feel the same way, or else you woulda told them the truth. You know I'm right. Besides, you'll be back home in a couple days, and they'll be none the wiser."

David's final sentence struck a chord with her. She always knew this trip was temporary and that she'd be back in Chicago sooner rather than later, but hearing her father say it out loud made her sad. He said it so casually, so matter of fact. There were many thoughts running through her mind. Did he have enough of her? Did he *want* her to leave in a couple of days? In her heart, she secretly hoped her presence there would remind him just how much he loved and missed her. So much so, he wouldn't want to live another day without her in it.

Hope stared over at him, but he seemed fixated on the ocean behind her. She gathered her courage and was preparing to ask him where their relationship goes from here, but David interrupted her before she got the chance. "Holy shit!" he exclaimed, pointing over her shoulder.

Hope turned around and looked out to the ocean but saw nothing. "What? I don't see anything," she said.

"Keep looking… keep looking," he repeated.

Just when she thought her father had truly lost his mind, she saw it. About fifty yards out to sea, a humpback whale was breaching. Hope's eyes bulged, and she stood completely still. As its tail smacked the surface, the biggest, most brilliant smile came over Hope's face.

By now, the rest of the passengers had also seen the whale. There was a buzz about the boat, and they all rushed over to get a better view. Mesmerized, Hope leaned against the railing and continued watching the whale surface and resurface over and over. Hope turned to her father, who seemed equally mesmerized by the large creature.

"Have you ever seen one before?"

With a hint of a smile, he shook his head and said, "Nope. Never."

She desperately wanted to throw her arms around him. He was smiling. She was smiling. And for the moment, that would have to be enough. Hope gazed to her left and saw the boat's railing was now lined with passengers. Almost every one of them had a camera pressed to their face.

"Oh my God," Hope exclaimed. "I need to get a picture of this."

She snatched up her camera and looked down at the counter.

"Only three pictures left," she said, turning to her father.

"Well, ya better make 'em count," he said, giving her a wink.

Over the next few minutes, they worked in tandem to get the best shots possible.

"Wait… wait," David ordered. "Get ready… get ready…aaaand SNAP IT!" he excitedly yelled.

Hope clicked the button and caught the whale at the pinnacle of its breach.

"Did ya get it?" he asked.

"I… I think so," she said with a smile.

Enthusiastically, David pumped his fist and shouted, "Yes!"

This was definitely the most animated she had seen him all week. Soon after their perfect photo-op, the whale headed further out to sea, and the boat made its way back towards the marina. With all the excitement going on, David made it the entire trip back without any ill effects of sea sickness.

"Thanks again," Hope said as they exited the boat onto the dock. "That was one of the grooviest things I've ever done."

"Yea, it was pretty… groovy," he said with a smirk.

"Are you making fun of the way I speak?"

"Not at all. Far be it for me to make fun of hippy talk."

She gave him a playful glare then looked down at her camera. "I can't wait to get these developed."

"No time for that now. We still have a lot of ground to cover today. What time is it anyway?"

Hope looked down at her watch. "Just after two."

David swung open the car door then barked over at Hope. "We better get a move on or else we'll be late for our next activity."

11

Hope pulled out her keys and started the car. "So, what's our next—"

"Chop, chop! Let's go! Less questions, more driving."

"Okay, okay! Where to?" she asked, smiling.

David pointed back to the main road and said, "Take this road to the other side of the island. We need to be there by two-thirty."

Hope headed back through town and towards the opposite end of Applewood. She had no idea where they were going, but wherever it was, she wanted to make sure her camera was fully loaded.

"Would you mind putting a new roll of film in for me?" she asked, pointing to the camera and film in the center console.

He released a giant sigh and acted as if Hope had asked him to do some major manual-type labor.

"It would save us time," she said with a hopeful smirk.

"Fine." he said.

Out of the corner of her eye, she watched his hands tremble as he feebly attempted to open up the film compartment. She immediately regretted asking him to do that for her. At one point, the camera slipped through his shaky fingers and fell to the floorboard.

"Goddamn stupid piece of—"

"You know what, I'll get it later. I forgot how tricky it is to change out the film in that camera."

His hands were shaking so much, even as he picked it off the floor, he nearly dropped it again.

"Seriously, it's fine," she repeated. "It really can be a pain to switch the film out."

Frustrated and embarrassed, David tossed the camera back into the console and huffed. "The goddamn thing is probably made in China, that's why."

Again, from the corner of her eye, she watched as he clutched at his satchel. Normally, this would be when David would take a drink and light a smoke, but this time he did neither. Hope was starting to think this was a conscious choice on his part. She was tempted to comment on this but decided against it. For as long as she could remember, one of her worst habits was biting her nails. It wasn't that bad of a habit, but at one point, she did make a concerted effort to stop biting them. About three weeks into it, her grandfather took notice and praised her for finally acting more *ladylike*. That comment was all it took for her to go back to chomping on her nails on a daily basis.

Even if her comments to her father were heartfelt and encouraging, she had a feeling it would backfire and cause him to drink and smoke in spite of her. She decided it best to keep quiet and drive on. From his pocket, David pulled out a crumpled piece of paper. He studied it for a second and said, "You wanna take a left onto Green Hill Road. It should be coming up soon."

"Okay," she said. "How about you give me a hint what our next activity is?"

"Nope. No hints." He attempted to focus on the upcoming street sign.

"Is it somewhere that you and Mom went?"

"There!" he said, pointing up to his left. "Green Hill Road."

She turned onto the road, but before she could resume her

questions, David looked at his paper and said, "In a half a mile take a right onto Hawkeye Road."

"Oh, I know where we are," she said. "This is the part of the island where most of the members of the Abenaki tribe live. I came out this way with…" She paused, not wanting to mention Adam's name.

"Ahh, Mister Sweet Talker brought you out here, huh?"

Slowly, she nodded and embarrassingly said, "He's probably taken many girls *sightseeing* out here."

"Eh, fuck that little punk! Besides, I don't think he'll be taking anyone sightseeing for a while. Not to mention, I don't think he'll be taking a normal piss for a while either."

The imagery of the previous night flashed through Hope's mind, causing her to let out a laugh. David joined in the laughter and pointed out, "He really did scream louder than a goddamn banshee, didn't he?"

Hope nodded and continued laughing. Less than a second later, her laughter was interrupted by David yelling. "*Whoa, whoa…* stop! Ya just missed your turn," he said, pointing to the road she just passed.

She hit the brakes, checked her mirror, and then backed up. "Sorry," she said, turning onto the road.

"Don't be sorry, just get going. We're supposed to be there in two minutes."

"You're really not going to tell me where we're going? Not even a tiny—" She cut off her sentence as her eyes read a small wooden sign on the side of the road.

ABENAKI STABLES – 1 MILE AHEAD

"Wait a second! Are we going horseback riding?"

David folded up the paper and shoved it back into his pocket. "No one's doing anything unless your foot gets a little heavier on that gas pedal."

Without thinking twice about rules or speed limits, Hope's foot pressed down harder causing the car to accelerate forward. Moments later, David curiously peered over at the speedometer.

"Maybe not so heavy on the foot, Speed Racer."

Hope gazed down and saw she was doing nearly twenty miles over the limit. "Holy Moly," she exclaimed, slowing down. "Sorry. Just got a little excited, that's all."

"That's okay," he said with a slight grin. "Nothing wrong with breaking rules and pushing limits. Feels kinda good, don't it?"

She also grinned but was quickly sidetracked by the wooden sign up ahead. It was larger than the previous one.

WELCOME TO THE ABENAKI STABLES
THE OLDEST & MOST SCENIC IN MAINE

"This is where we're going, right?" she asked.

"It is if you want to ride a horse."

Her smile and expression lit up the whole car, and even David couldn't help but grin at his daughter's excitement. Hope turned onto the dirt road and drove up and parked in one of the vacant spaces directly in front of the stable. From the car, she could see five horses milling about in their stalls. Hope shut off the ignition then made quick work of loading a new roll of film into her camera.

As they both exited the car, Hope anxiously said, "I can't believe I'm going horseback riding. This is going to be so—"

"Groovy?" David interjected.

She smirked and responded with, "Yes, groovy. And cool… and neat… and any other amazing adjectives you can think of."

Just then, a young Native American girl approached them from the stables. She looked to be around ten or eleven. The girl offered up a smile and a wave then said, "Hi. Welcome to our stables."

David curiously looked down at the young girl and asked, "You're the tour guide?"

The girl shook her head and giggled.

"Soon enough," a voice off to their left said. "Soon enough Brooke will be leading the tours."

They turned and saw an older Native American man approaching them.

"You must be Mr. Simmons?"

David nodded. "Call me David."

"Nice to meet you, David. I'm Daniel. And as my granddaughter said, welcome to our stables."

"Thanks. And this is my daughter, Hope," David announced.

Hope was slightly taken aback from hearing her father refer to her as his daughter. In the entire week, it was the first time David had verbally acknowledged it.

"Nice to meet you, Hope," Daniel said, but was quickly interrupted by David.

"Do ya want money now or when you get back?"

"I'm sorry, what was that?" Daniel asked.

"I said, do you want money now or when you guys get back?"

Hope gave her father a confused look. "What do you mean, *when you guys get back*? Aren't you going riding with us?"

David let out a loud laugh and looked at her as if she was nuts. "That would be a no. I think I'll catch up on some sleep in the car."

"Oh, come on! You have to go. It'll be fun."

"Sorry. Not happening. This body is far too old and broken to be climbing on one of those animals."

"I'll tell you what," Daniel interrupted, "if you come with us, the ride is completely free today... for *both* of you."

Hope gave a huge smile at the kind man then looked over at her father. David cleared his throat and said, "I appreciate it, but—"

"But nothing!" Hope said, stepping closer to her father. "If you don't go, then I don't go either!"

Hope wasn't usually the type to speak her mind or hold her ground, but at that very moment, she was bound and determined for him to join them on the ride. While David enjoyed seeing his daughter show a little moxie, he still had no intention of going out with them.

"I'm serious!" she repeated. "If you don't go, I don't go!" She straightened her back and crossed her arms. It was at that point David knew she might actually be serious.

"Goddammit it, Hope. Why do you have to be so stubborn?"

"Gee, I wonder where I get that from?"

Daniel and his granddaughter seemed to be enjoying their back-and-forth banter. Daniel finally stepped in and said, "If this broken-down fifty-something-year-old can ride with no problems, I think you'll be just fine. I promise, these are some of the most peaceful and gentle animals you'll ever meet."

"Pretty please," Hope urged.

With all six eyes looking over at him, David knew it was useless to resist. Slowly, he let out a defeated sigh.

"Yes!" Hope exclaimed, clapping her hands together.

"Okay then," Daniel said. "Let's go pick out a couple of horses for you two."

Reluctantly, David followed them towards the stables. Daniel scanned the horses then looked back over at his granddaughter and smiled. "What do you think, Brooke? Should we give Buttercup to David?"

Brooke giggled and nodded.

"Buttercup?" David said, less than impressed. "Can't I get one with a more manly name?"

"Of course you can," Daniel smirked. "How about I give you Thunder?" He pointed to the black stallion over in the last stall. As if on que, the horse let out a vociferous neigh. Not only was it the largest of the five horses, but it appeared to be the most vocal and active. While the other four horses stood perfectly still, Thunder's hooves shuffled about as he let out another loud neigh. David took a step back as his eyes nervously widened.

"Which one is Buttercup?" David asked.

Daniel and Brooke pointed over to the horse in the first stall, more specifically, the palomino *pony* in the first stall. Buttercup was half the size of Thunder and appeared to be much calmer.

"She's my favorite," Brooke said, walking towards Buttercup. "She's so sweet and gentle."

Without thinking twice about it, David blurted out, "Buttercup it is."

Daniel laughed then looked over at Hope and asked, "And you, my dear? Which horse would you like to ride?"

Hope scanned the horses, but her decision had already been made. From the moment she got out of the car, her eyes were fixated on the beautiful chestnut-colored mare in the middle stall. Its red highlights glistened in the mid-afternoon sun. The horse's large brown eyes seemed to be staring directly at Hope, almost beckoning for her to choose her.

"Can I ride that one?" Hope softly asked, pointing to the mare.

"Perfect choice," Daniel said with a smile. He then looked over to his granddaughter. "Why don't you get Buttercup and Starlight ready."

Brooke happily nodded and began prepping the horses for the ride. When she was finished, she led them out of the stalls and onto the gravel driveway.

"You're up first, my dear," Daniel said to Hope. "Have you ever ridden a horse before?"

"Nope. Never. Well, except for the merry-go-round at the fair."

He grinned. "I think you'll find this much more exciting. Okay, place your foot in the stirrup and swing your other leg up and over." Daniel started to help her mount Starlight, but as soon as his hand touched Hope, he gasped for air and recoiled backwards.

"Is everything okay? Am I doing it wrong?" Hope asked.

"Umm, no, you're fine," he said.

As he allowed his hands to once again touch Hope, a sensation ran through his entire body. It was extremely warm and calming and was unlike anything he'd ever felt before. When she was fully mounted, he paused a second longer then turned his attention over to David. "You're up next, Pops. Let me help you up."

David's pride kicked in, and he quickly spurned Daniel's offer. "I don't need help! I can handle it!"

Daniel smiled and stepped back. Luckily for David, his horse was much smaller than everyone else's, and ever though it took him a few tries, he finally was able to mount Buttercup on his own. After giving them a crash course in how to control their horses, Daniel swiftly mounted Thunder.

"Aren't you going with us?" Hope asked over to Brooke.

"No. I have chores to do," she said less than enthused.

Daniel watched as Hope gave her a sympathetic look. "I'll tell ya what, kiddo, if you think you can handle Patches, then you can join us."

And just like that, Brooke's face lit up and she rushed over to the second stall. The horse was slightly smaller than Hope's. It was a pale white color with multiple brown patches throughout her body and mane. Before they knew it, Brooke had Patches saddled up and ready to go. Brooke had no problem mounting Buttercup, but Patches proved to be more challenging.

"Need help?" Daniel asked, already knowing the answer.

"Nope. I can do it," she said with a stubborn confidence.

After three failed attempts, she finally was able to successfully mount Patches. Daniel gave her a proud wink and a smile. His look caused Hope to think about her relationship with her own grandfather. She couldn't remember the last time he had given her a look like that. She loved him dearly, but he was never the patient or prideful type.

"Everyone ready?" Daniel called out.

Hope and Brooke shouted back, "Ready!"

David responded with a grumble. Daniel took the lead and was followed by Hope, David and Brooke. Over the next hour, Hope was surprised by how many different landscapes were on this tiny island. They started off in a large open meadow and then wound their way through a thickly wooded forest. There were pristine streams, and at one point, they even came across a small scenic waterfall.

Throughout the ride, Daniel told them the history of Applewood; of how it was first settled by members of the Abenaki and Penobscot tribes. He also told of how the island was supposed to be the most magical place on earth. Between the breathtaking scenery and Daniel's history lesson, Hope was completely captivated. It took him a little while to get comfortable, but even David seemed to be enjoying himself.

Hope was so caught up in the moment, she kept forgetting to take pictures of the beautiful scenery around her. Luckily for her, Daniel stopped often and pointed out areas that might be deemed as the perfect photo op. In between snapping pictures of scenic areas, Hope found herself turning around and catching shots of her father up on his horse—to his disapproval, of course.

Although he didn't go into detail, Daniel did mention that the island was steeped in old Native American legends and folklore. On more than one occasion, she wanted to ask Daniel about the Dark Waters but could never bring herself to. It probably wasn't even a legend. Or more than likely, it was probably all just made up in her head.

"How's everyone doing?" Daniel asked, stopping his horse and turning around. "We'll be leaving the forest soon, and the next portion of the trail will be quite the contrast… but in a good way."

As soon as they exited out of the darkened forest, the sun immediately hit their faces, and its warmth coursed through their bodies. At one point, the sun was so bright, Hope had to shield her eyes from it. The horses followed the well-worn path up a large grassy hill. Off to their right was a smaller hill. It was dotted with dozens and dozens of three-foot round rocks.

Hope pointed over to it and asked, "What's that over there?"

Brooke looked over to her grandfather then sadly lowered her head. David also lowered his head, which made Hope wonder if her question was somehow inappropriate. Somberly, Daniel stared long and hard over at the rocks and finished with a look over in David's direction. Finally, he spoke.

"That is our sacred burial ground for the many brave men and women who lost their lives due to the… plague that hit the island hundreds and hundreds of years ago. We call the hill, Nemikwaldamnana, which means: We will always remember."

Hope had more questions but decided to remain quiet. The horses continued plodding up the path towards the top of the large hill. For the past twenty minutes, the fresh scent of pine had overtaken their senses, but the further they moved from the tree-line, it was replaced with a faint smell of salt air. As a matter of fact, the closer they got to the top of the hill, the more prevalent the smell became. It wasn't until all four horses reached the hilltop that the next portion of the trail was revealed.

Hope sat up as straight as she could, and a look of awe came over her face. There, stretched out before her, were the glistening waters of the Atlantic. It appeared calmer than the other side of the island.

"Wow. Beautiful," she exclaimed.

Even David seemed impressed with the spectacular view. After enjoying it for a few moments longer, they began to turn back toward the forest. For the most part, on the ride back, Daniel remained silent and allowed them to enjoy the peacefulness of their surroundings. At one point, he mentioned that he had come from a long line of shamans on the island.

When they returned to the stables, Daniel helped Hope climb down from Starlight. "I hope it was more fun than the merry-go-round horses," he said, smiling in Hope's direction.

With a huge grin, she replied, "Are you kidding me? This was one of the grooviest experiences I've ever had."

"That's hippy talk for she loved it," David said from his horse.

Daniel laughed then turned to his granddaughter. "Why don't you have Hope help you get the horses back in their stalls?"

"Okay," Brooke said, and then motioned for Hope to join her.

Daniel walked over to help David dismount from Buttercup.

"And how was it for you?" he asked, when David's feet landed back on solid ground.

"My ass will let ya know tomorrow," David shot back. He decided to cut his sarcasm short and managed a more positive comment. "It was good. Maybe even fun. I appreciate it... we both do," he said, looking at Hope over in the stalls.

Daniel reached out to shake David's hand. As their hands clasped, Daniel had a similar reaction as he did with Hope; he recoiled backwards, gasping for air. But unlike with Hope, there was no warm feeling coursing through his body. It was cold, ice cold. Daniel's face turned a pale grey, and after tightening his grip, he slowly placed his other hand on David's side; the same side he'd been clutching so many times throughout the week. Gravely, Daniel stared deep into his eyes. The whole strange encounter caused David to release his grip, also taking a step backwards.

"As I mentioned earlier, I'm the tribal shaman here on the island. If you would like, I could—"

David nervously laughed and interrupted. "Thanks, Doc, but I think we both know what's in me is even beyond your powers. Besides, this trip isn't about me." David's eyes looked over towards his daughter. "I just wanted to introduce her to the island… so she could see how special it was… and hopefully she'll remember this place one day."

The color was slowly returning to Daniel's face, and as he looked from Hope back to David, all he could do was offer a warm smile. "Can I get you anything while you wait for your daughter?"

"Maybe some Preparation H," David said, rubbing his ass.

Daniel let out a slight laugh and started to walk away. He took two steps and turned back around, focusing more intently on David, who was already slouched against the car. As David rested his achy muscles, he peered across the way at Hope helping Brooke take care of the horses.

"Do you know how lucky you are?" Hope said to Brooke. "I would love to ride horses all day."

Brooke shrugged. "I actually don't ride that much. More chores than anything." She glanced over to a pile of manure.

Hope giggled. "Still, a lot better than living in Chicago."

"You live in Chicago?" Brooke excitedly asked. "I've never been to a big city before."

"Eh, you're not missing much."

"Looks like you two have a classic case of the grass is always greener syndrome," Daniel said from behind them.

Hope turned and smiled.

"There's good and bad in everyone's home. The key is learning to appreciate the good more than concentrating on the bad."

199

Brooke rolled her eyes. "Grampa is always saying stuff like that."

"I only speak the truth," he said, rustling Brooke's hair. "Maybe one day all my ramblings will make sense… or maybe not." He shrugged and winked at his granddaughter. "Hey, Brooke, why don't you run inside and get David a nice tall glass of water. It looks like he could use some."

They all looked over to David, who was leaning against the car and wiping away the sweat from his forehead.

"He's had a busy day today," Hope said.

"Nothing wrong with that," Daniel said. "Would you like something to drink?"

"No thank you. I'm fine."

After Brooke scampered off to the house, Daniel stood back and watched Hope rhythmically stroke Starlight's neck and shoulder. At one point, Starlight leaned her head into Hope.

"That means she likes it," Daniel said.

Hope smiled and continued stroking. "Such beautiful animals, aren't they?" she asked.

Daniel nodded. "I really hope you enjoyed the ride today."

"I sure did. The scenery was amazing, and I loved hearing about the history of the island."

Once again, the image of the Dark Waters entered her head, but once again, she said nothing. She simply continued petting Starlight. Daniel intently focused his eyes on Hope.

"Is there something you'd like to ask me?"

Did he just read my mind? Hope removed her hand from the horse and slowly gazed over at the intuitive man.

"Umm… no," she hesitantly said, moving her gaze from the horse down to the hay-covered ground.

"Well, feel free to pet the horses as long as you like." He threw her a smile then turned to walk away.

Hope's brain told her to remain quiet, but her mouth had other plans. "Have you ever heard of the legend of the Dark Waters?" she blurted out.

Daniel stopped and slowly turned back around. "Ah, the Dark Waters, huh?" He placed a piece of hay into his mouth. "One of island's oldest legends. How did you hear about that?"

This time, her brain overruled her mouth. There was no way she could tell him that her eyes were able to see this strange anomaly. He would surely think she was a crazy hippy girl from the big city.

"Umm… I read a little bit about it at the place we're staying."

"I see," he said. "And where are you and your father staying?"

"A place called the Great Blue Heron Inn."

"Very nice," he said, nodding his approval. "Janice and I go way back. This island is full of old stories and legends, and the Dark Waters is certainly no exception."

"Is it really supposed to be a place where the Evil Spirit live?" she asked.

"It is." Daniel took a step closer, removed the hay from his lips, and then began to fill Hope in on the legend. "Like I mentioned earlier, there have always been mysterious and magical elements to this island. It's what drew my ancestors here in the first place. But for every good, there's an evil… and not long after settling here, that evil began to show itself."

"How?"

"By poisoning the island and its people from the inside out. Trees, plants, and even my people's souls were slowly decaying."

"Why didn't they just—"

"Leave?" he knowingly asked. "Because they knew, once healthy, this island had the ability to be the most magical place on earth."

Hope was completely engaged in his story. "What did they do?" she asked.

"They sent for the most powerful shaman in the region. He belonged to the Penobscot tribe further north. It is said, as soon as he stepped foot onto the island, he sensed the immense power of its magic. He also sensed the evil lurking within. It took him a while, but eventually, the mighty shaman was able to cast the Evil Spirit off the island, banishing it to the depths of the Atlantic. Unfortunately, not before half the tribe succumbed to the poison of the Evil Spirit."

Hope thought for a second and began putting two and two together. "That burial ground you showed us earlier... those deaths were caused by the Evil Spirit, weren't they?"

Daniel nodded.

"What happened next?" she asked.

As soon as the Evil Spirit was banished, the magic returned to Applewood. From that point on, the island and its people once again began to thrive."

Hope smiled at the happy ending but knew there must be more to the story. "Where does the Dark Waters come in?"

"Originally, the Evil Spirit was banished to the bottom of the ocean, but over time, it slowly made its way back up to the surface. And since then, mysterious and tragic events have occurred in that area."

"Do you believe it?" she asked.

"In the legend of the Dark Waters?"

"The Dark Waters... the Evil Spirit... all of it."

Daniel thought for a second. "Yes. Yes, I do. I know that probably makes me sound crazy, but—"

"No. Not at all," she quickly responded. Hope couldn't hold back her curiosity. "Have you ever seen it... the Dark Waters?"

Daniel let out a slight chuckle and said, "No. Never."

"Yet, you still believe in it?"

Daniel smiled then looked over at David, who was just finishing his glass of water that Brooke had given to him. Daniel turned back to Hope. "You don't have to see something to believe in it." He turned his attention to Starlight, and Hope watched as he gently stroked the horse's neck.

"Have you ever… met anyone who's seen the Dark Waters?" Hope asked.

Daniel shrugged. "I've known a few who claimed to have seen it, but…"

"You don't believe them?"

"Let's just say they weren't the most reliable people, and more times than not, they had the tendency to stretch the truth. Besides, they say it takes a person with a very special gift to be able to see the Dark Waters."

Hope's eyes moved from Daniel down to the hay-covered floor, and as she shifted her weight back and forth, she couldn't help but question herself. Was it all in her head? Or did she really see the Dark Waters that day? If so, that would mean she had the special gift Daniel spoke of.

Nope, no way, she thought. *I've never had a gift for anything… except passing my homework in on time and getting perfect grades.*

"Everything okay?" Daniel asked.

"Yea. I'm fine," she said, bringing her eyes back up to his. "But even if this whole Dark Waters thing is true, if people and boats just stay away from that area, it should be fine, right?"

"Unfortunately, it's not that simple. It is feared that the Evil Spirit will continue to grow bigger and stronger, eventually reaching our shores once again. And this time, it will poison this place from the outside in—once and for all, sucking the magic from the island."

Daniel's voice was filled with conviction and more than a hint of worry. Hope attempted to lighten the mood. "Well, you said yourself that you're the island's shaman now, so you can cast the Evil Spirit back to sea like the other shaman did. Right?"

This time it was Daniel's turn to let his eyes fall to the ground. "My abilities are nowhere near what his were. Not to mention, by the time the Evil Spirit returns, it'll be much more powerful than it ever was before."

A bolt of fear shot through Hope's veins, and a lump formed in her throat. She stood perfectly still for a moment and hesitantly asked, "How does the island get rid of it then?"

Daniel looked Hope straight in the eyes for a moment then turned his attention to David. "I think that's a story for another time," Daniel said, smiling back over at Hope. "I think your father is ready to go."

Hope looked over at her father. He'd gone from leaning against the car to full-on laying across its hood.

"Yea, it's been a pretty busy day for him so far," she said. "I should probably get him back to the inn for a nap… on a real bed." Hope started to make her way towards her car. She turned back to Daniel and said, "Thanks again for the ride. I loved it."

"You're very welcome, my dear. Hopefully our paths will cross again one day."

Hope just assumed this would be her one and only trip to Maine, but she gave Daniel a polite nod before attempting to wake up her father. David lay spread eagle with his back against the hood and his head propped on his satchel. She had no idea how anyone could be comfortable in that position, yet David seemed quite content as was shown by his loud snoring.

"Hey, you ready to go?" she asked, rustling his pant leg.

David shot straight up, nearly sliding off the hood. "Jesus Christ! Didn't anyone ever teach you not to scare a man while he's sleeping?"

"Sorry."

David climbed off the hood and did his best to stretch out his tight back and aching body.

"Are you ready to go?" she asked.

"I was ready to go twenty minutes ago," he mumbled.

Hope was feeling too good to let another one of her father's grumpy mood swings affect her. As she drove down the long dirt road, she thought about the day's events so far. If her day ended after the whale watch, it still would have ranked as one of her most favorite days of all time. But throw in a horse ride led by an authentic Native American—this day was without a doubt her most favorite day ever.

12

Before pulling onto the road, Hope looked over to David and asked, "Do you want to head back to the inn and take a nap?"

"Nope. Still got lots to do today."

Hope knew he was exhausted, but selfishly, the curiosity of what the next activity might be caused her to just go with the flow and follow his orders. "Okay then. Where to?"

David pulled out his crumpled piece of paper and did his best to focus in on the writing. The closer he brought it to his face, the more squinty his eyes became. He started to explain the instructions to Hope but quickly became frustrated. "Fuck! I can't read her goddamn writing!"

"Whose writing?"

"Janice wrote directions to the next place we're heading to. Here," he said, shoving the paper over to Hope. "You're the smart one… you figure it out."

Hope took the paper and patiently read through it. "We're leaving the island?" she asked.

"Yup," he said, reclining his seat back. "Janice told me the best flower shop in the area is located in that town. I'm just gonna rest my eyes. Wake me when we're there." He fidgeted in his chair for a moment then crossed his arms and closed his eyes. Before she'd even gotten a mile down the road, David was once again snoring loudly.

Not only was her happiness at an all-time high, her confidence was, as well. So much so, that as she approached the tiny bridge her mother used to jump from, her mind began to wander. She envisioned her mother standing at the edge of the bridge—young, beautiful, and full of confidence. She pictured her with arms outstretched as she bravely plunged into the waters below. It wasn't until Hope's car was almost across the bridge that her confidence peaked. She was about to do the unthinkable. She slammed on the brakes, causing her father to open his eyes and let out a scream.

"What the hell's going on? Did you hit something? An animal? A human? I've done both, by the way."

Hope didn't reply. Instead, she threw the car in reverse and backed up. She parked along the three-foot high wooden railing. David, still gathering his bearings, peered out the window. "Seriously, what in God's name is going on?"

Her heart was nearly pounding out of her chest, but she managed the words, "I'm gonna do it. I'm gonna bridge jump… just like Mom did."

David didn't have a chance to reply. With the car still running, Hope swung open the door and darted across the road. It wasn't until she climbed over the wooden railing that David actually knew she was serious. Grabbing his satchel, he popped open the door and rushed over to where his daughter was standing. He was about to inquire if she was going to put on her bathing suit, but he assumed it would probably ruin the moment. If she was going to jump, she just needed to do it—no swimsuit—no overthinking—just do it.

Her heart pounded. Her breath quickened. Her hands were clenched and sweating. "If Mom can do it, I can do it. If Mom can do it, I can do it." David stood still as she continued to whisper these words to herself. "If Mom can do it, I can do it."

"You got this, kiddo," David encouraged. "Just take a deep breath and jump. You'll be fine."

He was nearly four feet away but could still see how much her body was trembling. If she was smart, she would have just climbed over the railing and jumped without thinking. Instead, she stood perfectly still, staring down at the slow-moving water below. It was only about a ten-foot jump or so, but it might as well have been fifty.

"I can't... I can't do this," she said, turning back around towards her father. Both her hands were now tightly clutching the railing. "I thought I could, but..."

"But nothing. You can do this. You can absolutely do this." His tone was the most encouraging it'd been all week. "You're stronger than you think." David's eyes stared directly into hers. He took a long pause before repeating himself. "You're stronger than you think. You always have been."

Almost immediately, her trembling subsided. As David gave her a nod, she loosened her grip on the railing and turned back towards the water. She made a conscious effort to control her breathing.

"That's it... deep breaths," he encouraged. "Be brave. Don't let the fear take over. It'll all be worth it... I promise you that."

Hope closed her eyes and could literally hear her heartbeat slowing down. As her breathing slowed, her fears began to disappear.

"That's it, Hope. You got this. Now just close your eyes and do it... jump. Trust me, the exhilaration you'll feel afterwards will far outweigh the fear you're feeling now."

Hope remained quiet but allowed his words to resonate within her. With her arms outstretched, she prepared herself to jump. David took a step back and watched in anticipation. Unfortunately, the moment never came. Hope lowered her arms, let out a discouraged exhale, then slowly turned back around.

"I can't. I just can't do it," she softly said, without making eye contact with her father. "I'm sorry. I'm sorry I disappointed you."

She climbed back over the railing and expected her father to make some sarcastic comment about her chickening out. To her surprise, he did the opposite. "You could never disappoint me, Hope… never." He then turned and started to head back towards the car.

Still hanging on his comment, Hope stood frozen. For a moment, she thought she might cry. But instead, she channeled his beautiful words and allowed it to swallow up whatever bit of fear she had in her.

"If Mom can do it, I can do it," she blurted out.

David spun around and saw Hope climbing back over the railing. This time, she didn't think twice about it. She outstretched her arms, closed her eyes, and did it. By the time she made the jump, David had rushed forward and was leaning over the railing. Excitedly, he yelled out, "And don't forget to smile!"

Less than a second later, there was a loud splash as Hope hit the water feet first. David watched her disappear beneath the surface. At that point, his smile was replaced with a look of concern. He held his breath and waited… and waited. Finally, after what seemed like forever, Hope reappeared on the surface and began screaming.

"Oh, God, Oh, God!" David said aloud. "She broke something. Her legs… her back… maybe her whole goddamn body! Oh, God!"

It took him a moment, but as she began to swim towards the bank, he realized she hadn't broken anything at all. He also realized her screaming wasn't from pain but rather out of celebration. After she pulled herself onto the shore, she stood up and looked back over at her father on the bridge. "I did it!" she yelled. "Can you believe it? I did it!"

David released his anxious breath then let out his own celebratory yell. She climbed up the small grassy hill and eventually made her way back onto the road. He met her halfway, and neither one of them could contain their excitement.

"Did you see? Did you see? I did it! I actually did it!"

"Damn right you did! I told ya you had it in you. So, how do ya feel?"

She raised her hands in victory and yelled, "Invincible! And… and fffffffreezing." She lowered her arms and wrapped them around herself. "The water is soooo cold."

"No shit, Sherlock. We're in Maine… in April. What the hell did you think it'd feel like? Hot springs?"

They both laughed, and David motioned her to follow him back to the car. She looked down at her bare feet. "I lost my sandals when I hit the water."

"Eh. Minor price to pay for the art of spontaneity."

"I'm getting pretty good at being spontaneous and living on the edge, huh?"

"Relax, wild child. Ya still got a long way to go."

"Oh, come on! You have to admit, you're a little impressed with me, aren't you?"

David looked over at his soaking wet daughter and then glanced over to the bridge and said, "Maybe a little impressed."

"This must be how Mom felt when she jumped, huh?"

"Umm…" David's eyes shifted towards the ground.

"Umm what?" she asked.

"I might have twisted the facts a bit."

"She never went bridge jumping, did she?"

"Yes, yes she did. Many times, actually. Just… well… just not *this* bridge."

"You lied to me?"

"No," he said, almost offended. "I didn't lie. Just twisted the truth a tad. The bottom line is you both bridge jumped, and that's all that counts, right?"

The adrenaline was still pumping through Hope's body, which

made it impossible to be mad at anything. She gave her father a smirk and said, "I suppose it's kind of the same thing. Was the bridge she jumped from the same height as this one?"

"God no! Half as high—at most. To be honest, I can't believe you did it. You coulda broken your neck or something."

"What? Then why were you encouraging me?"

"What the hell did you want me to do? You were all gung-ho and had your mind set on jumping. It's the most fire I'd seen in you all week, so why would I wanna stop that? Huh?"

Hope had no response. If truth be told, she was glad he encouraged her and maybe even glad he had lied to her. She felt accomplished. She felt alive. They both took a step back and watched two cars drive over the small bridge.

"What time is it?" he asked, after the cars had passed by.

Hope looked down at her watch, gave it a few taps and shook her head in disgust. "Shoot! I forgot to take off my watch before I jumped. The water ruined it. First my sandals and now my watch. So stupid, Hope." Amusingly, David looked on as she continued berating herself. "It's not funny. I've had this watch forever, and those were my favorite sandals."

"You'll live," he said, turning away. "Besides, barefoot suits you better."

She dismissed his comment and continued to stand there shivering.

"You got clothes with you?" he asked.

"Yea."

"Well, get changed. We still got lots to do."

"You want me to change right here? On the side of the road?"

David shook his head. "You would never survive being homeless. What the hell is the big deal? Don't you hippies run around naked singing Kumbaya and shit?"

211

She desperately wanted to dispute his comment, but she couldn't, not completely anyway. "What? No. I've never run around naked," she said.

"And?" David said, leaning his head in closer.

She blushed then shrugged and mumbled, "I might have sung Kumbaya before, but it was around a campfire... fully dressed."

"Uh huh," he laughed. "Just go get changed in the back seat. And just in case people flock to see the big show, I'll stand guard for you."

"Fine. I'll go change," she said with a smirk.

While she undressed in the car, David paced back and forth fidgeting with his satchel. He needed a cigarette and a drink in the worst way possible. At one point, he found himself vigorously itching his forearms.

"Let's go, Hope!" he yelled.

"Okay, okay, I'm ready," she said, popping open the door.

Hope had chosen the nicest outfit that she brought with her. Her only wish was that she still had her beloved Birkenstocks, but she was happy with her flowing floral print gauze skirt and rust colored camisole. In a swift and well-practiced motion, Hope grabbed her wet hair and braided it to hang neatly over her right shoulder. She knew there was no way it would dry nicely if left to its own devices. Her hair always had a mind of its own.

They both climbed into the front seat. Hope started the car, put it in drive, then slowly drove over the bridge. She took one last look down at the water and proudly smiled to herself. It wasn't long before David had once again dozed off. Hope passed by the Great Blue Heron Inn and exited Applewood soon after. She followed the written directions and eventually entered the town of Gerrish Falls. At the stoplight, she took a left towards what was referred to as the Historic District.

Gerrish Falls was a lot bigger than Applewood with more of a small city feel to it. When she entered the historic district, the streets became narrower and were lined with old brick buildings. Main Street was filled with shops and restaurants, reminding Hope of a certain section of Chicago that she liked to roam around in. The buildings were nowhere near as high or as intricate as Chicago, but that only added to its charm. The tallest building was the giant church in the center of the square. Hope quickly glanced at the paper to see the exact address she was looking for.

"Miller's Flower Shop... 323 Main Street," she said out loud to herself.

No sooner did she say it, a sign reading MILLER'S FLOWER SHOP caught her eye just up ahead. She parked out in front next to the old cobblestone sidewalk. She shut off her car and turned towards her father, who was still sleeping soundly. Hope knew how tired he was and wanted to let him sleep, but she was excited to explore this new area.

"Hey... we're here," she said, giving him a little nudge.

As if ready to defend himself, His eyes popped open and he clenched and cocked his fist.

"Whoa. Relax," she said, raising up her hands. "It's just me, okay?"

"What the hell you waking me for?" he grumbled.

She pointed out the window to the flower shop. "We're here."

David straightened up in his seat and wiped the sleep from his eyes. "Good. About time. Let's get a move on."

Hope reached onto the floor of the back seat and grabbed a ratty old pair of flip flops.

"Don't you own any real shoes? Like ones that actually cover all of your feet?"

"At home I do, but I really don't wear them much."

"Whatever," he said. "Let's go."

David led the way into the shop and was immediately greeted by the owners, who appeared to be in their late sixties. Mrs. Miller was the first to greet them.

"Good afternoon," she said as the door shut behind them. Her glasses were attached to a silver chain around her neck, and she quickly lifted them to her face to get a better view. "How can we help you two today?"

David cut right to the chase. "Special occasion. We need a giant-ass bouquet of flowers… for an anniversary."

She smiled at his response and said, "I see. *Your* anniversary, I presume?" David didn't answer. He was too busy looking at the assorted flowers throughout the shop. "Do you have any idea what kind of flowers you'd like to get your wife?"

Hope bit her lip and looked down at the floor. Her stomach had the sick feeling again from hearing her mother mentioned in the present tense. David's only response to her question was an unhelpful shrug.

Politely, Mrs. Miller asked, "What kind of flowers are her favorite?"

Once again, he shrugged. He then turned to his left and said, "Hope?"

Her eyes shot open, and she slowly raised her head up and looked over at her father. Her body froze, and she felt her face turn red. He had put her in an awkward spot. She barely knew anything about her mother, never mind what her favorite flowers were. With both David and Mrs. Miller looking over at her, Hope bit down harder on her lip and turned a brighter red. She shifted her body away from Mrs. Miller and inconspicuously whispered to her father. "I don't know what her favorite flowers were."

David's response was neither inconspicuous or a whisper. "Then just pick out whatever you like. I trust your judgment. Well, not your judgement in shoes… or clothes… or boys, but I'll give you the benefit of the doubt when it comes to flowers." David reached into his pocket and pulled out some crumpled bills and handed them to Mrs. Miller. "This much worth of flowers, okay?"

Continuing to smile, she took his money and replied, "You got it. Shall we get started?" she said in Hope's direction.

Hope nodded and followed her to the other side of the shop. David didn't have the patience to join them nor the patience to wait around.

"I'll be outside," he said, already halfway out the door.

While Hope and Mrs. Miller wandered around picking out the perfect flowers, David found himself pacing back and forth on the cobblestone sidewalk. He also found himself people-watching; more specifically, watching people smoke. He desperately needed to shove a Marlboro into his mouth. Instead, he pulled out his Bic lighter and began to anxiously flick it on and off. About fifteen minutes later, Hope exited the shop, but to David, it felt like an hour.

"What do you think?" she asked, holding up the giant bouquet. It was so big that he could barely see Hope's face behind it. The bouquet was full of brightly colored flowers and had a white ribbon tied around it. David was definitely not a flower person, but even he was slightly taken aback and impressed with its beauty.

"Wow. That's… that's perfect. Absolutely perfect." The moment seemed to calm his nerves a bit, and he placed his lighter back into his pocket.

"Do you mind if we walk around a little?" she asked. "This town is super groovy."

"I suppose I could walk for a bit," he said. "Do you wanna put those in the car first?"

Hope paused in front of her car then looked down at the flowers. "I don't mind carrying them. I did this whole arrangement myself.

Pretty good, huh?"

David didn't reply but watched his daughter as she proudly lifted the flowers up to her nose. When she was finished breathing in as much fragrance as possible, she looked up at her father. "Don't they smell amazing?" she said, offering them up to David.

"I'm sure they do," he said. Without making an effort to smell them, he glanced over at the flower shop and muttered, "Anything probably smells better than that woman's God-awful perfume."

"I thought she was very sweet," Hope said. "And helpful, too." She then smirked and said, "But yea, her perfume was a bit on the strong side."

"Told ya! Smelled like a goddamn whore house or something."

Hope laughed. "I wouldn't know about that," she said, taking a final whiff of the bouquet. "Shall we walk?"

"I'm ready. You're the one standing around smelling flowers."

Hope cradled the bouquet and began walking down the sidewalk. About one block later, they entered the center of the historic district, known as Liberty Square. Potted flowers and plants lined the square, and there were a half dozen or so old wooden benches strewn about. There was a water fountain in its center, which was much larger than the one at the Great Blue Heron Inn.

Many people were milling about, but Hope's attention was focused on the person standing next to the fountain. He looked to be in his late twenties and had a guitar strapped around his shoulder. He was in the middle of playing "Hey Jude" by the Beatles and had more than a handful of people standing around watching him. Hope thought about the many buskers she used to see in Chicago's Grant Park. She would spend hours watching and listening to them play. It made her happy, but it also made her jealous of their talent. Even more so, she was jealous of their bravery and lack of self-consciousness.

The man's guitar case was placed on the ground in front of him and seemed to be filled with loose change and dollar bills. Hope, along with the others, stood still and watched intently. David's focus was more on Hope rather than the guitar player. He knew exactly what must be running through her mind. She probably wished that she had the courage to stand in front of people and play.

When the man finished, Hope adjusted the bouquet in her arms, making it easier for her to clap for him. She also joined the crowd by throwing some money in his case. "Great job," she quietly said, tossing in a couple of dollars.

"Thanks so much," he said. He then grabbed his bottle of water from the edge of the fountain and took a long sip. A few seconds later, he started playing "Hotel California" by the Eagles.

Hope made her way back over to her father. In the meantime, David had moved over a few steps to his right to be closer to a couple of middle-aged women. It wasn't them he was interested in; it was the fact that they were both smoking. David placed himself downwind and reveled in the bellows of smoke floating his way.

"Wanna continue walking?" Hope asked, not really noticing what he was in the middle of.

"You don't want to keep listening?" He motioned to the busker.

"I'm okay. Besides, I'm probably the only one in the world, but I'm not really a big fan of this song… or the Eagles, for that matter."

"Good. I fucking hate this song, too. Reminds me of a goddamn halfway house I used to live in. They said I could check out any time I like, yet I could never leave. Bunch of assholes who ran that place, I tell ya!"

David took one last inhale of the women's second-hand smoke then turned and walked away. Hope glanced at the busker one final time then followed her father down the sidewalk. It didn't take long before Hope's attention was back on the many cool storefronts. As they approached each business, she had a habit of saying the name of the store out loud. At first, this annoyed David, but eventually he softened and even started to be amused by her commentary.

"You do realize I can read? You don't need to announce every goddamn storefront we pass by." It wasn't his typical harsh use of the phrase *goddamn*. It was said with a sly smile on his face.

"Oh… sorry," she said, realizing what she had been doing.

"Are you actually gonna go in any of these stores or what?"

Excitedly, she nodded. "If you don't mind?"

"Why the hell would I mind? Go wherever you want."

"In that case, I want to go in there." She pointed up ahead to a store called Jackson Mercantile. "You coming?"

"Nope. I'm banned from that place."

"I thought you said you've never been to this town before?"

"I haven't. They have those stores all over the country."

Hope had never seen or even heard of this store before, but then again, this was her very first time outside of Illinois. Reluctantly, she took his word for it.

"What did you do to get banned?" she asked.

"I took a mannequin's head off with a baseball bat."

"Why would you do that?"

David's answer was quick and matter of fact. "The thing was looking at me all weird and shit."

She didn't put it past her father to do something like that, but still, she had her doubts on the validity of his story. She decided to keep her thoughts to herself and simply headed inside the store.

"Would you mind holding these while I go inside?" she asked, reaching the bouquet out towards him.

"What do I look like, your personal flower holder? I told you to leave them in the car, didn't I?"

"It's not a big deal." She recoiled the flowers back against her chest. "I'll take them inside with—"

"Relax, Hope. I was just kidding. Give me those things."

Hesitantly, she once again stretched her arms in his direction and said, "You really don't have to—"

"For Christ's sake, give me the damn flowers. You're gaining on the spontaneity thing, but you have a long way to go in realizing when someone is being sarcastic." He snatched up the flowers and with a wry smile said, "Have fun in the store. Oh, and word to the wise, don't decapitate any of the mannequins." He threw his daughter a wink then spun around and headed towards the square.

Hope entered the store and found herself laughing out loud at the first sight of a mannequin. She wandered around the aisles and eventually meandered from store to store along Main Street. Like so many times throughout the week, she felt like a tourist on vacation. That feeling caused her to pause and think to herself: *Was that all this was… a vacation? An escape from reality? Just a brief encounter with my father, only to once again go our separate ways in a day or so?* Whatever it was, she was secretly starting to wish it would never end.

After about a half an hour of exploring and making a few purchases, Hope decided to head back to the square and check on her father. Most of the week, she would have been worried about him going off and getting drunk, but for whatever reason, it hadn't crossed her mind all day.

When she finally got to the square, she spotted her father slouching on one of the wooden benches. His eyes were closed, and he clutched his trusty leather satchel on his lap. He looked peaceful. Just over his shoulder, a large pigeon sat perched on the back of the bench. The way the sunlight was shining down on him made Hope wish she had her camera with her. It just seemed like the perfect shot. The hustle and bustle of the square seemed to drown out his snoring, but it was still loud enough to hear nearly ten feet away. She approached closer but had learned her lesson about startling him while he slept.

"Hey," she whispered. When he didn't respond or move an inch, she raised her tone a notch. "Hey… I'm back."

Again, there was no response or movement. She took another step forward and repeated herself. This time, the only thing that could be heard was the pigeon flapping its wings directly behind David's head. It was enough to startle him awake.

"Jesus Christ!" he yelled, straightening his body up as much as possible. "What the hell ya doing scaring that thing off? It could have attacked me."

Hope smiled and shook her head at him. She was starting to get used to his overly dramatic reactions. "I'm pretty sure it wasn't one of those killer pigeons. I think you're safe."

"So says you! For your information, I was attacked by a clan of them in downtown St. Louis years ago. I still have the scars on my head to prove it. Wanna see the claw marks?" David leaned his head forward so Hope could get a better look.

"Sorry, but I don't see any scars or claw marks. And I think you mean flock, not clan," she said and laughed.

"Ohhh, that's right, I forgot. You're Miss College-Educated Know-It-All."

As she continued to laugh, she handed him the bottle of RC Cola she had in her right hand. "Here, I thought you might be thirsty."

"Well, yea. I nearly got pecked to death by a crazy pigeon. Of course I'm thirsty."

He happily took the soda and pounded down half the bottle. He followed it up with a long, obnoxious belch. When he finished, he noticed Hope was drinking a 7-Up. "Holy shit! Look who's drinking a soda pop. You're taking this living on the edge thing serious, aren't ya?"

"What? I'm not a prude. I drink soda… just not very often.

220

Usually, just on special occasions."

"And today's a special occasion?" he asked.

Without hesitation, she said, "Well, yea. It's your big anniversary, right?"

David smiled, knowing this was the first time all week Hope had acknowledged the big day. "Damn right!" he said, raising his soda towards Hope. She followed suit and clinked his bottle. David pounded down the rest of his soda and let out a final belch. "Top that!" he boasted.

Hope crinkled her nose and shook her head. "I'm not living on the edge that much. Besides, I'm still a lady, you know?"

This caused David to let out a giant laugh. "That's what your mother used to say. But eventually, she became a burping pro. Especially when drinking a cold beer. Hate to admit it, but I think she could outdo me."

She had a sneaking suspicion he was only saying that in hopes of getting her to attempt one. "I'm not falling for that," she said. "You also told me she jumped from that bridge, which was a lie."

"Not a lie… a twisted truth," he winked.

She giggled, took another sip, and then gazed down at her feet. "Oh, look! Look what I bought. Brand new Birkenstocks! I've been wanting a new pair for a while now, and they were way cheaper than back in Chi…" She stopped mid-sentence and her eyes focused on something familiar. It was tucked underneath the bench behind David's legs. "Is that… my guitar case?"

"Yup. Yup it is. I grabbed it when I put the flowers in the car."

She started to speak but paused. "Wait… how did you put the flowers in the car? I locked it."

David reached into his pocket and casually pulled out her keys. "They don't call me Pickpocket Pete for nothing!" He let out a proud, yet diabolical chuckle.

So many questions were swirling around her head. She focused herself then took them on one at a time. "But your name isn't Pete. I don't get it."

"Pickpocket David doesn't flow off the tongue very well. Pickpocket Pete had a much better ring to it. Besides, when you live on the streets, you never go by your real name."

Once again, Hope hated hearing or thinking about her father wandering the streets as a homeless person. She did her best to eliminate it from her mind, and she moved on to her next question. "When did you take my keys?"

"Remember when I *tripped*," he said in air quotes, "and bumped into you?" He let out another proud laugh. "Ha! Oldest trick in the book."

Now that those questions were answered, she moved on to the more pressing one. "But why did you get my guitar case?"

"Why do ya think, genius? So you can play."

Thinking he was totally joking, she burst out laughing. "Yea, right. There's no way I would ever do that. I told you, I don't play in front of people."

David pondered then said, "You also told me you were too afraid to jump off the bridge, yet you did it."

"That was different."

"Exactly!" he said. "Jumping off that bridge is way worse. The freezing cold water… the fact that you could have broken your neck. You don't have to worry about any of that playing guitar. Unless, of course, you suck and someone grabs your guitar and smashes it over your head… but even then, it's pretty much equal to the bridge jumping thing."

She looked from her guitar case to her father and realized he was completely serious. "I'm sorry to disappoint you, but it's not gonna happen." She knew this wasn't going to cut it with him, so she attempted to come up with some more legitimate reasons. "I don't really have anything prepared, and my throat's been feeling a little scratchy lately."

David was fully prepared to respond to her thinly veiled excuses. "I heard you the other night… you have plenty of songs prepared. And the only thing that's scratchy is your brain. You'll be fine."

"But… but I don't want to encroach on someone else's turf."

Her last-ditch effort was met with a big smile from David. "Lucky for you, the other guitar player isn't here anymore." David pointed to the other side of the fountain, and to Hope's dismay, the busker was indeed gone. "See, I took care of it for you," he said, winking in her direction.

"What do you mean you *took care of it?* What did you do? What did you do to the guitar player?"

He shrugged and said, "I just told him if he didn't move along that I'd take a baseball bat to his head. You know, just like I did to that mannequin back in the day."

Her mouth fell open, and she nearly dropped her soda. But before she could say a word, David burst out laughing. "Relax, Hope. I'm just bullshitting ya. Ha! You shoulda seen your face."

David's laughter quickly turned into one of his coughing bouts. At one point, it got so bad that a few people came over to see if he needed help. Although he couldn't talk, he angrily waved them off. When it finally stopped, Hope offered him the last of her soda. "Here. You can have the rest if you want."

He waved her off as well, then he bent down and grabbed her guitar case and said, "You gonna play or what?"

"No, no I'm not," she said, turning away from her father. "I… I just can't."

Undeterred, he again shoved the case towards her. And once again, she shook her head no.

223

"Your reasons for not playing are… well, to be quite blunt, your reasons are fucking stupid. Just play," he said, pushing the case within an inch of her.

It wasn't typically her style, but Hope had no choice but to resort to kindergarten tactics. She turned away from her father, crossed her arms in protest, then huffed, "I'm not playing, and you can't make me!"

He chuckled. "What are you, like, five?" He shoved the case closer and said, "You're right. I can't make you play, but… I can certainly embarrass you if you don't."

Curiously, she turned back around and looked up at her father, who had a diabolical smirk on his face. "What does that mean?" she asked.

"For starters, I'll strip down buck naked and take a little dip in this fountain right here." His eyes looked serious, but she thought for sure he was bluffing.

"Yeah, right," she said with a doubting smile.

"It wouldn't be the first time I skinny dipped in a fountain. But it would be the first time I did it while screaming that my abusive daughter forced me into it."

"You wouldn't dare." She looked him dead in the eyes. She thought there was no way he would really do this. Would he?

He put on his best poker face and said, "Go ahead, test me."

She looked from her father to her guitar case then back to her father. All his chips were in the middle of the table, and it was obviously her move. After a long pause, she called his bluff.

"I'm sorry, but I'm not gonna play."

David smiled. "Suit yourself." He reached down and started unbuckling his belt. Hope remained confident that he was still bluffing. Her confidence waned when his belt was fully unbuckled and removed from its loops. Her confidence completely disappeared when he unbuttoned and unzipped his pants.

Hope quickly glanced around, and before anyone realized what was going on, she blurted out, "Fine! I'll do it! I'll play." *This is exactly why I don't play poker or gamble,* she thought.

"Really? You'll play?" he asked.

"Yes. Just zip your pants up and put your belt back on," she whispered.

"With pleasure," he said with a victorious smile.

After he zipped up his pants and placed the belt back around his waist, he motioned to the guitar case. Hope let out a defeated sigh then slowly grabbed and opened it. David sat back down on the bench and watched as she fumbled with the guitar strap. When it was firmly on her shoulder, she returned the empty case to its spot beneath the bench. She gave her father one last desperate pleading look, to which he smiled and motioned towards the fountain.

"Your fountain stage awaits, rock star."

She released a resigned sigh and hesitantly turned towards the fountain. It was only ten feet away, but to Hope, it felt like she was on a pirate ship being forced to walk the plank. Actually, walking the plank seemed like a welcomed fate compared to this. Just when she thought it couldn't get any worse, her father added one last stipulation.

"Oh, and one more thing, Hope. No cover songs. Originals only."

Practically in tears, she spun back around and pleaded with her father. "Nooo. I can't. Not after last time. I—"

"Zip it, Hope," he interrupted.

She expected his next sentence to be filled with sarcasm, or at the very least, to repeat his skinny-dipping threat.

"Relax, Hope. Breathe. You got this. Remember, you're stronger than you think."

No sarcasm. No threats. Just encouraging words from a father she hadn't even met until a few days ago. His words weren't enough to calm her nerves, but they were enough to make her turn around and shuffle her way over to the fountain.

She did as he told her and took a deep breath—three, actually. It didn't seem to help much. Her nerves were still a wreck and her stomach remained in knots. She hadn't even strummed a chord, and yet, she already felt like she was going to throw up. Her posture was that of a caveman. Her shoulders were slumped low, her back bent like an old lady, and her eyes never made it above guitar level. David was certainly not the poster child of perfect posture, but even he shook his head and placed his hand over his face in embarrassment.

For different reasons, David was also a nervous wreck. He desperately needed a cigarette and a drink. While Hope continued to prepare herself, David scanned the square in hopes of spotting a group of smokers that he could go stand by. Not only were there no groups, but there were no individual smokers either.

"What the fuck is wrong with people?" he mumbled to himself. "Not one goddamn smoker around?"

Just then, he spotted three young adults all puffing away. They were hanging out on the sidewalk across the street from the square. David thought seriously about getting up and marching over there. He just needed to suck in some second-hand smoke. He didn't even care if they were smoking a shitty brand of cigarettes.

As he squirmed and twitched on the bench, his mind debated. Finally, just as he stood up to head across the street, he heard it—the strumming of a guitar. It stopped him in his tracks, and he sat back down and turned his attention over to his daughter.

Although she was strumming, her chords were unsure and lacked confidence. The lack of confidence didn't improve any when she started to sing. Her voice was shaky and quiet and was easily drowned out by the gentle splashing of the fountain behind her. She was out of tune and out of place, and she knew she was embarrassing herself. The first verse was nothing short of a disaster. Her voice cracked more times than she could count, but she didn't give up. In between the first and second verse, she managed to raise her eyes enough to look over at her father. He gave her a thumbs up and an encouraging nod. That, along with another deep breath, seemed to allow Hope to relax.

Halfway through the second verse, she closed her eyes and did her best to release her fears. By the time she hit the chorus, her voice had found itself again. It was louder and more confident, and it was just as angelic as David remembered from earlier in the week. In fact, it was so beautiful and angelic that the entire square fell silent as everyone turned their attention to this young guitar player.

Hope's eyes were still closed, so she had no idea people were watching and listening as intently as they were. When the final chord of the song was strummed, there was a brief moment of dead silence. At any second, she expected to hear people laughing at her or maybe someone screaming -*You suck*!

None of that happened. The opposite happened. It wasn't until she heard the loud sound of applause that she opened her eyes. There were at least a dozen people clapping—clapping for *her*. Hope's nervousness was quickly replaced with embarrassment. Through her blushing red face, a shy smile appeared. Before she had a chance to say a word, a loud voice boomed from across the way. "That's my daughter!"

She looked up to see her father giving her a standing ovation. Almost immediately, tears formed in her eyes, and she did her best to hold them back. David wasn't done there. When he finished clapping, he grabbed the empty guitar case and walked over towards Hope. He placed it directly on the ground in front of her and proceeded to toss some crumpled dollars and loose change into it.

David turned towards the small crowd and announced, "Come on people! I saw how much you were giving that hack earlier. Anyone can play someone else's songs, but it takes true talent to write originals."

227

Within seconds, people were digging in their pockets and one by one coming up and placing it in her case. She continued to blush as she politely thanked each of them. After the last person tossed a dollar in, David motioned to Hope to continue playing. This time, it didn't take half a song to get her voice and confidence in gear. From the very first chord, she was off and running. Even her eye contact had vastly improved.

David returned to his spot on the bench. He leaned back and proudly watched his daughter perform a nearly impeccable version of her song called "The Way Back Home." When she finished, the crowd, which had doubled in size, once again clapped loudly.

"Thank you," she shyly said, and watched as even more loose change and dollars were thrown her way.

Her songs were well-crafted, but it was her voice that really grabbed people's attention. The crowd murmured to each other and "angelic" was the common word used to describe Hope's voice. David continued to lean back on the bench, and for the moment, cigarettes and alcohol were the last things on his mind. Hope adjusted her strap, and without the need of her father's encouragement, she decided to play one last song.

"Thanks so much for listening. I guess I'll play one more," she said, giving the strings a quick tuning.

As the crowd clapped in approval, Hope stared down at her guitar and wondered what to play next. After a long hesitation, she decided to really go out of her comfort zone and play a new song she had just recently written. She'd only played it a few times in its entirety, and she made it a point to emphasize this to the crowd.

"Like I said, this is a brand-new song, so I haven't worked out all the kinks yet. I hope I don't screw it up too much." She wiped the sweat from her hand then placed the pick back between her fingers. She took a deep breath, gave a quick glance to her father, then softly said, "This is called 'Beautiful Regrets.'"

David listened to most of the song with his eyes closed. He wasn't sleeping or even tired any more. He simply wanted to allow Hope's words and voice to completely consume him. It wasn't long before a few tears escaped and ran down his weathered face. Hope had no idea, for her eyes were also closed throughout the song. When she finished, David quickly sat up and wiped his face with his shirt. It took him a second, but eventually he stood and joined the crowd in clapping. At one point, he placed his fingers to his mouth and gave his daughter a loud ear-piercing whistle. A huge smile beamed from her reddened face.

Although it was intended to be her final song, the crowd wanted more. Their cheers prompted David to hold up one finger towards Hope. She took a deep breath and pondered what to play next.

"I was ordered not to play any cover songs," she said in her father's direction. "But I think I'll end with one anyway. Besides," she smirked, "rules are meant to be broken, right?" David shook his head and returned her smirk. "I actually just learned this one yesterday. I hope you like it. Thanks again for listening."

When her guitar was fully tuned and ready, she calmly went into her version of "Can't Help Falling in Love." Once again, her voice and song choice caused David to get more emotional than he wanted. As soon as she finished, she had more than one person approach her and comment on just how talented she was. One elderly woman placed her hand on Hope's cheek and claimed she had never heard a voice so beautiful in all her life.

Because of all the fanfare, it took her almost ten minutes to make her way back over to her father. She approached him with the guitar in one hand and the money-filled case in the other. She placed the case on the bench and reopened it.

"I can't believe how much money is in there," she whispered in his direction.

"Don't be counting any of that now. Not very professional. Just put your guitar in there and you can count it later."

Hope nodded and placed her guitar on the bed of change and paper bills. When she was finished securing the lid on the case, she lifted it off the bench and asked, "Ready?"

"Yup," he replied. "Let's go get some dinner, rock star."

13

Hope placed her guitar in the trunk and climbed into the car and asked, "Back to Applewood?"

"Yup," he said, glancing at the clock in the car. "Reservations are for 6:30. We should just make it."

Hope put it in drive and quickly left the quaint town of Gerrish Falls behind them. Although they drove the first ten minutes in silence, David could tell by Hope's smile that she was reliving her big performance. About halfway across the causeway, just before entering Applewood, David blurted out, "You're welcome, by the way."

"For?"

"For getting your ass out of its comfort zone. And for allowing you to erase that shitty memory of your last performance in high school. I told you those kids were fucking idiots, didn't I? Yup, just another invaluable life lesson that I've taught you. I should charge you for that shit."

She smirked. "You can have all the money I made today."

She was half-joking, but she would have gladly given every cent to her father. She still had no idea how he was paying for this whole trip, but she knew he needed money a lot more than she did.

"I don't want your money, Hope," he said as they crossed back into Applewood. He gazed out his window and continued. "You just realize what your true potential is and we'll call it even, okay?" She started to laugh but quickly realized he was being completely serious. "Okay?" he repeated.

She nodded and softly said, "Okay." She paused for a few moments then followed with, "But you're right. I do owe you a thank you… for this whole day, actually. It's been one of the best days of my life."

David had no intention of letting the moment get too serious. "That's nice, but let's just concentrate on getting to the restaurant. I don't know about you, but I'm starving."

"What's the name of the restaurant again?"

"The Cliffside," David said.

"And you've never been there before?"

"Nope. I'm strictly going on Janice's recommendation. She's the one that made the reservation for us."

When they reached the other side of the island, David pointed up ahead to a small road sign reading THE CLIFFSIDE RESTAURANT. Hope turned left and headed up the steep hill. Nothing else was said as they both looked on in anticipation of this restaurant that Janice raved so wildly about. When the road finally leveled off, they found themselves driving along the cliffs high above the ocean. After a handful of sharp twists and turns, Hope entered the parking lot of the restaurant.

"Whoa," she exclaimed, gazing up at the building, which was perched at the highest point of the cliffs. "It's beautiful."

Even David had a look of awe on his face. "It's perfect," he said, smiling. He jumped out of the car before she had even turned the key off.

The wind was whipping and swirling about. David stood in the middle of the parking lot, closed his eyes, and let the wind hit his face as he breathed in the salt air. When he was finished, he motioned for

Hope to do the same thing. She originally laughed off his gesture, but when she saw his look become more adamant, she appeased him. With the wind in her face, she closed her eyes and took a deep breath of the salt air. When she reopened them, her father was grinning and staring directly at her. "That salt air is some good shit, huh?"

She couldn't help but to nod and smile along with him.

"Yup, this place is perfect!" he said.

"Good. I'm glad you like it." This whole anniversary thing was twisted and delusional, but Hope liked seeing her father excited and with a smile on his face. "Shall we?" Hope asked.

"Not looking like this," David said, pointing to his faded t-shirt. He reached into his satchel and pulled out a baby blue leisure suit. He threw the jacket on over his tee, and without hesitation, dropped his jeans around his ankles and proceeded to slip on the pants.

Hope looked around to see if anyone was watching then whispered, "You're really undressing right here in the parking lot?"

"Would you rather I do it in the middle of the restaurant? And it seems like you're the only one who cares... or is watching, for that matter."

With that, Hope rolled her eyes and turned away to give him some privacy. Not that he needed it, he would probably be fine with sitting in the restaurant in just his underwear.

A minute later, he called out, "All set! What do ya think?"

Hope turned back around and took in his entire outfit. Seeing as the suit had been stuffed in his bag, the first thing she noticed was just how wrinkled it was. The second thing that caught her eye was the fact that the suit was at least one size too small. David seemed oblivious to any of it.

"Where did you get that from?" she asked.

"Janice's dead husband," he said matter-of-factly.

Her eyes widened a bit, but all she could manage was a simple, "Oh."

"I didn't steal it, if that's what you're thinking. Janice offered it to me." David stretched out his arms and noticed the shortness of the sleeves. "I might be a little bigger than her husband was. But it looks okay, right?"

In any other circumstance, and on anyone else, the answer would have been, *you look ridiculous.* But this wasn't any other circumstance and this wasn't any other person. It didn't matter if this was their real anniversary or not—this week, this day, was very important to him. Hope was touched at just how much effort he'd put into the entire day. So, as she looked over at his short and extremely wrinkled suit, all she could say was, "I think you look… I think you look great."

"I kind of do, don't I?" he said, running his fingers along the giant butterfly collar. "Let's go eat."

From the moment they walked into the restaurant, everyone's eyes were on them. Hope knew they were focused on her father's entire outfit—dirty t-shirt and worn-out shoes included. Hope didn't seem to care. She was preparing to have a nice dinner with her father.

The inside of the restaurant was a little more casual than the exterior would have led you to believe. On each end of the dining room were two giant stone fireplaces, which were both lit and roaring. The hostess sat them in front of one of the many floor-to-ceiling windows overlooking the Atlantic.

"Is this okay?" asked the hostess.

Assuming her father would do the talking, Hope remained quiet.

"Does this work for you?" David asked in Hope's direction.

Beaming with excitement, she said, "Yes, very much so."

After they were seated, they both found themselves staring out the window. Daylight was waning, but they could still see the ocean down below. It seemed to stretch on as far as the eyes could see.

"Janice was right," he said. "This place is perfect."

Hope nodded in agreement and turned her gaze around the dining room. "Whoa, groovy!" she said, pointing across the way. Against the wall sat a large glass tank filled with lobsters.

"I bet they let us pick out which one we want to eat," David said.

"Really? That seems kind of morbid, doesn't it?"

"Not at all. Besides, if you order a steak here, I heard they let you go out back and pick out the cow."

For a split second, Hope almost fell for it. "Ha, ha. I'm not that naïve," she said.

To David's surprise, Hope revealed that besides haddock, she had never really eaten any seafood before. Because of that, he ordered a little bit of everything for them to try. As predicted, they were allowed to pick out which lobster they wanted, and as earlier stated, Hope wanted nothing to do with which lobster got boiled alive. She did get a good laugh when David reminisced about the lobster incident with Adam.

"You should have seen the size of some of those lobsters in the tank," he said, returning to the table. "Their claws woulda ripped that boy's pecker right off!" He said it loud enough for the table next to them to hear. Hope was laughing so hard that she didn't even care how embarrassing it was.

Their pre-meal conversation centered around telling each other their favorite foods. Although their lists differed quite a bit, they did agree on pizza—a deep-dish loaded with everything pizza, to be precise.

"Let me guess, you'd wash it down with a can of Schlitz beer?" she said, laughing.

"Actually," he pondered, "with that type of pizza, I'd prefer an ice-cold A&W root beer."

"Mmmm. In a frosted glass mug," she added.

"Well, yea! That's the only way to drink it!"

"One of my roommates and I go there for lunch sometimes."

David smirked and asked, "So, you *do* have friends, don't ya?"

"I suppose I kind of do."

Hope took a chance and asked what were some of her mother's favorite foods. She wasn't sure if it would set him off or not. It didn't. David told her about the many different places they used to go out to eat at. He elaborated so much that the conversation lasted right up until their meal was served. The first few minutes consisted of Hope trying to identify exactly what she was eating.

"What's this? What's that? Which sauce should I put on this?"

David was entertained, but he was also busy stuffing his face with as much food as possible. For the most part, Hope enjoyed each of the different kinds of seafood. Fried shrimp with cocktail sauce was her favorite, and whole-belly clams was her least. It took her a while to get her first taste of lobster, however, for David was having the hardest time getting it properly cracked open.

Hope started out being amused, but the more she watched him struggling, the more she realized it was due to his weak and shaky hands. She would have offered to help, but she had never eaten nor cracked open a lobster before. His frustration came with loud swear words. Luckily, Hope wasn't the only one watching him struggle. Their waitress approached and offered her assistance.

"These little guys can be quite tricky," she said in a calming voice. "Shall I?"

The waitress was way too cute, and her smile was way too polite for David to even think about snapping at her. Although embarrassed by his failure, David handed her the pair of lobster crackers. With methodical precision, she cracked open the lobster and ended with the comment, "There ya go. Now the fun part. Bon appetit." She gave David a wink, which seemed to further calm his nerves.

After she walked away, he looked over at Hope and confidently said, "That was French for *Have a good day.*"

Hope grinned but didn't have the heart to tell him he had his French phrases mixed up.

"Dig in!" he said, pushing the plate between them.

She started to pick up her fork and knife but was met with a disapproving glare from her father. "What?" she asked.

"Lobster ain't meant for utensils! Fingers only!"

It was more of an order than a statement, so Hope slowly lowered her utensils and began to reach for the lobster with her hands. Again, David glared at her.

"Now what?"

He handed her a plastic bib and said, "Here, put one of these on first. If not, you'll get shit all over your hippy clothes."

"You want me to wear a bib?" she said laughing.

David motioned around at all the other customers eating lobster and wearing bibs. "It's not my rule, that's just how it's done!" He then proceeded to tie a bib around his neck.

Hope continued to laugh but followed suit. When it was finally tied around her neck, she reached out and took a hunk of the lobster tail and began to raise it towards her mouth.

"No, no, no!" he huffed. "Ya got to dip it in hot butter first."

"Oh… sorry."

"Goddamn rookie," he mumbled, and then showed her exactly how it was done.

As it turned out, the lobster was Hope's favorite out of everything they had tried so far. "This is so good!" she said, reaching for more.

Over the next ten minutes, the only sounds that were uttered were oohs, aahs, and mmmms.

"Almost as good as an orgasm, don'tcha think?"

By now, nothing that came out of his mouth surprised her.

"Didn't I tell ya, there's nothing like a Maine lobster!"

"You were right," she said. "You were right."

Proudly, he nodded and leaned back, giving his stomach a satisfied rub. For a second, she feared he would undo his pants, but luckily it didn't get that far.

"This is the most I've eaten in years," he said.

"Agreed," she said, also leaning back in her chair.

As Hope stared across at her father, she couldn't help but giggle to herself. Despite wearing the bib, David managed to get butter and lobster juice all over his suit.

"Guess you should have worn a bigger bib," she said, now giggling out loud.

He looked down at the many food stains on his clothes. He attempted to wipe them, but it only made it worse.

"Goddamn it!" he yelled out, tossing down his napkin. "Oh, well, it's nothing that all-temperature Cheer can't take care of. Besides, it's not like her dead husband is ever gonna wear this again, right?"

Hope continued laughing and went along with him. "Good point."

"Wow!" exclaimed the waitress. "Looks like you two polished everything off. How was it?"

Hope looked up at her and said, "It was amazing!"

"Best meal I've ever had!" David said, slamming his hand down on the table.

"Excellent! I hope you saved room for dessert."

Hope rubbed her stomach. "Not me. I'm stuffed."

"Same here," David agreed.

"Well, okay then. Let me clear some of these plates, and I'll bring you the check."

Before she walked away, he called out, "Hold on... just out of curiosity, what kind of dessert do ya got?"

The waitress smiled and answered, "Tonight we have a peanut butter chocolate cake and a blueberry pie… both homemade and both delicious."

"Hmmm… can you pack one of each to go?"

"I sure can." She smiled then turned and headed away.

Hope gave him a look, to which he responded with, "What? We can eat it later, right?"

"Absolutely."

A few minutes later, the waitress returned with their desserts and the bill.

"Let me pay for dinner," Hope said, reaching for her bag. "You paid for everything else this week. It's the least I can do."

"Nope! Put your money away! I told you, this week was my treat."

Not wanting to argue and cause a scene, she simply put away her money and offered a sincere thank you to her father.

"Eh, don't mention it," he said. "That meal was worth every penny."

"Thanks for the whole week, actually. Especially today." Hope paused and said, "Although… I do find it a little strange that earlier in the week Janice asked me what were some of the things I wanted to do while I was here. Horseback riding, whale watching, and trying my first Maine lobster were on the top of my list. Don't you find it odd that we did all those things today?"

David was preoccupied with counting out his crumpled bills, but he did manage to mumble, "Quite the coincidence, I guess."

A sly smile formed on Hope's face. "You totally paid Janice to do some recon on me, didn't you?"

David threw one final bill down on the table then glanced over at Hope and said, "Nope. I didn't pay her one red cent. She did it for free."

Hope laughed. "But I don't get it. I thought today was supposed to be about Mom… about you and Mom?"

"Trust me," he said, pulling off his bib. "She'd love this."

He stood up and headed across the dining room towards the front door. Just like on their way in, many customers were looking over at David. His undersized suit was even more wrinkled than earlier and was now covered in various food stains. Hope assumed he was oblivious to their looks. It wasn't until they reached the car that he revealed differently.

"Ya know what everyone was staring at, don'tcha?"

She shrugged, pretending to not have a clue.

"They were gawking at your goddamn feet!"

"What? At my new Birkenstocks?"

"You can give them any fancy name you want, but they're still hippy sandals! Ya really think people want to look at someone's toes while they eat?"

Hope was more amused than offended. So much so, she didn't have the heart to tell him what they were *really* staring at. She started the car and decided on a different tactic. "Why should I be bothered by people staring at me? All week you've been telling me that I shouldn't care what people think. 'They're just blankety-blank idiots,' is what you told me, right?"

David soaked in her comment and nodded in agreement. "About damn time you listened to me. You're right, you should never care what people think. And if you want to be accurate, I never said blankety-blank idiots. 'Mother fucking idiots,' were my exact words!"

"I know," she laughed. "I was being polite."

"No room for polite in this car. But there is room for me to rest my eyes a bit." David reclined the seat back and made himself comfortable before closing his eyes.

"Don't get too comfortable. We'll be back to the inn in ten minutes."

Without opening his eyes, he said, "Back to the inn? What, are ya done for the night?"

"Umm, no. I just assumed you were tired and—"

"I am tired. Fucking exhausted, actually. But the day's not over yet. Head up to the lighthouse."

"Really?"

"Do I stutter? Yes, really."

"Okay. The lighthouse it is."

14

David's eyes remained closed as Hope navigated towards Harbor Cove Park. As she watched her father sleep, a sad smile formed on her face. She remembered him telling her how special the park was to him and her mother. She assumed it would stir up a lot of emotions for her father, but she had no idea just how much. Just as she pulled in, the last two cars were on their way out. It was now dusk, and the lack of lights made the gravel parking lot feel desolate.

"Hey, we're here," she called out to her father.

"What?" he said, squirming in his seat.

"We're at the park."

He let out a sigh and sat straight up. "About time," he said, opening his door and climbing out. "Are ya coming or what?"

She joined him outside the car and asked, "Do I need to bring anything in particular?"

David thought for a second. "Do you have a blanket?"

"No, I—wait… actually, I do." She walked to the back of the car and opened the trunk. "When I first got this car, Grampa made me a roadside emergency kit to keep in my trunk." She unzipped the bag and pulled out the rolled blanket and said, "I'm not sure how big—"

"That'll work," he said, peering into the bag. "What else ya got in there?"

Hope listed each item, and expected at any second, David would have a sarcastic comment towards her grandfather. Instead, he surprised her by saying, "This bag was a really smart idea. Good for him."

"Umm, yea. Grampa is famous for giving me practical gifts."

"Take that, too," he said, pointing to the flashlight.

She handed it to him then zipped the bag and shut the trunk.

"There's nothing wrong with practical… as long as you mix it in with some fun." He flicked the flashlight on and said, "Personally, I woulda got you a pair of fuzzy dice for your car."

The thought of fuzzy dice hanging from her rearview mirror caused her to laugh out loud. David spun around and shined the light directly into her face.

"Hey! I'm serious! You need to take the time to enjoy yourself once in a while. Life is way too short to be so serious all the time. Got it?" He sternly repeated himself, making sure she knew it wasn't rhetorical. "Got it?"

She nodded. "Yea… got it."

"Okay, good." He turned back around and led the way up towards the park. Before ascending the stairs, he shined the light on the sign to the left.

HARBOR COVE PARK – OPEN DAWN TO DUSK

Without looking at her, David called out, "That's right, we're breaking the rules. Deal with it!"

Hope smiled and followed her father up the steps and into the darkened park. There was still enough light to see the many flower gardens and trees. For the longest time, the only sounds that were heard were their footsteps on the gravel paths. Hope followed close behind, watching her father take it all in. Finally, he spoke. "Jesus Christ… this place has changed." His statement wasn't loud or angry. In fact, it was more on the quiet and sad side.

"Changed in a good way or bad?" she asked.

"Just changed, that's all. It wasn't even a park when your mother and I used to come here."

"Really?"

"Nope. There were a few clearings, but besides that, there were nothing but apple trees up here."

Hope glanced around at the beautifully landscaped park and found it hard to picture it covered in nothing but trees. She then focused on the lighthouse. "I bet you guys used to love to look at that," she said, pointing to its bright red light slowly rotating around.

"The lighthouse? Nah. It was the sky. It was the sky we focused on. The stars were the only lights we cared about. We would lay here for hours looking up at them."

Hope absolutely loved the image of her parents looking up at the stars together. She gazed up at the sky, but it wasn't dark enough to make out any stars yet.

"Don't worry," David said, joining her upward gaze. "They'll be out. Soon enough they'll be out."

With that, he tossed down the blanket and lowered himself onto it. Of course, he moaned and groaned the whole way down, mumbling something about his old, broken body. When he was finally settled, Hope sat down next to him. She knew there must be a thousand thoughts and emotions going through his head, so she remained as still and quiet as possible. Off in the distance, they could see flashes of lightning followed by the faint rumbling of thunder.

"Think it's coming this way?" she asked.

"Nope. I think she's staying out to sea."

"Good. I would hate for it to ruin this beautiful night."

She looked over to her father. They both knew she was referring to more than just the temperature. David turned his attention back to the night sky. This time, the lightning was more than just a flash. Long, jagged bolts, violently stretched from the sky to the sea. The thunder that followed was a bit louder than the previous round. David watched as Hope bit down on her lip and nervously grabbed a handful of the blanket.

"Don't tell me you're scared of a little thunder and lightning?"

"Not so much the lightning… just the thunder."

"You're more afraid of a noise rather than a bolt of lightning?" he asked.

"Yup. I hate loud noises. I remember when I was little, I didn't really understand the concept of thunder. I remember constantly asking, 'What if the thunder get us?' Grampa tried to explain until he was blue in the face, but I just didn't grasp the fact that thunder was just a noise and that it couldn't hurt you. I actually like watching the sky light up…" Just then, there was another rumble of thunder. "But I could definitely do without that noise," she said, cringing.

"Well, I wouldn't worry too much about it. I already told you, it's heading further out to sea. If not, I'll do my best to protect you from the thunder." He laughed to himself as he continued staring out at the ocean.

"Did Mom like Christmas?"

"What?"

"I know it's kind of random, but for whatever reason, it just popped into my head. Nana and Grampa aren't really huge fans of it, but I love Christmas. It's my favorite holiday."

David took a long pause and said, "It was Maggie's favorite as well."

Over the next hour or so, their conversations were an even

balance of back and forth. Unlike most of their earlier talks, David held back on his typical sarcasm, and never once did he abruptly change the subject. This was the most open she'd seen her father all week. Their conversation was going so well that Hope decided to take it up a notch. Without thinking too hard on it, she blurted out, "Did you ever get my letters?"

Immediately, David's contented look turned uncomfortable, and he looked away from his daughter. Hope went on to explain when and how she found out about her parents.

"Nana and Grampa were all I ever knew, so it took me a while to start to really questions things. It took them even longer to answer me honestly. I was probably four or five when they told me the truth about Mom dying soon after I was born. I asked what happened to you... but they didn't really have an answer for me."

"Of course they didn't," he mumbled.

"Grampa told me I should ask Uncle Jeremy. He was still living in Chicago at the time, and he used to visit me once a month or so."

"Did you? Ask him?"

Slowly, she nodded. "He told me you were really, really sick and that you were in and out of special hospitals. I asked him when I could see you... when I could meet you for the first time. He told me I was too young to visit the hospital and that you just needed to rest while the doctors made you better."

David continued to look away.

"I figured since I couldn't visit... maybe I could write you instead. Every night before I went to bed, I wrote you a letter and drew you a picture. And whenever I saw Uncle Jeremy next, I begged him to mail them to you. He used to tell me not to get my hopes up... that you might be too sick to write back."

Hope remembered licking the stamps and giving them each a kiss as she placed them on the envelope. She decided not to share that little piece with her father.

"I know they got mailed because I personally put them in the big blue mailbox myself. He also told me not to tell Nana and Grampa about the letters. Back then, I didn't really get why, but as time went on, it became obvious how much Grampa—"

"Hated me?" David said, still looking away.

Hope bit down on her lip and pressed on. "Every day I waited for the mailman to come, but... but you never wrote back. I remember I even made you a Father's Day card. I made a giant heart out of glue and glitter."

Anxiously, David's leg began twitching. His right hand fidgeted on the blanket, and his left hand nervously rubbed where his beard used to be.

"Did you ever get them? Or even read them?"

He shrugged and mumbled, "I barely remember last week, never mind all those years ago."

He struggled to his feet and took a short walk over to one of the benches. It was obvious she had pushed too hard. She desperately wanted to discuss this further, but she knew she needed to take her foot off the gas a little bit, at least for now. Hope climbed off the blanket and joined him on the bench. She crossed her fingers that her next question wouldn't cause a similar reaction.

"How old were you when *your* mother died?" she hesitantly asked.

"What? My mother?"

"Uncle Jeremy said she had cancer?"

At any moment, she expected him to snap at her or to say something sarcastic about his brother. Instead, David's fidgeting slowed, and as he stared into the night sky, a moment of calmness fell over him.

"I was ten when she died. Lung cancer. You think I smoke a lot? She smoked like a goddamn chimney. Both my parents did. Our house was never the same. She was the glue that held it all together."

Hope pushed a little further. "What was she like?"

Surprisingly, David was quick to answer. "She was a free spirit but was strict when she needed to be. My father was the bread winner, but make no doubt about it, my mother ran the ship. And she had a great sense of humor. Why do ya think I'm so fucking hilarious?"

Hope rolled her eyes but found herself laughing at his comment. David thought for a moment and said, "Speaking of people who loved Christmas, my mother was crazy about it. We were always the first ones on our street to get a tree and the last ones to take it down. Yup, she certainly went gaga over that silly holiday. As soon as Thanksgiving was over, the Christmas decorations would come out."

"That's exactly how I am! Nana and Grampa never really shared my enthusiasm though, but they do let me decorate until my heart's content."

"Yea, my father was never big on the whole Christmas spirit thing, but my mother always won him over. My brother and I used to argue over what to put at the top of the tree. He wanted an angel. I wanted a star."

"Did you alternate each year?"

"Nope. My mother never wanted either of us to feel left out, so she put both of them on the top."

"Sounds like she was a pretty groovy woman."

"She was one of the best people I've ever known."

Hope sadly smiled and said, "I wish I could have met her."

Without making eye contact, David replied, "She woulda loved you… and she definitely woulda spoiled you."

"Really?"

"Yep. She woulda spoiled you rotten." The smile on his face made Hope glad she had asked about his mother.

"What else? What else can you tell me about her?"

David's eyes were locked on Hope, but his mind was lost in nostalgia a million miles away.

"She loved to cook. And she definitely loved to laugh. Like, really laugh. When she got going, she sounded like a goddamn cackling hen."

Hope giggled and shivered from a quick blast of the ocean air. David took noticed. "We can get out of here if you're getting too—"

Cutting him off, Hope blurted out, "No. I'm fine. Just a little chill, that's all. I like being here."

Another burst of cool air blew in, but this time, Hope did her best not to react to it. Seeing this, David stood up and took off his jacket and handed it to his daughter.

"Here. You need this more than I do."

She knew it would be pointless to argue with him, so she politely thanked him and slipped the warm jacket over her chilled body.

"Did I ever tell you I spent a whole winter living on the streets of Baltimore?"

The last time he told her that story he said it happened in Cleveland. Either way, she knew better than to call him on it. The more time she spent with him, the more she realized just how unwell he was; both his mind and body. Hope was worried that the jacket thing would distract him from telling her more about her grandmother, but luckily for her, he picked up right where he left off.

"She also loved to sing... my mother did. And she was amazing at it, too. Come to think of it, that's probably where you get your beautiful voice from."

Hope loved hearing that about her grandmother, but even more, she loved hearing her father offer such a sweet compliment. It was out of character, but very much welcomed.

"You really think my voice is beautiful?"

"Well, yeah. If I thought it sucked, I wouldn't have made you get up in front of all those people today. You don't think I'm that much of an asshole, do ya?"

"No. I—"

"One of my earliest memories is of my mother singing 'Twinkle, Twinkle Little Star' to me and my brother. It was her go-to lullaby for us. Of course, she did it in her own way. She did it with such a unique flair that every time I hear it the normal way, I immediately become bored with it."

"She sounds like a wonderful woman."

"Yea, she was. And so was your mother, for that matter. A better woman than I ever deserved. That's for damn sure."

Hope enjoyed hearing about her grandmother, and it seemed her father liked talking about her. It also seemed to make him less fidgety. But like so many times that week, David's mood was about to drastically change.

"What about your father?"

"What about him?" he snapped. "I'm sure my brother filled you in."

Nervously, she shrugged. "All he told me was your father went away."

David burst out laughing. "Ha! Is that what my brother said? That our father *went away*?"

Hope nodded and hesitantly said, "What's so funny? I don't get it?"

"Forget it. Just forget about it."

And just like that, David's body began to twitch and fidget again. Vigorously, he started scratching his right arm and then his left. When he was finished, his arms were bright red as if he'd used sandpaper on them. Hope had no idea what flipped the switch in his mood, but she knew better than to pursue it further. She really was enjoying their night, and the last thing she wanted was to say something to ruin it. He seemed to be at his calmest when talking about his mother, so she decided to head back down that road.

"What did your mother look like?"

"Jesus Christ! Enough! Enough with all the damn questions. What the hell do you want from me?"

It was dark out, but Hope could still see the fire and anger in David's eyes.

"I… I just want to know things about you. I just want the truth."

"Bullshit!" he snapped. "Trust me, you only wanna hear what you *want…* not the truth. Not the cold, ugly truth."

"Yes I do. I do want the truth," she said, attempting to hold her ground.

Her response seemed to amuse him, and he leaned back on the bench and let out a laugh. "Fine! You want the truth? You got it! When my fucking brother told you my old man *went away*, that was his polite way of saying that he blew his brains out on his bedroom floor!"

Hope covered her mouth in shock and immediately regretted pushing for the truth.

"It's so fucking easy for Jeremy to say our dad just went away. He wasn't the one who found him." David looked his daughter straight in the eyes and said, "Is that enough truth for ya?"

He didn't wait for a response. He grabbed his satchel from beneath him then opened it up and pulled out his bottle of vodka. Shakily, he untwisted the cap and proceeded to guzzle down nearly all of it. When he finished, he let out a satisfied, "*Ahhh.* Almost made it the whole day." He shrugged and said, "Oh well. Fuck it!"

He put the cap back on and placed the bottle into the satchel. He pulled out a fresh pack of Marlboros and held them up to Hope and said, "Dessert time."

After placing one between his lips and lighting it, he stood up and walked away. Hope immediately felt sick to her stomach and placed her head in her hands. Why? Why did she have to push so hard? Half the time, what came out of David's mouth was nothing but lies and twisted truths. But she could tell this time was different. Sadly, she knew he was telling the truth. The grandfather she never knew had committed suicide.

Internally, the future psychologist in her started to analyze her father's past. The sadness he must have felt when his mother passed away at a young age... the trauma from finding his father on the floor... and then his wife suddenly dies during childbirth. Any one of these things on their own would cause most people to fall into a deep, dark depression. But experiencing all three? She'd never wanted to hug and hold her father as much as she did at that moment. Not only was her heart breaking for a grandfather she never met, but for a father she never got to truly know.

David continued to stand by the edge of the cliff smoking one cigarette after another. Knowing he needed some space, Hope watched from a distance and remained on the bench. After his third cigarette, David polished off the rest of his vodka then proceeded to toss the bottle off the cliff and into the waters far, far below. After lighting another cigarette, he stepped back from the ledge and began walking up the darkened path. Helplessly, Hope watched as he walked further away from her. She wanted to chase after him. She wanted nothing more than to wrap her arms around him and tell him how much she loved him. She wanted to, but she didn't. She was still reeling from what he'd just revealed to her, and her body felt paralyzed.

As the cool night air continued to blow in, she snuggled deeper into her father's jacket. It was tattered and worn, and it reeked like Marlboros, but there was just something about it. She couldn't put her finger on it, but it made her feel safe. She also couldn't put her finger on it, but the night sky gave her a comforting feeling as well.

Hope leaned back on the blanket, instantly becoming mesmerized by the number of stars that were now visible. Even on the outskirts of

Chicago, she had never seen it so pitch black and painted with so many bright stars. Like her father's jacket, the stars seemed to fill her with a safe and calm feeling. It didn't take long for her eyes to close and for her to doze off.

She had no idea how long she'd been out, but when she woke up, her father was seated next to her. With a lit cigarette between his fingers, he stared out at the lighthouse; its red light methodically rotating around. Hope sat up and wiped her tired eyes. She didn't know what to say to her father, but she didn't need to. David spoke first. His tone was calm, honest and straightforward.

"I was a freshman in high school, and Jeremy was a junior. He usually stayed after for some sort of practice... baseball or basketball or whatever. On that particular day, I had detention, so I was forced to take the late bus home. Anyway, when I finally got home, I noticed my father's car in the driveway. I thought it was a little strange because he usually didn't get out of work until after seven or eight. As soon as I walked in the front door, I knew something was wrong. I just felt it. I called out for him, and when he didn't reply, I headed straight for his bedroom. His door was shut... it was never shut. He actually rarely ever used his bedroom. He usually just passed out drunk on the couch every night."

Any bit of sleepiness Hope had was completely gone. She was wide awake and listening intently to her father.

"I knocked on his door, but... I knew there'd be no reply. I just felt it. I knew. But nothing could prepare me for seeing him lying on the floor... surrounded by the largest pool of blood I'd ever seen."

Nearly in tears, Hope threw her hand to her mouth.

"Next to his right hand was his gun, but... but that wasn't what I was focused on. In between his fingers of his left hand was his cigarette... and it was still burning. The goddamn thing was still burning. That's when I realized... I must have just missed it. For the longest time, all I could think of was what if I didn't have detention that day? What if I wasn't such a fuck up? I woulda been there... I coulda stopped him."

"Oh Dad, it's not your fault," she said, clutching his arm.

David took the final drag off his cigarette then flicked it off to his right.

"I know," he said. "It took me a while, but... but I realized it would have eventually happened whether I was there or not. I always remembered him being a drinker, but it got worse after my mother passed away. It's like he just shut down and became so angry at the world. Of course, my brother and I bore the brunt of it."

Hope said nothing, but continued clutching his arm.

"And the older I got, I realized that not only was he a drunk, my old man was fucked in the head, too. Where do you think I get it from? My brother got his athletic ability, and I got his fucked-up brain."

"I'm so sorry, Dad. I... I never knew."

David brushed off her comment. "Why would you? Although, I am surprised your grandfather didn't blurt it out."

She shook her head no and said, "And neither did Uncle Jeremy."

David let out a chuckle. "Of course he didn't. My brother never talked about stuff like that. He was the master at ignoring the truth. Hence, telling you our father *went away*. Eh, whatever. I can't really blame him. I wouldn't want to admit that my father and brother were fucking crazy."

"Dad, stop. Mental illness and alcoholism are diseases."

This time, David's chuckle was louder and longer. "Mental illness? Alcoholism? Are those the proper college terms? Why don't you just call them what they are? Bat-shit-crazy drunk seems more appropriate, doesn't it?"

"That's not funny. None of this is funny."

Instead of piling on with more sarcasm, David softened his tone and agreed with Hope. "I know. It's not funny. And neither is abandoning your kiddo when she needed you the most. You must have hated me all these years, huh?"

"No. Not at all."

Incredulously, David looked over at Hope.

"Seriously, I never hated you. Especially when I learned more about…"

"Me being a drunken nut job?"

Hope shook off his sarcasm and continued. "I will admit… there were many times I wished you… I wished you fought harder to get some help. Especially when the alternative was not being in my life. But I never hated you, Dad. Never."

"I think you're being too easy on your old man. I'm sure you hated me, especially when you were little."

Again, Hope shook her head. "No, I didn't. I guess I always knew why you left and never came back."

"And why is that?" he asked, pulling another cigarette out of the pack.

"A part of you blamed me for Mom's death… you probably still do."

David was in the process of flicking his lighter but stopped cold, and he curiously turned towards his daughter. "What the hell are you talking about? Blamed you?"

"I'm the one that caused it… if it weren't for me…" Her voice trailed off, and she did her best not to make eye contact with her father. Although her head was down, David could tell her eyes were full of tears, just waiting to escape and cascade down her cheeks.

"Please tell me your goddamn grandparents didn't tell you that?"

Sadly, she shook her head no. David's heart was completely shattered for his little girl. In the twenty years since he left, he never once considered that Hope would blame herself. His shaky hand started to reach over to console her, but he stopped short. As he searched for the right words to say, he finally got around to lighting his cigarette. After a couple of puffs, he addressed his daughter.

"Did you know that I never went to Maggie's funeral? I couldn't. I just couldn't. She was my everything. Do you wanna know what I did instead? I spent the entire day getting plastered at a bar. I got so fucking drunk that I don't even remember where I passed out that night. After everything Maggie had done for me, that's how I honored her memory."

Hope wiped the tears from her cheeks then slowly turned and continued listening to her father.

"Ya see, not only was I fucked in the head like my old man, but I inherited his love of booze. Ironically, I had my first ever drink and smoke the night of his funeral. By the time I met your mother, I was an obnoxious drunk. And that's putting it politely. Because of her encouragement, I eventually stopped drinking." He took a long pull off his cigarette, and after bellowing smoke into the air, he laughed. "I never quite gave these things up, though."

He gazed down at his cigarette and flicked its ash onto the ground next to him.

"Not only did she get me to give up the booze for a while, but because of your mother… your beautiful, beautiful mother, I even started to see someone for my fucked-up head. Don't get me wrong, my shrink was a fucking idiot. We just never had a connection. Everything he did and said was strictly textbook. It was like he was some sort of robot."

David's foot began to nervously twitch back and forth, and once again, his fingers began to scratch at his bare arms. It was obvious to Hope just how uncomfortable he was talking about all of this. She wanted to tell him that he didn't need to continue, but these were the types of things she had wanted to hear about all these years. David

256

took a long pause then spoke.

"A few weeks before you were born, I got laid off from my job. I didn't tell Maggie. She was so excited and focused on becoming a mother... I just couldn't break it to her. I figured the last thing she needed to hear was that I was unemployed... and drinking again. I spent the first couple of days driving around trying to find another job, but no one was hiring. By the end of the week, I was so goddamn stressed out... I felt like a huge fucking failure. From that point on, I just pretended to go to work. I'd either hit the bar or drink in my car for the day. Maggie knew... she must have, but she never said a word. Like I said, she was so focused and excited about bringing you into the world."

A somber smile appeared on Hope's face, and she remained listening to her father.

"She was excited, but she was also nervous and scared. She kept telling me something was wrong... that she didn't feel right. You weren't due for another month, so I told her she was just being paranoid and overly dramatic. Yup, that's right, I used those exact fucking words."

David briefly made eye contact with his daughter, but her sympathetic look only caused him to ashamedly turn away. After a brief pause, he continued. "Late one afternoon, I came home from the bar and found a note from your mother. It said *Something's not right. I think the baby is coming. I called my parents to take me to the hospital.*"

David didn't pull one out, but he nervously began fiddling with his half-empty pack of Marlboros. The crinkling of the cellophane wrapper was all that could be heard as they both sat in silence.

"By the time I got to the hospital, she was already in the ICU. They wouldn't let me see her, but I did get the chance to hold you. You were so goddamn tiny. Tiny, but a fighter. I could tell right away how strong and special you were. You were definitely the miracle we

257

had prayed for. About an hour later, they told me the news… your mother was gone. The doctors were trying to explain the complications she suffered, but I didn't really hear a word they were saying. All I kept thinking was that I should have been there for her. If I was at home instead of the fucking bar… I could have gotten her to the hospital quicker… and maybe she wouldn't have…"

Angrily, David tossed the pack of cigarettes against his satchel. His left foot and leg were twitching faster than ever. Hope sat quietly and watched as he ran his fingers through his hair. He picked up his lighter and began flicking it on and off. Hope could see the pain and regret pouring out of her father. When he finally stopped flicking, he turned to his daughter. "I'm so sorry, Hope… I'm so sorry. Your mother and I were cursed from the beginning… I'm just so sorry you got dragged into it."

Once again, tears streamed down Hope's cheeks. She started crying so hard that she couldn't even ask what he meant by her parents being cursed. David desperately wanted to console his daughter, but instead, he reached over and slid his satchel closer and opened it. Hope assumed he was searching for another bottle of booze, but to her surprise, he carefully pulled out a single rose. He had taken it earlier from the bouquet and placed it in his satchel.

Without eye contact, and without saying a word, David stood up and made his way to a giant ledge extending out over the cliff. Hope sat perfectly still and watched from a distance. He was just far enough away that it was hard for her to hear very well, but David appeared to be talking to himself as he stared out to sea. The moon was only half full, but it was enough to illuminate the ocean far below. With the rose clutched in his hand, he spoke to his wife.

"Oh, Maggie… I'm sorry I couldn't be the husband you deserved… or the father our daughter needed."

That one simple sentence was all it took for the years of pent-up guilt to come pouring out. As soon as the first tear released from his eye, it was as if the flood gates had opened, and he began sobbing uncontrollably. In the midst of crying, he quietly called out, "Why? Why did you believe in me? Why?" His voice became louder. "You knew I was bad news. You knew I was fucked up in the head! You knew we were cursed! You KNEW it!"

With tears now pouring from his eyes, he angrily flung the rose off the cliff. When it hit the crashing waves below, his anger switched back to remorse and sadness. "I'm sorry... I'm sorry... I'm so, so sorry, my love."

By now, Hope had made her way over and gently placed her hand on her father's shoulder. David seemed unfazed as he continued crying and talking to his wife. Words flowed from his mouth, but they made absolutely no sense to Hope. Rather than complete sentences, it was more like incoherent babbling. His crying made it even harder to decipher any of his ramblings. "We had a good run... and each and every time, I fell more in love with you."

When he finally finished talking to his wife, David turned away from the ocean and faced his daughter. As soon as his eyes looked into hers, he once again lost it. But this time, he didn't ignore his desire. He took a step forward and took her into his arms—like he had wanted to for the past twenty years. Hope had also dreamt of this moment, and with his arms wrapped tightly around her, she also lost it. She didn't even attempt to hold back her emotions.

Through his tears, he began to apologize to his daughter. Once again, most of his comments didn't make sense, but Hope was able to catch the gist of what he was saying. He voiced his regret of how sorry he was that had left her and that he should have tried harder to get better. When he was finished, Hope tightened her embrace and repeated, "It's okay, Dad... it's okay. It's all going to be okay."

Eventually, she guided him away from the cliff. Just as they arrived back at the blanket, he experienced another one of his coughing fits. When it finally slowed, he clutched at his abdomen and painfully lowered himself onto the blanket. After his emotional outburst, she assumed it would only be a matter of time before he searched out his bottle of salvation for a nice long swig. But he didn't. He just sat there, still trembling and anxiously twitching.

It went against her better judgement, especially after his coughing fit, but she grabbed his pack of Marlboros and offered one to him. After everything she had just heard, and after everything he had been through in his life, the least she could do was provide him the brief satisfaction of a smoke.

His shaking hand quickly took it from her. He lit it then sucked in a long satisfying drag. About halfway through his cigarette, he looked up at Hope and asked, "You've never smoked at all?"

"Nope. I've always thought it was kind of a dirty, disgusting habit. No offense," she said with a smile.

"None taken," he said, taking another puff. "It's a totally disgusting habit. I can't imagine what my lungs look like. Probably as black as the sky is right now."

David finished off his cigarette and flicked it straight ahead. He watched Hope's eyes fixate on it as it continued to smoke and smolder in the grass. He let out a chuckle. "Every part of your being wants to go stomp that out, doesn't it?"

She looked from the cigarette to her father and then back to the cigarette. "It really does," she said, and then stood up and proceeded to walk over and put it out with her foot. She even carried the extinguished butt back over to the blanket.

"You're too much," David said, laughing.

Using his satchel as a pillow, he lay on his back and let out an exhausted sigh. Not that it was a bad thing, but this had been one of the longest days he could remember. He had reconnected with his little girl, which at one point in his life, he didn't think would ever happen.

Hope joined him on her back, and as they both gazed up at the stars, David curiously asked, "I bet you've never even had a drink, have you?"

She shrugged. "Not really. I mean, I've tried alcohol, but it's not really my cup of tea."

He smirked. "Lemme guess, your actual cup of tea is tea?"

Hope laughed and replied, "It kind of is."

"Your mother used to be a tea drinker. Not me. Black coffee and a smoke were my breakfast of champions." Slowly, David's eyes closed shut, but he blinked them open enough to ask, "Your grandfather still drink scotch?"

"Yup. He has one glass every night at—"

"Seven sharp," David said. Hope nodded. "Looks like some things don't change. He was always so goddamn regimented with his schedule."

Again, David's eyes fell shut. This time, it would be a solid minute before he forced them open.

"I never saw eye to eye with your grandparents, but I knew they would do a better job raising you than I ever could have."

"That's not true," she said, turning to face him. "That's not true at all."

"Yes, it is. Everything about my life is cursed… I guess I've always known that. Most of it was out of my control. But what I could control was not dragging you down with me." Hope started to respond, but David held up his hand as if to let him finish his thoughts. "When I came home from school that day and found my father on the bedroom floor… lying in a pool of blood… it's been thirty years, but that vision still haunts me… I never EVER wanted that to be you… finding me."

"Oh, Dad, you don't know that would have happened."

He continued to mumble as he slowly dozed off. "The only

difference between me and my dad was he owned a gun and I didn't. I chose to overdosed on pills and vodka instead."

"Huh?"

"It was right after your mother died. That's when they placed me in the loony bin... or the *special hospital,* as my brother referred to it."

"I... I never knew."

"It was actually your grandfather who found me. So, yea, your grandparents have every right to hate me... and so do you."

"Oh, Dad, I don't hate you. I've never ever hated you."

Unfortunately, Hope's words fell on deaf ears. David was sound asleep and was already snoring. She desperately wanted him to know that she didn't hate him. For a second, she thought about waking him up and repeating herself, but as his snoring grew louder, she knew he needed his sleep.

Hope once again placed her back against the blanket and focused her attention on the night sky. She still couldn't believe the number of stars that were twinkling down at her. Although she had taken an astronomy class back in high school, she'd never really seen this many constellations, not in person anyway. As a matter of fact, most of the things she learned in life were from books rather than actual in-person experience.

As the waves crashed off in the distance, and as the stars twinkled down at her, Hope thought about how perfect the last twenty-four hours were. So perfect, in fact, she didn't want to close her eyes to sleep. She was afraid that when she awoke things would go back to normal. She didn't want normal. She wanted her father back in her life. And after this past week, she was pretty sure he wanted the same thing. She knew her father still needed plenty of mental help and probably some medical help as well, but she was determined to do whatever she needed to do to make him better. When her eyes finally gave in and closed for good, she fell into a deep sleep. It was deep but short-lived.

Around five in the morning, she felt a tugging on her jacket. She rustled around but ultimately ignored it and continued to sleep. A few seconds later, she heard her father's voice. "Hope… come on… get up." At that point, David switched from tugging on her jacket to yanking on her hair. There was no way Hope could ignore that. She brushed his hand away and managed to open one eye.

"What?" she asked.

David was sitting up and staring straight ahead. "I thought you might wanna check this out."

"Check what out?" She struggled to sit up.

He motioned past the lighthouse, and there, peeking its head out from the horizon was the sun. The sky was filled with deep purples and bright pinks. Hope's other eye, along with her mouth, shot open in awe. "Oh my God," she gasped. "It's… it's so beautiful."

David said nothing but nodded in agreement. From that point on, Hope also said nothing. The two of them just sat there and watched the sun slowly and brilliantly make its way above the lighthouse. When the colors had all faded, and when the sun was high enough in the sky, David climbed to his feet and outstretched his arms. "We should probably head back to the inn," he said.

Hope nodded. She stood up and gave the blanket a good shake before folding it. David placed his hands on his lower back and arched his spine as if to give it a good crack.

"You would think I'd be used to sleeping in uncomfortable places, but this old back ain't what it used to be. I'm very much looking forward to climbing back into my bed at the inn. I figure we can get another four or five hours of sleep before checking out. You definitely need to get some sleep if you plan on getting back to Chicago by your Sunday morning deadline."

Hope stopped folding, and her smile slowly faded away. Did her father just say *you*? If *you* plan on getting back to Chicago? Didn't he mean *we?*

"Luckily for me, I don't have a deadline… or a specific place to be. I just go where the road takes me… or until I run outta smokes and booze," he said and laughed. He then proceeded to light his first cigarette of the new day.

Hope didn't find this amusing one bit. This wasn't how her mind saw it playing out. Not at all, actually. She took a breath, softened her stance, and then pushed the smile back onto her face. Without hesitating or thinking too much, Hope blurted out, "You should come home with me… back to Chicago."

Again, David let out a laugh. It wasn't until he looked over at his daughter that he saw just how serious she was.

"I know of some great places where you can get the treatment and help that you need. And I promise, I'll be with you every step of the way. I promise."

David looked deep into his daughter's eyes. They were filled with innocence and hope. It was a look he hadn't seen since before his wife passed away.

"Oh, honey… this was a great week, but…"

Hope ended his sentence there. She wasn't about to let him ruin her visions of happily ever after. "It's not too late! This can be our do-over… our new beginning." David continued to show apprehension, and Hope continued to press. "We can make this work. I know we can. I swear I can be there for you… just like Mom was. I swear." Her eyes pleaded with him as she moved closer. "Please say yes, Dad. Please."

By now, she had his hands in hers, and as she clutched tighter, she looked up at him with the most hopeful eyes she could muster. David knew it was no use to argue. With his cigarette still dangling from his lips, he conceded and gave her a slight nod. She released his hands, and with a joyful smile, she wrapped her arms around her father.

"It's going to be okay," she said into his ear. "It's all going to be okay. Everything happens for a reason, and this week proves it."

She held her hug for a few seconds longer then finished folding up the blanket. Together, they made their way down the path and back to Hope's car. Before he got it in, he took a final puff off his cigarette then tossed it to the ground. This time, he appeased his daughter by stomping it completely out.

David reminded her to drop him off at his car, which was still parked at the diner from the previous morning. Hope's eagerness remained throughout the car ride. "So, we'll get some rest then leave around lunch time?" she asked.

David stared out the window and mumbled, "Sure, whatever you want, kiddo."

After picking up his car, he followed Hope back to the inn. No sooner did he climb out of his car, Hope hit him with some more excited comments. "Kind of a bummer that we have to take separate cars back to Chicago, but it'll be fine. We can stop whenever you want to get food or to rest. Whatever you want. I just have to be back by noon tomorrow."

David turned towards his daughter and asked, "Have you thought how you're gonna explain all this to your grandparents?"

"Not exactly. But don't worry, I'll take care of everything."

"I'm sure you will, kiddo. I'm sure you will."

As they walked by the Henderson's car, David smirked and said, "Maybe you should invite the happy couple to follow us back to Chicago, too?"

She giggled but put her finger to her lips for him to talk quieter.

"Eh," David said, waving her off. "I'm sure they're still sound asleep. Let's hope they check out before we get up."

Hope continued to giggle as she quietly turned the door knob and entered the inn. About half way up the stairs, they were greeted by a soft whisper from behind. "Well, good morning you two."

They turned around and saw Janice standing in one of the doorways.

"We didn't wake you up, did we?" Hope asked.

"Oh, no. Not at all. I've been up for an hour or so. Just catching up on some reading."

"What time do we need to check out by?" David asked.

"Whenever you want. I have one or two couples checking in later today but that's about it. Like I said, our busy season isn't for another month or so. Just let me know when you're ready to leave, and I'll make sure I get a good meal in you first."

"Thanks," said Hope.

"I'm going to bed," David murmured, and continued up the steps and into his room.

Hope remained on the stairs and offered up a quick apology. "Don't mind him. He's just exhausted. We had a long day."

Janice looked up at Hope. "I'd ask how it was, but I can tell by your smile that it went pretty well."

Hope's feet were firmly planted on the stairs, but it felt as if she was floating on a cloud.

"Today was one of the most amazing days I've ever had! I'll fill you in on all the details when I wake up," she said, letting out a giant yawn. She climbed a couple more stairs then turned back to Janice and eagerly said, "Let's just say, my father is coming back home with me. I know, I know, it's going to be a lot of work, and we'll never get back all the years we missed, but... it'll work out. I'll get him the help he needs, and... yea, it'll work out." Again, she yawned. "Like I said, I'll fill you in on everything when I wake up."

With that, she widely grinned and scampered up to her room. Janice held her supportive smile until Hope was out of sight, and then a sad look of skepticism fell over her face.

Hope entered her room but was way too excited to sleep. In her mind, she kept replaying the events of the past twenty-four hours. She thought about writing in her journal but was too excited even for that. As she sat on the bed, her thoughts turned to her grandparents. What *was* she going to tell them? More importantly, how was she going to keep her grandfather from blowing his top? Multiple scenarios ran through her mind. One of which, involved her father and his trusty baseball bat.

"No, no, no!" she said to herself. "No negative thoughts. Positive thinking only. Positive thinking only." She continued this mantra and climbed into bed. As excited as she was, it was only mere seconds after her head hit the pillow that she fell fast asleep. It was an even deeper sleep than back at the lighthouse.

Over in David's room, it was a different story. He was just as exhausted, if not more, but sleep was the last thing on his mind. He still had some unfinished business left to do. He dug into his satchel and eventually pulled out a tattered old notebook and a pen. He flipped through it until he found an empty page and then proceeded to do what he hadn't been able to for twenty years.

15

It was exactly 11 a.m. when Hope's eyes finally opened. Even though she had only slept for a few hours, she awoke with a spring in her step. It was as if it was Christmas morning. To her, it was even better than Christmas. Before getting up, she stared up at the ceiling and thought about the lyrics to one of her favorite John Denver songs.

"Today is the first day
Of the rest of my life
I wake as a child
To see the world begin"

Today *was* the first day of the rest of her life, and she couldn't wait for it to begin. With a beaming smile on her face, Hope jumped out of bed and headed straight across the hall to her father's room. After knocking three times without a response, she knew it was up to her to get him going for the day. He was always extra grouchy and irritated when he first woke up, and she assumed this time would be no different. Normally, she would have given him space and let him wake on his own, but she was nearly bursting at the seams and eager to hit the road with him. She gave it two more quick knocks then slowly twisted the door knob.

"Time to get up, sleepy head. The highway is call—"

The rest of the sentence died in her throat when she realized the room was empty. His bed was already made and there was no a trace of him or of any of his belongings. Hope's heart sank, but she refused to let the negative thoughts take hold.

He probably just woke up early and is downstairs waiting for me right now, she thought. *Janice is probably giving him something to eat, and he's enjoying his last cigarette in Maine.*

She repeated these thoughts and headed back to her room. Hesitantly, she made her way towards the window. She closed her eyes, took a deep calming breath, and then opened them. As she gazed out the window, her heart sank even lower than before. The only cars left in the driveway were hers and Janice's. The Hendersons' car was gone, and more importantly, so was her father's. She felt her eyes well up, but she fought with all her might to keep the tears at bay. Again, she tried to spin it in a positive way. *Maybe he just ran to the store for some supplies for the road*, she thought.

At this point, she didn't even care if his supplies were cigarettes and alcohol. She would have gladly welcomed the sight of either one of his bad habits. In an attempt to reverse the tears that were forming, Hope laid on the bed and looked up towards the ceiling. She widened and strained her eyes as she willed herself not to cry. After a handful of deep, meditative breaths, she forced herself off the bed.

With each step she took down the stairs, she tried to convince herself that her father was just at the store and would be back at any moment. In her heart, she didn't really believe it, but she wasn't ready to face the truth—the truth that he had once again left her alone. It wasn't until she ran into Janice downstairs that it hit her. Without saying a word, Janice's face said it all. Hope didn't even try to hold back her tears this time. They slowly fell out and ran down her cheek.

"I'm so sorry, sweetie," Janice said, giving Hope a sympathetic embrace. "I know how much you wanted things to be different."

"Whatever. It was one of the stupidest ideas I've ever had. Like, he was really going to come back to Chicago with me and start over? Happily ever after is just in the movies, isn't it?"

"Oh, honey." Janice hugged her tighter. "I wish I knew the right words to say to you."

"Me too." Like a river, Hope's tears poured onto Janice's shoulder. After a few quiet minutes, Hope pried herself away and began wiping her face. "I'm sorry about your shirt."

"I'll put it on your bill," Janice said, trying to lighten the mood.

"Don't forget to charge me for all the therapy sessions, too."

"Nah, those are on the house." Janice continued to smile as she placed her arm around Hope and guided her towards the sunroom. "Come and sit. Let me go get you some tea. Tea makes everything better. At least that's what I tell myself anyway."

Janice headed into the kitchen and returned with a tray filled with assorted muffins and two cups. Graciously, Hope took the tea, but her stomach wasn't ready for any food. It was still tied in knots with a sick, empty feeling in its pit. Janice sat and listened as Hope filled her in on the previous day's events. From bridge jumping, to horseback riding, and everything in between, Hope recounted each of these stories with a giant smile on her face. She even told Janice about the lobster incident with Adam. That particular story caused both of them to laugh out loud. It wasn't until she thought about the early morning conversation with her father that her smile faded into a sad frown.

"I can't believe I actually thought he'd come back to Chicago with me. I must be the most naïve girl in the world."

"Oh, honey, not at all. I'm sure there's nothing he wanted more than to return with you and to have you back in his life. I think we both know alcoholism is a disease, and if it was that easy to overcome, he would have done it years ago to be with you." Janice paused, unsure if she should keep offering up her thoughts. Ultimately, she continued but treaded lightly. "I'm no expert, and this is certainly none of my business, but I think your father's condition goes beyond just alcoholism."

"Are you talking about his mental state?" Hope asked.

Janice nodded. "Again, I'm no expert, but I think your father has a lot of demons up in his head. Demons that have nothing to do with you."

Hope thought about her grandfather's suicide and knew her father had been fighting demons long before she was even born. Although she thought about telling Janice, she ended up keeping the facts about her grandfather to herself. Besides, by the look Janice was giving her, it was as if she already knew everything and understood completely.

"This has been the craziest week of my life, and I have no idea what the point of it was. No idea at all."

The tea had cooled down, and Hope took multiple sips. Janice stared over at her, once again searching for the perfect words to say. "One of the big sayings on this island is *everything happens for a reason, even if we can't see it at the time*. I know those seem like hollow words, but I promise you, it's the truth."

Hope gave Janice a polite smile and finished the rest of her tea. Just then, the grandfather clock struck twelve. Hope placed the cup back on the tray and let out a long sigh. "I think I need to hit the road. If I'm not home tomorrow morning, they'll really get suspicious."

"Drive safe and take plenty of breaks. And… and try not to overthink things, Hope. Trust me, sweetie, this week was a good thing." Janice then picked up the tray and began to carry it towards the kitchen. At the doorway, she stopped and turned back to Hope. "While you go gather your things, I'll pack you some goodies for the trip." Before Hope could say a word, Janice rushed off towards the kitchen.

Hope found herself taking one last look around the library at the mahogany clock, the fireplace, the extra-cushiony chairs on either side of the window, and in the far corner, the large hand-carved Great Blue Heron statue. She then turned to her left and soaked in the centerpiece of the room—the books. Closing her eyes, she breathed in their scent. Along with fresh-cut grass and campfires, the smell of old books was at the top of her list of favorite smells. Before heading upstairs, she took a mental snapshot of the entire library and vowed that she would one day have a room like this in her own house.

It didn't take long for Hope to gather her belongings, for she had already packed before she went to bed earlier that morning. Her small suitcase and macramé bag sat neatly next to the door in eager anticipation of the trip back home with her father. Sadly, she picked them up and headed back down the old, creaky staircase for the last time.

Janice was already waiting for her by the front door. She had a picnic basket in her left hand and held it out to Hope as she approached. She winked and said, "Just a few things for the road."

"You really didn't have to do that."

"Oh, nonsense. We can't have you surviving on fast food and gas station snacks, can we?"

"But what about the basket? I don't want to take your—"

"You can return it the next time you visit," Janice said, once again giving her a wink.

Hope took the basket from her and graciously replied, "Thank you."

"It was no trouble. Just a few things to tide you over until you get back to Chicago."

"No—I meant thank you for everything this week. I don't know what I would have done without you here. You went above and beyond for me... for both of us, actually. I just want you to know..."

"You're welcome, dear. It was my pleasure. You breathed a little life into this old inn."

"I don't know about that… but thanks."

Janice moved closer and placed her hand on Hope's cheek. "You don't give yourself enough credit. You're much stronger and more special than you think. Don't ever forget that."

Her comment caused a few tears to fall from Hope's eyes. They were the exact same words her father had said to her a day earlier.

"Oh, honey," Janice said, wiping Hope's tears away. "It's all going to be okay. I promise you."

Janice wrapped her arms around Hope's neck. Hope lowered the basket and suitcase to the floor and returned Janice's hug. She held it for longer than originally planned, but it felt right—it felt needed. When the long embrace ended, Hope wiped the remaining tears from her face and picked up the basket and suitcase.

"Do you want me to carry something out to the car for you?"

"It's okay, I got it," Hope said, walking onto the porch.

"Ahh, spoken like a strong, independent woman," Janice said as she smiled and joined her on the porch.

Hope let out a little laugh. "I certainly don't feel very strong… or independent, for that matter."

"You are. Trust me. It took great courage to make this trip out here. Especially not knowing what was in store."

Hope shrugged. "I guess so."

It was met by a warm look from Janice. "Be careful driving and pull over as soon as you get tired."

Hope couldn't help but smile as she walked down the steps. Janice's comment sounded exactly like something her grandmother would have said to her.

"I will," Hope said, standing on the walkway. "Well, goodbye. And thanks again for everything."

"Goodbye *for now*," Janice clarified. "We'll see each other again."

Hope smiled back then turned and headed towards her car. She placed the suitcase and basket in the backseat. She threw Janice a final wave then took her bag off her shoulder and opened the driver's side door. She started to toss her bag onto the passenger's side but stopped cold when she saw what was already on the seat. It was her father's satchel and placed on top was the bouquet of flowers they had purchased the day before.

Slowly, Hope climbed in the car and lowered her bag onto the floor. Even as she closed the door, her eyes never strayed from the flowers and satchel. Her heart was racing, and she knew it was only a matter of time before she would once again be overcome with emotion.

As if waiting for Hope to fully drive off before she went inside, Janice continued standing on the porch. There was no way Hope was going to let Janice witness her breaking down once again. After a few long moments, she finally pulled her eyes off the satchel and started her car. She forced a brave smile and looked over at Janice one last time before exiting the long, winding driveway.

The marina was as far as Hope got before she jerked the wheel to the right and pulled into the lot. Being a Saturday, there were dozens of people awaiting the next whale watch. Not wanting to be around anyone, Hope parked in the vacant lot of the Rusty Anchor. Again, her eyes focused in on the flowers and satchel next to her. After taking several deep breaths, she reached over and grabbed the bouquet. With her eyes closed, she deeply inhaled their sweet scent, and she couldn't help but wonder if the flowers were meant for her the whole time. It was more of a fleeting thought, for her attention was now focused on a white envelope sitting on the satchel. Across the middle, her name was written in large letters. In multiple spots, the blue ink was smudged.

After a bit of hesitation, she picked up the envelope and carefully opened it. Inside was a one-page handwritten letter. Normally, Hope was a fast reader, but in this case, she had to take her time. It wasn't by choice, but rather because her father's handwriting was so shaky. Many of his sentences were barely legible, and she was forced to read through them multiple times to get their meaning.

My baby girl, Hope

I'm sorry for leaving yet again, but trust me, it was for the best. I've always wanted nothing more than to be in your life, but it's just not in the cards. There were so many times I tried to clean myself up and get the right help so I could be a part of your life. I swear I tried! But the truth is, I'm much too broken and fucked up for anyone to fix, including you. I need you to know how much this week has meant to me. Seeing you, talking to you, laughing with you... it meant everything to me. I don't know a lot of things, but I do know that your mother is smiling down right now at the amazing woman you've become. I even think she's smiling down at me too for introducing you to this place. I know being here this week might not make any sense to you right now, but it will. One day, when the time is right, it will... and you will shine like you were always meant to. You were right, Hope, everything does happen for a reason... this week included. But just not the reasons you think. I promise, though, it'll all make sense one day. I promise.

It kills me that you've spent all these years blaming yourself for your mother dying or for me leaving. You need to know that NONE of this was EVER your fault! You also need to know that you and your mother will forever be the most beautiful things that have ever happened to me. But unfortunately, I fucked it all up, and now, all I'm left with are regrets... beautiful, beautiful regrets. You'll forever be in my heart.

Love,
your father.

As she finished reading the final sentence, a couple of tears dropped from her cheek onto the letter. Up until then, she hadn't even realized that she was crying. She read through the letter one more time before folding it up and placing it back into the envelope.

Just then, a black pickup truck rumbled through the dirt parking lot and pulled into the space next to her. The man climbed out of his truck, and with the dust cloud still hanging in the air, he shot Hope a curious look. Hope recognized him as the bartender from earlier in the week. She gave her tears a quick swipe then lowered her head to avoid any further eye contact.

The man walked to the front door, unlocked it and headed inside. Hope assumed he was there to get the tavern ready to open. He probably thought she was there just waiting for him to open so she could get the first drink of the day. The sad truth was, if ever she was going to drink, now would be the perfect time.

As soon as the door closed behind him, she turned her attention back over to the passenger's seat. The entire week, she hadn't seen the satchel leave his side. She knew how important his cigarettes and alcohol were to him, and she just assumed that's why he guarded it so closely. The satchel always appeared to have some heft to it; heft that went well beyond just packs of cigarettes and bottles of vodka. On more than one occasion throughout the week, Hope was tempted to ask him what else he had stashed away in it, but she knew exactly how he would have responded. It would have been a sarcastic quip, or more than likely, he would have shot her a *None of your goddamn business* response.

Her curiosity was more than piqued, yet, with the satchel only a foot away from her, she was apprehensive to reach over and grab it. He would never leave her his booze and smokes, which meant whatever was in there would probably cause more tears to fall. Putting off the inevitable, Hope once again picked up the bouquet. A sad look came over her face as she admired each of the flowers that she had hand-picked the day before. She was quite proud of her beautiful arrangement and took another long whiff of their scent. When she was finished, she placed the flowers on the floor and slowly grabbed hold of the satchel and slid it onto her lap. The outside of the bag still carried the strong smell of cigarette smoke. At this point, Hope would have given anything to have her father there next to her smoking like a chimney.

Hope ran her fingers across the worn-out leather and wondered how long her father had owned the old satchel. She also wondered if he had owned it back when he was with her mother. The questions in her mind could have gone on forever, but she knew she needed to cut to the chase and answer the main question of what was inside the satchel.

Finally, she unbuckled the two tattered straps and opened it up. She wasn't sure what would be inside, but she surely wasn't expecting what she found. A puzzled look came over her face as she slowly pulled out a stack of old spiral notebooks. The covers were various colors, and some of them were so old and worn out that they didn't have covers at all.

The puzzled look remained on her face as she opened and flipped through the first notebook. Most of the pages were either barely hanging on or had become completely detached from the spiral binder. The more she flipped through, the more confused she became. The pages were filled with scribbles, and every so often, there were random sketches. The scribbles weren't even complete sentences. They were incoherent thoughts at best. The sketches weren't much better either. The penmanship was even worse than in his letter, and there seemed to be no rhyme or reason to any of it. Each notebook she opened was the same. Not all the pages were written on, but the ones that were, made absolutely no sense to Hope. The only thing she knew for sure was that her father was even more mentally ill than she had realized. She tossed the notebooks down onto the seat. "These are nothing but gibberish," she uttered.

Like so many times in her life, she was torn between feeling sorry for her father or being angry with him. But just like every other time, the anger quickly dissipated, and her heart couldn't help but break for him. It was now obvious by the contents of the notebooks that his mental state was worse than she thought.

Through the windshield, she watched the bartender flip the CLOSED sign to OPEN. Less than five seconds later, two trucks sped into the lot and came to a sliding stop in front of the tavern. Two men, appearing to be in their forties, exited their vehicles and headed inside. Normally, Hope would have shaken her head and pre-judged the men for drinking so early in the day. But this time she didn't. Before you judge a man, walk a mile in his shoes. Hope had always been fond of this saying, but after being so close to her father that week, it truly resonated with her.

After the men entered, Hope's attention returned to the notebooks. There was one left that she hadn't yet examined. By the looks of it, it appeared to be the oldest of the notebooks. The cover had long since fallen off and many of the pages were crinkled and folded over. Assuming it was the same as the others, she picked it up and half-heartedly began flipping through it. Her attention was immediately caught by what seemed to be a full-page letter. By far, the writing was the most legible out of all the other notebooks. What really caught her eye was the first sentence which read: *To my baby girl, Hope.*

It was the same salutation as the letter he had left for her, and she just assumed this was the rough draft for it. As she continued reading, however, it became apparent that this letter was written many years ago—fifteen, to be exact. His letter was short, but it sucked Hope's breath away, and once again, tears fell from her eyes.

To my baby girl, Hope.

Thank you so much for your letter and drawings. I love them! They are by far the best part of my day. I'm so sorry for not being there for you right now. I miss you so much. I promise I'll get better and come back to you soon. I promise! Be good for your grandparents and keep writing and drawing those beautiful letters!

Love, your father

As she read the letter, two more cars pulled into the parking lot. The men gave her a curious look as they walked by her car. Hope was too overcome with emotion to even notice or care who saw her crying. The first part of the notebook was filled with unsent letters to her. Most were half-written, and some were scratched out in frustration. Even though the rest of the notebook was filled with blank pages, Hope chose to focus on the unsent letters.

"He *did* get my letters… and he *did* write back," she said, smiling through her tears.

Right then and there, it didn't matter that David never actually sent the letters. He wrote them, and to Hope, that was all that mattered. That's all that would ever matter to her. She read and reread them over and over again. From the first letter to the last, she could tell the difference in his mental state. The final few letters were harder to understand and were mostly filled with broken sentences and random thoughts.

By the time she closed the notebook and glanced up at the clock, she realized she needed to hit the road. She neatly stacked up the notebooks, and as she began to place them back into the satchel, she noticed there was something else in there. Hope dug her hand to the bottom and pulled out some sort of necklace. The entire necklace was made out of beautifully multi-colored seashells. The smile on her face grew as she held it up to the sunlight. Most girls, especially her age, wouldn't be caught dead wearing something as gawdy as this, but she knew it was totally her style. She loved that her father knew that as well.

"Aw, Daddy," she said aloud. "Thank you... for all of this." Hope placed the notebooks in the satchel and carefully draped the necklace on her rearview mirror. She then started her car and made her way out of Applewood and began her long journey back to Chicago.

***

Just as Hope was leaving the island, David was pulling his car into a rest area. He'd only been driving for a few hours, but the emotion and exhaustion from the previous day had taken its toll on him. He found a quiet and shady spot and parked his car for a well-deserved nap. The cigarette dangling from his mouth was just about gone, and after one last drag, he extinguished it in the nearly overflowing ashtray. As usual, he followed it up with a nice long pull from his bottle of vodka. David tossed it to the floor and began to lean his seat back. Before he closed his eyes, he glanced over to his right. There, on his passenger seat, was a large stack of papers. David reached over and picked them up. Slowly, he removed the rubber band, which was tightly wrapped around it.

One by one, he looked at each piece of paper. It was every single letter and drawing his daughter had sent him all those years ago. Besides his cigarettes and vodka, they were the only things he kept from his satchel. A sad smile appeared on his face when he came across the glitter-filled Father's Day card. The final two items in the stack were photographs. The first was a picture of David holding Hope in the hospital soon after she was born. He held it close to his face, and with his smile still beaming through, he spoke aloud. "Shine on, baby girl. Shine on."

He then picked up the final photo, also holding it close to his face. It was of him and Maggie back in their younger days. His eyes went back and forth from picture to picture.

"We did good, Maggie. We did good. Let's pray it's enough."

16

Six months later – October 1981

Hope never told her grandparents about her trip to Applewood. As a matter of fact, it would be nearly six months before she breathed a word of it to anyone. Unfortunately, it would be under the saddest of circumstances. Hope had just started her senior year of college, and as usual, her social life was pretty non-existent. More than ever, she was laser-focused on her future. She was determined to be the best therapist and to help as many people as possible.

Sadly, Robin had graduated, and for the time being, all that was left in the house were Darcy and Dee. Hope didn't seem to care that they were in the process of bringing in another one of their friends to replace Robin. She was just biding her time until graduation and was as determined as ever to finish with a perfect GPA.

Darcy and Dee, on the other hand, were set on enjoying their senior year to its fullest. Hence, just after 1 P.M, they were sound asleep and were so hung over that they didn't even hear someone knocking on the front door. Hope had been up since 5 a.m. and had just returned to the house a few minutes earlier. She spent her weekend mornings volunteering at the Chicago-Reed Mental Health Center. Eventually, her stint there would be short-lived. It was just too depressing and emotionally exhausting.

With a piping-hot cup of tea in her hand, Hope stood up from the chair and walked to the front door. She assumed it would be a gentleman caller for one of her roommates. The word gentleman was used loosely—very loosely. It never ceased to amaze her at the type of guys Darcy and Dee attracted.

Before she opened the door, Hope closed her eyes and attempted to guess what this horny college boy might look like. She'd become somewhat of an expert at this game, which sadly spoke volumes about her own social life, or lack thereof. She also knew better than to limit her guess to college boys. Just last week, a history professor came calling for Dee—a married professor.

Today's guess was a six-foot preppy frat boy. In anticipation of once again winning her silly little guessing game, Hope turned the knob and opened the door. Her eyes popped open and her jaw dropped. It wasn't a frat boy. It wasn't even a professor. As a matter of fact, it was the last person she expected it to be. Well, maybe the second to last person.

"Uncle Jeremy?" she said, stepping back surprised. "What are you doing here?"

"Nice to see you, too, kiddo."

"I'm sorry. I didn't mean it like that. I just haven't seen you in…"

"A long time. Too long of a time," he said, and then outstretched his arms and moved in to hug his niece.

Hope started to do the same but realized she was still holding the cup of tea. Awkwardly, she placed it on a hutch next to the door, spilling half of it on a stack of magazines.

"As you can see, I'm still a giant klutz," she said, wiping her hand on her pants.

Jeremy laughed as he gave her a long embrace. Despite having the same eye color, Jeremy and her father looked nothing alike. Jeremy stood at least four inches taller and had a more fit and athletic build than his brother. Not to mention, their smell was completely opposite. Instead of cigarettes and BO, Jeremy sported the fragrance of Brut by Faberge.

"It's so good to see you, kiddo," he said, stepping back to admire her. "Although, I guess I probably shouldn't be calling you kiddo, huh? You're like a full-grown woman now. I think the last time I saw you, you were yay big." He lowered his hand just below his waist.

Hope remembered the exact moment she last saw her uncle. She had just started third grade and he had taken her out for ice cream. Before he dropped her back off at her grandparents' house, he explained to her that he had accepted a job offer that would require him to move to Germany. Hope was heartbroken. It wasn't like they hung out a lot to begin with, but in Hope's eyes, her uncle was the one and only connection she had to a father she'd never met.

"Wait," she said puzzled. "How did you know where I live?"

"I stopped by your grandparents' house first."

"Oh boy. How'd that go?"

"It went fine," he said with a smile.

"Are you back in town on business?"

"Something like that," he said, losing his smile.

Hope continued her barrage of questions. "Is Aunt Katrina with you?"

"No. I'm here by myself."

Before she had a chance to fire another question at him, he said, "Do you have plans today? I thought maybe we could go grab something to eat and hang out a bit."

Hope was exhausted from her early morning shift, and she still had plenty of studying to do, but there was no way she was going to back out on spending time with her uncle.

"That sounds perfect! Let me just go grab a jacket."

A few minutes later, they headed out and climbed into his rental car. As Jeremy slowly drove through the campus, a nostalgic smile flickered across his face.

"Wow, it's been nearly twenty-five years since I've been back to the old college."

"Does it look different?" she asked.

"Not at all, actually. It looks completely the same." Jeremy pulled over to the side of the road and pointed to a building on the hill. "That was my dorm my freshman and sophomore year."

"No way! Mine too!" she excitedly replied.

"A lot of memories. A lot of memories," he said, continuing to stare up at the building. "I remember the fourth floor permanently smelling like pot and vomit."

Hope scrunched her nose in disgust and said, "It still does. Thank God I was on the first and third floors."

They both laughed, and Jeremy pulled back onto the road exiting the campus. It was mostly small talk as they drove through the streets of Chicago. His college hadn't changed a bit, but he was shocked to see just how much the city itself had changed. Many of his old stomping grounds were now torn down and replaced by skyscrapers.

"Jesus, I can't believe how much has changed since I was a kid," he said, turning onto Michigan Ave. A few minutes later, a huge smile came over his face and he pointed up ahead. "Now that's what I'm talking about! It's nice to see not everything has changed."

"The Billy Goat Tavern?" she curiously asked.

"Don't tell me you've never had a burger there?"

Slowly, Hope shook her head no.

"What? How the hell do you live in Chicago all these years and have never been here?"

Hope shrugged and smiled. The way he said it reminded her of her father. Even his facial expression and inflection were the same.

"Well, my niece, prepare yourself for the best burger of your life!"

Jeremy couldn't believe she had never heard of the Billy Goat Tavern, so he spent the first part of lunch explaining the history behind the iconic Chicago restaurant. He even spoke of the many times her father had accompanied him to the Goat for beers and burgers.

On more than one occasion, she was tempted to tell her uncle about her trip to Maine months earlier, but for now, she decided to keep the conversation more lighthearted. They mostly talked about her college experience and her future plans.

After lunch, they made their way to Grant Park for a walk. Hands down, Grant Park was one of Hope's most beloved and relaxing places in the city. Throughout their walk, she made sure to point out some of her favorite spots of the sprawling park. Hope also found herself asking question after question about what it was like living in Germany all these years.

"It sounds beautiful over there."

"You should come visit sometime. Your aunt Katrina would love to show you around. She knows all the cool spots."

She beamed. "I would love to! Maybe after I graduate and get some money saved."

"Don't worry about the money. My treat."

"Uncle Jeremy, you don't have to—"

"Consider it our graduation present to you," he said and winked. "It was really nice hanging out with you today. Long overdue."

Hope nodded. "Yea, it was a nice surprise seeing you show up at my door. How long are you in town on business?"

His demeanor seemed to change as he looked away and shifted around on the bench. "Um... not long. Not long at all," he said, fidgeting with a loose thread on his shirt.

Hope didn't really notice his shift in mood. She was too busy watching a couple of squirrels darting back and forth in front of her.

"Hopefully we can see each other again before you leave. Just let me know so I can rearrange my—"

"Hope," he interrupted, "I need to tell you something. I've been trying all day to find the right time to tell you…"

Hope's attention turned from the squirrels to her uncle. Her brown eyes saddened as if she knew exactly what he was about to say.

"Your father passed away."

Even though she knew what he was going to say, his words left her numb and in shock.

"I'm sorry, Hope. I should have told you right away, but… but I just didn't know how to…"

"When? When did he pass away?"

"Thursday. He actually called me about a week ago out of the blue. It was the first time we had talked in I don't know how long. He joked that he was in the hospital for some routine maintenance, but I could tell there was something up. I knew it was serious when he spent most of the conversation apologizing for being such a shitty brother over the years."

Hope's heart ached and felt empty, but her eyes remained dry. Her uncle's eyes, on the other hand, were already welled up.

"Before we hung up, he made me promise to always look after you."

Tears fell from his eyes, and as Hope watched them roll down his cheek, she leaned over and hugged her uncle. Neither said a word during their embrace. When they finally released one another, Jeremy spoke. "A few days later, I received a phone call from the hospital he was in. This time, it was one of the nurses telling me he was gone."

"Did she say how?" Hope asked.

"Apparently, he'd been suffering with cirrhosis of the liver. Ultimately, he died from renal failure."

Hope's head sunk into her hands. She vaguely remembered learning about that very thing in a class years earlier. It was all making sense to her now; her father's coughing, the sharp pains in his side, and even the constant itching of his skin. She was overcome with emotion, but more than that, she was upset with herself for not putting two and two together.

"I should have known," she blurted out. "I should have seen the signs."

"What?" he said puzzled. "What are you talking about? How on earth would you have—"

"I saw him earlier this year. Back in the spring."

"What? Where?"

Hope took a deep breath then gave him the short version of how she tracked him down in Maine. Or more specifically, how he *allowed* her to track him down.

"And when I woke up that last morning… he was gone."

"Oh, Hope, I'm so sorry."

"It's okay," she shrugged. "I should have known he was never coming back to Chicago with me. I should have known." Hope shifted and squirmed on the bench and finally stood up. "Do you mind if we keep walking?" she asked.

"Of course," he said, rising from the bench.

For the next five minutes, the only sound between them was the crunching of leaves beneath their feet. After a loud sigh, Jeremy spoke. "David had it wrong. I was the one who was a shitty brother. I should have been there for him more. I should have been there for *you* more. Maybe I never should have even taken that job in Germany."

Hope locked her arm into his and said, "Aww, Uncle Jeremy, it's not your fault. I'm not sure what you or anyone else could have done."

"It's always been easier for me to just ignore problems and hope they magically get better. It's like, if I don't acknowledge them, then they don't exist."

Hope knew he was referring to more than just his brother. She remembered her father telling her how her uncle never really faced up to their father's death.

"Not to mention, it's pretty goddamn pathetic that this is the first time I've seen you in years."

"Seriously, Uncle Jeremy, it's okay. I always knew if I really needed you, you'd be there."

He smiled over at his niece and said, "Your father must have been so proud to see what kind of woman you've grown up to be."

"Thanks," she said, lowering her head and blushing. "Despite what you might think, he was proud of you, too."

"Ha! Let's not get carried away," he said. "He did start every conversation with, 'How's the Nazi thing going?'" Both of them laughed as they continued up the path through the park.

"Did you ever tell your grandparents?" he asked.

"Huh?"

"About you going to see your father back in the spring?"

"Oh, gosh. No way! They would have flipped out on me for sure."

"Yes, they would have," he said, chuckling. "But what I still don't get is why your father chose Maine. It just seems so random."

"What are you talking about? He chose it because that's where he originally met my mom." A puzzled look came over his face, but before he could respond, Hope continued. "Not to mention, that's where you two used to go in the summer with your aunt and uncle." Hope slowed her speech when she realized none of this was still making sense to him.

"Hope... neither of our parents had any brothers or sisters. We never had an aunt or an uncle. Not to mention, I've never been to Maine in my life, and I'm pretty certain your parents have never been there either."

"But... he showed me all the places where he romanced her... where they had their first kiss... the little tavern where they met."

"I'm sorry, sweetie, but none of that was true. Not at all. Your father had a lot of… mental issues in his life, and it's obvious that his memory was twisted and tangled when you saw him."

Hope stopped and gasped. The disappointment she felt was like a punch in the gut. It was like a child finding out the truth about Santa Claus, the Easter Bunny, and the Tooth Fairy all at the same time. She placed her head in her hands and mumbled, "I'm so stupid… so naïve."

"Oh, honey, no you're not. Not at all." He clutched her arm and led her over to another bench.

A few minutes after they sat, Hope turned to her uncle and asked, "So how did they meet? Like, for real?" At that point, he looked away as if to avoid eye contact. Her big brown eyes and soft voice pleaded with him. "Tell me… please."

Jeremy looked back over at his niece and knew she deserved the truth. "As you might have guessed, my brother was always a bit of a wild child. More than a bit, actually. But it was soon after our father… *went away* that he really started to lose it."

Hope knew exactly what *went away* meant, but she didn't bother telling her uncle that she knew the truth about what happened to his father. Jeremy's euphemisms didn't end there.

"David's behavior started to become more erratic… more violent. Not only violent with others but with himself. At one point, he had a major meltdown at school. Apparently, he started talking nonsense and threatened multiple times that he was going to hurt himself. Long story short, he was removed from school and put into a… a special hospital."

It was pretty obvious that Hope knew exactly what he meant by special hospital, but still, he couldn't force himself to use the words *mental institution* or *psychiatric hospital* even.

"Anyway, it was there that he met your mother."

290

"What?" she said, confused. "If he was a teenager… my mother would have been way too young to work there."

Jeremy took a long, thoughtful pause and looked directly into Hope's eyes. It was then that she knew exactly what he was about to say. Still, hearing the actual words sent a bolt of sadness through her body.

"Your mother was also there as a patient… also for threatening and attempting self-harm."

Hope's mouth dropped open. "I… I never knew that."

"Apparently, in the short time they were in there, they had fallen in love with one another. Even when they both were released, they continued seeing each other. Of course, your grandparents were completely against it. They thought David was a bad influence. They used to refer to him as evil and poisonous."

Evil and poisonous? Hope thought to herself. *That's way worse than unsavory.*

"Their relationship was rocky at best. Over the next few years, they broke up and got back together more times than I could count. But I will tell you this, they loved each other with all their heart, and they really did have a unique bond." Jeremy stood up to stretch his legs and back. He then smiled over at Hope and said, "Your father used to say that not only was Maggie the love of his life, but she was the love of all his lifetimes. I always thought that was a pretty cool sentiment."

Hope's face lit up and a smile returned as she recalled her father telling her that same quote. "Yea. I think it's a beautiful sentiment," she said, joining her uncle by his side.

It would be just after sunset when he dropped Hope off back at her place. They said their goodbyes and both promised to stay in better touch with one another. Before he drove off, he once again extended the invitation for her to come visit him in Germany.

291

17

5 years later – Oct 1986

Although Hope and her uncle stayed in close contact throughout the years, she never did make the trip over to Europe. Actually, she didn't make many trips outside her own state either. As soon as she graduated, she wasted no time jumping into the real world. One of Hope's favorite professors used his connections and landed her a job as a court-appointed therapist for the City of Chicago. Basically, she dealt with family-type matters, as in, child custody evaluations or the ever-growing cases of child abuse.

With a steady paycheck coming in, it wasn't long before Hope proceeded to move out of her grandparents' house. Her apartment was on the outskirts of the city, and although it was extremely tiny, it was hers—completely hers. She did make it a point to swing by and check in on her grandmother as often as possible. Sadly, due to an unexpected heart attack, her grandfather had passed away that previous Christmas. When it happened, Hope's first instinct was to abandon her lease and move back home, but her grandmother was adamant that she stay put. Hope knew how stubborn her grandmother could be and that it was pointless to argue with her.

Hope visited her every day after work, but it didn't take long for her to realize that the house was too big and lonely, and the upkeep

292

was just too much for her grandmother to handle. On multiple occasions, Hope tried to convince her to sell the house and move in with her but was angrily shot down each and every time.

After nearly a year of grieving and denial, her grandmother finally came to terms with the inevitable, and she begrudgingly placed the house up for sale. Instead of taking Hope up on her offer, she chose to make a clean break from Chicago and decided to move in with her sister up in Minneapolis. Even though this was probably the best situation for her grandmother, perhaps selfishly, Hope, couldn't help but feel sad. Considering her lack of real friends, Hope knew that once her grandmother moved away, she would be left all alone in the city.

Just like her college career, Hope threw everything she had into her job. She quickly became a full-blown workaholic, and even when she wasn't working, she was volunteering at one place or another. Either way, her social life was completely non-existent. She did, however, love attending free concerts throughout the city, especially in Grant Park. Occasionally, she would abandon her frugal ways and pay top dollar to see a show. Her last big expenditure came in June of '83. That's when she drove out to Aurora, Illinois to see the Grateful Dead. Even though she attended it by herself, it was the highlight of her twenties.

On the rare occasions when she wasn't working or volunteering, she was engaging in her favorite pastime—reading. Once in a while she would read fiction, but mostly, she read about the philosophies of different cultures. She never really subscribed to a specific religion. She always saw herself as more of a spiritual-type being.

Throughout her search, she held a special place for Native American culture and beliefs. It was that same passion and curiosity which led her to discover the origins of the seashell necklace her father had left her years earlier. Besides free concerts in the park, Hope enjoyed attending local Native American powwows. In particular, she loved the annual powwow held by the American Indian Center of Chicago. Each year, she would return home with more than a few hand-woven bracelets and one or two new dreamcatchers to add to her collection.

As Hope prepared for one particular powwow, she dug through her closet looking for something warm and comfortable to wear. It was extremely windy and brisk, even for Chicago. Hope was a simple girl, but even she was getting sick of her small, limited wardrobe. Just as she was about to close the door, something caught her eye. On the floor of the closet, partially hidden by her long-flowing dresses, was a cardboard box. Hope slid the box out and placed it onto her perfectly made bed. Carefully, she opened it and sadly smiled as she admired its contents. Inside the box was everything her father had left her. David's satchel lay at the bottom of the box and still contained his notebooks, which now had the dried flowers from the bouquet pressed between their pages. Folded neatly on top of the satchel was David's old leather jacket. The final item in the box was the seashell necklace. Hope rarely ever wore it, never mind leave the house with it on. It wasn't that she didn't like it, because she absolutely loved the necklace. It was just hard for her to wear it without getting extremely depressed about her father. It was that same reason why she kept the cardboard box buried in the back of her closet.

For whatever reason, though, today was different. Proudly, Hope placed the necklace around her neck then reached down and picked up her father's jacket. Her smile grew when she realized it still smelled of cigarette smoke. She always believed that certain songs and smells could transport you back in time. The smell of his jacket was the perfect example. For a brief moment, she was back on that tour boat in Applewood seeing her first-ever whale. It was settled. She would wear both the necklace and jacket to the powwow.

Upon arrival, she did what she always did first; she entered the circle and had one of the Native Americans perform the smudging ritual on her. It would be a ritual that she would one day adopt for her own house and office. She meandered through the powwow taking everything in. This event was always one of her favorite days of the year.

Throughout the afternoon, Hope received multiple compliments on the necklace, but none bigger, and none more important than at the very end of the day. Hope had just finished purchasing her annual dreamcatcher when an old woman from the next booth waved her over.

"Beautiful... simply beautiful," the woman said, causing Hope to blush.

It took her a second, but as she moved closer, she realized the woman was referring to the necklace. Hastily, the woman fumbled with her glasses, which were sitting next to her on the table. All the while, she motioned Hope to come closer.

"May I?" she asked, reaching out her bony fingers.

"Of course," Hope said. She removed the necklace and handed it to the woman.

After meticulously examining it, the woman explained that due to the type of shells and specific technique used, its origins were somewhere up in the Northeast.

"It was actually given to me in Maine a while ago."

"Ahh, I see. Probably Abenaki or Penobscot," the woman said. "Necklaces like this were usually worn by the wife of a great chief. This is an exquisite piece of history." She handed it back to Hope and said, "You should be very proud of your heritage."

Hope let out a tiny giggle. "Oh, this doesn't belong to my family. It was just given to me, that's all."

The woman's lips curled into a smile. "Necklaces like this aren't randomly given... they're passed on." Before Hope walked away, the woman grasped her hand and said, "You have an amazing light and energy about you, my dear. Unlike any I've ever seen."

Hope blushed and looked away. She was never good with compliments. "Thank you," Hope finally said, making a little eye contact.

Long after Hope left the powwow, the old woman's comments stuck with her. She could never prove that a great chief was one of her ancestors, nor could she trace that the necklace actually came from her family line, but at the end of the day, Hope didn't need definitive proof. From that point on, she chose to believe in the possibility of it all. She convinced her heart and mind that she really was a descendant of a great chief from Maine.

***

Before heading back to her apartment, she decided to stop by and check in on her grandmother. Even though Hope had been there all week helping her pack for the big move, it was still quite a shock to enter into such an empty house. So empty, in fact, Hope's voice echoed when she greeted her grandmother.

Most of the larger pieces of furniture were still there, but all the things that make a house a home were gone. They were already packed and loaded on the U-Haul, which was parked out in front. She couldn't believe how cold and lonely the house seemed. Gone were the antique lamps, the giant clock above the mantle, and most of all, the many, many photographs and pieces of artwork. They had adorned the walls for as long as Hope could remember.

"I didn't think Uncle Barry was coming with the U-Haul until next week?" Hope asked.

Barry was her grandmother's brother-in-law from up in Minneapolis.

296

"The friend he has helping him could only do it this weekend," her grandmother replied. "I'm not sure why he rented such a big truck. I'm really not bringing much with me. Photographs, clothes, and some of my favorite fine china, that's it. Oh, and my bed. I'm not sure I could sleep on anything else. My sister and Barry said I should just get a new one, but why would I do that? There's nothing wrong with my bed. Besides, it knows my body perfectly. There's no way my back would do well on a stiff, new mattress."

Neither of her grandparents were ever good at being sentimental or talking about their actual feelings, but Hope knew the real reason she wanted to keep the bed. It was her grandmother's way of forever remaining close to her grandfather.

"I definitely think you should keep your bed," Hope said. "You know, for your back's sake."

Her grandmother gave her a slight smile then turned her attention to Hope's tattered leather jacket. "Oh, honey, if you need money just ask. You don't need to be buying clothes… or necklaces at a thrift store."

Again, Hope smiled and said, "Trust me, Nana, I'm fine."

There was no way she was going into the origins of the jacket and necklace, so she quickly switched subjects and asked, "So, if that's all you're taking with you, what are going to do with everything else?"

"I'm just going to leave most of it all here. Whoever buys the house can do what they want with it. Everything else will probably just go to the dump."

"Really?"

"Yes, really. My sister's place isn't that big. I'd never have room for all of this. Besides, it's just stuff. It's just stuff."

Hope assumed her grandmother was putting on a brave face. There was no way you could be married and live with someone for nearly fifty years and consider everything *just stuff*. There was no way.

"Where are Uncle Barry and his friend now?" Hope asked, changing the subject.

"They're down in the basement going through your grandfather's tools and whatnot. I told them to take what they want and get rid of the rest."

There was a hint of sadness in her voice and in her eyes. Quickly, she turned away and began retaping a box. Hope and her grandmother always considered those tools junk, but deep down, they both knew how much they meant to him. A look of sadness was now on Hope's face as she watched her grandmother pretend to be packing.

"Remember we used to call them Grampa's toys?" Hope said in her grandmother's direction.

Her grandmother paused a second then turned and said, "The guys must be thirsty. Can you bring them something to drink? I think there's some soda pop in the fridge."

By now, Hope was well aware of her grandmother's refusal to get too emotional or sentimental—at least not in front of her.

"Sure, Nana. I can do that."

Hope grabbed a couple of root beers from the kitchen and made her way down the narrow and rickety stairs. She'd lived there all her life but rarely went down into the basement. Besides the oil tank and furnace, the only thing down there was her grandfather's work bench. There were only a few lights, so between the darkness and the many cobwebs, the basement had always creeped her out. But the main reason she never went down there was due to the fact that her grandfather was adamant about not wanting anyone disturbing his tools. Considering that she and her grandmother had zero interest in wandering around a creepy tool-filled basement, they were just fine with that.

Ironically, even though the wall of tools stretched nearly ten feet across his bench, Hope had no idea what her grandfather had actually done with them. She never really remembered him doing any woodworking projects. The only thing she ever remembered were transistor radios—lots of them. For many hours, especially on the weekends, he would spend his time tinkering and repairing the radios. As far as she knew, he didn't do it for the money. To him, it was just a hobby to pass the time.

She remembered one time coming down into the basement and trying to show interest in his work. After about her third question, he looked down at her and said, "I think this stuff is a little too complicated for you. Why don't you run up and see if your grandmother needs a hand in the kitchen?"

It was condescending, for sure, but Hope was never too offended. In truth, she really wasn't that curious about his radio repair. She was just trying to show a little interest in his hobby in hopes of becoming closer to him.

When she arrived in the basement, Hope handed the drinks to Barry and his friend, Frank. Barry was close to the same age as her grandfather, but he could have easily passed for at least ten years younger. Seeing as her grandparents rarely traveled outside of Chicago, Hope didn't really have much of a relationship with her uncle Barry or Aunt Linda. At most, they would see them once a year. The only time she remembered visiting them in Minneapolis was about ten years ago for Thanksgiving. There weren't a lot of people there, but she recalled how social and full of life everyone was. She considered it her most favorite Thanksgiving ever.

Hope had no interest in football, nor did she understand a thing about it, but even she got into the big Thanksgiving game. Hope asked plenty of questions, and Barry and the others happily answered each and every one; something her grandfather would never have had the patience for. The Lions won on a last second field goal, and not only did Hope yell the loudest, but she also participated in the ritualistic high-five celebration.

The socializing didn't end there, for Hope found herself in the middle of multiple conversations on many different topics. A lot of the topics were right up her alley. They ate dessert, they laughed, and then ate more dessert as they played board games well into the night. The long ride home the next day was a different story. The only socializing was listening to her grandfather mumble and grumble about football and TV in general. Things like: "There's no place for that silly garbage, especially on Thanksgiving." Or, "If they ever come down to our house for Thanksgiving, there'll be no damn football on TV, I'll tell ya that!" When he wasn't complaining about the previous day, he was huffing and puffing about the long drive and the wear and tear on his Plymouth Valiant.

"Thanks for the drinks, kiddo" Barry said, snapping Hope out her Thanksgiving flashback.

By now, Barry and Frank had pretty much packed everything up into various crates and boxes. As Hope stared at the now empty wall of tools, she felt guilty for remembering her grandfather that way. He might not have been the most social or emotional type of guy, but Hope knew he loved her. His tough love was only to prepare her for the real world, and although she had only been on her own a short while, some of his life lessons were already coming in handy.

"Want a radio?" Barry asked, laughing as he pointed to her right.

Hope looked down at the giant box. There must have been a few dozen radios stacked up. Some looked in better condition than others.

"What are you going to do with all this stuff?" she asked.

"We're taking most of the tools with us, but as far as the radios are concerned, they'll probably go to the dump with a bunch of other stuff. There's no telling if they even work or not."

Hope was never very interested in her grandfather's radios, but they were his passion, and she couldn't bear to see them just thrown out. "Actually, I think I will take one," she said. She leaned down and chose a dark grey transistor. Its condition appeared to be one of the better ones, but for Hope, it didn't really matter if it worked or not. "Let me know if you guys need another drink," she said, moving towards the stairs.

Both men nodded in appreciation. Barry then shot Hope a question. "Hey, ask your grandmother what she wants us to do with that."

Hope followed his finger to the back wall of the basement. The nearest lightbulb was some distance away, so it was difficult for her to make out exactly what he was referring to. She stepped closer and adjusted her eyes to the darkness. On the floor in front of her sat a three-foot wide chest.

"We found it underneath those," Barry said, motioning to a couple of dust-covered blankets. "Ever seen it before?"

"No... I don't think so. What's in it?"

"No idea. It's locked."

"Hmm, I'll go ask Nana about it." Hope headed upstairs and found her grandmother in the kitchen packing up some leftovers for her.

"Don't want you to starve over the next few days," she said, snapping the Tupperware lid shut.

"Thanks, Nana."

"How's it looking down there?"

"Empty," Hope replied, sitting in one of the kitchen chairs.

Her grandmother let out a tiny sigh and said, "That's exactly why I had *you* go down there and not me. I just can't bear to see it that empty. I always hated that dingy old basement, but... but Raymond loved it down there... tinkering away on his radios and whatnot."

Sadly, Hope smiled and nodded. Before she had a chance to reach out and grab her grandmother's hand, her grandmother swiftly changed the subject. "So, how's the boyfriend situation going? Are you dating anyone?"

Since you last asked me three days ago? Hope thought, but didn't say.

"You're certainly not getting any younger. You do realize, by the time I was your age, I had already been married a solid five years."

Hope didn't respond. Instead, she turned the tables and switched topics. "Oh, by the way, Uncle Barry wants to know what you want to do with that chest downstairs?"

Her grandmother snapped the final Tupperware lid then curiously said, "Chest? What chest?"

Hope shrugged. "It's black with a silver latch and hinges."

And just like that, the expression on her grandmother's face changed, leading Hope to assume the chest was another sentimental item belonging to her grandfather. Without waiting for a reply, Hope warmly smiled and said, "I'll tell them to pack it on the truck for you."

Hope stood up, but before she exited the kitchen, her grandmother softly called out, "It was your mother's."

"What?" Hope asked, stopping in her tracks.

"That chest was your mother's," her grandmother repeated. "She had it since she was little. We actually bought it at a yard sale. Yard sales were where your grandfather bought most of his silly radios. Your mother said it was the perfect treasure chest for all her treasures." Her grandmother gazed off at nothing in particular and paused a moment before continuing. "She kept it at the foot of her bed. Still not sure what she kept in it, but to her, they were all her treasures. She took the chest with her when she moved in with your father."

Just then, a light bulb went off in Hope's head. She *had* seen the chest before. It used to sit at the foot of the bed in her mother's room. For several years after her death, Hope's grandparents left Maggie's bedroom untouched. It was like a sad and depressing memorial to her mother, yet the door always remained shut. Hope remembered getting scolded numerous times for curiously poking her head in her mother's old room. That's where she saw the chest.

When Hope was around four or five, her grandparents finally decided to do something with the room. They boxed everything up, got rid of the bed and dresser, and turned it into a sewing room. Ironically, her grandmother never actually used it for sewing, and Hope was still ordered not to step foot in there.

"I had Raymond bring it back here after your mother…" Like always, she couldn't bring herself to say the words. "When we finally cleaned out your mother's room, I just assumed your grandfather got rid of the chest, but he must have put it down in the basement instead."

Hope placed her hand on her grandmother's arm and sympathetically said, "I'll definitely make sure they pack it on the truck for you."

What happened next totally caught Hope off guard. Her grandmother reciprocated by grabbing Hope's arm. "No. It's not coming with me. I think *you* should have it."

"Really?"

Her grandmother nodded and said, "Yes. I think Maggie would like that." Instantly, tears formed in Hope's eyes—her grandmother's eyes as well. Before it became too emotional, she pulled away from Hope. "I'll make sure Barry drops it off to you before they leave town tomorrow."

18

Just as promised, first thing the next morning, Barry and Frank brought the chest over to Hope's apartment. When asked where she wanted them to put it, there was no hesitation in her voice. She had them place it at the foot of her bed. Hope was running late for work, so she followed the men outside and said her goodbyes.

"Thanks again for dropping off the chest. And thanks for helping Nana with the move. This whole thing has to be so hard on her."

"Don't worry, Hope, she'll be fine. I think moving in with us is the best thing for her. I know Linda is looking forward to having her sister there. I give it a week, and they'll probably be giggling with each other like little school girls. Either that or pulling each other's hair out."

Hope laughed, mostly at the thought of her grandmother giggling. She could count on one hand the number of times she had heard her laughing—like, really laughing. Three of those times were while watching the *I Love Lucy Show*. Her grandmother rarely watched TV, but when she did, she loved Lucille Ball.

"And I know you're a working woman now, but you should come out and visit us soon. Long overdue."

"I would love that," Hope said, giving him a hug goodbye. She waved to Frank, who was already in the truck, and then she headed towards her car.

"Oh, Hope," Barry called after her. "I almost forgot…" He dug his hand into his polyester khakis and pulled out a key. "Your grandmother found this. She's pretty sure it goes to the chest."

Her smile grew as she took it from him. "Thank you. Thanks so much."

She wanted in the worst way to rush upstairs and see if it indeed was the right key, but she was already running late for work. She clipped it onto her keychain then rushed off to work for the day.

***

It was just after six when she returned back to her apartment. Like always, she was completely exhausted—exhausted and famished. Besides a late morning bagel, she hadn't eaten a thing the entire day. On more than one occasion, she found herself thinking about her grandmother's leftovers sitting in her fridge, but what really consumed her mind was the newest addition on her keychain. So much so, she completely ignored her grumbling stomach and headed straight for her bedroom.

She tossed her bag and jacket on the bed and hastily dug her hand into her pocket. She knelt in front of the chest, took a deep breath, then placed the key into the lock and twisted. The sound of the click caused her heart to race even more. With both hands on the lid, she lifted it open. Hope didn't know what to expect, but she certainly wasn't prepared for the first thing that caught her eye. There, laying on top, was a stuffed teddy bear with a giant bow and note tied to it. The note read:

To our bundle of joy, Mommy & Daddy love you to the moon and back!

It was obvious that this was intended to be their first-ever gift to their newborn baby. Hope tightly clutched the bear, and just like that,

305

the first of many tears began to fall from her eyes. When she finally composed herself, she returned her attention back to the chest. Underneath the teddy bear were stacks and stacks of vinyl records. Some were full albums but most were 45s. Each one she looked at, her smile grew bigger and bigger—none bigger than when she came across "Can't Help Falling in Love" by Elvis.

Other than the vinyl records, the only things left in the chest were two leather-bound diaries. The first one appeared to have been started when her mother was a teenager. What started off as typical feelings of a teenage girl, slowly changed into something much different. Her mother's thoughts became scattered, and that was putting it politely.

Hope had a hard time understanding exactly what her mother was talking about and an even harder time reading her erratic and messy handwriting. It was eerily similar to her father's notebooks. She remembered her uncle telling her where her parents had actually met—a mental institution. When it got to the point where Hope couldn't understand a single word her mother was writing, she closed the diary and pushed it away. Her heart ached for her mother's mental illness. Her heart ached for both her parents.

Needing a break, Hope stood up and headed into the living room. She had no particular destination in mind. She just needed to walk around and clear her head, which was spinning in an emotional overload. She made her way over to a table in the corner of the room. On its center sat a small glass fish bowl with two goldfish darting about. She gave Jerry and Siggy (Garcia and Freud) a pinch of food, and then, as if drawn back, she returned to the chest in her bedroom.

Hesitantly, she picked up the second diary and opened to the first entry. It was dated a few years later than the first, and Hope could tell a distinct difference between the two. Her mother's handwriting was once again legible and her thoughts more cohesive. One of the early entries explained why:

I've been so tired and blah lately. Part of it is the fact that I'm pregnant, but I think it mostly stems from the new medication they have me on. The medication is a double-edge sword. It keeps me semi-normal, and more importantly, it keeps me out of the institution, but it seems like the pills drain all feelings and emotions from me. I hate walking around like zombie.

At that point, Hope moved from the floor to her bed, crisscrossed her legs and continued reading some of the other entries:

I still can't believe I'm going to be a mother! I keep thinking – I'm 19... I'm ONLY 19! I'm not really sure if I'm ready for this. I'm so nervous, anxious, and scared, but I'm determined to be the best mother possible.

Couldn't take it anymore! I left my parents' house and moved in with David. It's not much, but it's ours!!! I'm not sure what's worse, my parents constantly fighting with me or the fact that they're not even talking to me now...

Oh my God! David proposed to me! But because of money issues and the fact that I'm a fat cow right now, it'll just have to be a town hall wedding. David promised that one day we'll do it right, but I could really care less. I don't need a "real" wedding, I just need him by my side for always and ever. Nobody thinks this will work, but I know the truth. We promised to be together for eternity, and no matter what that thing throws at us, we WILL succeed! Our little miracle will make sure of it.

As Hope continued reading her mother's diary, it was like an emotional rollercoaster. For every sweet and happy entry, there were equally as many sad and heartbreaking ones. Some of them talked about how stressed her father was concerning money. There were mentions of how he was also on some sort of medication, but he was starting to refuse to take it because he didn't like how it made him feel. Her mother also wrote that she feared he might start drinking again.

The entries were more sporadic, and there certainly weren't as many as the first diary, but Hope read each and every one. When she finished, she closed the diary, let out an extended yawn, and glanced down at her watch. It was just after 10 p.m. Time had flown by. She was exhausted, but she was also starving still. Before heading into the kitchen to reheat her grandmother's leftovers, she placed everything back in the chest—everything except the teddy bear. From that point on, she kept the bear close to her.

She started to shut the lid but stopped. She made her way over to her closet and gathered all of her father's things: His jacket, satchel, notebooks, and the seashell necklace. If this was indeed a treasure chest, it was only appropriate that her father's belongings be placed in there with her mother's. Hope rarely had guests over to her place, and she wasn't worried about anyone breaking in, but nonetheless, she locked the chest and placed the keychain back into her pocket.

Her grandmother would have chastised her for using a microwave, but Hope was much too hungry to properly reheat everything in the oven. In the meantime, she also made herself a hot cup of tea. Starving, she made quick work of the leftovers, and then she brought her tea back to her room and climbed into bed.

Hope loved that both she and her mother kept diaries. Actually, the more she thought about it, the more she realized that it had been a while since she had written in hers. Placing the tea on the nightstand, she opened the drawer and removed her own diary. Her last entry was almost three months earlier. A new entry was definitely overdue.

Unsure what to write, she leaned back against the headboard and began chomping down on the end of her blue Paper Mate pen. There wasn't a pen or pencil in the house that didn't have bite marks on them. She always claimed it helped her to think and concentrate better. It must have worked, because within minutes, she was writing up a storm. She wrote about her mother's treasure chest and each and every item inside.

After reading my mom's diary, I guess Uncle Jeremy was telling the truth about their relationship. It was rocky and sometimes volatile, and it had more ups and downs than I could count. But despite all of that, I know they loved each other deeply. I know it.

My father used to say that not only was my mother the love of his life, but she was the love of all his lifetimes. I still get chills when I think of him saying that. It's one of the most beautiful things I've ever heard.

I know now that my parents really met in a mental hospital... a far cry from the romantic version my father painted of them in Applewood. Sadly, those were just stories he made up in his head. That being said, I can't help but think of a phrase he had written in one of his notebooks: "Truth, like beauty, is in the eye of the beholder."

I didn't really understand it at the time, but maybe now I do. Because from this point on, whenever I think of my parents and their love story, I'll choose to believe my dad's version. Maybe that makes me as crazy as him... as both of them... but I don't really care. All I know is the thought of them in Applewood looking up at the stars together...

Hope pulled the pen back, paused, and then finished with:
...makes me happy. Extremely happy!

Hope's long entry that night served as future motivation for her to keep up with her diary more. As a matter of fact, she turned it into a nightly ritual. She'd make herself a cup of tea, climb into bed, grab her diary and begin writing. Sometimes it was a whole page. Sometimes it was just a few sentences. Either way, each and every time she wrote, she had her lucky teddy bear right by her side.

19

Journal entry:
June 10, 1987

Some people have jobs that are physically taxing, but mine is more mental...
100% mentally exhausting. Ironically, I got into this field to help people... to make
a difference. Unfortunately, more times than not, it just doesn't feel like I am. It's
one thing when people purposely seek you out for therapy; at least then, you actually
know they want to be helped. But working as a city-appointed therapist, most of
my clients have no desire to be sitting in front of me—especially kids. No matter
how many cases of neglect or abuse I've dealt with over the years, it never gets any
easier. Today was no different.

My latest clients are two teenage boys. Their files are incomplete, and all I
know is they've been in multiple foster families, suffering abuse in at least one of
those homes. They've recently been placed into the Boys Home of Chicago, where
they'll probably stay until they're 18. The police report from their last home was
heart wrenching.

I've met with the boys together and also separately. The city pays for three
sessions, which, if I'm being honest, is a joke. There is no way I can gain trust and
break down walls in just three sessions. Like I said, it's much easier when people
choose to seek therapy rather than be forced into it.

Today was my third and final session with the boys, and I'm no closer to
helping them than on day one. One of the brothers still hasn't even said a word to

me. He just sits there with the saddest, most pain-filled eyes. I know this sounds weird, but the boys kind of remind me of my father and uncle… what they would have been like as teenagers… after losing their mother, and then tragically their father. I still can't imagine how my dad must have felt finding his own father laying on the bedroom floor. My dad and Uncle Jeremy had no one to help them through it, just like these two young boys have no one. Heartbreaking beyond belief!!

I know I can't help everyone, and I know you're not supposed to get too attached to your clients, but there's just something about these two boys… I can't put my finger on it, but there's just something different about them. Maybe one day our paths will cross again, but until then, I hope they can find the peace and comfort they need to take all that pain and sadness from their eyes.

The End

About The Author

Jody grew up in the Kittery/York area of southern Maine. He originally started out as a screenwriter. As of now, he has written nine feature-length screenplays ranging from dramas, to dramedies, to comedies. Not only did Jody grow up in Maine, but he makes it a point to utilize and represent his state as much as possible. From Maine's scenic rocky coast, to its remotely pristine backwoods, to its eclectic characters; all serve as backdrops and pay homage to his beloved state. His ultimate goal is not to just sell his scripts, but to have them filmed right here in the Great State of Maine.

Unfortunately, searching for the proper financing has been a long, tiring, and at times, disheartening process. Feeling helpless in the whole "funding" process, Jody decided to reverse the typical Hollywood blueprint. That blueprint being: It's almost ALWAYS a novel that gets turned into a screenplay and not a screenplay which gets turned into a novel. Jody's thought process was simple: It's much easier to self-publish a book rather than self-finance a movie, and who knows, maybe, just maybe, this will be a screenplay that gets turned into a book only to eventually get turned back into a movie! But even if this wild idea never comes to fruition, at least by turning it into a novel, the *stories* themselves will be able to be enjoyed by the public. Whether it's two or two million people who buy his books, Jody is just happy that they are no longer collecting dust in a desk drawer.

Other books by Jody Clark

"Medillia's Lament"

"Livin' on a Prayer – The Untold Tommy & Gina Story"

"The Wild Irish Rose"

The Soundtrack to My Life Trilogy
Book one – *"The Empty Beach"*
Book two – *"Between Hello and Goodbye"*
Book three – *"The Ring on the Sill"*

Available at

www.vacationlandbooks.com

I do most of my posting & promoting via my Facebook profile

Feel free to *friend* me!

Jody Clark (vacationlandbooks)

Made in United States
North Haven, CT
12 March 2022

17062768R00193